The Seven Deadlies

Charles L. Stafford

ISBN: 0990893510
ISBN 13: 978-0-9908935-1-6
Library of Congress Control Number: 2014918985
CreateSpace Independent Publishing Platform
North Charleston, South Carolina

Dedication

For Cord, Cameron and Linus.

Acknowledgements

I AM FOREVER grateful to my wife, Sarah, my parents, my mentors (Patrick McCord and Chris H.), my Write Yourself Free workshop comrades (Chris, Debbie, Jeffrey, Laura, Nathalie, Wendy), the gang up in the Tower of Power and my HP for making all things possible.

Prologue

FOUR INCHES TALLER in her patent leather platforms, Bea had to stoop to see through the peephole. Her pad was on the third floor of Waterbury Mews, all the way at the end. She turned to check her hair in the vanity mirror on the wall next to her door. She knew her hair was perfect, but pecking at it with her pinky helped her think.

Ridiculous. She was just jumpy. There was no one out there and besides, today was her day for a little justice! She was all decked-out for the interview. She'd selected just the right palette of subliminal "yes" colors, from her swank new pantsuit - a throbbing aubergine, right down to her go-go-green runway shoes! She was damned if she'd be late, not today.

She moved a blond lock with her pinky. On the other hand, one bullet to the head and she wouldn't need a job. Fucking Howard – no, she couldn't do that. It wasn't entirely his fault...

She stooped, stared into the empty hallway and scoffed.

Just ninety-nine percent of it; for starters, it was Howard who had set her up in this pad three years ago. He'd spotted it from the car during one of their roundabout midnight rides near the Club. Back then, Rocco sported her one break per shift. The other girls got two. She put up with it. Getting on that slimy hog's good side wasn't worth the extra twenty minutes, not even close. Besides, she had Howard.

Howard stopped trying to poke his finger in her ass (God, he was annoying about that), hit the brakes and tugged at her hair bun. She reached over her head to swat at his arm.

"*Careful*, Howard, watch the ears! I have to go back to work you know!"

"Sorry," he let go. "But take a look, Beebee, look!"

She rose up from his lap and looked out his window. The sign read, "Waterbury Mews. Estate Living. City Style."

"Sounds pricey, Howard." She sat up and fixed the satin black kitty ears pinned to her bun.

"I'm going to set you up, Beebee! Nothing but first class for you, baby! Champagne, caviar and a penthouse apartment, nothing but the best, I'm serious. Top floor, baby, your dancing days are done."

Howard was speeding as usual; he was always pinching her Black Beauties.

"Howard, we got to get back to the club. Rocco's going to miss me."

"I'm serious."

"Yeah, right, so am I," Bea shimmied up her miniskirt and sat back in her seat.

Howard drove her back to the club looking like his ice cream had melted.

Howard Zuckerman was a lawyer, dull, really.

But, low and behold, he *was* serious! He rented the pad on the condition that she quit dancing at the KitKat, so she did. Things were sweet and homey for a while, right up until a few months ago when he split. Worse still, her landlord hadn't heard a word from him either. She spent all of June hunting for Howard, well, technically at least. She hit all the haunts in Waterbury, went by his office, and finally drove to his house. It was empty, a For Sale sign by the mailbox. The bastard had packed up the wife and kiddies and blew town.

Her landlord wasn't interested.

She tried to get her gig back at the KitKat Club. Rocco sucked on his rank cigar and told her there wasn't room in the stable for a broken old mare.

Rocco was a shit.

Howard Zuckerman was a shit.

The landlord was a shit.

When would she ever learn?

And now this! she pressed her ear to the door, but heard nothing. She took a deep breath and unlocked both deadbolts. She held the doorknob and peeked into the hall one more time.

Nobody there.

Of course, even a moron like Owen wouldn't just stand there in front of her door. Prison must've taught him that much.

"You're being ridiculous," she chided herself.

She eased open the door just enough to peek her head out and look to her left down the long, carpeted hallway. The hall was empty and quiet, lit well enough to show the worn track running down the center of the awful rose-red carpeting.

"Ridiculous," she muttered.

Bea stepped into the hall and closed the door behind her. She pinned her old attaché folder with her resumé under her arm and bolted both locks. She swished down the hall in her bell-bottom slacks, taking strides as long as her platforms would allow. She held her purse strap to her shoulder to keep it from slipping off the pressed Dacron blazer of her new suit. She hadn't worn a business suit since she got shit-canned from her secretary gig at Waterbury General back in '68. It seemed like lifetimes ago.

Up Against the Wall Motherfuckers!

What a hoot!

She and her pal in Procurement, Margie Muller, used to stir thing up wearing their Emma Peel knockoffs to the office. A bit of a heifer, the other girls in the office tolerated Margie; but Bea's groove thing was too much for them. They spread all sorts of dirty rumors about her, most of them false. One thing was for sure; she wore the hell out of those hot pants.

The hospital let her go anyway.

Protest was all the rage, but boring, really, until she saw John and Yoko in bed. That was more her style. She caught on to the flower child thing and then Owen Farring caught on to her. He was a wiry, pseudo hippy from just north of Naugatuck.

Fact was, Owen Farring was all business, big business, the trunk of his pale yellow '68 Barracuda Fastback loaded with dime bags and sheets of blotter acid and 'ludes and Black Beauties and God knew what else. They got all high and muddy at Woodstock and Owen made plans. He made a killing up at that farm, a killing.

"It's the gold rush of '69, Beetle Bug. We're gonna strike it rich in San Francisco," he'd promised.

Instead, she ended up freezing her tits off in a Columbia, Missouri jail cell. She gave Owen up to the DA. Owen got ten years in the Missouri State Pen. That windy Columbia winter whipped sense into her. She woke up to a simple truth; stripping in clubs paid a helluva lot better than dancing in the streets. She dumped her clogs and flowers for heels and pasties. It was still groovy. Nudity was beautiful; shame was a right-wing thing.

"Up against the wall motherfuckers," Bea chuckled, swishing her bellbottoms past the world's slowest elevator to the fire exit at the end of the hall. She opened the steel door and paused on the cement landing. Hearing nothing, she let the door close behind her. The snap of the metal latch echoed down the empty stairwell. The cement stairs descended like a squared off corkscrew, with a landing every half story. She took the stairs slowly, pausing on the landing half way between her floor and the second to peer down over the railing. Nothing but a fat tabby cat licking his haunches on top of a filthy mattress on the ground floor; dumped down there by one of her slob neighbors, probably the cat too.

People refused to take care of their own.

"Pathetic," she muttered and then hurried down the remaining flights, going as fast as her platforms would allow.

She shoved on the exit door and the cat followed her out into the sunny parking lot.

She slowed down, reassured by the sticky August heat and the open space. She had to relax. She needed this gig.

The late night phone calls couldn't be Owen. It was just some kid making crank calls, or some perve getting his jollies. Owen still had, what, four years to go? And what would he want with her anyway? What was she supposed to do, go to jail for his drugs, for his fucking gun that he never said boo about?

She crossed the lot to her teal blue Tempest. She unlocked the door and tossed her purse on the seat and slid in. She kept her attaché flat on her lap. The car was hot as blazes. She rolled down her window, started the engine and pressed in the lighter. She reached in her purse for her little silver pillbox and her smokes. She put her pack of Virginia Slims on her attaché, opened the lid of her pillbox and gave it a little shake. She fished out a blue Valium from her multicolored stash of capsules and pills.

Margie Muller still had her job in Procurement. She was no Emma Peel, but a doll all the same.

Bea swallowed it down and then tongued out a butt from her pack of Slimes. The lighter popped. She lit up and then unfolded the attaché in her lap. She nailed her resumé dead center with a smoke ring. She looked pretty good on paper. Good enough for Mr. Salvino Mancuso of Tartusville, that's for damn sure. She put the car in gear.

"What the hell?"

Fucking cops can't ticket here! She shifted back into Park and reached out her window for the ticket under her wiper blade. The scrawl in thick black marker caught her eye.

"SEE YOU REEL SOON BEATLE BUG"

⊷═▷ ◁═⊶

The half hour drive to Tartusville and the extra Valium helped settle her nerves. Outside the door of the Mancuso Refuse Company, Bea checked her reflection in the chicken wired window. She fluffed her feathered strawberry blond hair. All of a sudden, it was "Farrah hair." Every skinny teen queen across America was doing the Farrah Flip. She was no ditzy angel on the boob tube, facts were facts; that Hollywood bitch stole her look.

Bea dismissed the thought. She had to have her smile going, inside and out. This job could solve everything. If she played it right and this Mancuso guy was for real, she'd get that little slice of justice. She straightened her suit jacket and opened the door.

Bea stepped onto the uneven hardwood floor of the small, smoky office. A beehived old crow sat behind a small desk next to an interior door with "Salvino M. Mancuso, Proprietor" stenciled on the frosted glass. The walls were lined with black file cabinets. Bea approached the receptionist's desk but the woman kept her eyes on her work, stabbing a smoldering butt into an ashtray. Above her beehive hung a large color photo of last year's Patriots. Bea spotted Jim Plunkett in the center. He was a sexy monkey that one. Next to the Patriots hung another color photo, this one of four hardened, middle-aged men in tank tops. They stood beside a huge bloody fish strung up by its tail, sneering into the camera like a Sea World lynch mob.

Bea waited while the woman poked at one ember and then the next, her lips tight with concentration. Bea looked around at the framed pictures on the walls. There were shots of dump trucks and guys in coveralls; a black and white of tired, dirty soldiers standing shoulder to shoulder, cradling their rifles; another black and white of a ribbon cutting ceremony at the front gates of the Tartusville Refuse Center.

A violent hacking thundered from behind the interior door.

The beehive cocked to one side but her assault on the ashtray continued.

"Excuse me," Bea said.

"Oh my Lord, young lady! You gave me such a start!" The woman slapped a hand to her shapeless knit sweater. Peach was not her color.

"I'm sorry to startle you. I'm Beatrice Vacarie. I have an appointment with Mr. Mancuso."

"Oh, of course you do, dear, one sec," she glanced back at Mancuso's door. "He's not doing so well today," she confided in a whisper. She waited for the coughing to stop before ringing him on the intercom. "Mr. Mancuso, Miss Vacky is here."

"Who?" the intercom speaker rattled.

"Vacarie," Bea said.

"Miss Vackery," said the receptionist.

"Yeah, yeah, yeah." The intercom clicked off.

"He'll see you now." She smiled and tilted her beehive toward the door.

Bea walked into his office. Salvino Mancuso stood behind a steel desk with Old Glory stretched on the wall behind him. He rested his lit cigar in a marble ashtray and held out his hand.

"How you doin'?" his deep voice crunched like flats on gravel, "Sal Mancuso."

She took his hand. His grip was stony. Bea recognized his face from the fish photo. He'd lost weight, but his shoulders were broad and his neck thick and solid under a large round head. He had a full head of tight Italian curls, more salt than pepper. With his wide nose and brutish chin, he was not handsome, but the spark that shot from his black, bloodshot eyes steered him clear of ugly. Sal Mancuso looked quite a bit like a pot-bellied Jim Plunkett. Sick or not, he looked like he could break Owen like a pretzel.

Not that that would be necessary.

"Have a sit," he said.

"Thank you." She sat sidesaddle on the chair with her back arched. He rubbed his chin and gazed at her legs. This one wasn't shy. She crossed one ankle over the other and opened her attaché.

He lifted his cigar off the ashtray. "Do you mind?"

"Oh no, I like the smell." Bea handed over her resumé.

"Good, that's good," he glanced at the paper. "Oh, Vacarie," he murmured. His eyes scanned down the page. "So, Ms. Vacarie... says here you graduated college in two years?"

"Yes, I graduated in '64. Garland's a Junior college," Bea smiled.

"Mhm... And then you went to work in Waterbury?"

"At the hospital, yes."

"Says here you were a nurse?" Sal Mancuso raised his dark eyebrows.

"Well, technically I was a coordinator—"

"Says nurse," he puffed his cigar.

"Well, I was, basically," Bea shifted in her seat and rested her hands on his desk. "They were short staffed. You know, with Vietnam heating up and all."

"Yeah... Then you moved to Missouri?"

"I needed to care for my sick mother."

"You're from Missouri?"

"No, my mother moved there."

"And then you came back?"

"To Waterbury, yes. She died."

He eyed her over the page. "Then you got a job as a... a legal aide? What's a legal aide?"

"It's like a coordinator - lawyers instead of doctors." Bea laughed and fanned herself. "I'm a bit warm, Mr. Mancuso. Do you mind if I take this off?" She watched him as she eased out of her blazer. He put down her resumé, rested his cigar on the ashtray and leaned back in his chair.

"Here it is then," he said, "I'm after sort of a live-in secretary, you get me? Someone to help out around the home front, house-wifey stuff." He folded his hands behind his head. "You know, shopping and cleaning and cooking and whatnot."

"I'm not a maid, Mr. Mancuso."

"I got a maid. A maid don't cut it."

"Well, why not get a live-in maid?"

"Did I not just say a maid don't cut it?" He looked up to the ceiling. "There's some nurse-type-stuff too."

"I see, no family then?"

"What?"

"No wife, kids?" Bea asked softly.

"Is this your business?" He glared at her.

"Oh, my goodness, I'm sorry, Mr. Mancuso. It's just surprising to see a man like you without a woman to take care of him, that's all."

"What the fuck is that supposed to mean?"

Bea waved her hands, "No! No! It's a compliment, really, Mr. Mancuso. You're obviously a... a... a successful, handsome man. I just assumed—"

"You're something, you know that?" He crushed his cigar out in the tray. He looked her up and down from across his desk. "Call me Sal, I ain't mayor yet," he coughed out the joke.

"Okay, thank you, Sal. I'm just saying it's hard to imagine—"

"I don't need the hassle," he shrugged.

"Oh, I'm hip to that," she risked a wink. "So, you were telling me about the job?"

"I just told you about the job."

"You want a nursemaid."

Sal's face flushed. This one had a temper on him.

"You know what? Forget about—"

Sal's coughing fit came on him before he could turn away. He covered his mouth with a handkerchief, using both hands. He coughed his face from red to purple. Veins bulged on his neck and twisted along his temples. He sucked in a breath and then coughed some more.

Bea circled around his desk. He leaned over the arm of his leather chair. She rested her hand on his convulsing back. He sat up and wiped his mouth and chin between heavy gasps.

"Freakin' sonofabitch!" he groaned and spat into his hanky.

"Can I get you anything? A glass of water?"

"Yeah, yeah, that would be good." He pointed, "Bathroom!"

Bea hurried into the bathroom. She rinsed out a mug of old coffee and filled it with water from the rust-stained sink. Her soles clomped on the floor as she returned to his desk. He took the mug with a nod. She sat down in her chair and dug through her purse. Sal gulped. Water spilled down his cheeks.

"Thanks," he said, drying his neck with his shirtsleeve.

"I have something that might help," Bea rummaged through her pillbox.

"Sorry, honey, I'm way past cough drops."

Bea shook her head. She picked out two black and orange capsules and two yellow pills.

"Here, one of each for now and a couple for later," she said and placed them on his desk.

"What're they?" He nudged them with a knurled fingertip.

"Beauties and Percs, they'll help," Bea replied.

He gave her a long look before swallowing the pills. She gathered her things and stood to leave.

"I hope you feel better, Mr. Mancuso." She had her hand on the doorknob when he spoke again.

"So where'd you get the, uh, helpers?" he asked.

"A girlfriend."

"Where does she get 'em?"

"From work."

"You known her a long time?"

"Since forever, Mr. Mancuso." Bea smiled.

"Call me Sal."

"Okay, Sal."

"So I'm thinking maybe I was wrong. I'm thinking maybe you should come by and see my place. Interested?"

"I'd love to."

"Good, tomorrow afternoon then, work it out with Dolly – tell her my place. She'll give you the address." Sal picked up his phone and dismissed her with the back of his hand.

"See you then, Sal." Bea smiled, turned on her go-go green platforms and sashayed out his office door.

Chapter One

AT THE TOP of the staircase Eddie Musso's new Guccis slid like Teflon on Amy's red and gold Persian runner. He lunged for the polished oak banister.

"Jesus Christ!" Eddie cursed, the pulse in his temples quickened to an aneurysmal pounding.

He clutched onto the banister with one hand, his gym bag in the other and slowly limped his way down the stairs, babying his reconstructed knee. It had been giving him pain day and night lately; the icy ache no longer confined to the low end of the barometer. His head throbbed with each descending step. Despite the double shot of minty fresh Scope, the smoky taste of peat from his Glenfiddich nightcap clung to the back of his throat.

At least it was Friday. He'd feel better soon enough, maybe even yabba-dabba-do-it out of the office a little early and soak in some me-time at Madigan's with that sweet barmaid. Sweet Sandra, with her short shorts and that little butterfly tattoo hovering just above her nipple; she knew all about adding value.

Eddie made it to the cool, white marble tiles of the dark center hall landing. Amy still hadn't gotten around to installing the goddamn chandelier she'd insisted they ship back from Florence. It sat in their garage between his 2006 BMW M5 and her dinged-up Tahoe in a box big enough to house a gorilla. Squeezing himself in and out of his sweet new car in his own damn garage depressed him.

The kitchen floodlights blazed indirectly from around the corner. Hadn't he shut everything off last night? He limped around the corner, squinting his dry eyes. Beyond the kitchen table and then the granite kitchen island, he saw Maggy holding her chestnut brown ponytail back and stretching up for a peek into a pot she had cooking on Amy's professional Thermador range. It was too early to be so bright, too early for daddy time, but she was his little girl. He stretched on his happy face.

"Well, hi-dee-hi-Maggy-pie! What're you doing up?"

"Hi Daddy! I'm cooking you breakfast."

"You are? Well ain't you sweet!" Eddie set his gym bag on the kitchen table and caught a whiff of what smelled like burnt vinegar. Maggy had laid out his place setting, a spoon and a small glass brimming with orange juice. Under the glass a wet circle spread from the top right corner of the placemat. It reminded him of her drawings. She liked her suns big and shining from the corners, thick and waxy with Crayola yellow and orange. He smiled, though at the moment he was in no condition to handle one of her food experiments.

"What's for breakfast?" he asked.

"Oatmeal! It's pretty much done I think."

"What a surprise!" The four Advil he'd washed down chewed at his gut. "Need a hand?"

"Nope, I can do it all by myself."

"Oh, that I know, Maggy-O."

"You just sit and have your juice."

Eddie hesitated as Maggy gripped the handle of the saucepan with two hands. "You sure you got that?"

"Daddyyy!" she reproved. Eddie shrugged and sat. Maggy turned the pot upside down over a cereal bowl beside the stove. Eddie held his breath and wished for a make-believe breakfast. Maggy peeked up into the overturned pot, snorted and gave it a shake. The oatmeal fell in a viscous wad along with Eddie's hopes.

"And there we are," she said as if to a studio audience. She picked up the bowl, held it with both little hands and walked along the island, her eyes on the prize. She set it down on his placemat.

"Bon appetite!"

Eddie clapped his hands together and rubbed them with delight.

"Ooo yummy," he said. The oatmeal was brick red. He sliced out a chunk with his spoon and blew on it.

"Its got sugar and cinnamon and special secret ingredients."

Eddie nodded his head and chewed. He flushed down the bite with his juice. His mouth burned and his belly rippled. He swallowed more juice, compounding the effect. He held up his glass.

"May I have some water, honey?" he choked.

"You don't like it," she pouted.

Eddie cleared his throat. "Are you kidding? This is the best oatmeal I've ever tasted!"

"Really? Even better than Mommy's?" she asked with a hopeful smile, minus two front teeth.

Eddie reeled her in with his finger to tell a secret. Maggy turned her ear to him. He whispered, "Well, I wouldn't want to hurt Mommy's feelings, but between you and me, this is the best damn oatmeal I ever ate."

Maggy stepped back and pointed with delight. "You said damn!"

"Oops!"

"Don't worry, I won't tell," she said.

"Phew!" Eddie handed her his glass. "How 'bout that water?"

She took his glass to the sink. Eddie looked down into his bowl. There was just no way. He poked at the dark mound in his bowl.

"What are the red specs?"

"Red pepper flakes! There's hot sauce and paprika in it too. It's Cajun style. I know you love spicy stuff."

"Mhmm, that I do."

"Here's your water."

He smiled, took the glass from her and gulped down the water. "So, what're you wearing there, Maggy-bear?"

"It's my dance costume, uh-doy!" she slapped his shoulder. "Tonight's the recital," Maggy twirled on her bare feet. "You're coming aren't you?"

"Uh-double-doy! obviously! but you can't wear your tutu to school, can you?"

She stopped spinning and stood facing him, her hands on her hips. "Mommy says I can."

"Then I guess you can," Eddie scooped a small lump and swallowed it like a pill. "Maggy-Pie, honey, I'm running a little late for work, would you mind if I took this delicious breakfast to go?"

"Do you promise to eat the whole thing?"

"Yup."

"Lick the bowl?"

"Yup."

Maggy crossed one arm across her waist, set her elbow on it and held two fingers to her mouth as she considered. The pose was classic Amy, though somewhat less intimidating coming from his six-year-old. "Yeah, I guess that would be okay."

"Thanks, honey," Eddie pulled her close for a kiss on the forehead and a one-armed hug. "Thanks for breakfast."

"Have fun at work."

"I'll try," Eddie said as he stood up. He picked up his bowl and gym bag, "I'll see you tonight for the big show."

"Recital," she corrected. She walked with him through the kitchen.

"Recital, yes," he said. He raised his bowl to Maggy, sent her an airmail smooch and walked out the back door into the garage.

The garage door opened to a gray, damp morning, reminding him of last night's dicey ride through heavy rain. He circled around the back of his Beemer, stepping over his tire tracks. Still wet... He must've gotten home later than he thought, no wonder he felt so crappy this morning. He set his bowl of fire on the damn gorilla box and opened his car door, tossed his gym bag into the passenger seat and squeezed inside. He backed out and shut the bay door with the clicker.

"Shit!" he forgot his bowl.

He idled in the driveway, staring up at his bedroom windows above the garage. If he opened the door again he'd risk waking Amy. Nope, not worth it, he'd just have to take his chances. If Maggy spotted his breakfast on top of the box, he'd just have to come clean and tell her he forgot it. He rolled down his steep driveway and turned onto the street. The wheel felt chunky. He really was in rough shape.

The clock in the dash read 6:30, ugly-early, but he wasn't about to go to any AA meetings in nearby Weston, or Trumbull, or anywhere near Stamford either, for that matter. It was worth the extra miles to avoid any chance of running into someone he knew. He'd done a masterful job containing the DWI, damned if he was going to fuck it up now. Hell, he'd already hoofed it up as far as Waterbury! He had to admit it though; the damn DWI had done him the biggest favor of his career. He'd have AA to thank when he got his seat in the executive dining room of the United Tobacco Company.

Wipers going, radio on and air conditioning blowing, Eddie wasn't sure he had a flat until he was at the entrance of his cul-de-sac.

"Christ," he grumbled and cut the engine. He got out, turned his suit collar up against the fine drizzle, and checked the front end.

The rim of the passenger side quarter panel was crushed inward. The tire was completely fucking flat. When the hell did that happen? Eddie yanked out a torn branch wedged up under the broken plastic rim of the wheel well. He put his hands on his hips.

"Well, let's get'er done," he said in his best cowboy drawl.

He stripped down to his undershirt and shoved his jacket, tie and oxford shirt in the car. He pulled the jack and spare from the trunk and set to work. He inspected the damage as he cranked the jack. He'd been moving, that much was for sure given the long parallel gouges in the quarter panel. It was too much damage for an animal, even a big dog. His stomach flipped.

"Oh no, please no," Eddie mumbled and leaned under the well for a closer look. He wiped his hand under the front bumper and inspected his fingers. He saw no sign of hair or blood, no cloth, nothing red, just black dirt and leaves.

"Okay, okay, good, we're good. Thank you, Jesus."

Eddie removed the lug nuts and replaced the flat with the spare. It was a real spare; his M5 delivered on its premium image. If the spare had been one of those Asian mini-tires, Eddie's future Purchase Interest for a BMW would have dropped from top box to bottom, the old DWNB. Definitely Will Not Buy, or, as he used to say working in New Products, "Definitely Will Need Booze."

He tightened the last nut. The back of his undershirt was soaked through. He must've swiped a guardrail coming home. He wasn't sure if that was memory or imagination, but whatever, no blood, no foul. He got in the car, pealed off his undershirt and started her up. He fishtailed out his cul-de-sac and gunned it for the highway.

He'd always been lucky.

Hell, discovering he had a knack for marketing was even dumb luck. But he had a gift for building strong brands, for creating marketplace synergies. He knew how to capitalize on consumer insights - check that, sorry Legal - *adult* consumer insights. In Big Tobacco Land there was no such thing as consumers, only adult consumers. He was a brand guy, a premium brand guy at that. He cared enough about his loyal adult consumer base to provide for them only the finest, 100% American grown tobacco products. His adult consumers worked for a living. They were the heart and soul of this country, everyday blue-collar heroes, the salt of the earth. These men (less than 5% of his adult consumers were female, he was working on that monster opportunity) deserved the best tobacco, not just in terms of quality and value, but also in terms of integrity. Eddie managed brands that stood for something real, for American values, for freedom, for Fortitude. Hell, take any white male Marine between the ages of 25 and 34 or factory worker between 35 and 54 and chances were better than good that, if he used tobacco, it was one of his brands.

Eddie raced north on Route 8 in the opposite direction of his Stamford office, his wet ass baking dry on the seat. According to his little white AA booklet, there was a 7:30 AA meeting at The Our Lady of such and such church up in Tartusville. He'd be late, but all he could do was hope whoever was running the show wouldn't be a Nazi prick about signing his probation sheet.

Across the highway divide, southbound traffic was light. He had another ten miles or so on the highway before the Sycamore Lane exit. The church would be easy to find and hopefully this meeting would be as packed as all the others. Truth was, that since his brainstorm for the upcoming national roll out of Fortitude Lights, he really didn't mind going to the meetings. It was great market research. Every meeting he'd been to so far just reiterated the genius of his new product sampling plan.

So he didn't need a segmentation analysis to know that these meetings were full of opportunity. These were his people, his future adult consumers. Shit, psychographics alone demanded he leverage Alcoholics Anonymous! And if they wouldn't play ball, then he'd just revise his brand plan. His strategy ensured the successful launch of Fortitude Lights. And that was just the boost he needed to climb that last slippery rung of the corporate ladder. Fortitude Lights would hit a four share in year one and lock him in as the next V.P. of Marketing at UTC.

"Ah shit," he banged the steering wheel. Legal had banned the use of the word "leverage." He'd have to come up with another word for his presentation to the brass.

Eddie exited onto Sycamore Lane. He felt better, his hangover drifting through him like a fast moving front. He blew by the dumpy little mom and pop shops along Tartusville's main drag and hung a left into the church parking lot. Our Lady of Perpetual Forgiveness, now that's a brand promise.

"Complement!" Eddie exclaimed. A perfectly benign, ambiguous term, Legal would love it.

And Amy probably wasn't even up yet.

Chapter Two

ZELLA WHIMPERED FROM under the bed. It was the beagle in her. She sounded as if she'd swallowed one of her chew toys.

Jonathan peeked at the morning. Gray light cut through the slats of his white window blinds. He'd stayed up too late watching movies. His boss made him do it.

"It's okay girl, thunder's long gone. Nothing's going to get you, it's okay," Jonathan cooed from his damp pillowcase. Zella had survived the thunder, but she would not escape the tumors that bubbled up from beneath her coarse coat. Jonathan grunted. He was thinking in Roman-speak, it was that gladiator movie, too many movies.

Darn it, he always waited until it was too late.

"You need to know the products, Jonathan. You haven't seen enough," Brent had said, handing him a stack of DVDs. Brent was a good boss. The other clerks called him names. "Blockbuster Brent" was the nicest by far. Jonathan kept his mouth shut. It was a good job. He wanted to keep it.

He'd fallen asleep in his comfy chair during *Goodfellas*. It was hard to follow. At some point during the rainstorm, thunder boomers came from across the lake. Zella's howls woke him up. He held her in the dark. Lightning lit up her lumpy snout and the thunder felt close enough to rattle the siding loose from the house. The booms echoed far in the distance before either of them were calm enough to crawl into his bed.

Jonathan curled in a ball and pulled clammy sheets over his head. He needed more sleep. Beads of sweat formed between his man-boobies. Droplets slid through his blond chest nest bound for his damp mattress. More droplets followed. They slid down his forehead, his armpits, in between his flabby thighs.

His cell phone rattled and rang on his bedside table. He pawed for it, but missed the table entirely. He yanked off his sheet and reached across the clutter of plastic cups and wadded Kleenex for the phone. He flipped it open and held it at arm's length.

It was a man's voice, but screechy like a girl's. "Good morning, Jonathan! Francis van G. here with your 6:55 wake-up call! It's Friday, August the sixth in the year of our Lord 2006! Remember, Karl's our qualifier this morning—"

Francis?

Francis! Jonathan jolted upright, flipping the phone shut accidentally. He turned on his side and wedged himself upright to check his alarm setting: Off.

"Sons of boogies!"

He flipped open his phone, scrolled down and found "Mother" in his recent calls. He pressed SEND and tucked the phone between his slick shoulder and stubbled jowl.

She picked up on the third ring.

"Umm, yes? Hello?"

"Mother, it's me. Hi. I mean, good morning."

"If you say so," her voice was raspy. "I've got a rancid headache."

"I'm sorry. I overslept. I'll be by to get you in like twenty minutes."

"Oh for God's sake! this is why you call at the crack of dawn?" She sounded like her cheeks were full of marbles. "And here I thought you might be calling out of concern."

The line went dead.

Jonathan sat up. He toed his Captain America boxers up off the floor and slid them on, yanking the waistband up and over his hips. The boxers were damp and waxy with day-old funk. Jonathan took three deep breaths and pushed himself up onto his feet. He pulled on sweatpants, sneakers, a t-shirt and then tiptoed through Blockbuster cases and dirty clothes.

Boogers! he bent to gather the cases in easy reach.

"What am I doing? I'm supposed to be hurrying!" he dropped the cases and ran into the bathroom. He positioned himself in front of the toilet, penis out, arms to his sides. He tinkled with his legs spread wide enough to catch a whiff of his sweet, rank butt-crack bouquet.

And it was a bouquet. He must think of it as a bouquet. This time around he was told he must think nothing but positive thoughts about himself.

"Johnny, you smell like a courageous gladiator, like, like... like Spartacus."

He liked that movie.

He gripped the banister on his way down the narrow staircase to the kitchen. His kitchen was a small, square room directly beneath his bedroom. The cabinets were white vinyl veneer. The stove and refrigerator had yellowed with grease and age. Jonathan opened the refrigerator and reached for the last Egg McMuffin, the sole survivor from yesterday's McMuffin binge. He unwrapped it, and doused the stiff egg with Tabasco.

Dirty dishes filled the sink. He had to get to those. Mother didn't live here anymore, but she'd go ape if she saw them all the same. She'd moved out the day after his twenty-first birthday.

"I need reliable, caring care," she'd insisted as she polished off her sloe gin fizz. "Sunny Brook Farms Luxury Assisted Living Center" was written in script letters above the fancy gated entrance.

Breakfast in hand; he hurried back through the house toward the front door.

"Zella, I'll be back, girl! Eat something! We'll watch a movie and maybe go for a swim later, okay? Be a good girl!"

Jonathan crossed his weedy driveway to his yellow '92 Cadillac El Dorado. It looked good. He'd saved up and bought it himself, thank you very much. Stuffing the last of the McMuffin in his mouth, he wiped his hands on his sweats and plopped himself onto the driver's seat. He kneaded the wheel before starting her up. The sweet stench of stale beer and rum compelled him to prayer.

"Thank you God for this sober day. Today is Your day. You are in charge. I am in Your care. If it be Thy will, please help me to stay sober today. And God, if it be Thy Will, I ask You to put an end to Mother's suffering. I humbly ask You to gather her in Your glory. Have mercy on her." He mouthed a silent Our Father, except for the "forgives," which he shouted.

⇥▶◉ ◉◀⇤

Jonathan pulled out onto Lakeside Drive. He turned onto Sycamore, plowing the Caddy through debris left over from the storm.

The Program says pray for those still suffering. The Program says wait until they're ready. Meanwhile, be strong for them both. He was on a good sober clip this time and he could see that Mother was miserable with fear and vodka.

"Who says I'm miserable? Life's just life, that's all. We're just like the ants in that awful farm you used to keep. You work your ass off to build something decent—always for somebody else mind you—and then you die of exhaustion or sun bake, or you, you, you get squashed in a massive earthquake—"

"Not at all, mother, life is like a river," he reassured her. "We've all got to go with the flow."

"More like a flood, Zippy. We all drown eventually."

He made it to the security gates of Sunny Brook Farms Luxury Assisted Living Center in ten minutes flat. The guard checked him in and he drove up the hill, admiring the golfing lawns on either side of the drive. The Main House came into view, and then his mother's red hat and then Nurse Lisa. The two women waited for him side by side on an Adirondack love seat nestled in patch of wildflowers slung low from the rain. Mother wore her big sunglasses and had her long gray hair stuffed into her red bucket hat. He pulled up to the curb and Nurse Lisa opened the passenger door.

"Good Morning, Lisa," Jonathan tried not to look at her chest.

"Good morning, Mr. Vacarie. Here she is."

Lisa helped Mother into her seat. She plunked down with a boozy sigh.

"You have yourself a nice morning, Bea." Nurse Lisa shut the door. His mother's familiar scents of cigarettes, mints, camphor and vodka flooded the car. Jonathan cracked open his window.

"Oh, you too dear," she murmured as they drove away. She dipped her sunglasses at Jonathan. "No good morning for me?" Her voice was rougher than usual.

"Good morning, Mother."

"Well? Shall we?"

"Need help with your seat belt?"

"Oh, I've got it," she said and slapped away his hand. "Just drive."

Jonathan waved to Lisa in his rear view mirror. At the bottom of the long drive, the gate at the security house swung open and they were on their way to The Our Lady Of Perpetual Forgiveness.

"I'm glad you're coming," he said.

"You had us waiting out there forever. My feet are cold."

"I'm sorry."

"There you go with the useless apologies. When will you learn to be on time?" She huffed. "You're sick you know that? You're really sick."

"I know."

"And you need help."

"I'm getting help," he said and punched the Caddy up the ramp onto the highway.

"Not your AA nonsense! Real help! From a professional! Father McMullin for example," she huffed and puffed.

"Mother, AA isn't nonsense—"

"Oh, how would you know?" she scoffed.

"Well, I'm still glad you're coming," he said.

"I'm not sitting next to you," she squeezed her purse against her tiny waist and stared out her window.

"Mother, you get the message from any seat in the room, 'cause meeting makers make it."

"Oh, shut up."

⊷⊨◉ ◉⊨⊶

The church basement was cool and damp. Jonathan walked with his mother to the circle of chairs arranged at half court, in the center of the large, rectangular hall.

"Mother, we're all in the same boat," he whispered.

"No, we're not," she said and shrugged his hand off her elbow.

Jonathan took a seat on his folding chair along with the rest of the meeting-makers. He straddled the old half-court line. His mother took a chair directly across the circle from him. She crossed her arms over her dark blue cardigan sweater, her rose-red bucket hat pulled low enough so that the brim touched the frame of her Whopper-sized sunglasses.

The elastic band of her hair net peeked out beneath the edges of her hat. She turned to her left and sneered in the direction of Francis. Francis sat up straight in his mime costume and whiteface. Francis always wore the same thing, a black T-shirt under a baggy white tuxedo that hung off him like huge pajamas. He smiled at Jonathan with his black lips and then pushed up his wide sleeve to check his watch. Francis was their meeting leader. Jonathan looked past Francis toward the stage. The old home team hoop was stowed away, facing the ceiling.

As a kid, Mother had insisted he play basketball, said it would help him get coordinated, said it would help him make friends. She was always right, but sometimes right didn't make any sense.

The basement ceiling was no more than fifteen feet from the floor. Any shot from the outside had to be a line drive, unless you were good enough to bank one off the ceiling. The kids who figured that out went off to play in real gyms.

The parents used to sit and watch from these same metal folding chairs, lined up along the sidelines. Most parents sat in silence, except his mother.

"Shoot it!" she'd shout whenever and wherever he had hold of the ball.

"Shoot it! Shoot it!"

He stood out of bounds right next to her chair, searching for someone to pass to.

"Just shoot it!"

So he shot it. The ball bounced off a beam and rolled out of bounds across the far sideline. The referee blew his whistle. The coach put him back on the bench. His mother threw her hands up and shook her head. He pulled his curly hair until it hurt. Chalk up another loss for the boys of OLOPF.

Jonathan toed at the corner of a loose floorboard. It was the first Friday of the month and that meant someone was going to tell their story. In The Rooms they called this "qualifying." Qualifying was an honor and an act of service. The speaker shared his experience, strength and hope. Jonathan liked the experience part best. Facts were facts. He had a harder time paying attention during the strength and hope parts, when people started talking in slippery terms that were hard for him to hang on to. But he was trying. He was in the chair. He was almost 13 weeks in this time around.

This morning King Karl sat in the hot seat next to Francis. It was his nickname for the man. It was a good one. Karl was big, very big, especially across the shoulders and chest. Karl sat with his back straight and his hands on the blackened knees of his stained jeans. His forearms popped out from the rolled sleeves of his waffle shirt. Karl craned his neck from side to side, teetering on his chair like three scoops on a cone. Chocolate colored tattoos covered his vanilla white skin. He was mostly bald, save for some cream-white stubble. His skull was sprinkled with brown, nut-shaped scars.

Francis checked his watch again and spoke.

"Welcome, everyone, to the Friday morning meeting of Alcoholics Anonymous. I'm Francis and I'm an addict."

"Hi, Francis," Jonathan replied along with the room.

"On the eve of his tenth anniversary, I've asked Karl to share his story with us today. Karl has the kind of sobriety I admire. I tell you without reservation that he is a meaningful and inspiring part of my program." Francis bowed his head and extended his hand toward Karl. "May I humbly present to you, Karl."

Jonathan clapped along with the others. He looked to his mother across the circle. The wrinkles around her mouth were still as stone. Karl got on with it. He spoke slowly. He thanked Francis, told his sobriety date, and began his story. Jonathan studied the wooden crossbeams overhead. Every dozen feet or so, a thick support beam ran across the ceiling from one sideline to the other. Save for a lucky line drive from the baseline, there was no way to sink a basket from the outside.

"Shoot it, Johnny! Shoot it!"

He'd no idea she was drunk, all he knew at the time was that he and the other OLOPF Junior Juggernauts didn't stand a chance.

And then it was Karl's deep voice that rumbled along the floor and up to his ears.

"...shameful things to be doing, you know, shameful. Shit, I had a wife and my little boy to care for. But that didn't make any difference at all. God I hated

Kissette, thought I didn't deserve all her bitching and black girl bullshit. I had a right, right? I worked hard and I played hard, my right, yeah right.

"So anyway, like I was saying, we took Dumb Willy along with us for the ride. We stopped at the store and made him buy us a bottle and he did and we drank that bottle down right there in the parking lot and sent him in for another. Then we hit my buddy's pipe while Willy drove. He chauffeured me and Jack around town and I remember laughing at the idea and punching Jack's arm and Willy glancing back at us over his shoulder. Willy was a short little dude. He might have had some Chinese in him or something, maybe not. I don't know. Anyways, his chin barely showed up over the seat. We rode around until the sun went down and came up on some woods and we told Willy to park. We smoked every last bit of Jack's rock, and then, well..."

King Karl paused. He looked down and wrung his monster hands in his lap.

"Well, you know, we um, we were all crazed and one thing led to the next and then Jack dragged Willy out of the car and well, we um, we had our way with him." He swayed his knobby head from side to side. "When we were done we threw him in the back and Jack drove us on out of the there. Now and again I'd look over the seat at poor Willy all curled up, shaking and crying like a baby."

King Karl sat up, took a huge breath and pressed his palms into his eyes.

"The man cried like a baby in the back seat of his own car... his own damn car. So, yeah, well, I got mine for that. I got my eight years up at Osborn."

The gym was silent.

"Am I getting this right?" Mother blurted out from under her red hat. "You raped a *man*?"

It was her first share.

Jonathan cringed and squirmed in his metal seat. She'd reeked when she got in the car. Maybe he shouldn't have brought her. He raised his hand to hush her, but put it back in his lap. In AA, you weren't supposed to interrupt.

"I'm sitting here in the basement of *my own church* that I have been attending since *before any of you was even born*, listening to some drunk convict tell me he's a backwoods butt fucker?"

"Madam—" Francis started.

"Don't you madam me, you... you fancy-pants freak."

"My apologies, your name is?" Francis asked.

"Never you mind my name, you... you... you *clown*!"

"A mime, madam, and that is quite enough."

"You're probably sitting there getting all worked up you... you... you *loon*."

"Excuse me, Karl," Francis put his hand on King Karl's shoulder. "Madame, you're drunk. You need to be quiet or you need to leave."

"What? me? he's the rapist!" she stabbed a finger at Karl. "You're out of your mind! You're all out of your minds!"

Francis stood up and raised his hand over his head. He must've been good at basketball, tall as he was. His sleeve bunched under his skinny arm.

"I move for an emergency group conscience," Francis said.

Jonathan looked around at the other faces. Maybe this sort of thing happened a lot.

"Let her say her piece," King Karl said. Karl looked at her. His face was cherry red.

"But she's drunk!" Francis said.

"Don't mean I haven't offended her," Karl said.

"Offended? Offended? Is that what you call it?" she screeched from behind her dark lenses. "I call it faggot porn. What in God's name does faggot porn have to do with staying dry?"

"Sorry, Karl." Francis halted her with his hand like a traffic cop. "Madam, final warning, either be quite this instant or I'm going to have to ask your..." Francis looked at him with his black half-moon brows way up on his white forehead.

"Son," Jonathan admitted.

"Your, uh, son to escort you out." Francis shook beneath his big jacket. His scowl twisted the cheery expression painted on his face.

Jonathan rose from his chair. The greasy heat of eggs and Tabasco bubbled down from his gut. He felt like an upside down volcano, rumbling and about to blow.

"Mother, I think we should go."

"You sit down, Zippy!"

Jonathan's stomach cramped. Sweat rolled down his temples. He dropped back onto his chair. A blip of oily heat escaped into his underpants.

She pointed at him. "You're the one who dragged me here. 'You should go to a meeting, Mommy,'" She tossed a hand at the circle while her other hand stayed in her lap, locked on her purse. "So here I am with... with I don't even know what! And I'm subjected to this big ugly buttfucker's confession? 'There's a Higher Power Mommy.' Really? And who's your Higher Power there, Johnny boy? Ronald McDonald? Wendy? Who? Mayor McCheese?"

Jonathan grimaced and doubled over. He mouthed silent put-ups.

You are a valiant gladiator with buns of steel. No one is here to judge. It's my body to control. God is with me. He does not will for me to poo myself. His will be done.

He clenched his butt cheeks together with all he had.

"Madam, that is enough!" Francis shouted.

"You're damn right it is, you freak!"

Francis ignored her. "By a show of hands, who feels this woman aught to leave this morning?" He raised his hand.

Jonathan looked around. Only he, his mother and King Karl kept their hands by their sides.

"That's it then. The group has spoken. We ask you to kindly leave. You are welcome to return in the future, but now you must go."

"You can't throw me out of my own church! You... you... you *clown*!"

"Jonathan, please escort your mother outside," Francis said

"He'll do nothing of the sort. I'm perfectly happy to get away from you bunch of drunken perverts."

"As you wish."

She stood up with a huff. Her chair skittered behind her, upended and toppled to the floor with a clang and a thud. She swept her glare in a wide arc and stomped for the door. The door opened toward her as she reached for it and she stumbled backwards. A tall man in a business suit and tie reached out his hand.

"Whoa there, pardon me, ma'am," he said.

"Oh shut up," she grumbled and shouldered her way past him.

Jonathan hugged his stomach and doubled over in his seat. He heard the basement door slam shut.

Chapter Three

WHAT IN THE world was keeping that fat ass?

Beatrice Vacarie stood by his piece-of-shit Caddy, hands on her trim, aching hips. She kept her eyes on the stairway leading up from the church basement. She couldn't imagine what he was up to. For all she knew, he might not leave the meeting at all - make her wait in the drizzle until she caught her death. He knew full well that summer colds are the worst. God knows she'd nursed him through dozens over the years.

"Well, low and behold," she murmured and sucked a drag off her Virginia Slim. Out the door he came, bobbing up the steps from the church basement, his little head of greasy curls leading the way. Her fretting had been preposterous of course. Her Johnny didn't have the balls.

"You get tired of dancing with the devil down there?" she called across the lot.

He stood panting at the top of the stairs.

"Taking a breather are you? I don't blame you." She took a last drag off her Slim, aimed the butt and flicked it into a puddle. She drew her shoulders back and raised her chin.

"I'd like to go now, please," she said, her tone firm.

Never had she allowed Johnny to trifle with her, not in all his years of troublemaking and certainly not now. This dry spell had been going on for months and his self-righteousness was nearly past her ability to endure. His head was so full of twelve-step hot air that she wouldn't have batted an eye if he floated over to her, toes dangling over the wet asphalt. This too shall pass; wasn't that one of their little sayings? Lord knows, she could only hope.

Johnny's head never was right-sized though; it was squat, just like the rest of him. And now that he'd packed on all the pounds his head sat on his bulky, round shoulders like a shrunken trophy on some witch doctor's shelf.

It was funny how things changed for the worse. Baby Johnny had his father's gorgeous wolf-blue eyes and her cute pug nose. She'd seen the resemblance the moment the doctor wiped the mess off and handed him over.

"Congratulations, Mrs. Mancuso, it's a boy," said the doctor.

"It's Vacarie," Bea corrected.

"A boy!" Sal exclaimed from the corner of the delivery room, cradling his portable oxygen tank in his lap. He pulled his mask aside and craned up his neck to see the newborn. "How's he look? He look like me? Does he look like his old man?"

"The spitting image," she said.

"Are his eyes open?" Sal asked.

"He's plenty curious," she said.

Sal pushed himself up out of his chair to get a better look.

"Those ain't my eyes," he grumbled and dropped back in his chair. He put his mask back on.

"Those would be mine, Sal," she lied.

Of course Jonathan didn't look anything like him, but by then Sal was in no shape to see it. Sal was too busy dying. Those last months in his house drained her youth away. All the needy cries and all the goddamn diapers and all the late night feedings and those nasty Similac spills that hardened like Elmer's Glue on the stovetop; it all sucked her dry to the bone.

Sal finally mustered up the decency to die, just before Jonathan's third month. At least that cut her burdens in half for a while; one less mouth for her to feed, one less diaper to change, one less ass to wipe, one less whiner to appease. He died a dad, just what he'd wanted.

But as Johnny grew, the less he resembled her or his father. Johnny ended up no taller than her, just five-foot-six though his father stood a full six-foot-two. And the wonderful features they'd passed to him; her fare skin, his magnetic eyes and wavy blond hair, seemed misplaced on his little head and stubby frame.

He was her golden cross to bear, a handful since day one of school—impetuous and short-tempered and the teachers always harping on and on about testing him for this, that or the other thing. They simply refused to accept the fact that some people were born stupid, plain and simple.

It's no wonder a girl drank.

Johnny shuffled across the parking lot, sweat dripping down his flat, round face, his arms extended out to his sides like a summer snowman.

"Mother, what was that all about?"

"Don't you 'Mother' me."

"You can't say things like that in a meeting!"

"Like what? What exactly did I say other than the truth? You feel more sober after hearing where that jailbird likes to stick his wick? I know I don't. That's for sure."

"You've been at it this morning," he pointed his fat finger at her.

"And thank God for that! Gave me the courage to take a stand for what's right, now didn't it? You see any of those other twerps do anything? Do you have any idea of the sort of riff raff you're cavorting with in there?"

She rolled her eyes. Of course he doesn't.

"Cavorting?" Johnny raised his eyebrows.

"Hanging around with," she clarified. "That faggot hulk is the Devil himself, spewing his filth at all of us. What else could I do? Someone had to say something!"

"The Devil, Mother? Seriously?"

"And did my own son stand up for me? No, of course he didn't. You... you... you coward!"

He turned a deep shade of red. "Get in the car, Mother."

She crossed her arms and replanted her feet and waited for him to get the message. He stepped beside her and opened her door.

"Thank you," she said.

Bea somehow misjudged her altitude and bumped her head, dislodging her red bucket hat. She scrambled and caught it before it fell on the filthy, wet asphalt.

"Are you alright?" he asked.

"What do you care?"

He closed her door without even a hint of warning.

"You want to take my knee off?" She fogged the window with wasted breath.

She sighed. What a disaster that would have been! She popped the dents from her hat and brushed off the drizzle. It was a chic, fabulous hat. She glanced over her shoulder at the church door and then pulled it back on.

Johnny loitered uselessly by her side of the car. How her house survived with just him in it was a mystery. The little lummox could hardly keep up an ant farm! Lord, if that wasn't the sad truth. She still had to help him with his checkbook!

"I'll be right back," he said.

And just like that he deserted her!

"Give me strength," she muttered. She rummaged in her purse and pulled out one of her little nippers of Popov.

Chapter Four

... YOU SHOULD go out to that parking lot and pound the piss out of that old bitch.

Karl Warth's old mind stopped raging when he heard the basement door bust open. Karl turned in his chair to see. Fat Jonathan's blue eyes was wide open but still too tiny on his wet, flat face. He waddled up the stairs to the bathroom by the stage. Karl turned back to the circle to listen to the woman's share. He heard a toilet seat slam on porcelain, but if he sat still and listened hard enough, his new mind would set things straight.

"I'm just so ashamed all the time, you know? It's everything. I'm a phony," she swept her big hands down her front. "This is a costume. I'm a costume, you know? Everything you see is a lie. It isn't me. I'm just off the farm, for God's sake!"

Her name was Nellie. She was a familiar type, with her shiny blue high heels and those skintight jeans that came up high and choked her calf meat. These ones always had big calves, smooth and sexy, pumping those high heels along. The calves were the be-all and end-all on these bitches. The rest of her just showed her hard living. A roll of belly peeked out from under her top. The little hoop she had stuck in her navel when she was a proud young teen now hung sad and low, like the guide ring off a bull's nose. She'd slipped her leopard print raincoat down off her shoulders. Strands of bleached hair, yellow like corn, swept past her pale-skinned blades as she skipped her eyes around the group.

"I have an obsession, you know?" she dropped her head and hid behind that long hair. "Well, yeah, that's an understatement. I have lots of obsessions.

I collect obsessions. Can you imagine? An obsession with obsessions? I know, I know, that sounds crazy. That's what my sister says, anyway. But then she goes ahead and feeds me, you know, in her own special way. I guess that's enabling, right? But she's always been the strong one, strongest by far. It's a mess. Everything's so damn complicated! But I'm trying to simplify, you know? I really am. I mean, I come to the meetings, I listen to everyone and God knows I know I have a problem, lots of problems..."

Nellie paused. She rolled her long, red fingernails against the sides of her chair. The metallic taps circled in the silence. And now she locked on him with her pleading, painted eyes. She was familiar all right. Her cheeks were drawn inward; as if she couldn't set 'em right after all the sucking she'd likely done. Karl bent over and rested his elbows on his knees of his jeans, stained to black from pine tar.

"I just have a hard time saying no, you know?" she said.

He nodded. He got that. In this damp basement she was what she was - all worn out and stringy. But damned if she wouldn't be the late-night queen over at the Lounge, or King's, or hell, maybe even Billy's Topless. She was the kind of woman that drew a man's last-call attention.

Fuck that chick's lights out.

Dark days, old mind in charge, when the morning came up harsh and he'd look over and see what he drug down with him. He knew all that fear; worrying sick over what you caught and you'd feel your pecker tingling and getting little pinches and pains that you didn't have before. And then the only thing you could do was to hit it again because that 80-proof was the only medicine that worked. And you'd do it again and again until you couldn't do it any more.

"Everything is just so hard all the time..."

Tapiddytap.

"Still, I put a few good weeks together or even a month or two here and there. You know, not doing anything bad, not drinking or drugging or," she took a deep breath, "or any of the other stuff. And then I start to feel good, really good and then, I don't know, something comes up, life, you know? The bills and this shit-hole of a town and all that fucking reality you know? And the walls of my crummy apartment start closing in on me, I'm serious, it gets to feeling like a cage in there and I have to get the fuck out! And the only thing that seems to stop those walls from squishing me like an ant is a bottle, or my hair or a pill or... or... whatever."

Tapiddytap.

"But I pray and pray, you know? I say the serenity prayer like a million times a day and I ask for His help and tell myself that it's His world and all the other things I learn in here and still I end up on the corner stool at King's."

Tapiddytap, tapiddytap.

Karl's nod wasn't goodhearted like the others. It didn't come from identifying or sympathizing. He was nodding because he liked that corner stool at King's. It was his old mind nodding.

He'd tap that skank and it wouldn't be nothing but a thing, nothing at all.

Karl shifted in his seat and looked around the circle. His old mind was fucking with him. He was out there right now, getting all juiced up. Sometimes there was no stopping it. The bad thoughts just slipped on in.

Slippery as this chick's beat-up box.

All bad, his old mind didn't need booze to be thinking drunk. Bare fact was he had a disease of the mind, a sickness of the soul. He knew it. He knew he had it bad. It was dug in deep like a tick about to burst; stuck so deep in his heart that no matter how many 24 hours he put together, the urges would come. And when they came, they came on strong.

Those long nails dragging down his back, taking skin, leaving tracks.

He shifted and crossed his legs. He called on Him to break the spell.

"Thy will not mine, Lord," Karl prayed silently mouth and swiped the sweat from his temple.

"Sometimes it's just so hard to be honest, you know? I wish I could be honest like you," she swung her hair and looked at him. "But I can't. I mean, like, I just lie sometimes, like a reflex you know? Like a button gets pushed and the lies fly out of my mouth before I have a chance to shut it. Stupid shit, you know? Like yesterday I'm down at the Sev-Club and I run into a guy I know, you know, from the life. He's got a Big Gulp in his hand and he goes, 'wanna a sip?' and I say sure and take a sip, but I don't even want it, you know? I'm lying, right? I'm lying all around." She threw her hands up, "Oh Christ! I'm so mixed up in the head right now. I'm not even making sense. I'm sorry."

Nellie looked at him, just plain desperate.

"No, it's alright. You're making perfect sense," Karl said. He gave her a smile and hated himself and, with a nod, encouraged her to continue, but she was all done.

Chapter Five

Officer Joe Batina rubbed his raw eyes and replanted his feet on the old gym floor to stop his knees from bouncing. His gaze kept drifting downward to the day-counter's belly button ring. She was laying it out there the best she could, good for her. He sat in the circle with the old stage and blue curtain at his one o'clock. The home team basket was drawn up on its hinges in front of the stage, the old wooden backboard facing the low ceiling. Francis the freakin' mime sat on the edge of his seat, listening. Hell, who was he to judge? Francis's knees weren't jumping like Bolivian beans.

A toilet flushed backstage. Joe watched the kid, Jonathan, creak down the stairs by the side of the stage. The kid waddled to half court and plunked himself down in his same seat, to Joe's right. Joe winked when the kid caught him staring. The kid nodded with an apologetic half-smile and smoothed back his mop of greasy blond hair.

The day-counter clicked her nails on her chair and told on herself. Joe nibbled his numb front teeth on his rubbery tongue tip, nodding as she spoke. He knew more than he cared to about how all those lies had a way of doing end arounds, or sneaking up from under, or hitting from behind. No shame in counting days, no shame at all.

Joe glanced to his right. The kid listened with his squat little eyes half shut. His mismatched lips hung open, his full bottom lip drooping below his flat, thin upper lip. He raked his stubby fingers through his tangled curls.

He could stand a trim himself. Maybe he'd get up a little early this afternoon and drop by Vic's for a buzz. Working nights messed him up, worse than ever now at fifty-two. Fifty-freakin'-two and back on graveyard! What he wouldn't give to be back in his thirties like the nail-tapper here! Fuck-a-duck, even his forties would do! He could've done it all different, could've stuck with the meetings. He'd still be working the cush shifts back in Elkton, still be coming home to Denise, still be eating crabs down in Chesapeake City on summer Sundays. He'd be being and doing a lot of things.

He hadn't eaten since yesterday morning. There was a hollow, queasy buzzing in his stomach. His knees were bouncing again. He pressed his scarred fists on his thighs, squeezing the rim of his cap in his left hand. Joe belched up little gas bubbles and wrinkled his crusted nostrils at the stench of his foul monkey breath. He had to get down some real food after the meeting. He could use a cheesesteak. Good God could he use a cheesesteak! But they got no idea how to make 'em up here, not a clue.

He'd forgotten all there was to despise about good old Tartusville.

Joe shifted sideways in his chair. He adjusted his holster and unstuck the butt of his Sig Sauer from his rib, the same spot he'd plucked it from a minute ago. Just off his shift, he had that particular variety of jitters that came with spending the night behind the wheel of his cruiser. Sitting DWI on a Thursday was either feast or famine and last night was famine. So now he was stuck with the damn jitters, bleary but sure as hell not able to sit still. He was so damn tired. His eyes felt gritty, every blink scuffed like his lids were made of sheets of 600 sand paper.

The Xanax wasn't doing the job. The blow was running the show. He only used what he had to, the bare minimum, just enough to stay alert. It was a work thing. What else was he gonna do? Coffee went right through him. He wasn't forty anymore.

"You ain't forty no more, hon!"

Ah, Denise, God love her. Denise was no cheesesteak, just another one of those Perryville girls who loved to party. How the hell was he supposed to know they weren't for marrying?

Joe sat up and focused on the newbie's share. She was gonna cry. That's all right.

The kid had cried when he came in a few months back. He'd made an impression straight off, what with his rat's nest of blond hair and wet eyes as blue and familiar as fresh bathwater. Poor kid was no more than five foot six and two twenty if he was a pound. Every time he opened his mouth he'd sweat like a glass of iced sweet tea in the sun. He'd wring his pudgy hands and turn four shades of purple and little drops of sweat would roll down from his temples onto his thick neck.

Well, no freakin' wonder! Now Joe got it. Who wouldn't be trying to eat himself to death with that drunk old Norma Desmond for a mother? His mother! Jesus Christ almighty, grandmother maybe. What a piece of whiskey-work she was. His freakin' mother, who'd've thunk it.

The bile bubbles from his stomach tasted like sour aspirin. Drugs not withstanding, he'd been back in-program for six months now. Got right on with the meetings as soon as he'd landed back in town. If he boozed, he was done. He wouldn't get another shot. Shit, if he hit the Beam again, he wouldn't want one. He was no druggy; he was a boozer.

Yeah, yeah, he knew all about the lies.

Thirty years! Thirty freakin' years since his first meeting. Fresh out of the academy, back then he was a squeaky clean rookie on the Elkton P.D. He hit meetings over the line in Newark, down in Smyrna, up in Wilmo. But he was a floater. Spent a year drifting from one room to another, hanging out in the back. When he shacked up with Denise, he figured he was cured. And he was, spent the next fourteen years dry as a nun's nipple.

And it took a few years for the wheels to fall off, but they did. Lost everything, just like they'd said in the rooms and now he was right back where he started. Fuck-a-duck.

He knew he had to kick this shit in a hurry or it would put him underground. Had to do it just the way he'd shut off the booze on his way out of Elkton. But Tartusville was a small town. Booze was one thing. Drugs were another. He couldn't get it done here. He'd have to find a regular meeting out of town, Waterbury maybe, someplace he could dig in and come clean.

He glanced over at Jonathan. None too bright, but he'd heard enough about God-shots to know one when he saw one. And Jonathan was a God shot, no doubt about it. The kid sat there, hands wedged between his thighs, teaching Joe just what all it meant to be powerless. The kid was his walking, talking reminder that things operated outside of anybody's control. God made the plans. And God had a plan for the kid just like He had a plan for him. And Joe would share about all this if he could, but he wasn't really in any condition to be sharing. How was he supposed to go sharing something like that? He was Tartusville P.D.

Joe tuned back into the blond woman, while he scanned the faces in the circle. On his left sat another fresh one. He was all flash in his slick suit, checking his heavy gold watch time after time. Must be nice, laying down - what - ten large on a watch like that? Slick, no doubt, was here on a nudge from the judge. He had a three-inch-long scar that cut down the middle of his forehead and a bum leg that he stuck straight out into the circle. Aside from that, he looked like your standard corporate prick. His scar popped red off the pale skin of his forehead. He slouched in his chair, looking bored, but Joe recognized the look in his eyes. He was just like the rest of 'em that came crawling into the rooms. Slick had a truth in him that he didn't yet choose to believe.

Joe replanted the rubber soles of his shoes flat on the floor. The blonde had it bad, all decked out in her do-me duds, rolling her fingernails along her metal chair. He held his hat in his lap and willed his knees still. Jonathan raised his head up from his hands. The kid smiled at her, full of goodwill and shame.

Slick nudged him and passed him a pen and the clipboard. Joe scanned the typed phone list for his name. Joe B., there he was, and there was the kid, Jonathan B. printed right below! Well good for him. The young buck was getting with the program. Joe took a fresh copy, and now he had a brand new number to avoid calling. He passed the clipboard along to Jonathan with a little smile.

"No, it's alright. You're making perfect sense," Karl said to the woman.

Joe looked to Francis and raised his hand. Francis acknowledged him with a double smile from behind his whiteface. Takes all kinds to make this world.

"Good Morning, Joe."

"Morning everybody, alcoholic Joe here."

"Hi Joe."

"I just wanted to get my hand up this morning. I got a lot of stuff running between these ears and that's never a good thing. Thanks for your story, Karl, and thanks for your share," he nodded at the blonde, "sounded honest to me." He took a deep breath. "You know I was just thinking about God and His strange sense of humor. He does have His way of telling us stuff, don't He? I mean, ya'll know... excuse me, you all know," Joe winked at Karl, "You can take the man out of Maryland, right? Anyhow, He told me something this winter now didn't He? I mean, my old lady tossing all my shit out in the snow is a strong message right? He's telling me to go home, get help, right? So here I am, back home." His knees were bouncing again. He leaned forward on his thighs.

"So, anyway, so there I was again, blaming God instead of thanking him. I was just sitting here complaining to myself about the fact you can't get a decent cheesesteak! You believe that? Never mind the fact that it was God Himself that got me a spot on the WPD - but no, I got to bitch and moan about cheesesteaks and The Cooper test and the Poly and the exams. I got to bitch about the 6 weeks back at the academy. I got to moan over working nights, poor freakin' me. But all that moaning keeps my eye off the ball, right? Keeps me from having to come clean - helluva thing, right? So, here's some cleaning. My program's a little bent at the moment..." he paused.

Francis edged forward in his seat.

"You see, I got family in the graveyard here. My mother's back there for one, been there since forever. And you know what? I been in town since January and I still haven't paid her a visit! Always some freakin' excuse, but not today, not today."

Joe looked around the circle. His shoulders had snuck up toward his ears and he craned his neck, making like it was stiff. Nothing to do now but keep it going.

"You know, back in the day, me and my kid brother - God, I used to be such a freakin' prick to that kid - called him Numb Nuts, Jimmy Numb Nutz, but that's a whole 'nother story. Anyway, we'd go visit her, you know, freshen up the flowers, kneel and say a prayer 'cause we knew she'd like that. But you know it didn't take much time for us to fall out of the habit. It didn't take much more than a year before Jimmy and me'd turn it into something to do when we were out boozing and carrying on. Ya'll - you know, like maybe we'd drop by after we'd been out fishing all day or tearing it up at Titans football games. Shit, we'd show up in the middle of the night so busted up that we'd get lost in the headstones and Jimmy'd complain that there should be signs—"

Jimmy used to laugh his skinny ass off. Joe rubbed his nose.

"So we'd finally stumble onto her grave and maybe drop an empty in the little copper tube that was meant for flowers, you know, like a joke. We'd laugh it up like a couple of red-eyed ghouls. And it was funny, but it wasn't funny at all, right? She was a good woman, our mother. She took good care of us. She did right by us, seriously. God took her out quick with cancer." Joe looked down at his shoes. "Anyhow, whatever. What I'm getting at is that I tell myself over and over, 'today's the day,' right? So today - I'm saying it out loud - today, I am going to pay my respects." He looked back up at Francis who now sat all the way back in his chair with his arms folded.

"I got to say I'm always amazed coming to these meetings. I know I need 'em now more than ever. God knows I'm so full of my own bullshit. But at least I know that much…"

Chapter Six

THE COP WENT on and on.

Bullshit or not, Eddie had to admit; it was worth driving a half hour north to get to this holy house of fruits and nuts. He stretched out his achy knee and crossed his arms over flexed abs. He felt a hundred percent better, good really. He'd get his car into a body shop next week and the flat tire mystery would be a thing of the past, no harm no foul.

And while this group was much smaller than he'd hoped in terms of his research, these Tartusville drunks were way, way out there, crazy as all-get-out. Between Jackie-O-Hammered the drunk old battle-axe shoving him at the door, Nervous Nellie the nail tapper, and Ichabod the creepy mime, he'd found himself some great entertainment. All except for the poor fat kid with the tiny head of curly hair - Eddie felt bad for him. The guy looked pretty roughed up when he slumped back in his chair with a look of horror on his not-quite-right face.

By comparison, Eddie had it made. He was living the standard American Dream with Amy and Maggy, and their four-bedroom center hall colonial complete with fence, lawn and tree swing. He had the business suits and the high paying corporate gig to which he was one hundred percent tied and vested. Come bonus time, he got to chase another big fat carrot of stock options on a stick two years long.

The cop rambled on like he'd been out chasing crack instead of criminals. He looked like he might bounce right off his chair. Too much time spent blowing lines in the Dunkin' Donuts parking lot. His jaw moved sideways as he spoke.

"Look, I know I'm not supposed to cross talk, but I think it's okay to tell you - Nellie is it? - that I respect what you're doing, what you're trying to do. Your, you know, your um stick-to-it-tive-ness, your um..."

"Persistence?" Eddie suggested.

The mime extended his long arm toward Eddie and popped up his index finger. "Please my friend," he whispered and then drew back his finger until it met his pursed, black lips.

Eddie shrugged, un-fucking-believable. He imagined the lanky clown all liquored-up and sloppy, swigging booze from a make-believe jug and belching with his hands. A good mime is a terrible thing to waste. Eddie rubbed the smirk off his face and turned back to Officer Hoppy.

"Yeah, that's what it takes, persistence. You got to stick with the program. And that's no bullshit, I tell you what." The cop's deep-set eyes fell to the floor. The fat kid dropped his head into his hands again. The tattooed mountain next to the mime nodded his scarred head. Nervous Nellie wiped tears off her smudgy cheeks. Eddie knew the score. All these Gomers from the Valley were deep into each other's business.

Still, the guy did have a point. Persistence was what it was all about. In fact, it was just that degree of commitment that had him well on his way to penetrating America's top two percent. This little DWI episode was just a hiccup, an aberration along a multi-year success trend. People like him, with a sufficiently sophisticated perspective; recognized blips like these were simply part of the model. He knew his model. He was the hard-working family man that had a few more than he intended and got himself a little wake up call from a cop with a quota. What could be more statistically consistent, more predictable, hell, more understandable? He should have a forecasting algorithm built for young success stories; just load in a few relevant data points for your current DWI probability index. He'd make a mint.

"It's no cakewalk is what I'm saying. I mean, what's better than kicking off the boots and cracking a cold'un and watching the Birds on the tube, right? I was Elkton PD! I was Policing Through The Community! It said so right on my badge. And when I was off the clock, I deserved a reward. I deserved it, right? I thought I was really living, like I was the man, the freakin' man," the cop grunted.

And here the cop had stumbled onto the kicker. The Man - that measly quarter gram of Bolivian bink had complicated things. Hell, if it weren't for the blow, he'd have just come clean with Amy. At least it happened in New York. Out-of-state meant off the radar.

He'd managed to keep the whole thing contained with the help of a high priced attorney and a new checking account, piece of cake. And though he was no Listerine guzzling Kitty Dukakis, the judge had slapped him hard on the wrist. For the next three months he had to walk the line; get his signatures from these corny meetings, and show up for his probation appointments. No sweat, by Thanksgiving the whole thing would be ancient history.

"And Denise would ride me constantly. 'Hon, you're living in a fairytale,' she'd say it all the time. All her freakin' badgering just made me thirsty...'" the cop yammered on.

Eddie glanced at his watch. Fifteen minutes to go. This morning he'd get his presentation through Legal and then up to his boss. After lunch he'd approve few layouts and then it was off to Madigan's.

No, that wasn't the plan. He had Maggy's thing tonight; that was the plan. That was better all around. He'd update his calendar and lean in on the start time a bit. A parenting commitment was a rock solid reason for skipping out early. UTC was all about family, all about work/life balance. Plus Maggy was so excited, already wearing her special dance outfit. She was a cutie, his little Maggy-Pie. Eddie smiled. That was the plan.

"And Denise was right, I got to admit." The cop refused to shut up, running a shaky hand through his thick, salt and pepper crew cut. "So I've got to remind myself of that every day. There's just no such thing as a couple cold'uns. Persistence, right?" The cop caught Eddie's eye.

Eddie nodded and then looked down and rolled his gold wedding band around his finger. Women were nothing if not persistent, that was for damn certain. And, gacked-up or not, the cop was singing a familiar tune. Something had happened to Amy somewhere along the line, motherhood most likely. Motherhood had changed her, stiffened her. Of course Maggy wasn't to blame, but since her little homecoming Amy's nagging trended upward in frequency and degree. She got on his ass more and more, and not just about drinking, about everything; tracking dirt in the house, waking up too late, waking up too early, getting home too late, buying the wrong Cheerios, installing the wrong kind of baby locks, or the right kind of locks on the wrong cabinets. In Amy's eyes he couldn't do enough and what he did do he fouled up. And this was coming from the proud owner of a six thousand Euro chandelier that never made it out of the garage. All she had to do was make one call to an electrician, but he'd given up on that front. He'd rather squeeze into his M5 than poke the bear.

"I suppose I'm sorta in a fairytale right now. Things are moving along okay, but I see what's coming. I know, I know." The cop sighed. "But that's the rub, right? You put that fairytale through the warsh and what you got before you is one nasty nightmare…"

Eddie thought of Sandra washing mugs behind the bar at Madigan's, sizzling in her tank top and short shorts. Those firm, smooth crescents of her tiny ass bopping up and down behind that cozy wooden bar, sweet Jesus, talk about fairytales! It was his favorite joint, and not just because of Sandra. He liked the bar, felt at home propping his elbows on the stained oak bar, resting a foot on the sturdy brass rail. He'd sip his beer and watch the regular Joes throw darts.

"So I'm gonna put an end to this freakin' little fairytale I got going. I been around the rooms plenty long enough to know certain things just ain't worth flirting with…"

Sandra did love to flirt. Was that yesterday? Eddie pinched his eyes shut but could only recall her little butterfly tattoo floating on top of those sweet saline dreams.

"How'd you get it?" She'd pointed to his forehead.

"Motorcycle accident."

"Can I touch it?"

"If you dare."

She slid her index finger along the length of the scar that ran from the top of his forehead to the bridge of his nose.

"Sexy," she smiled.

"Yeah," he chuckled, "I wish."

She touched his scar once more, sending a tingle through him that landed in his lap.

"You know what I wish?" She pointed to his hands.

"What's that?"

"I wish you didn't have that ring on."

Eddie opened his eyes, sat up in his chair and flexed his aching knee. That woman was pure pixie dust, but not tonight. Tonight was Maggy's night.

The cop was finally wrapping it up. "So I'm gonna walk back in that bone yard and pay my respects and maybe that'll help me remember, help me wake up to the fact that this ain't no fairytale world I'm living in. It's either that or I'll be taking my dirt nap right along side 'em. Thanks for letting me share."

"Thanks Joe."

"Thanks," Eddie said reflexively with the rest. The black bags under the cop's eyes looked almost fluffy, like he could pull them up over his eyes like a veiny quilt. Good old Officer Joe looked like he's been up since Tuesday.

Eddie's Blackberry buzzed in the breast pocket of his pinstriped suit. He checked it and frowned. He had specifically told Sandra, *no emails*. UTC had a thing about email security. Legal had IT monitoring everything.

"HI! C U later hand some?" Well, with an ass like hers, Sandra's spelling was forgivable. A little harmless flirting, that's all. Still, Legal had a zero tolerance policy for personal emails, or anything resembling fun for that matter.

Chapter Seven

JONATHAN'S STOMACH WAS quiet now, but his poop-hole smoldered like a spent shotgun shell. Jonathan heard bits and pieces of the policeman's share. He heard about the mother. He heard she died. How they loved her! The shame shivered in him like warm vodka.

Last week he turned thirty. He and Zella celebrated with cake and ice cream because that's what you do on your birthday. It was in all the movies. He prayed a rock solid prayer that evening in front of his Fudgy the Whale cake. The whale had one candle stabbed into it's middle. Counting out thirty candles was too much trouble. He prayed to stay clean and dry, like Jesus. He prayed for Zella to get better. He prayed for his mother. He prayed for the day to end and it did.

Officer Joe's gruff voice rolled along in the background like a mood, and he prayed a prayer of a different sort.

Thank You, God, thank You...for giving me the courage to return to this chair, clean and dry. Thank You. Thank You for helping me stand up to her. Thank You. Thank You for making me Your fearless gladiator.

Jonathan propped his chin on his fingers and stared to his left at Officer Joe. The cop returned his gaze. He took his hat from off his bouncing knees and turned it in his hands. He looked like he didn't sleep much.

"Thanks, Joe," said the circle.

"And thanks to everyone for a great meeting." Francis said as he stood up between King Karl and the new lady, Nellie. He reached for their hands and the rest followed his lead. Everyone joined hands. Jonathan held hands with Officer Joe and the businessman.

"Will you take us out, Jonathan?" Francis asked with a smile.

"Um, how does it go again?" He flushed.

"A moment of silence for those still suffering..." Francis started.

"Oh yeah, right, okay... Some silence for the sick and suffering..." Jonathan looked at Francis. "Our Father who art in heaven..." The businessman dropped Jonathan's hand before the end of the prayer.

Jonathan had nothing left to do but head for the door. He felt a hand on his shoulder.

"I'm happy you stuck around," Francis said. He had his black hat back on.

"Oh, right, yeah me too I guess..."

"Jonathan, it's all part of the program. You'll see." Francis perched his hat on the back of his head, far above his white forehead.

"I didn't know you guys wore cowboy hats," Jonathan said.

"It's not a cowboy hat, my friend, it's a Fedora. And the hat you're probably thinking of is a beret. But everything evolves you see, even we mimes. Besides, this hat is quite versatile. I can wear it high and happy, or low and sinister - like so," Francis angled it down over his forehead. His eyes narrowed and hardened and Jonathan stepped backward.

"Uh, yeah...wow," he managed.

"Versatile, right?" Francis returned the hat to its happy position.

"Excuse me, Francis is it?" The businessman limped in between them.

"Yes?"

"Will you sign this for me?" He handed Francis a sheet of paper and a silver pen.

"Sure thing, and you are?" Francis asked.

"Eddie. Eddie M."

"Jonathan, may I use your back?"

"Sure," Jonathan stood still. He felt Francis spread the paper on his back and sign it. He handed it back to Eddie. "I hope we'll see you again, Eddie."

"Oh definitely, I got a lot out of it," Eddie grinned.

"I'm happy to hear it. Did you get a phone list?"

"Uh, no, maybe next time," Eddie shrugged.

"Next time then, copies are by the coffee. This is Jonathan by the way."

"Nice to meet you," Jonathan said.

"Yeah, sure, you too," Eddie replied. Instead of offering his hand he folded his paper and pocketed it. He turned and limped for the door without another word.

Francis shrugged. "You have a phone list, right?"

Jonathan nodded.

"Suggestion. Make use of it, okay? Everyone's on there. Make some calls. It makes things easier, I promise...and just call the men, mind you," Francis winked.

"Okay, I'll do that," Jonathan said. He followed Francis outside and up the stairs. The concrete steps were still damp. Some dark clouds lingered. Francis turned to him.

"Listen, Jonathan, I didn't realize, that is, I didn't know she was your mother. I'm terribly sorry. I'd like to speak to her, you know, make sure she knows she's welcome to come back," Francis said.

Jonathan looked across the lot. Through the fogged rear window of the Caddy he could make out her red hat. Beyond his Caddy, at the far end of the lot, he saw Officer Joe walk through the iron gates of the graveyard.

"I'll tell her," Jonathan said.

"Well, alright, perhaps that's best," Francis said. He clapped his hands and rubbed them together. "Well, it's prime time for mime time as we say in the biz. You have yourself a good day, Jonathan. And don't be afraid to use the phone, okay?" Francis patted him on the back.

"Yeah, will do," Jonathan said, distracted by the sight of Nellie hurrying to catch up with King Karl. He was nearly twice her size.

"Uh, hey, Francis?" Jonathan started but Francis had his cell phone up near his ear.

"Gwen, can you give me just a moment?" Francis cupped the phone against his chest. "Saints and sinners, we just love to mingle," he explained. "I have to take this. May I suggest that, just for today, you wear your life like a loose garment, okay?"

Francis wiggled his arms and legs. His extra wide cuffs flapped on his slippered feet.

"Like me," he smiled and tipped his hat and turned toward his old station wagon.

"Any day now!" Mother shouted from her window.

"Will do," he mumbled as he shuffled to his car. "Will do."

Chapter Eight

"Listen, I got to get to work. You just hang in there, okay?" Karl said. He kept his hands in his pockets and leaned his backside against the door of his pickup.

"Easy for you to say," Nellie said. "You're the one with all the time. You're the one doing the service. What am I doing?" She wiped tears from her cheeks with the heels of her hands and then ran her forefingers under her eyes to try and contain the black smear of mascara. "I'm a mess," she said with an embarrassed smile.

"You're just where you're supposed to be right now," Karl said. It's all he could think to say. He knew the words were right, even if he wasn't.

"You leave that girl alone you damn devil from Hell!" The cry came from Jonathan's old Cadillac as he drove past. Karl shook his head and watched them tear off. He glanced at Nellie and climbed into his truck. She caught hold of his door.

"Can I call you?" she asked.

"Why don't you call one of the ladies? Did you get a phone list?" Karl asked.

She shrugged, bit her lower lip and looked around. The church parking lot was empty, save for the two of them. Karl reached for his wallet and handed her one of his cards. She took the card, squeezed his hand and read aloud, "Karl (917) 555–3324, DON'T PICK UP - CALL ME. That's some card. Thanks, Karl."

"Use it if you have to. I really got to get going," he said and shut his door.

As it was he was already going to be late picking up Marcus and that was bad enough, never mind having no trust for himself when it came to twelve stepping this poor girl. First things first, and he had his ninth step to be doing, his living amends to Marcus and the boy's mother. The best he could do was hustle over and pick the kid up and get to the job. They'd be late and maybe Alec would give them some heat, but probably not. They had tree work this morning on account of the storm and Alec would already be high up in a tree cutting limbs. So he'd get the chipper started and have Marcus get going on collecting the felled limbs and sawing them down to fit in the mouth of the chipper. Tree work was good for him and his boy, between the screaming of the chainsaws and the wailing grind of the chipper, there wasn't a need or chance for talk. He could work side by side with Marcus and not say a word and let his mind work it's magic, make believe the silence between them was just because of all the noise instead of all the hate.

And the boy did hate him, hated him with all his teenage might. But Karl could pretend otherwise, at least until Alec called for a break. And then the boy's silence would go back to being hate. And Marcus'd step off on his own and drink his water and smoke his Marlboro with his back to him. But the break would end and the sawing and the grinding would start up again, and Karl could go on pretending he was Marcus's dad instead of his fucking father. It's a feel good lie.

Karl took a right on Main and drove north to Sycamore. He passed through town, all the storefronts quiet and gray. A couple shopkeepers swept wet leaves and sticks off their sidewalks into the gutters. He turned onto Sycamore and crossed over the railroad tracks, making a point to lift his feet off the cab floor for luck. On his right the Tartusville Station platform extended down the line, a sole commuter looking down the line and then down at his watch. The roads were drying under a sky that was clearing out but the trees would stay slick all morning and he imagined old Alec curse his way up a pine, the iron claws strapped to his shins slipping on the bark.

Bet that fucker was climbing and cursing him like he had something to do with it. Cursing him like the weather was his doing. Cursing him! Getting set to blame him for the fall.

Course none of that was fair, or even true, Alec wasn't like that at all; but his old mind still loved to get him all worked up.

He turned onto Railroad Avenue and rolled past one decaying row house after the next, standing shoulder-to-shoulder and bearing down on Karl like he was to blame for their ugliness. And maybe he was. Maybe Alec was lying on the ground right now with his back broke. Maybe Nellie was hitting the bottle already. He pulled over behind Kissette's Civic. The old brown paint flaked off the front of her house like peels of burnt skin.

Marcus wasn't outside.

The front door was shut. He pressed his foot on the brake and twisted the wheel between his fists.

"Please just come on out," he muttered.

If you stay dry and stick with the program long enough, you get to that place where you know your mind ain't your friend. Your mind is something else. You stay in long enough and you start to grow a new mind. A mind that speaks to you from a new place; it's the start. But this new mind is just that, it's new. It don't have much of a footing. It comes and goes, gets buried and surfaces. They tell you to keep on coming till the miracle happens.

The miracle ain't the birth of that new mind. The miracle is the rearing of it. The miracle is the battle, the battle between your old mind and your new, baby mind. But your old mind has no intention to surrender, even though your baby mind is telling you that your old mind is what got you in all the trouble. The one that dragged you through the shit until you were completely covered and ugly, smelling bad, looking bad, being bad. And the more time you put in the more you started to believe your baby mind. The stronger your baby mind got. But the battle still raged from time to time, no matter how long it's been since your last drink or drug.

He shifted into Park and then craned his neck, looking up at the roof of his cab first, before gazing back at her door. The middle reflector, the number two, had fallen off the door. Her white house number, 124, read like it had a tan ghost caught in the middle.

Next thing you learn is that that new mind, that baby mind, isn't your mind at all. It's God's mind. And then you have to learn to operate on faith and that isn't an easy thing to do when all your life you've been operating on your fears and your needs and your lust for blood and pussy. And on a morning like this, when you wake up with God's mind strong in your heart and head, only to get a taste of the real world and your old mind comes screaming back, comes on up from the grave you thought you'd finally put it in, well, then you know you have no business trusting yourself. And if you're lucky you stop and do nothing, you hole up and don't come out until you feel like you can make a move without hurting yourself or somebody else.

It was coming up on 9:00. Where was Marcus? He shifted in his seat.

"Just come out, boy." He took his hand off the wheel and diddled his door handle with his finger.

All the damn work and the lazy kid can't get himself out of bed on time. All the damn work and the kid still hated him.

Keep on keepin' on they say. Shit anyway, Nellie was just starting out on her rocky path full of burning, hard facts. Maybe he did have something to offer her. Maybe he could help her through the flames. Maybe he was all she had. And what kind of program was he working if he avoided some clear-cut twelve-step work?

So what if she made him hard just by looking at her?

His old mind just loved to do its thing. But his dug-in old mind and his precious defects weren't good enough excuses to ignore a call for help, right? This might just be God tapping him on the shoulder and giving him a chance to do something good. Nellie was a drunk in need of some help. And if he was the only one there for her right now, who was he to turn her away?

He should be calling his sponsor. But shit, didn't he already know what Chris was going to tell him? Wouldn't Chris just reach through the phone and slap him upside his lumpy head and tell him to do what God was asking of him? He needed to be doing what all the other AA folks had been doing for each other for years. He needed to be a servant. He needed to be selfless.

"You want to keep it?" he could hear Chris's growly voice rattle off one of those questions that already had the answer sewn up in it.

"Then you got to give it away," Karl said aloud. He cut the engine, got out of the truck and walked up the crumbling cement pavers to Kissette's door. He climbed the three steps leading onto the porch. The door jerked open only as far as the short steel security chain would allow.

"What the fuck you doin'?" Kissette snarled at him sideways.

He shrugged and raised his hands in peace. "I've been waiting. We're late."

"Get the fuck off my porch."

"We're late, that's all."

"Last time, Karl, get the fuck off my porch or I'll—"

"Or you'll what?" He bit down on the inside of his cheek. When he tasted iron he knew his new mind would do the talking. "I'm just here to hustle Marcus along. We're late."

"He'll be out in a minute. Meantime, you get off my porch. And don't be doin' that again."

"I'm sorry."

"Don't you ever come up here."

He pointed. "You know you've got a number missing?"

"What?" She scrunched her nose and cocked her head. Her hair was cut short like a man's.

"You cut your hair," he said.

"What?"

"I said the two is missing in your one-two-four and your hair's all gone."

"Get off my porch, motherfucker," She hissed and slammed the door shut.

"It's just different, that's all," he said to the door. He rubbed his head with his rough hands. His fingers rolled over his nubby scars. He took his time walking back to his pickup. The sun cut beams through the clouds.

He started the truck and scanned the radio before and clicked it off. He gripped the wheel and gazed at Kissette's front door. He'd buy a new number 2 reflector and give it to Marcus. A living amends, this was his living amends, his chance for a clean slate. He'd begged forgiveness from Kissette like a basehead begs for a rock. She had none to give. Under his waffle shirt his skin sweat with a burning, foul resentment that flowed through his veins like water on fire, like that river in Philly (or was it the Hudson?) - the one that caught fire from all that fucking pollution. Set itself ablaze. There was no other way to clean it.

He'd better call Chris.

Karl picked his cell phone up off the dash. He scrolled through the numbers he'd last dialed, found Chris's and was about to press SEND when a call came in. "RESTRICTED" showed in place of a number.

"This is Karl, who's this?"

"Hi, it's Nellie. I'm sorry to call you so soon. I feel so lame."

"You alright?" He watched as Marcus came out the front door.

"Yes...well, no, not really."

"Not drinking are you?"

"No, well no, but..." Her voice sounded wet and shaky.

"Where're you at now?" He reached over and swung the passenger door open for his son.

"I'm home."

"Well, that's good. Any booze in the house?"

"No, not really, some wine maybe, I don't know. No, nothing. Can you talk?" Karl heard her blow her nose. Marcus ducked into the cab and folded himself into his seat. The boy was a damn weed, healthy as they come. Thank God Kissette didn't carry on like he had done, or there'd been no telling what Marcus would've come out like. Hell, he might've turned out like Jonathan, one of them odd looking alcohol syndrome babies. Nope, she done good by Marcus, he was pit bull strong and pushing six four at seventeen.

"Yeah, sure, go ahead." He put a finger up to Marcus.

"I mean... can you come by?" she asked. Marcus eyed him.

"I can't right now, I'm on the way to work."

The boy shook his head and looked out his window. Karl switched the phone to his left ear.

"Karl?"

"Yes?"

"Can you meet later?"

Karl flushed and glanced at his son, "Well... How about we meet at the church around lunch time?"

"I, I don't think I can leave my place. Can you come by here?"

"Listen, I'll call you at lunchtime and we'll figure it out, okay?"

"Okay..."

"Just hang in there until lunch."

"Okay, okay. I'll do it. I can do that. Thanks, Karl, I can do it. I'll see you for lunch though, right?

"Right."

"Okay, okay, great, I'll see you for lunch then. Right here, here at my place. That will be great. I have food, you don't need to bring anything."

"I've got to go now, okay? You can do it. Say a prayer."

"Okay, I can. I will. I'll be fine. I'm fine now, Karl. Thanks, really, I'm fine now." She hung up.

Karl took a deep breath and put the truck in Drive.

"Hot lunch?" Marcus muttered out his window.

"What'd you say?"

Marcus turned and looked him in the eye, "I said, hot lunch?"

"She's from the rooms. She needs help."

"I bet."

"You don't know shit." Karl said, though he knew he was wrong. The boy knew plenty.

Chapter Nine

JONATHAN DROPPED INTO the driver's side of his Caddy.

"So you just figured I'd be fine out here, is that it?"

He shut the door. He prayed a quick one with his eyes shut. An answer shot back, don't pant, breathe. Jonathan took a deep breath through his nose. The sour, greenish stink of his mother's vodka breath caught in his throat. He gagged and cranked down his window.

"Mother..."

"Does it look like I'm fine?" The red rims of her eyes looked about to blister.

"I'm sorry, Mother. I had to go to the bathroom. I thought I better stay."

"You thought," she parroted back. "You thought it better to leave your mother out to soak in the cold rain. That's what you thought."

"But you were in the car—"

"And catch her death of cold—"

"No, Mother, that's not—"

"While you hob knob away in there with all your AA buddies." She pulled a balled tissue from her purse and dabbed the end of her sharp, red nose. "I just don't see how a son is able to make that decision."

"It's stuffy in here," he said. He cracked his window and started the engine. The wipers lurched across the windshield. He sucked fresh air through his mouth. "You were fine."

"Well, sure, as far as you were concerned." She stuffed the tissue back in her purse and pulled out a half empty pony bottle of Popov. She unscrewed the cap and drank at him. "See what you make me do?"

"Mother, put that away," Jonathan pulled forward slowly, swinging the long front end around toward the bright red pickup truck across the lot. "Mother, I'm not going to tell you again." He watched the bottle from the corner of his eye as she tipped her head and shook it dry. The final drops hit her yellow tongue and she smacked her lips.

Jonathan rolled the Caddy by King Karl and Nellie.

"You leave that girl alone you damn devil from hell!" his mother hollered from her seat.

Jonathan groaned and stepped on the accelerator. In the rear view he saw King Karl looking after them. Jonathan tore out of the parking lot and hung a wide right onto Main Street. An oncoming car leaned on the horn. He stuck his arm out the window and flipped the guy off.

"Have you lost your mind?" she gasped. "You're going to get us killed!"

"You're kidding me, right?" Jonathan fixed his eyes on the road. Sunny Brook Farms was fifteen minutes away. All he had to do was get her there, just breathe and get her there. He just had to drop her off and avoid doing or saying anything he'd regret. He'd just drive and pray for her. He'd forgive her for being the nasty drunk that she was, that she'd always been. He needed to remember that his mother was sick.

"Oh look, Johnny, there's the store. Stop the car," she pointed out his window to the liquor store across the street.

"No," Jonathan said.

"What? Stop the car. We did your little errand—"

"We went to a meeting."

"Like I said, now you can do this for me."

"It's closed, Mother."

"It is not. Stop the car! Oh look what you've done - you've gone right by! Now you've got to turn around."

"I'm not turning around, Mother. The store is closed."

"What do you mean it's closed?"

"It's like nine in the morning. Stores don't open until eleven."

"So? We can wait."

"No we can't".

"Oh you are so difficult, Johnny. You make everything so difficult."

"Whatever you say, Mother."

"Stop the car!"

"Are you telling me how to drive?"

"I demand you stop the car this instant and let me out."

All he had to do was forgive her. He pressed on the gas pedal and weaved through Main Street traffic.

"Why do you insist on driving like a lunatic?"

"Please be quiet, Mother."

"We're better off having me drive. Slow down, Johnny! Watch it! Johnny!"

All he had to do was get her to the home.

"This is not the way to Sunny Brook." She pulled a new pony bottle from her purse. She cracked it open, finished half of it and tilted it at him.

"Stop all this craziness, have some."

"Get that away from me and shut your trap!"

"What? What did you say to me?"

"You heard me." Jonathan veered hard left and then back right. She held the bottle out for him. She didn't spill a drop.

"Do yourself - better yet - do us both a favor and have a drink, Johnny. And for God's sake, slow down!"

All he had to do was drive three exits up the highway, less than five miles. Sunny Brook was not far off the ramp. All he needed was the strength to forgive. That's it.

She polished off the bottle. "You have no right to treat me like this. Kill yourself if you like but you have no right to endanger me! You're sick, Johnny. You know that? You're sick and I feel sorry for you."

He cut the wheel right and skidded up the steep entrance-ramp. He floored it right up until the string of red lights from the bumper-to-bumper traffic lit up his windshield.

"Look out!"

"Sons of boogies!"

He jammed on the brakes. The Caddy slid sideways. He yanked at the wheel to turn into the skid. The Caddy veered back to his right, banging the passenger side up against the cement guardrail. His rear view mirror was gone in a grinding flash. They came to a halt. Jonathan clutched at the wheel, panting.

"You're crazy you know that? Crazy!" she pounded at his shoulder with the side of her fist. "You could have killed us both!"

Jonathan's stranglehold on the steering wheel tightened until his forearms ached. Traffic was at a dead stop.

"So we're just going to sit here?"

Breathe. The trick was to breathe - breathe and pray, pray and breathe. God give him strength, guide him to do the right thing, have mercy on him. Have mercy on them both. Have enough mercy to shut her up, just for a moment, just until he was able to see straight, to think straight.

"Well fat-ass? What's the plan? You just going to sit there and have one of your hissy fits?"

"Mother, please be quiet and let me think."

"What's to think about?"

"How to get you home."

"Without killing me, I hope."

"I know," Jonathan muttered. He kept his eyes closed and his hands on the wheel.

"Don't get smart with me. You're a real piece of work you know that? Mr. Sobriety, Captain Twelve-Step, Peter Peaceful, what a bunch of hooey! You... You... You're a maniac is what you are. An unemployable, unappreciative, lazy, good-for-nothing drunk!"

"Mother, I have a job." He opened his eyes and turned to face her. "Will you please stop talking?"

"Oh, is it something I've said? Do you need a moment to reflect? Maybe you need a little time out? Well by all means, please. This seems like just the time. Maybe you'd feel better if you took a little nap. That's just the thing to do on THE GODDAMN HIGHWAY!"

"Right." Jonathan looked over his shoulder, shifted into Reverse. He steered the car down as best he could along the shoulder of the ramp. The side of the Caddy scraped along the guardrail. Cars honked. At the end of the ramp he backed onto Main Street and shifted the car into Drive. The Caddy lurched forward.

"We'll just have to take Main instead."

"With all the lights? That's going to take forever!"

"I know."

Main Street ran more or less right along with the highway. At each intersection was another convenience store, or liquor store, or both. His mother got quiet as they drove out of town. They passed split-level houses, yards cluttered with plastic kiddie pools and rusty cars and barking dogs and woodpiles and overturned flamingoes. In another mile, the houses thinned out. The forest grew up against the guardrail and the miles clicked off easier. Sunny Brook wasn't far now. His mother snored with her mouth up and open and her hat pressed against the headrest. Her arms lay folded on top of her purse in her lap.

Thank you, God.

Sunny Brook Farms came up on his right. He turned in and approached the gatehouse, wheels rumbling over the cobblestone. He pulled up to the window and the guard smiled, his hair high and tight, a radio microphone clipped to his black blazer.

"Good morning," the guard greeted them.

"Hi, good morning, I'm dropping off Ms. Vacarie," Jonathan said, his mother out cold beside him. The guard peeked around Jonathan's head.

"Ah yes, of course, Ms. Vacarie. One moment please," the guard turned to his computer monitor and typed. He pushed the talk button on his walkie-talkie.

"Ms. Vacarie arriving. Have a nice morning folks."

The iron gates swung open slowly. Jonathan drove up the hill. He liked the tacky hum of his tires as he rolled along the smooth, damp asphalt. Cherry trees and blood-red azaleas and white and blue impatiens lined both sides of the drive. Through the glistening blooms and leaves flashed the deep green of the golf course. Jonathan drove up to the main building at the end of the cobble stoned cul-de-sac. He stopped in front of the big gold awning. Beneath it stood Nurse Lisa, waving.

"Mother, we're here," he nudged her.

"Huh? Oh," she blinked and straightened her hat.

The passenger door opened. Nurse Lisa's cleavage and then Nurse Lisa leaned in to say hello. She gently tapped his mother's shoulder. Mother was out again. Nurse Lisa caught his eye. He looked away and adjusted the rear view mirror.

"She's very tired, Nurse Lisa."

"Mmm, I see," she nodded. "And how was your drive, Bea?" she asked in a loud voice. She reached for Mother's elbows with both hands, hands as soft as Charmin. He just knew it.

His mother jerked awake and clamped down on her purse. "Oh, hello Lisa, you gave me a start." Mother held out her arm and Nurse Lisa helped her out of the car.

"Get some rest, OK? I'll call you later. Thank you, Nurse Lisa," Jonathan said with a daring smile.

He watched Nurse Lisa's backside as she guided his mother through the grand entrance of Sunny Brook Farms.

He rode his brakes down the hill and enjoyed the view.

"Zella would love this place," he said aloud.

Chapter Ten

"YOU LEAVE THAT girl alone you damn devil from Hell!"

Officer Joe looked over his shoulder.

"Freakin' nightmare, poor bastard," he mumbled and continued down the path. He walked with his eyes down. Raindrops collected on his black patent leather shoes. He swished through the tall wet grass that grew thick on the un-kempt footpath of the Our Lady Of Perpetual Forgiveness cemetery. He plodded on, the sun peeking out from the clouds here and there, occasionally dropping a ray on one stoner or another.

The old headstones nearest to the church were the straight up, no nonsense ones. The here-lies-a-rocky-ground-farming-son-of-a-buck type tombstones, brownstone slabs pocked by lichen and age. Deeper in, the markers showed more imagination, shapes varied, sculptures appeared, lots of saints, lots of angels.

He came up on the marble Mary statue that he knew to be just up the lane from his mother's plot. This was a biggun', as they say, so even in his tweeky exhaustion, he couldn't have missed it. The pedestal alone stood six feet off the ground. The big, merciful Mary, the big V.M. stood with her hands together and her eyes on God. Joe paused to look up at her, thought to cross himself, forgot all about it and remembered again only after he'd swished on up the path. His mother's tombstone came up on his right.

Here lies Mary Mancuso Batina, b. Dec 3, 1935 d. May 22, 1971

No frills, Uncle Sal had insisted. He'd also insisted on including the Mancuso name. Well, it was better than Lofthus, Jimmy's middle name, and a hell of a lot better than the one she'd stuck him with, Saul. God love her, she didn't play favorites when it came to bible beating - Old T, New T - it was all The Word far as she was concerned.

Joe knelt beside the empty copper flower urn centered in the ground before her headstone. The dark green copper stuck out sorely from the burnt summer grass that surrounded it.

His head buzzed from the exertion of dropping to his knees and his knees pained from there.

"I'm back, Ma, sorry I didn't come by sooner, but you know..."

He didn't have anything else to say. The backs of his legs cramped. He rolled off his knees and slid himself up to lean his back against her stone, resting with the empty flower tube between his legs. Cool wetness seeped through his blues. It felt fine and he thought maybe he'd just sit for a minute. He scanned the graves. He was alone. He dug the vial out of his front pocket and helped himself to a quick blast to take the edge off.

Maybe he'd just hang for a while, soak in some R-and-R. He knew, he knew all right, freakin' signs were clear. Signs were right on the money, right Mom? Freakin' blow, freakin' Jimmy, he tipped his hat over his eyes. It was quitting time...

⋆▸▬◉ ◉▬◂⋆

Jimmy Batina hoisted a ratty box spring, hoping that brown stain was rust, and dropped it into the compacter pit. He peered in after it. Smoke from the Marlboro dangling from his lips caught him in the eye.

The dump was always a fucking zoo on Saturdays. It was no surprise. Still, his big brother, Joey, was all worked-up in his little hut by the compacter. He barked orders out his window from over the distorted blare of his transistor radio. Jimmy could make out the new Aerosmith tune.

Sweet Emotion, good tunage.

"Hey, Numb Nutz! Get the freak over here!" G.I. Joey shouted, all frantic like it was the second coming of Tet or something.

Dick.

Jimmy rubbed his eyes and turned back to the line up of cars and pickups looking to unload their lifetimes' worth of crap. Idling vehicles burning gas and stuffed to overflowing with black garbage bags and old rugs reeking of cat piss and abused Play School kitchens and forts, so stained and sticky that even The Salvation Army took a pass. A lifetime's worth of other people's shit passed him by on a daily basis. Jimmy flicked his butt into the compacter pit.

"Yo Numb Nutz! Hey, Jimmy! Yo!" G.I. Joey shouted.

His brother called it the control booth but it was really just a shed with a toggle switch. G.I. Joey sure had worked his way up the ranks of Shit Mountain; only 21 (or was it 22?) and now he was the switchman, the pacesetter. He was Mr. Throughput this hot summer of seventy-five. He was Mr. Large and Almost In Charge at the Tartusville Refuse Center.

And so Mr. Missed-My-Shot-in-'Nam, the muscle-headed Captain with the Kung Fu Grip was ruling all over his world. At home, Jimmy couldn't leave a dish in the sink or (heavens to Murgatroid!) miss a visit to Uncle Sal's or a drop of piss on the toilet seat without hearing about it.

Christ, Mr. Muscle-head had karate'd his ass just for bailing on senior year! He'd come to on the kitchen floor with Joey holding a bag of ice to his jaw.

"What kind of retard-ard-ard... Quits high school-ool-ool... A year to go-go-go?" Joey's voice had that whippety wah-wah pedal throb.

How could someone actually prefer knockouts over nitrous?

Jimmy'd squinted and tried to make out one of the Joeys hovering over him. The underside of his brother's chin was a mound of scar tissue from his years of Titans Varsity Football. And he tried to understand, but how could he? It made no sense.

"Dude..." What else could he say?

And it made even less sense because, the thing was, Joey could be all right. Sometimes he'd have a few pops and the lid would loosen on that jar head of his. They'd have some laughs. He'd turn human. But sometimes he'd have a few pops and just turn.

Jimmy watched the steel wall of the compactor squeeze the box spring until the frame splintered with a few sharp cracks. It could crunch a piano into the size of a shoebox, no problemo. It was one badass piece of engineering for sure, crushing the world's unwanted into little manageable chunks.

"Jimmy! What're you doin'?" Joey shouted out over Perry's screaming guitar and Kramer's slow rolls.

"Working?" Jimmy shrugged.

"You see the cardboard dumpster?" Joey pointed out into the yard. "You see it's overflowing?"

Jimmy turned to look. He blew a low whistled. "Yup."

"Well, work on that! Do your freakin' job!"

"Okay, I'm on it, alright? Take a fucking pill, Saul."

"I'll give you a fucking pill," Joey shouted back over the electric drone of the compactor. Up from the pit came the sharp cracks of wood snapping or plastic splitting or bones breaking, or whatever the fuck. Jimmy scuffed his Pro Keds across the concrete of the staging bay, dodging between the Saturday morning honey-dolts who dumped their old lives into the compactor, each one of them peering into the pit, hoping to catch a glimpse of their shit getting eaten by the machine as if their shit were something special, as if they had that tasty treat that would make the monster belch, all giddy with yum yums.

Jimmy walked out from the shady stench of the transfer station and crossed the asphalt yard to the recycling area. It was already blazing hot; the sun baked him inside his new coveralls. His new uniform wasn't making life any more worth living. The uni was standard issue for all the guys at the dump, slate blue with a white, oval patch with your name stitched on it.

Joey had taken a sharpie to his. A thick black line cut through the center of his name and just below it, in Joey's best block letters read, "Numb Nutz."

It got a big laugh from the guys yesterday at quitting time.

"I'm not wearing it," He'd said. He downed his Piels and threw the uni back at his brother.

"Come on bro, don't be like that," Joey stuffed the uni under his arm, fished another beer out of the cooler and threw it over to him. Franky couldn't let it lie.

"Jimmy fuckin' Numb Nutz - so what? Better than 'Grace Kelly faggot face,'" Franky P. snickered.

Franky P. was the foreman, the head cheese. He was always quick to point out that, with the exception of his two tours in the shit, he'd been running the show nearly as long as Jimmy'd walked the planet. According to Franky, he was "East Coast Untouchable." All his brothers were "Staties." He'd pour himself into his car and shout out his window, "Mama says no pinchin'!" as he tore off the lot. Joey said Franky was a war hero. Franky said Jimmy was too pretty to be working a man's job.

"Better than Blue-Eyed-Dream-Boat-Puss-Boy," Franky said and swiped beer foam off his chin.

"I don't think that would fit on the patch, Franky."

"Watch your mouth, Jimmy," Joey warned.

"Yeah, watch yourself, pretty boy. Don't matter to me whose nephew you are, or niece or whatever."

"Bro, it's just a freakin' joke," Joey said.

Jimmy grabbed the uni out from under Joey's arm.

"Who gives a fuck, right, Franky?"

"Right on, Numb Nutz," Franky smiled and showed off the gap where his two front teeth used to be.

What a dump.

Jimmy bent over to grab a cardboard box off the ground and the heat rushed into his head. Someone had a brand new Magnavox Odyssey, nice. He reached inside the box and pulled out the Styrofoam packing. Looks like that same some-one was just too darn busy to bother taking out the packing, much less flattening the box. Surrounding the big steel dumpster was box after boxy box, all as three-dimensional as you please. Jimmy tossed the packing aside, put the box top-side-down and punched at the taped seam. He got it flat and picked up another.

The sun picked at either side of his thick, blonde pony tail and sweat dripped from his nose as he broke down boxes. The work was dull, which suited him just fine. Nothing to think too hard on, nothing to plan out or organize or even finish. The dump was the finish, the never-ending finish line, the bottomless pit. He and the boys just kind of hovered about, moving things along, swapping paper for ashes, pulverizing the putrid, burying the lifeless.

His skull started to give him those little pains right where his horns would go. It was time for a break. Jimmy searched the yard. Franky was nowhere in sight. Joey was deep into his crushing thing. He craned his flattop out the control room window as if keeping an eye on the waist high rim of the compactor made a fuck of a difference. He wouldn't be able see if there was an elephant down in the steel gut of that thing, not a head, not an ear flopping, not a not even a trunk, raised or otherwise.

Jimmy dried his face in the crook of his arm. He walked around the dumpster and continued on to the chain linked fence at the far side of the yard. On the other side of the fence was a small stand of trees, city trees, with beer cans and Baggies and hair curlers and used rubbers and MD 20/20 bottles and all kinds of living scattered about the skinny trunks.

He turned his back to the fence, leaned into it and looked up into the canopy of branches that cut through and above the razor wire. It made for a nice, country shade. This was his sweet spot. He scanned the yard and, when he was satisfied of his invisibility, he dug out the tin Sucrets box from his pocket. He took out his one-hitter that looked more like a brass Louisville Slugger than a pipe. In the box he'd crumbled some black opium in with his Maui buds. And this wasn't Falls River basement Maui. This was Maui Wowie Maui. The sticky stash clogged his one hitter most every load, but, alas, there was no chasing dragons at the office.

He jammed the pipe full and held it in his teeth while he pocketed the Sucrets box and dug for his Zippo with his other hand. In a fast sweep against his thigh, he popped the lid, lit the Zippo and sparked up. He sucked at the pipe until it was kicked and held the hit while he reloaded. When it was set to go, he exhaled, and lit up straight away. Power hitter, that's what he was, just playing some major league ball. Behind closed lids he enjoyed the fireworks of capillaries popping. Everything went silky-smooth and super-duper.

Jimmy opened his eyes and, God, if he didn't fucking love the dump.

Chapter Eleven

Joey's breath reeked of peppermint schnapps but unless you were in the car with him you'd never guess. He steered the Pinto perfectly straight, kept his speed slow and steady. "Speed kills," he'd say. He said it every time he drove with a few drinks in him, for luck or something. The more he had in him, the more he'd say it. He always drove slow on the way to Uncle Sal's.

"Speed kills little brother, speed kills."

Joey sat low in his seat, hanging his wrist over the steering wheel. He had the sleeves of his army surplus jacket pushed up to his elbows. He rode the brakes down Sycamore, the worn pads on his Pinto whining like pinched puppies. Jimmy yawned. He wondered why every minute of a Sunday felt so early.

"You think Uncle Sal's got waffles?"

"Not likely, bro."

Jimmy reloaded his one hitter and sparked it up, out of turn. He stuffed the smoke down deep, loading up all those little lung sacks. Strictly kind-bud in his stash today, Joey gave him shit about opium. Fuck the opium; he'd been chasing dragons in his bedroom all morning. Captain Clean would freak if he knew about the dragons.

Treetops passed by his window one after the next, dying leaves hanging on to branches like they might go green again someday. Jimmy held his breath and counted trees, trying to lock down if they were marking depth or distance? When he'd plunged as deep as he could go, he sat up, pursed his lips and blew out the open crack of his window. Air fluttered on the tip of his nose like wings from a bubble butterfly, if there was such a thing, which now that he thought of it, there should be.

"You might have passed that along, bogart," Joey said.

"What?" Jimmy looked over at his brother, a desert dog dangling from his thick lips. He was an inch taller than Joey, but Mr. Muscle didn't fit in his seat. If he sat up, his flat top brushed the frayed nylon of the roof liner. If he hung back, one shoulder wedged up against his door and the other got into Jimmy's space. His legs were short, that was the thing. He was like a bizzaro iceberg, rock hard and upside down. Jimmy stifled a giggle. The guy could drive though, he had to give him that.

"I said, you might have passed that one my way."

"You want another?"

"Oh no. I'm just pointing out that it was my turn."

"So...you don't want another?"

"Whatdyathink, Numb Nutz? Yeah, I want another!" Spittle fluttered from Joey's mouth onto the dash.

"You don't have to yell."

"Who's yelling?"

"You were."

Joey looked over at him, incredulous. "You know what? Forget it."

"Okay," Jimmy shrugged and looked back out his window. The leaves clung to the trees in all that windy wind, the reds, the golds and greens. They had color, but it was dead color, a sootiness about them like they were blackening from the inside. The blackness was hard to spot, but it was there. You just didn't see it with your eyes; you saw it with the rest of you, your soul or something. Like your soul could see death even when the rest of you couldn't. And it was all over those leaves. He tapped the one-hitter out into the ashtray.

"What're you doing?"

"What?"

"You going to clean out the tray?"

"What?"

"You gonna clean out the tray?"

"It's filled with butts."

"Yeah those are my butts and this is my car and that's my ashtray. You want to dump shit in my tray, go ahead, but you're cleaning it."

"You're serious?"

"As cancer," Joey growled, nodding in slow motion. He turned his attention back on the road and nestled deeper into his slouch.

Jimmy cranked his window down, yanked the tray out of the dash and held it out the window at arms length. He dumped the butts and gum wrappers and dried boogers and whatever-the-fuck out onto road. Ash blew back in the window.

"What the fuck, retard?" Joey switched wrists on the wheel and swung at the air. "The shit's blowing in the car!"

"There, it's all clean and nice-nice, okay? Happy?" Jimmy shoved the tray back in the dash. He wiped his sooty fingertips on his jeans and then brushed the ash off his Neil Young Harvest t-shirt.

"That's it," Joey said and pulled the car over. Jimmy sat up and pulled his t-shirt off. If it was go-time, he didn't want the asshole to rip it. He braced himself in case Mr. Cranky Pants was jacked up enough to throw down before they even got out of the car. Joey was a heavy hitter, but he lost more power than he knew when he was drunk. Jimmy might avoid an ass kicking if he could tie him up quick enough.

"What're you doing now?" Joey looked at him funny, like he was drooling or something.

"Getting ready," Jimmy said. He wiped the back of his fist across his mouth. Nope, no drool, bone dry in fact.

"Ready for what?"

"What?"

"We're here, Numb Nutz."

Jimmy risked a sucker punch to look out his window. A flock of pink plastic flamingos stood, one legging it on Uncle Sal's dead lawn. He was baked to a fine crisp indeed.

"Well, you gonna pull in?" Jimmy asked.

"Do you not see the fucking car in the driveway?" Joey pointed and the two of them stared out the windshield. Parked dead center on the steep downhill driveway, blocking both garage bays, was a powder blue Tempest. The right front quarter panel ahead of the wheel was bashed in and the corner of the bumper was rusting out. The rest of it looked pretty sweet.

"Whose is that?" Jimmy asked.

"How the freak should I know? A friend of his, I guess."

"And who's that?" Jimmy pointed to the yellow 'Cuda parked by the curb down past the far side of Uncle Sal's driveway. "Sweet ride. Sal having a party or something?"

Joey leaned close to the windshield. "What's that shitball doing?"

"Smoking a butt."

Joey turned and glared at him. "Jesus freakin' Christ! I mean what's he doing just sitting there?"

"I dunno."

"I don't like it," Joey mumbled. He bent over, round cheek face flat against the wheel and reached under his seat. He sat up and held the wadded towel in his lap with both hands.

Jimmy exhaled out his window, "Hey man, you don't need that fucking thing." Joey's gun was one of those snub-nosed jobs like the fuzz carry. He kept it tucked under his seat, wrapped in one of mom's old blue and white striped dishtowels.

"The hell I don't." Jimmy followed Joey's gaze out the windshield.

The guy in the 'Cuda wore big Buddy Holly shades. He had a skinny head, stringy black hair to his shoulders and a stringy chin beard and mustache to match. "Looks like Jesus got himself a hotrod," Jimmy joked.

"What freakin' planet are you on? This ain't funny."

"He's nobody, what? Dude, you have one hit and you're paranoid."

"You know, that's why I do what I do and you do what you do."

"I try not to do too much."

"Exactly. I'm gonna see what this shitball wants with Sal."

"What would he want with Sal?"

Joey gave him another look and unwrapped his gun.

"Okay, that was maybe a stupid question," Jimmy shrugged. "Still, you don't need that thing."

"Better to have it and not need it."

"You couldn't shoot anybody," Jimmy said.

"Bro, you are without a freakin' clue."

Jimmy took another drag. "Bullshit," he said through a cloud. "Let's just go inside."

"Stay put. I'll be right back," Joey stuffed the gun in his pants and swung open his door. He ambled down the middle of Sycamore toward the 'Cuda like the new sheriff in town.

Douche.

Jimmy rubbed at the worries crawling up his neck. Joey stood on the double yellow line in front of Sal's driveway. Stringy Jesus started up the 'Cuda. The engine shook the hood. That was more than a 318 rumbling.

"Joey..." Jimmy pulled his door latch.

"Hey, buddy, can I help you?" Joey shouted.

Jimmy pushed open his door, "Joey!"

Stringy Jesus punched it. Rubber smoked under the backend and the 'Cuda shot out from the curb, straight at Joey.

"Joey!"

Joey dove to his right as the 'Cuda roared past him. Jimmy heard it tear down Sycamore as he ran over to his brother. Joey hopped up off the ground.

"Holy shit man, you okay?"

"Fine," Joey brushed off his jacket. "You recognize him?"

"No."

"You see his plates?"

"No," Jimmy said.

"Motherfucker," Joey closed his eyes and scratched hard at his flat top. "All right. Better go see on Uncle Sal," he said.

Jimmy double-timed it to keep up. "Joey, what's going on?"

"Did I not say I dunno? I DUNNO."

"So whose car is this?" Jimmy pointed at the Tempest.

"Just hang back a little, all right?" Joey said. He pulled his gun from his pants and held it tucked in his right jacket pocket.

Joey stood in front of Jimmy on Sal's stoop. Joey tried the gate. It was locked as usual. He motioned for Jimmy to stay put. He pressed the doorbell and stuffed both hands back in his jacket pockets. They waited. On the steps, Jimmy shuffled his feet through fallen leaves that didn't yet know they were dead.

Joey glanced back at him with a strange smile, "Forget something, Numb Nutz?"

Jimmy glanced down at his bare chest. He jumped when the door opened, but Joey didn't flinch.

Good God, he was crispy indeed... It was Farrah. Farrah stood behind the gate, welcoming them with a smile. Her kittenish green eyes and feathered blond curls... He'd never hallucinated Farrah angels before. If it weren't for the white skirt and top, he might just be back in his bedroom, rubbing out another one to her poster on his wall. Farrah, his Farrah, smiling and sassy in her red one-piece, her skin creamy, her right nipple rock-hard. And here she was, looking down at him and smiling and he didn't know any better.

Chapter Twelve

SWANK AS IT was, Sal's guest room shared a wall with the master bedroom. Bea hadn't had a decent night's sleep in two week with all his snoring and coughing. And being the rigid prick he was, moving across the hall to his den took plenty of convincing.

"The boys'll be here soon," he protested.

"Pleeaase, Sal, I'll be super careful. I'll move everything piece by piece," Bea cooed as she tickled the underside of his balls.

"I got all my memories in there," he mumbled, flat on his back on top of his blue satin sheets. It was true. His den was a shrine to Omaha Beach; from his decorations and gear to jars of empty shells and sand.

"I was born that day, you know." That was true, too. She stroked his limp little wiener.

"No shit?"

"I'll set everything up in the guest room just the way you have it. I promise."

"You'll need to do more than that."

She unbuttoned her sweater and promised to do things that would make him forget he was sick. She teased him to throbbing.

"The boys..." he moaned.

"Shh, we have time," she whispered. She straddled his hairy chest. She told him how she couldn't help but play with herself whenever she had on her crotchless panties. She lifted the hem of her white mini skirt.

"It's true, watch," she licked her fingertips.

Sal fixed his bloodshot eyes on her hand as she reached down between her legs. She closed her eyes. Jim Plunkett came to mind and she moaned.

"Enough fuckin' around," he grumbled and pushed at her hips.

"You be patient," she scolded and licked her fingers again. She shimmied backwards over his stomach and gave a little squeal when he slipped inside her. It took all of two rolls of her hips before he came with a single grunt.

Bea bounced on him harder, trying to get there. He shriveled out. She stopped and opened her eyes. He was asleep. Bea sighed; at least he hadn't coughed up a bloody storm this time, thank God. She lay down beside him and tried to finish herself off, but gave up. Not even Jim Plunkett could compete with Sal's wet snores. She got up and tiptoed across his zebra skin rug in her white stilettos.

In his bright, clean bathroom, she longed for a snooze in Sal's oversized Jacuzzi or a luxurious steam in his Swedish shower. She stood in front of his stone pedestal sink with shiny brass fixtures that resembled a rising swan. It looked like it was hand-sculpted She wet a washcloth under the swan's beak and scrubbed her crotch. She tossed the cloth in the hamper. She didn't do laundry.

Bea buttoned up her white sweater. The buttons strained across her lacy bra, just enough to call a man's attention. After all, a nurse must be inviting and sweet, but certainly not tarty. She fixed her skirt and checked her hair in the mirror. She turned sideways, put a hand on her hip and pursed her lips. She could have made a mint at the Kitkat in her little nurse number.

She smiled. To hell with the Kitkat! She'd stumbled on The Trifecta Man, single, rich and tidy. Tidy! Stepping into Sal's drab, single story ranch house had been like slipping behind one of Monty Hall's winning curtains.

"So which one was it Sal, basic training or your mother?" she'd asked Sal while he gave her the grand tour.

"What?" he flicked on the garage light.

"Who made you such a neat-nick?" she pried, admiring her reflection in the window of his spiffy red Ferrari.

"Basic! Basic's a wet dream!" he snapped. "It's like I told Joey a hundred times!"

"Sorry Sal, I didn't mean to—"

"Bragg was a fucking blow job in the breeze! A grunt's life begins and ends in the motherfucking trenches. Either way you come out - on your feet or in a bag - you come out different. Believe me, you get pinned down nose to asshole in shit hole after shit hole and you learn to love clean."

She closed his bedroom door behind her and clicked down the marble hall to the kitchen.

So what if he was an irascible male chauvinist pig? Fact was this little piggy had his nose in a whole lot more than Tartusville garbage. The gun rack in his den and the iron gate guarding the front door told her that much. Sal had himself his own little Mafioso fortress right here in dreary Tartusville.

Bea relaxed at the kitchen table, sipping her Budweiser and flicking through the channels. A color TV in the kitchen, with a remote, no less! She took a drag and imagined old Owen wetting his pants on the front stoop, begging Sal for mercy. She'd get the rest of her things out of her pad and Owen would be ancient history.

Bea'd just lit her second Virginia Slim when the doorbell rang. She snatched the ashtray off the table and hustled over to the sink to douse her cigarette and dump the last of her beer. She checked her face in the window above the sink, fluffed her hair and gave herself a wink for luck. She hurried down the hall, smoothing the front of her white skirt. She unbolted and opened the front door.

"Well, hi there! You must be Sal's boys," she smiled cheerfully through the iron bars of the security gate.

"Uh, yeah, hi, nephews actually," said the dark, muscular one with the fatigues and the flat top. Bea unlocked and opened the gate. The other one had no shirt. Her eyes stuck on his naked chest.

She looked back at muscles. "So you're Joey, right?"

She extended her hand. Joey struggled to free his hand from his pocket. Boys are so awkward.

"Uh, yeah, right. How you doin'," he took her hand. His palm was wet. "And you are?"

"Hi, Bea Vacarie, I'm your uncle's new, um, nurse-slash-assistant. He didn't mention?" she asked, squeezing his hand and smiling.

"No, no he didn't," Joey said. He looked her up and down before meeting her eyes again. She knew the look, the bug eyes, the loose jaw.

"Well, here I am. Please, call me Bea," she turned to the shirtless beauty. "And you must be Jimmy."

"Uh, what? Yeah, yeah, Jimmy. Hi," he looked up to her from the lower step. He was stoned, very stoned. Below his drooping, delicate blond lashes his aquamarine eyes looked like blue diamond islands floating on bloody seas. She couldn't keep from staring at the boy.

"So good to meet you! What a treat!" Bea blurted.

Bea pulled her hand from Joey's and, without time or opportunity to rid it of his sweat, thrust it toward Jimmy. He took it gently and she sandwiched his hand between hers. His chest was slim and tone, smooth and hairless all the way to his belly button. From there, she followed a narrow trail of dark blonde fuzz to the waist of his worn jeans. She clamped her lips back together. Her hands lingered. Jimmy's hairline ran straight across his forehead. His hair was dirty blond like Lee Majors', only longer. He had it tied back in a thick ponytail. Oh God, she did have a thing for men with long hair.

"Come on in, gentlemen. Your uncle's asleep. I was just about to make some coffee, any takers?"

"Hey did you see—"

Joey squeezed his brother's forearm and cut him off with a sharp look. He smiled back at her.

"Sounds great," Joey said.

Boys. She led the way to the kitchen, Joey right on her high heels.

In the kitchen, Bea pulled a can of instant from the cabinet above the television while the two boys sat in silence at the round kitchen table. She put the kettle on to boil. She spoke as she watched the gas flame.

"So I hear this is the tradition, right? You boys come over most every Sunday?"

"Mostly," Joey replied.

"So Sal's your...?"

"Our mother's brother, she died a while back. Uncle Sal's kind of looked out for us since."

"I'm so sorry," Bea turned, and, in seeing Jimmy first, turned back to watch the water refuse to boil. She rubbed her shin against the back of her calf. She should have worn stockings.

"Thanks, we're over it though. It's been a while. Truth is, Mom and Uncle Sal didn't really see eye to eye. She was... how should I put this? She was a believer."

Jimmy chuckled.

"A believer?" Bea asked.

"Yeah, you know, a woman of God."

"I see."

"Uncle Sal's not much for God."

"No, I don't suppose he is," she said quietly.

"Mom'd make him say grace," Jimmy muttered. He didn't seem to be speaking to anyone in particular.

"Really?" Bea turned again, having a good excuse to stare.

"Uncle Sal always said something like, um... 'Thank you God for this freakin' meal and my big hairy balls,' or some other crazy shit." Jimmy glanced up at her and blushed. "Sorry, crazy *thing.* He did it every single time. And every single time she'd jump on him and—"

"And we'd keep our heads down, right, Jimmy?" Joey said with a laugh.

"Right."

They fell silent. Bea spooned Maxwell House into three mugs. Steam rose from the kettle and she poured.

"Milk and sugar, Joey?"

"Uh, what? Yeah, okay," Jimmy said.

"I take it black, thanks," Joey replied. He glared at his brother. Joey looked up at her and rolled his dark brown eyes. He stretched out his arms and folded his hands over his head. His biceps were so large they filled the sleeves of his jacket. He flexed them; right one first, then the left, then both. "So what's your story? You gonna be here often?"

"Yes, I'll be living here." Bea brought the mugs to the table and sat down across from Joey.

"Living here?" Joey asked. He sipped and tipped his mug in compliment to her coffee.

"That's the deal, yes. I have my own place at the moment. But your uncle needs someone here at night, so that's me."

"So... You gonna have any nights off?" Joey asked with a grin.

"We haven't worked out the specifics."

"Let me know when you do," Joey winked.

Bea smiled politely. She glanced at Jimmy. He looked down into his coffee. He'd been staring.

"Hey, that reminds me, would you big, strong boys be willing to help me move the rest of my things?"

Sal shuffled in through the swinging door, still in his satin bathrobe and slippers.

"Afternoon gentlemen," Sal said.

"Well hello there, Sal, you're up! The boys and I were just having a little get to know you," Bea said.

"You got a coffee for me?" Sal sat at the table.

"Absolutely," Bea got up and walked to the stove. "You want milk?"

"And sugar," he said.

Bea opened the fridge. She couldn't resist. She bent over and felt her mini skirt cling and rise. She knew what boys liked.

"So, how you doin' Uncle Sal?" Joey asked.

"I don't know how I'm doin'. You tell me," he said. He motioned to Joey like he was expecting something.

Bea handed him his mug and sat down in her chair. God knows what he had to be cranky about.

"Well, this is nice," she said.

Sal tapped her on the shoulder. "Hey, go do something for a minute."

Bea narrowed her eyes and forced a smile. "Okay, sure, Sal, I'll go see about the den."

"Good, you do that."

Pig. Bea stood up from her chair. "Will you boys be staying for lunch?"

"Bea," Sal looked up at her. "Please, a minute."

"Okay, okay," she said. That was better. She winked to the boys and went off to plan her new room.

⊷┝═◉ ◉═┥⊷

Uncle Sal didn't speak until the door stopped swinging.

"Put down the freakin' coffee," Uncle Sal said it low and stern. His voice sounded like his throat was coated with sandpaper. He glared at Joey. Joey put down his mug. Jimmy did the same; he'd had more than his share of static today already.

"Hey, Uncle Sal, I got to tell you—"

"You got something for me?"

"What? Was I supposed to—" Joey flushed.

"Tell me you didn't forget," Uncle Sal tilted his head.

"No, no I didn't. 'Course not, I just didn't get to it yet."

"Did I not tell you to lean on that freakin' shitball? Did I not specifically say Friday?"

"Yeah, yeah I know, Conklin over in Watertown. You told me. I just didn't get to it. I'm sorry, Uncle Sal."

Jimmy shifted on his seat and his chin on his chest. His heart was banging for dragons. He kept his eyes stuck high in their sockets and peeked at the two of them.

"Don't you bullshit me Joey, you forgot. Just say it."

Joey looked down at his hands folded on the table. "Okay, yeah, I'm sorry."

"Say you forgot."

"I forgot." Joey sounded like he might cry.

"You need to get your head out of your ass, soldier. So this is how it's gonna be. Your gonna add," Sal paused to count on his stubby fingers. "Your gonna add forty points to the number and you're gonna get your sorry ass in that shit-box of yours and haul it over to Watertown. You're gonna do him like I told you and your gonna bring back my fucking scratch. We clear?"

"Yeah."

"What's that soldier?"

"Yes sir, Uncle Sal, we're clear." Joey stood up and tucked in his chair. He stood there with his hands on the back of the chair. He took a deep breath and leaned down to Uncle Sal. "Listen, Uncle Sal, I gotta tell you about this guy hanging out in front of your place."

Sal raised his thick eyebrows. "What guy?"

"I didn't recognize him, some squirrely looking cat in a yellow 'Cuda. I called him out and he nearly ran me down, right Jimmy?"

Jimmy nodded.

"I don't know nobody with a yellow 'Cuda. What'd he look like?"

"Like a speed freak Jesus," Jimmy said.

Sal glanced at him sideways and then looked up at Joey.

"Pretty much," Joey shrugged.

"I don't know no strung out Jesus and that means he's a nobody."

"But, he was scoping your place—"

"Did I just say he's a nobody? If he comes back, then maybe he's a somebody. Until then, he's a nobody. Now get the fuck outta here."

"Can I come?" Jimmy asked. Hanging out here with a pissed-off Uncle Sal meant death to his buzz.

Sal pushed himself up from the table and patted Jimmy on the shoulder. "This ain't for you, kid." He said it almost kind. "This is Joey's thing," he nodded to Joey and walked out the swinging door.

"Freakin' Numb Nutz," Joey snarled and dug his fingers into his flat top as if he was looking to pull it clean off his head. He turned and stormed out the back door, slamming it behind him.

Jimmy's gray matter rattled. He blew on his lukewarm coffee.

The swinging door flew open, startling him. It was like living in Looney Tunes, all this coming and going. Nurse Vacarie appeared, heals clicking on the kitchen floor, her golden curls bouncing on her shoulders. Jimmy peered down at her perfectly curved calves. Joey's rage hung in the room like a dog fart.

"What going on?" she asked, a little breathless. She looked to the back door.

"What?" Jimmy said and coughed. The hair on the back of her head was tangled and matted. She must've caught a catnap.

"What was that all about?" she asked.

"Hmm? Oh, uh... Joey just had himself a little rage-o-rama."

"What about?"

"I dunno, somethin' about somethin'."

"So he left?" she asked.

"Yup."

"Is he coming back?"

"He better, he's my ride," Jimmy raised his mug. "This is really good coffee, Nurse Vacarie."

"Please, it's Bea," she said with a smile and touched the tip of his nose.

Chapter Thirteen

KARL TORE A bite off his cherry protein bar and offered it to Marcus. Marcus ignored him and stared out his window as if he was interested in each and every split-level ranch and saltbox they passed. The work was a few more miles down Sycamore, just shy of the highway. Tree work was good, steady work. Alec had a standing contract with the Tartusville H.D., so storms were moneymakers, just another thing for him to be feeling grateful for. And with tree work you damn sure knew you were doing something for the money.

The damp road shined. Small patches of dried asphalt popped up here and there. Karl fixed on the sticky hum of his tires. It was easier than messing with the radio. All Marcus listened to these days was that hip-hop bullshit with everyone piping off about how much money they're making off the rest of us sorry slobs, every song the same, every rapper going on about his money and his bitches and his boof at the cluuub. The lady rappers were slightly better, at least there was some truth to their booty power.

Still, he took his sponsor's advice. "Speak the language," Chris had said.

So Karl introduced some old school rap to the boy, what little he knew of the old school at least. Karl played him some Grand Master Flash and Rick James and Wu-Tang Clan. He wanted so bad for Marcus to hear some truth and all Karl knew for certain was that it couldn't come from him.

Marcus rolled down his window and lit up a Marlboro. Fucking kid was going to kill himself.

"You're gonna kill yourself smoking, you know."

"Where we going?"

"Just down the road bit."

"Power lines?"

"No. Alec said it's just clean up."

Marcus took a deep drag and exhaled out his cracked window. They passed by the last of the houses, and the woods leaned over the road. The road hummed along, and he glanced at Marcus here and there.

"Friggin' monkey work," Marcus spoke at the windshield.

"What's that?"

"I said it's monkey work."

"It's good work," Karl snapped. His old mind clicked in surging heat up his back.

Fucking ingrate.

He gripped the wheel. His God mind tried to keep it light. "Well, I suppose it is, what with all the tree climbing and all," he forced a smile.

"We don't even climb no trees."

"Yeah well, you got to train for that job, get certified and get a license and all."

"So, he's a trained monkey, good for him."

"You think what Alec does is easy? Handling a chainsaw hanging from a rope fifty feet off the ground?"

"Doesn't seem all that complicated."

"Why not just be happy with the work you got?"

"Because I ain't no monkey."

"So, you calling me a monkey?" Karl snapped again. He couldn't help it; the boy provoked him, picked at his sore spots.

Just like his mother.

"Whatever," Marcus shook his head and looked out his window.

The boy had a talent for raising the devil. Karl shifted and sat up straight behind the wheel, clutching it with both hands while his two minds wrestled. His God mind soared on and on about tolerance and gratitude. Marcus was talking to him! Really saying something! This was a blessing! Don't you see it, you dumb fuck? Don't you crush it with your judgments and your rage! Your boy is reaching out to you! It's The Promises!

Karl crushed the wheel. His forearms ached.

The arrogant little shit could just fuck off.

His minds grappled and left him with a bundle of spiritual phrases, each with a smoldering fuse. Every thought in his head needed to be decoded and disarmed. He finally spoke, slow and careful.

"So... Senior year starts soon... Big deal... You must be excited, right?" He took a breath. "You have what you need?"

"I'm all set," Marcus said. He lit up another smoke.

"Jesus, kid, you got to put those things down," Karl said.

Marcus rolled his eyes. He dragged his way through a good quarter inch of the butt, young lungs. Dense tobacco smoke clouded Karl's view of Alec's wood chipper parked along the roadside.

"Blow that shit out the window please," he shot Marcus a hard look.

And save for the difference of 80 pounds and his boy's tight Afro, damned if Karl didn't get the very same look back. Everyone's a mirror; that's what they say in the rooms. Course that just makes it hurt worse, the poor little son of a bitch. Karl rolled past the wood chipper, hitched to the back of Alec's light duty dump truck. It was one of those trucks with the plywood sidewalls, covered from top to bottom with rakes and ladders and hedge trimmers and shovels all bungeed to eye hooks. Karl pulled over and parked. Marcus opened his door and stuck a foot out.

"Wait, wait a sec," Karl reached for his shoulder.

"We're late," Marcus looked back at him, eyes thin and impatient.

"I know, I know... Look, Marcus, it's just, well, it don't have to be like this, you and me. You know?"

"Like what?"

Karl closed his eyes for a moment. "Look, I love you, Marcus. I always have, always will."

The corners of the boy's mouth turned down like he'd bit into something foul. Karl sat still, aware of his breath through his flat nose. He waited. Marcus' lips screwed tighter; his chin moved just a hint from side to side.

"We're late," Marcus said, hopped out of the cab and slammed the door shut.

Chapter Fourteen

Jonathan pulled forward far enough to make room for the next customer, the McDonald's bag warming his thighs. He'd made it for breakfast! He dug in, nudged aside Ronald's heavenly hash brown and went for the first Egg McMuffin. He tore off the wrapper and squeezed on three packs of ketchup. He bit down and chewed in slow motion, just like on the TV. He cradled the bite in his puffed cheeks. How did they get the eggs so perfect?

He didn't swallow until his mouth filled with a salty lather of pork bits and cheese. Just for today he could be certain of one thing - he got his break. He took another bite and repeated the routine, but the magic of the first mouthful was gone. By the time he finished the last bite, he didn't taste much at all.

He pulled into traffic, one hand on the wheel, one hand aloft with cool, greasy pink drippings sliding down his wrist. He took the highway back to Sycamore, and headed east for the lake. He hung a right onto Lakeside Drive. The sun shined through the clouds and the leaves glittered in the tress. Jonathan drove along Lake Tartusville. The sun added cheer to the old summerhouses and shacks by the lake.

He smiled. He'd done a good job so far today. He'd been to a meeting, said his prayers, spoken to other alcoholics, cared for his mother, said "no" to a bottle, filled his belly and all before ten in the morning! He hung a left onto his gravel driveway, and drove through the tall weeds that grew in as thick as a Zella's coat. He got out of the car and walked around the house. He crossed through the knee-high grasses of his small backyard into the stand of birch, maples and pines that bordered the lake. The air cooled and the light went flat in the shade. A few yards down the old deer path, sunlight jumped off the lake and lit up the lichen like fireflies. Jonathan passed quietly over leaves and needles until he was once again in the sun, by the shoreline.

"Thank You for this beautiful day."

He walked along the shore and stretched his arms wide. The water was calm, only a few bass boats to be seen and they were on the far side, near the dam. Jonathan matched his breathing to the rhythm of the gentle lapping of the water.

"Thank You for the peace in this moment."

He clasped his thick hands together and rose them skyward. He was certain the miracle was within reach. Don't quit until the miracle happens. That's what they said. That was the deal - just don't quit quitting. "Recovery won't be hurried along. It takes its sweet time." That's what King Karl always says.

He stood and searched the shallows for spawning beds. He waved at the blue gills suspended in the clear, calm water. The rain had stopped. The storm was over. He stepped up to the water's edge. He peered over his belly in a search of more fish, absently picking at a dried clump of ketchup on his shirt. He sprinkled the pickings into the water, but the fish did not bite. He discovered several more spots on his t-shirt. He scratched and picked at the spots one at a time until he'd forgotten about the fish entirely. He turned back for his house, picking and scratching at the stains. He climbed his deck stairs up onto his back porch. His mother's empty chair swing swayed in the gentle, swirling breeze.

Jonathan slid open the glass door leading into his kitchen. The stench hit him immediately. To his left, Zella lay on the kitchen floor, wheezing. Behind her, a black trail of poodoo led from the kitchen past the Formica dining table and into the family room. She'd done her nasty business all over the wood floors. She was always good that way, always stayed off the rugs, even as a puppy. His chin quivered.

"Oh Zella, oh no, oh jeez," he moaned.

He knelt by her and propped her head on his lap. The tumor over her left eye now pressed it completely shut. He bent down and she met him nose to nose. She sniffed at him as if to say hello, as if to apologize for the mess, as if to reassure him that things were a little rough at the moment but were sure to be fine after a good walk.

"Oh Zella, I am so sorry girl."

His tears dripped on the short white fur on top of her head.

"You just take it easy girl. I'm going to call the vet."

He lay her head back on the floor and rose to his feet. He reached for the phone book off the top of the refrigerator. He leafed through the white pages. He grunted when he realized he didn't know who he was looking for and flipped back to the yellow pages. He read through the vets. One was as good as another at this point. He'd end up lying next to Zella on a cold tile floor or maybe on some horrible death blanket they'd provide that would reek to Zella of the hundreds or maybe thousands or even millions of doggy souls that passed before her. No, horrible death blanket!

A big fancy advertisement with hearts in all four corners caught his eye. It must be a good choice, what with the hearts and all.

DEATH WITH DIGNITY. YOUR PET, YOUR HOME, YOUR TERMS, YOUR LOVE.

He glanced down at Zella. Her eyes were shut and she panted with wheezy breaths. He dialed the number.

"Good Morning, Peg Lohber, D with D." Her voice sounded chipper.

"Is this Death with Dignity?"

"That's right, this is Peg Lohber, D with D, may I help you?"

"Oh, uh, sure great, my dog is dying I think. No, actually I know. She's dying."

"What's her name?"

"Zella. I'm looking at her right now and she's on her way. I don't know what to do. She's struggling for breath."

"Did she get hit? Is she injured?"

"No, she's sick, cancer I'm pretty sure."

"I see. Is she drinking or eating?"

He checked her bowls. "No, no food at least. I can't tell about the drinking. She um, she lost her uh, she pooped all over the place."

"Oh my, yeah, that happens toward the end. What kind of dog is Zella?"

"She's like a pit bull terrier mix."

"So cute," Peg sounded sincere.

"She's my best friend," he wiped his eyes.

"And you are?"

"Jonathan Vacarie."

"Well Mr. Vacarie, I'll be candid, okay?"

"Okay."

"Great, from what you're describing it doesn't sound like we have a lot of time and it sounds like Zella's very uncomfortable. So here's the headlines. I can euthanize Zella in your home where she's most comfortable and assist you with the remains. Where are you?"

"By Lake Tartusville."

"Great, you're pretty close then, that helps. I charge based on time and materials. I'm guessing Zella's in the 40 pound range so given her size and travel time and urgency..." Jonathan edged the top third of his ass up on the kitchen counter while she calculated. "It's going to be in the three to four hundred dollar range."

"Three to four hundred, I see," he said, scratching his head.

"That's without any bells and whistles - caskets or that sort of thing."

"Four hundred to kill my dog, then," he confirmed.

"No, to put your dog out of her misery. To provide her with a merciful end, that's what D with D is all about."

Jonathan thought that sounded right, but he wasn't sure about the numbers. "So it's four hundred for a merciful killing then? Is that right?"

"Euthanize, Mr. Vacarie, not kill," Peg said.

"Euthanize, right. I didn't know mercy cost that much."

"Mr. Vacarie, mercy's cheap. Drugs are expensive."

He eased off the kitchen counter and rubbed his tingling rump. Zella snuffled at his feet. She had been a cute pup, all ears and tail.

"Alright, I get it. I mean, uh, I want it," he rubbed his hand on his forehead. "I mean, yes, please come," he said. Zella's hind legs twitched. "What should I do now?"

"Keep her company, maybe find a blanket to keep her warm. She's a short hair, right?"

"That's right," he said with a nod.

"Be brave, Mr. Vacarie, be strong for her."

Jonathan wiped away more tears, "Okay, okay, but well, when can you get here?"

"You live by the lake? I'll be there inside an hour. Give me your address."

She was quiet while he racked his brain trying to remember.

Chapter Fifteen

"Come on Numb Nutz, last one, I gotta go." Joey shifted the Pinto into gear.

Jimmy held his hit as long as he could, but his lungs conspired against him. The revolution started from an upward spasm, deep in his gut. There was no stopping the murphatroid. He clenched his lips and smoke shot out from his nostrils. His lips vibrated with each spasm, like a bugle boy blowing reveille, or taps. In a coughing fit of freedom he surrendered his hit out the window toward Uncle Sal's flamingos.

Joey slapped his back again and again, like that was gonna fix it.

"Damn bro, maybe you should ease on the cheese," Joey said.

Jimmy horked an ashy tasting glob into a leaf pile by the curb. He clutched his Sucrets box in one hand and his bat in the other. The hot end of the bat felt fine between his fingers. He was good.

"I'm good," Jimmy raised his left arm. "I'm good, dude, you can stop."

Joey quit hitting. "Look, I'll be right back. It's just a quick thing in town."

"Not Watertown?"

"Naw, the guy's practically around the corner," Joey checked his mirrors.

"You swear?"

"Bro, I swear, alright? What the freak are you griping about anyway? You get to kick back with the Naughty Nurse!"

It would be so cool if she were from Naugatuck. Wait.

"Wait..." Jimmy pointed at his brother, who was definitely further away than he appeared. "I thought that was you."

Joey grinned. "You bet your ass that's me." He took a sip of his beer and set it back between his legs. "But, I tell you what I'll do, I'll let you warm her up for me."

"Dude, I ain't you. Make it quick," Jimmy got out of the car. He stood, gaining altitude way too fast. He used the door to keep himself upright while he waited for the scenery to catch up.

"Jesus Numb Nutz, shut the door already!"

Jimmy turned for Uncle's Sal's and closed the door in one super-smooth, deft motion. Joey peeled out. Jimmy cut through the leaf pile and walked softly through the flock of flamingos to his Uncle's front door. Her Tempest was parked just like last week, smack in between the two garage doors. He rang the bell.

"Well, hello there, Jimmy." Nurse Farrah-Vacarie opened the gate. Her teeth weren't pearly like Farrah's, but they were perfectly straight. Her nipples pinned her pink halter-top to her boobs, or maybe it was the other way around. She wore the same white mini-skirt - but no heels this time - just white stockings over her feet. He chubbed up right there in the hall.

"Where's Joey?" she asked. She stood on her toes to peer over him.

"He had something to do. He said he'd be back soon."

"Well then, it's just us," Nurse Vacarie smiled, reached for his shoulder and gently pulled him inside. "I was just about to make Sal some lunch. He's glued to football on the TV. He's been going on and on about the season opener," she rolled her green eyes. "I know zero about football, you a big fan?" She squeezed his shoulder.

"No, that's Joey."

"Well, are you a fan of tuna sandwiches?" She looked in his eyes and rubbed his back. His shifted from foot to foot, all of him tingling like he'd become a bursting sack of electric baby spiders. He checked his stiffy, pointing uncomfortably downward in his jeans. His Felix The Cat t-shirt hung low over his waist, thank God.

"Oh yeah, tuna, yeah."

She scampered her fingernails down his back and called into the living room, "Sal, Jimmy's here!" she pushed him along, her hand on the small of his back. "You go say hi to your uncle and I'll get going on lunch."

Jimmy and his hard-on stepped down into the living room. The game was on the TV. He recognized the Patriots. The other team was green.

"Hey, Uncle Sal," Jimmy said

His uncle sat in the middle of the couch with his feet up on the coffee table. His satin robe was tied loosely around his medicine ball belly. His face was a pale gray, like he'd scrubbed with dirty bleach.

"Hey kid - is she getting lunch?"

"Yup."

"Where's your brother?"

"Out."

His uncle mulled on that for a moment. "Wadaya mean he's out? We got the Pats on here! Where's he at?"

"He had to do something, I dunno," Jimmy shrugged. "He said he'd be back soon."

Uncle Sal grunted.

"You watching the Pats?" Jimmy wedged himself into the corner of the couch.

Sal turned to look at him with a black eyebrow raised, thick and fluffy like a caterpillar on the move. "So how you doin', Jimmy boy?"

"I'm doing okay, Uncle Sal, you?"

"Hanging in there," Uncle Sal said. "Go turn it up, will ya?"

Jimmy got up and squatted in front of the TV and turned the volume button. The announcer's voice seemed louder, but he couldn't be sure because the language he spoke was foreign. Maybe he'd turned the wrong button. He looked over his shoulder. His uncle sat spread eagle, his big, hairy balls hanging in full view. Uncle Sal leaned to one side and waved him out of the way.

"Sorry," Jimmy muttered and slid sideways. He sat cross-legged on the floor. The Patriot's quarterback got hammered from behind.

"Sonofabitch!" Sal shouted, "This Grogan's a freaking bum."

"Yeah, no doubt, no doubt," Jimmy mumbled. He looked into his lap and wiggled his fingers. Hello Jimmy. Hello fingers. Where's Joey? We surely could not say. O frabjous day! Callooh! Callay!

"Here we are!" Bea stepped down into the room with plates in each hand. "Hope you're hungry."

"As a horse!" Uncle Sal said. He arched his back and his belly bubbled like gum. "Must've been that special medicine."

Bea handed Uncle Sal a plate. Jimmy watched her white feet pad toward him, wading through the blue shag. He reached up and took the plate from her. She'd cut the Wonder diagonally. The tuna tasted fine.

After lunch, Jimmy took their plates to the kitchen. The lights were off and the afternoon sun came soft through the windows. He put the plates in the sink and sighed as he sat at his regular spot at the table, facing the sink. It was so nice and quiet. He was so nice and alone. All he had to do was wait for Joey to get back.

He picked at a petrified lump of gum wedged between the underside of the tabletop and its metallic rim. He inspected his fingertip. It might have been Bazooka. It was too old to tell by color. He sniffed. The sweet banana-ramic whisperstink was unmistakable, Juicy Fruit. He reached under the table and probed some more, stroking the ribbed surface of the gum with the tip of his finger. It felt like a peach pit, a four sticker for sure. He had to see it, see if the Juicy Fruit had transformed into a peach pit. He bent over and craned his neck sideways to look up under the rim. It had turned! Out of nowhere fans suddenly cheered.

"Oh shoot, no, no, no! Rats!"

The floor shattered behind him.

Jimmy banged his eyebrow on the rim of the table. He sat up, pressing his palm on the pain.

"Jimmy! My God you gave me a start!" Nurse Vacarie stood at the kitchen door, balancing teetering teacups on top of a stack of plates she held cradled in her arms.

"Whoa, uh sorry, about that. Umm... need a hand?" He smoothed his hair back and cinched up the hairband on his ponytail.

"Aren't you sweet. I'm such a klutz!" Bea rolled her eyes. "I was just bringing in some of my things from the car."

"Here let me," Jimmy got up and rubbed the Juicy Fruit finger on his jeans. He gathered the surviving teacups off the top plate. His knuckles brushed against her breast. He blushed and turned quickly for the counter.

"You're not watching the game?"

"Naw."

Nurse Vacarie knelt to pick up pieces of the fallen cup. She'd put her heels on. Her skirt rose high on her thighs, above the frilly hem of her stockings. White straps buttoned to her stockings disappeared under her skirt. Jimmy searched the floor by his feet, but couldn't find a thing to pick up.

"I got tired of it. I'm no Joey," he said.

"Sit, sit, I've got this," Bea motioned to him with her chin. She rose up oh-so-flamingo and dropped the broken pieces in the trash. She put her hands on her hips, looked at him and sighed. She sat beside him and put her hand on his knee. The electric spiders returned, stampeding from her fingertips. She leaned toward him, showing cleavage that outsized the real Farrah by a cup size or two for sure. She smelled like lilacs and her bosom shimmered like hot, white sand. She stroked his eyebrow with her fingertip. He shivered.

"Are you okay?" she asked with a concerned pout.

"Uh...oh yeah, I'm good."

"Really? Is there anything I can do to make you feel better?" She shifted her hand on his thigh. "You poor thing."

"Uh...I'm good, Nurse Vacarie, thanks though."

She gave his thigh a slap. "I told you, silly, it's Bea."

She leaned closer, tilting her head. Her golden, feathered hair fell over her shoulder. He heard uncle Sal swear at the TV and glanced over his shoulder to the kitchen door. He pressed his forearms against his lap, squeezing his hands between his legs.

"Jimmy, you mind if I ask you a personal question?" She didn't wait. "How old are you?"

"Eighteen."

"Is that the truth?" She looked unconvinced.

"Yup. Turned eighteen in July, July tenth, fifty-seven." He proved it.

She smiled and squeezed him just above his knee. It tickled. "If I ask you something else, you promise you'll tell the truth?"

"Uh, yeah, sure."

"Do you like me, Jimmy?" Her hand slid an inch up his leg and the spiders zinged and flittered.

"Well, sure, you know, I guess. I mean, yeah," he shrugged.

"I know, I know, you get that feeling about people, right? I do anyway. Sometimes I just know. You know?"

"I know," Jimmy said.

They giggled.

"It's not crazy," she reassured, she moved closer. She leaned over, met him nose to nose and slid her cheek along his. Her breath tickled in his ear.

"Really?" his voice cracked.

"Really," she cooed. Her lips touched his earlobe and the spiders convened briefly on the nape of his neck before cascading down his spine and piling into his raging boner. Jimmy adjusted himself with his forearm. Bea pulled away from him and grinned. He sat hunched over, dumbstruck, embarrassed and on fire, spiders everywhere. She stood up and smoothed her skirt.

"So anyway... I was hoping you boys could help me move the rest of my stuff today. You think Joey will be back soon?"

"I think so," Jimmy said. He swiped sweat off his temple.

"Does he know his way around Waterbury?"

"I think so."

"Terrific! Then how 'bout you and I get a head start, you know, to pack. I'll leave him a note with my address. And we'll just hang out until he gets there. Sound good?" She smiled.

"I guess, but—"

"It'll be more fun than football, I promise. Let me just go see if that's alright with your uncle. You sit and, and, and relax for a minute - be right back." Bea got up, grabbed a beer out of the 'fridge and did a little shimmy out the swinging door.

Callooh! Callay! O frabjous day!

He chortled in his joy.

Dude.

Chapter Sixteen

BEA PUT THE Budweiser down by Sal's feet on the coffee table. He stared at the TV with his right hand tucked under the belt of his robe. He had an awful habit of picking at his belly button.

"Sal, I hate to say it, but this looks like the only beer in the house," Bea announced with a frown.

"What?"

She had his attention. "This is it for the beer, babe."

"You check the garage?"

"I checked everywhere," she said with a touch of desperation.

"How is this freakin' possible? It's Sunday for Chrissakes! How we supposed to watch football?" Sal lurched forward and coughed into his palms. He wiggled his fingers for her to pass him the Bud. He picked at the pull-tab with the knurled tip of his index finger.

"Well, I could run back to my place," she suggested.

"You got beers at your place?" He kept his eyes on the can, his lips tight with determination. The ring snapped against the tin top with a taunting pop.

"I think I have most of a twelve pack."

"Well then, by all means," Sal waved her along, "do it." He got his beer open and let the tab hang from his finger. He slurped at the foam.

"Mind if I take the boys along? They can help me move the rest of my stuff."

Sal perked up, "Joey's here?"

"No, not yet. I thought I'd take Jimmy now and leave Joey a note. We can do it in all one trip with both cars."

"Fine, fine, hurry up. I'll tell Joey if he gets here."

"I'll leave my address on the kitchen table."

"Yeah, yeah, fine. Hurry up," Sal waved her off. He was back in the game.

�„⊷═⊙ ⊙═⊶„

Bea poked her butt out the window; the ash blew off in the breeze. She drove fast, stealing glances at Jimmy on the straightaways. He stared out the windshield, looking like he was going to jump out of that silky smooth skin of his.

"Well, what *do* you like then?" How could anyone not like KC And The Sunshine Band? She turned the dial in search of another station.

"Um, you know, Zeppelin, Floyd, The Who—"

"I saw them at Woodstock." She listened to a few notes of classical and kept turning.

"No way, you did Woodstock?" Jimmy said.

"Sure did," she chuckled to herself. This was the first time she didn't utterly regret the fact.

"You saw Hendrix?" he asked, those aquamarine eyes filled with wonder.

"Trust me, baby, I saw it all," she said.

Jimmy smiled, finally. "I like new stuff too—"

"Ooo, I love these guys!" she turned it up and sung along. "Oh, come on, it's The Captain and Tennille! You know the words," she poked him and then caught up with the song, showing Jimmy the palm of her hand.

"Whatever," Jimmy turned red.

Bea laughed, though she knew well enough this was a bad idea. On the other hand, if she didn't have a little fun here and there, what was the point? She'd end up winding herself into a tight, bitchy little knot. It wasn't *horrible* riding on Sal's little wand. But Sal had brought her to a certain state of randiness, not the screwing so much as the sheer potential of the situation. Things had progressed so smoothly and quickly that she'd refused herself any satisfaction. She was afraid of jinxing it.

Now she wanted satisfaction, wanted it bad. And this cute little wayward Adonis with his tone, hairless chest and arms, not to mention the promising bulge in his blue jeans, was too much to resist. All the stars had aligned. Sal would never know. All the things that she had coming her way were finally arriving in delicious style.

Bea braked hard and the tires of the Tempest screeched as she cut the wheel and swung into the entrance of Waterbury Mews. She rolled along slowly, searching the lot. No one in sight and most of the spots were taken. She caught her breath at the sight of a yellow trunk.

"What?" Jimmy looked at her.

She sighed; it was a Challenger.

"Not a thing, we're here," she said and parked in spot 320. She cut the engine. Jimmy turned to her, looking uncertain and timid, yet with cheeks flushed to rosy. She reached over and squeezed the lean, rounded bulb of his shoulder. He was such a beauty this boy, with his thick, dirty blond hair tied back in a ponytail. All those middle-aged men claiming some sort of imaginary connection between baldness and virility were kidding themselves. She tucked a loose strand back behind his ear. If it weren't for the ghost of Owen haunting her, she'd climb up on him this minute and get the ball rolling. She opened her door and slipped off her seat.

"Come on," Bea said in a breathy voice. Her weak legs surprised her.

"Uh, yup, right behind you," Jimmy said. His ponytail flipped toward her as he yanked on his door handle.

She reached for his hand and hustled him across the lot. Cool breeze drew goose bumps on her arms but her blood streamed through her, hot as firewater.

And that was just the ticket.

Safe inside her double locked door, Bea sat beside Jimmy on her pleather love seat in the middle of the living room. A few overstuffed moving boxes, the couch and her bed were all that was left to move.

Jimmy choked on his Johnnie Walker.

"You okay?" she asked and took the drink out of his hand.

"No, yeah, I'm fine," he blurted. "Just went down the wrong pipe is all." He cleared his throat.

She put the glasses on the floor.

"So…here we are," she whispered. She put her arm over his shoulder, curled up to him and touched his top lip with the tip of her tongue. He kissed her tongue gently before their lips met. Either his instincts were good or he'd had a bit of experience. She caressed his chest through his t-shirt and lowered her hand to his lap. He slid his hand up her thigh and under her skirt, maybe a bit more than a bit. She felt along the length of him, and unbuttoned his jeans. He shuddered, maybe not.

"Take these off," she commanded. His nervousness drove her crazy. She felt as if all of her gushed to overflowing. He shimmied out of his jeans while she tugged at his boxers with both hands. His ass skittered forward on the couch with a farting warble.

"That wasn't what it sounded like," he said.

She smiled, got up from the couch. She kicked his feet apart and stood between his legs. She pulled up her skirt, tore at the buttons of her garter and stripped off her panties. All of him was perfect.

Bea straddled him, guiding him with her hand. She eased herself down but he held her up by her hips.

"I don't have a—"

"It's taken care of.

"I've never done it without a—"

She held his shoulders and pressed herself down on him.

"Oh Jesus, holy sweet Jesus" he moaned.

"Relax," she whispered. She trembled as she slowly raised her hips. Had she ever trembled like this? She eased down on him again. She pressed his head between her hands, but there was no need to coddle him. She was already there. She grabbed fistfuls of his thick hair and shoved herself down.

"Oh my God, oh shit!" she screamed. She shut her eyes and came, and then came again. "Oh… Holy shit!" and again! Her screams came from a distance, she'd lost her bearings in a flood of ecstatic disbelief. Jimmy clutched onto her thrashing hips and arched his back. His thighs went rigid beneath her. She forced his head back by the hair and bit his bowed neck.

"Oh no," he croaked and she felt him, felt all of him, bigger and bigger and she came again.

Bea slumped forward onto his chest. Good God she needed that.

She'd just caught her breath and he was already up and ready for more. Jimmy was something special. He didn't need any more direction. She clung to him and they screamed like alley cats.

He lasted longer this time; how long she hadn't a clue. A couple minutes? An hour? She slumped off him, sweaty and exhausted. She'd have to find another top. Her halter was drenched. "I have to go to the bathroom. You should get dressed."

"One more time?" he asked with a hopeful smile. Incredible.

"No, baby, we gotta stop," she touched his nose. It was damp and puppy cute. She got up on tired, shaky legs and gathered her things off the floor.

"So um, did you enjoy that?" he asked, a fragile look on his face.

"Thoroughly," she said.

"I've never done it," he paused.

Bea flushed, there was just no way.

Jimmy held up his hands. "No, no, no. I mean, I've done it, just never like that before, you know never with a, or without a, or um…"

"This isn't high school, Jimmy," she said with a little chuckle.

"Exactly," Jimmy nodded and smiled. He pulled on his boxers and then his jeans. He buttoned them over his sexy, toned abdominals. He tried to stand but fell back onto the couch.

"Wonder wobbles, right? Me too," she said.

"Wonder what?"

She patted her thigh, "Wonder wobbles, you know, legs like Jell-O," she explained.

"Uh, yeah, right," Jimmy said as if he'd misheard her. He reached for her hand and searched for the words she already knew were coming. She considered running off to the loo to spare him the anguish.

"You know how you were saying you just had this feeling?" he asked, holding her hand and looking up at her.

"Mmhmm."

"Well, I'm having that - big time. You're… um, you're awesome."

"Thank you, so are you," she said, but shouldn't have. This was not the time for honesty.

"I'm really into you."

"Yes you were," she said with an offhand giggle.

"I'm serious," he said.

She nodded, "I know." She bit the inside of her lip but said it anyway, "Me too."

"I think I, I mean I—"

She freed her hand and held up a finger. "Hold that thought. I have to pee like crazy!" She hurried off down the short hall for the bathroom. She knew this was a bad idea.

She flushed toilet and heard her door buzzer.

"Joey's here!" Jimmy called out from the front room.

"Okay, I'll be out in a sec!" She hoped she had a decent blouse in the bedroom.

Bea heard Jimmy unlock the bolts. She twisted hard on her old faucet handles and cold water dribbled out the rust stained spout. She scrubbed her hands and heard her front door slam shut. It took forever for the hot water and she realized how much she loved Sal's swans. She turned the water off and shook her hands in the sink. All her towels were packed. She pushed opened the door a crack and called to the boys.

"There's beer in the 'fridge!"

"Mighty white of you, Beetle Bug." Owen wedged the door open with the squared toe of his black boot. He leaned over to get a look at her and smiled. The teeth he had left formed a brown, jagged row. "Now, these were probably overkill," he raised his right hand and pulled off the brass knuckles.

"Jimmy!" Bea gasped.

"Turns out lover boy's got himself a glass chin," he lamented with a little shake of his long, scraggly chin beard.

"You get away from me! You... You... You...!" Bea stammered. She tugged with both hands on the doorknob but Owen yanked on the door and the knob slipped out of her damp, shaking hands. He narrowed his beaver brown eyes, shook his head again and sighed like he was bored to tears. He grabbed her by the hair.

"You and me, we're going for a little joy ride - be just like old times."

He slapped the scream right out of her mouth.

"You do that again and I'll skip the joy part."

Chapter Seventeen

KARL SURVEYED THE damage from his truck. Damn wind had come through like God's whip. Along the roadside, a dozen trees lay strewn about, some whole, some broke in pieces. Two fat white pines had fallen across Sycamore. The road crew had cut a path for traffic but left the remains. He and Marcus would have to saw up those tops across the road and drag them back for chipping.

Karl got out of his truck and followed his son's trail into the shade of the woods. His boots sunk into the soft forest floor. The damp leaves and pine needles lied to him with cool whiffs; he'd be sweating soon enough.

Some twenty paces in, Marcus stood beside Alec's red and yellow ropes coiled by the foot of sugar maple. Marcus had his eyes up the tree, guiding the red equipment line. Thirty feet up, Alec had tied his wiry self to the maple, a yard or two beneath the jagged breakpoint where the wind had snapped the top half of the tree sideways. The top of the tree lay cradled in the branches of a neighboring oak, stuck fast under its own weight.

Alec hauled on the red line. Midway up the maple, between Marcus' feeding and Alec's gobbling, a chainsaw dangled, loop-tied to the red line. It bumped its way up between the limbs.

"You boys arrived just in time," Alec called down. "Took me a while to get up this slippery bitch." Alec motioned at Marcus. "More to the left now, Marcus."

Eyes on Alec, Marcus stepped to his left, hesitated and took two steps to his right.

"Ayuh, that's the ticket!" Alec shouted. "Hey, Karl, I'll be up here a while clearing limbs. I got to get a good knot on her. She's wedged pretty tight for now, different story when we cut her loose. Tricky. Don't have a good sense of her yet."

"We can get going on the pines, clear off the road," Karl called.

"Ayuh," Alec untied the chainsaw from the red line and clipped it to a strap affixed to his safety harness, which was really no more than a length of old climbing rope doubled around his waist and looped around both his thighs. The strap was about four feet long and the chainsaw hung from it now, just below Alec's feet.

Karl gawked at the sight. No amount of money would get him up in a spot like that. Man might be made for climbing, but he was made for falling too. Bad enough being thirty feet up a broken tree, never mind working a chainsaw. No, not for him, he was a ground guy. And he was just fine with ground-guy money. On the ground all he had to worry over was getting brained by a falling log. Shit, dropped from Alec's perch, a three foot section from a tree like this would cut a trench deep enough to bury a coon hound.

Alec shouted down. "Marcus, send up the blue heave-to line will ya?"

Marcus searched around his feet.

"It's in my duffle!"

"Got it!" Marcus hollered. He tied the blue line to the end of the red one. "Okay!" The blue line slid up through Marcus's loose grip and the knot rose above his head.

"No need to guide it," Alec called down.

"We'll get at the pines," Karl called up.

"Ayuh," Alec grunted. Karl watched Alec size up the tangle of leafy limbs above him. He glanced over at Marcus. All three of them gaped upward like hungry, baby birds.

"Let's get at it," Karl said. He patted Marcus on the shoulder. Marcus didn't move. "I'll start up the chipper. You start sawing up the pine across the road."

"How 'bout you do that and I get the chipper going?" Marcus said, still looking up.

"How 'bout you just do what I tell you."

"Whatever," Marcus shrugged and walked back toward the road.

The cocky little shit needs a big boot up his ass.

Karl followed Marcus and sucked in the green air. His God mind steered his attention to the red flash of a cardinal darting between branches. He rolled up his sleeves. The air under the trees was cool enough to raise black goose bumps on top of the old jail ink that littered his arms. Like the rest up in Osborn, he'd done his time stoned, bored and senseless. Like the rest, he'd marked his time inside with a sick-souled pride outside. He did his time in the pit of incomprehensible demoralization, though he wouldn't come to know that phrase until he was long out of the joint.

Karl stepped out from under the trees and the sun kissed his cheek right there by the side of the Bandit 65XP wood chipper. Marcus stood waiting in the road on the other side of the Bandit, his big hands half-tucked in the pockets of his low-slung jeans.

"You remember how to start it up?" Karl asked.

Marcus came closer and peered at the engine. "Just give it half throttle and turn the key."

"And choke it quick when you turn the key. Quick though, or it'll flood. Then slow with the gas."

"Yeah, yeah," Marcus said. He turned the key. The engine sputtered and caught, chugging through burps of exhaust.

"Easy on the throttle!" Karl shouted over the noise.

Karl walked alongside the rumbling chipper to the back of Alec's truck. He pulled a chainsaw off the steel bed and laid it on the ground. He took out two hardhats, the yellow shells sooty with sap and gear grease. Stuffed into the rubber straps of each was a pair of safety glasses. Both hardhats had ear protectors, little black cups fixed to the sides that resembled old headphones. Karl slid put on the glasses and squeezed his head into the straps of the hardhat. He clamped the headphones over his ears. They took the edge off the scream of the engine. He stepped over the trailer hitch and walked back to Marcus.

"Easy on the throttle! Here!" he shouted and handed Marcus the other hard hat, "Glasses too!"

"Yeah, yeah, yeah! I got it!" Marcus shouted back.

It felt good to shout at the kid, real good, and he couldn't tell if it was his old mind or his God mind feeling the pleasure. He got under the blow spout of the chipper, unlocked the rotor and pointed the spout into the woods. He walked around to the business end of the chipper and put his hand on the safety bar that ran across the topside of the mouth.

"Hey!" he shouted to get the boy's attention. "Hey!"

Marcus looked over at him.

"Push the bar for Reverse, right?"

"I know!"

"And don't be reaching in there for nothing!"

"I know!"

"Once that feed wheel gets a hold of something—"

"Jesus Christ, I KNOW!"

Karl shook his head. "I know you know, and I don't give a shit. I'm telling you anyway."

"Dad, I know, okay?"

Karl shrugged and walked back to the hitch for his chainsaw, scary fucking thing. It used to be the scariest thing his old mind could imagine was some kid calling him dad. And then for a time it felt better than any hit or shot he ever took. But nowadays Marcus was stingy with the word, avoided it as best he could, so the highs were few and far between. And when Marcus did let it slip, it hurt Karl's heart to hear it. Especially a dad like the one he'd just let fly. He'd goaded this one out of the boy. This one wasn't no voluntary dad. The boy might just as well have called him Motherfucker. Kissette loved to call him Motherfucker.

"Motherfucker, you owe me $900! Two months! Don't you start with your lying, Motherfucker! Motherfucker, what gives you the right? As far as I'm concerned, Motherfucker, you ain't the boy's father, you just some funky uncle junky comes around."

The bitch poisoned his boy, turned son against father.

"There's another chainsaw in the back of the truck," Karl shouted.

Marcus waved him off. Karl crossed Sycamore and backtracked to the farthest heap of wood. Piled on top and on either side of the trunk were saw-cut limbs left by the road crew. He stood over the tangle of it and wondered where to start. Underneath the fresh cuts lay the bulk of the work. The pine's shattered branches splayed out from under the trunk like broke spider legs. Trees fell just like anything else, not gentle and clean but hard and messy. He yanked a couple of cut limbs off the top of the pile. They were heavy old limbs; thick, sticky limbs too big to get a grip on. He tucked one under each arm and dragged them across the road.

As he crossed, he watched Marcus feeding the chipper. Thick limbs bumped hard against the steel hopper from the force of the grind wheel tugging the wood through the choke hole leading to the rotary blade. And then came the whirling howls of shredding wood followed by the clatter of bits spewing out the spout some twenty feet into the woods. Sugar coated as it was by the sweet, minty smell of fresh cut pine; the chipping struck him strange, just like his qualifying this morning, as if he was a party to something ugly.

Back when Alec showed him how to chip the wood, ugly was all that came to mind. He'd listened to Alec, standing a stride away from the Bandit with his arms crossed tight.

"Listen, Karl, I'm just saying, best thing to do is never get comfortable with it. I just stay scared of the whole fucking idea. Machine's dangerous enough, but that's not even the real worry. Nope," Alec poked a sooty finger at the gray hair by his temple, "It's the man working it - that's the worry. Chipping is mindless work. That's the thing see? Feeding it one stick after the next, over and over and over again. That's what you need to be afraid of. Mind yourself, Karl, you get bored, restless, your mind starts wandering, you start forgetting just exactly what it is you're dancing with and, well, there you are, all ground up and spit out the other side."

Karl dropped his branches down behind Marcus with a grunt. His son picked one off the ground like it was nothing.

"Feed 'em trunk first!" Karl shouted.

Marcus flashed him a look out the corner of his eye, his mouth tight with a go-fuck-yourself scowl.

Karl's God mind knew the difference between one kind of hatred and the next, knew how they all had their different flavors. Some hate had that sour aftertaste that stuck in your throat like cheap tequila; some hate was more like spiced rum. It went down sweet and easy and came up just the same. But his boy's hate burned him from the inside out, like he'd drunk down a bottle of Drano and passed it along. It ate away at the both of them.

Marcus shoved the cut branch into the hopper. The big limb shuddered as the Bandit chewed it up. Needles rained onto the pavement. The engine chugged and strained and it smelled like Christmas in a coal mine.

Chapter Eighteen

THE HOLLOW KNOCK on the glass door woke both of them with a start. Jonathan dozed cross-legged on the kitchen floor, back wedged against the counter with Zella's head resting in his lap. She growled weakly in the direction of the sliding glass door. He looked up, glanced at the old cuckoo clock on the wall, the wooden arms showed ten-thirty. Outside, a woman dressed in light blue like a doctor tapped on the glass.

Jonathan struggled to his feet, his legs and back stiff. He paused at the door, and stared at her through the glass. She smiled at him. Like most folks, she was taller than him. Her bright green eyes met his directly. She had a sharp nose above smooth, full lips and a firm, Roman chin. She wore a black, long-sleeved t-shirt under her blue top and a do-rag on her head, black with red flames. Out from the back of her cap hung a dark red, braided ponytail. She carried a baby blue blanket folded under her left arm and a medical bag in her hand. She pointed to the floor behind him. He slid the door open part way.

"Mr. Vacarie? I'm Peg Lohber, D with D."

"Hi." Jonathan stood motionless for a moment. The woman tilted her head and eyed him with an odd expression. "Yes, right... come on in," he slid open the door and stepped aside.

"Let me guess, not what you expected?" She extended her hand. He took it. Her grip was stronger than his. "That's okay, me neither. Anyway, I get that a lot," she said.

"Get what?"

"You know, what's a girl like you doing - blah, blah, blah. It's usually house-wives though. Hi, Zella, may I?" She'd moved around him before he had a chance to register the question. She dropped to one knee and held the back of her hand out to Zella. Zella lifted her head, sniffed and gave another low, weak growl. "I know girl, I know. You're right."

Zella rested her head back on the floor and exhaled.

"She knows," Peg Lohber said.

"She does?"

"They always know. Animals don't do denial, that's something reserved just for us humans." She stroked Zella with two long fingers. "I've had lots of experi-ence with animals, believe me."

Jonathan hovered above them. He studied the biker crest on top of her head. He shifted his weight. His right foot tingled painfully. He picked a potato chip crumb from between two tiles on the counter. Mother loved her tile. He squeezed the greasy shard between his thumb and finger. It broke into bits but did not disintegrate, leaving him unsure of what to do.

"Have you said goodbye, Jonathan? I'm sorry, may I call you Jonathan?"

"Hmm?" he pulled his fingers from his mouth. "Oh sure, doctor, of course. No, I haven't, should I?"

"Call me Peg," she smiled. "And yes, I think that would be best."

"Would you excuse me a second?" He shuffled out of the kitchen and down the narrow hall. He walked into the living room and stood between the two dog-worn couches. Zella had made both of them hers; chewing the corners, forgetting her fuzzy dog bed ever existed. In the evenings she'd stretch herself out, digging her nails and worming her way from one end to the other. Jonathan wiped tears off his cheeks. He lifted a cushion off one of the couches and re-turned to the kitchen.

"Can we get her up on this?" he asked, placing the cushion on the floor near the sliding glass door.

"Perfect," she said.

Jonathan coaxed Zella up onto the cushion. Zella didn't budge.

"Alright girl, here we go," Jonathan slid his arms underneath her and trans-ferred her gently onto the cushion. "It's nice, it's your plop-plop."

"Plop-plop, that's cute," Peg said.

"Just our silly stuff, you know," he sniffled.

"Silly stuff is what makes the world go 'round. Why don't you two take a moment? May I?" She draped the death blanket over Zella, and then grabbed her medical bag off the counter, stepped around the cushion and into the dining room. She sat at the head of the table, in his mother's seat. He heard glass containers click on the tabletop. "I'll be a minute with the meds. Take all the time you need."

Jonathan bent over Zella and scratched her behind the ear. He tucked the blanket around her. It smelled like bleach.

"You're a good girl. You've always been a good girl. I'm so sorry. I'm so sorry," he paused to wipe his cheeks and under his nose. He snorted. "I don't know how to do this. What do you say?"

"You're doing fine. It's just company, that's all. She feels you. That's the comfort. You don't have to say anything if you don't want."

"Okay." Jonathan bent over and touched his forehead to Zella's. He felt her breath rustle the hairs on his chest. His tears dropped past her snout, some landing on her paws. She looked up at him.

"Bye bye," he choked. Peg returned with two syringes in her hand and a stethoscope around her neck.

"Are you ready, Jonathan?"

"Yes," he said and bit his lip.

She knelt beside them. "This first shot is a sedative. It puts her to sleep. The second shot will arrest her heart and she'll pass. Okay?"

Jonathan nodded and Peg gave the first injection. Zella's eyelids drooped shut and she started to snore.

"Oh, she's snoring," Peg said with a little smile.

Jonathan nodded, though he wondered why. Peg's face got serious and she injected Zella for a second time. The snoring stopped. And then everything stopped.

"Jonathan? Jonathan? Can you hear me?"

How many trips had he made to Sunny Brook? How many trips to Our Lady of Perpetual Forgiveness? How many times did he hear he was no good? Good for nothing, a dope, a loser, a child? Zippy the pinhead! How long had he waited for God's mercy? He looked down at Zella, the tip of her tongue stuck out from her mouth. Maybe he'd lay down next to her and ask for a shot of his own.

"Jonathan? you okay?"

He looked up at Peg. Her green eyes narrowed, her head tilted to one side. She had a tiny diamond stuck in her right nostril. He noticed her ears were pierced several times over, though most of the holes were empty. She scowled. "Hey, give me something here. Are you with me?"

"Yes. I'm here."

"Phew, good, had me going there for a second. Can I get you a glass of water or something?"

"Yes, please," he struggled to his feet and got as far as the dining table. He sat heavily in his regular seat, to Mother's right. He listened to her rummage through the kitchen cabinets and run the water in the sink.

"Here," she said and sat beside him.

"Thanks," he drank the cup dry and set it down beside her medicine jars. A cell phone sounded from her medical bag. She pulled out the phone and checked the number.

"You need to get that?" he asked.

Peg shook her head. "No, it's just my sister," she rolled her eyes. "She calls a lot, you know, family."

"Yes I do."

"You have a sister?"

"Nope, it's just me and my mother."

Peg turned to look in the living room. Her thick pony tail, shiny red with wisps of orange trailed down her back like hot lava.

"And no wife I'm guessing. What about a girlfriend?"

"Nope."

She looked back at him. Her eyes looked like sweet green apples. "Boyfriend?"

Jonathan flushed, "No."

She folded her hands in front of her and leaned toward him. "So who takes care of you?"

"What do you mean? I take care of myself."

Peg nodded slowly.

Jonathan rubbed under his nose. He looked in the kitchen, making a point to keep his eyes off the floor. He looked into the living room and then back at Peg.

"Why are you staring at me?"

"I'm sorry, I'm not." She reached into her bag and pulled out a pad and pen. She rolled up her sleeves and then wrote on the pad. Her arms were covered in flames of black-green ink.

"Well, my mother used to live here," he explained. "We roomed together for a time."

"Oh, I see," Peg said. "So, you want me to take care of the remains, right?"

"The remains? Oh, right, yes, please," he stammered.

She was staring again. This time she looked annoyed. "Look, I'm just going to charge you $300, okay?"

"Three Hundred?" His stomach flipped.

"Mr. Vacarie, I told you that on the phone."

Jonathan buried his face in his hands. A moan escaped him. "I don't have it," he peeked through his fingers.

"What?" Peg looked around. She looked like she didn't believe him.

He dropped his hands to the table. "Oh, boogers! I grew up here, okay? My mother moved out a long time ago. She still helps me with my finances, okay? I'm not great with numbers, okay?"

"She moved out?" Peg didn't seem to believe this either. "Where is she?"

"She's living over in Sunny Brook Farms."

"Very nice," Peg said. She guided her fiery hair over one shoulder. "Do you work?"

"Yes I have a job!" he snapped. "I work at the Blockbuster in Seymour. I'm in line for assistant manager as a matter of fact." He crossed his arms.

Peg sat in silence. She put her pen down. "Look, how about you just write me a check and post date it?"

"My mother cosigns my checks."

"Sounds complicated," Peg said.

"You have no idea. She's a drunk you see."

"Really? I'm sorry," she said. She ran her hand down her braid. "I had one of those."

"One of what?"

"My father was a drunk," she said.

"Really?"

Peg shuddered. It reminded him of Zella shaking off a fly. She reached over and held his shoulder. "I tell you what, if I didn't move out of my parents' house, I would have killed the both of them."

"Really?" Jonathan asked again.

"Oh you betcha, with pleasure."

She sat back in her chair. Jonathan picked up the little bottles and read the labels absently.

"She's a drunk, a mean, miserable drunk," he muttered.

"Hmm. Gotcha...Him too. He was a pig farmer."

"Who?"

"My father. He was a pig farmer, a hundred head at any one time."

"Cute."

"What?" she cocked her head sideways.

"Pigs are kind of cute, right? All pink and fat and rolling around oinking in the mud."

"That's the sows you're thinking of, not the boars. The boars are big, scary fuckers. Nasty animals, actually, eat anything, anything at all," she sighed. "I hated that man."

"Yeah, I know the feeling."

Peg looked up to the ceiling. "You know, when we were kids and living on the farm, there were always cats, cats everywhere. You have a cat?"

He shook his head.

"They just show up, feral, you know? Wild. You couldn't take 'em in. We used to sneak milk out to them behind the barn. After a while they got used to it, used to come out and greet us, my kid sister and me, meow like crazy, probably a dozen maybe more. God, they'd raise hell at night, all that fighting and screwing. My father got to bitching a blue streak about them, all bleary eyed and sleepless at the table.

"So we kept on feeding them, right? I did it just to torture the bastard. He'd be up inside me with his fat fingers - late night, you know - and those cats would be outside screaming. And I tell you what. They were a comfort. They kept me whole, you know? My sister too. Anyway, one day he gets it in his head to trap 'em, one at a time, baiting a catch cage with Star-Kist, one poor pussy after the next. That man was hell on a pussy. He'd put on his work gloves, yank a skinny tom out of the trap and brain it with a ball peen.

"So then of course, we're trying to shoo them away, my sister's throwing rocks at them when they came looking for milk. I felt so bad, like I'd doomed them, right? Each night the ruckus would dwindle and I'd feel so damn bad, until my father would come in and give me something real to cry about." She lowered her eyes.

"Jeez."

"Sometimes he'd miss the kill shot and the tom would still have some life in it. What'd he care though, right? He'd just dump it in the feed bin, still twitching and call 'em in. 'Soooey! Getchya kitty, 'mon getchya kitty!'" He'd snicker and then head off to reset the trap again. And those boars, they did not leave a trace, believe me."

"That's uh..."

"Horrible, yeah, I know."

"So..."

"So, well, he died and I got the hell out of there. Went to live with my boy-friend's family. I was a sophomore."

"What about your mother?"

"She was useless."

"And your sister?"

"She's F.U.B.A.R., she left the farm after my mom died. She's a real townie nowadays."

Peg took a deep breath but didn't say anything more. Jonathan nodded as if he took her meaning. He looked over at Zella on her cushion. His stomach gurgled. Apparently, Sausage and Egg McMuffin's were not the answer for the shits. He wiped sweat from his forehead. He held up one of the bottles. He sounded out the word.

"So-mu-lose. Is this the lethal stuff?"

"Yup."

"Strong, I take it," he said.

"Oh yeah, 6cc's will drop a 120 pound sow."

Jonathan rolled the bottle between his fingers.

"You know, Jonathan, alcohol abuse wreaks all kinds of havoc on the body, not just the liver. It affects everything, even the heart."

"She is miserable," he turned the bottle in his fingers.

"It's a disease, a disorder. It affects how people think, makes 'em unpredictable, mean. I feel bad for you both."

"It's hard to... to.... watch," he admitted.

She tilted her head, her green eyes piercing. "Euthanasia is a tricky business, Jonathan, expensive too."

Jonathan fixed his eyes on hers. "What do you mean?"

Peg reached over and squeezed his hand. "I think you know what I mean," she said. "You're her only family? No aunts or uncles? Cousins? Long lost siblings?"

He shook his head, "nope, just the two of us."

She looked him in the eye. "I think we can help each other. I think I can help your mother."

"You do?"

"Like I said, Jonathan, euthanasia's not cheap. It's going to cost you."

"You can help my mother?"

"I can put her out of her misery," she plucked the bottle from his hand. She held it by the cap and jingled it like a bell. "You know the last thing I did before I left that goddamn farm?"

Jonathan shook his head.

"I fed the pigs," she grinned at him with her nostrils flared. He jumped when she howled at the ceiling, her red hair hanging behind her like a bloody rope.

"Soooey! Soooey! C'mon, getchya daddy! Getchya daddy!"

Jonathan laughed. She was nice, trying to cheer him up and all.

Chapter Nineteen

JOEY LEANED HIS elbows on the edge of the kitchen sink, feeling a little green. The blood in his stomach wasn't sitting well with the Jim Beam. He spat and scrubbed his hands under the cold water. The blood on his palms was mostly from his nose and washed off easy enough. His nose had finally stopped pissing blood; it just dripped now and again. Freakin' big, buck-toothed deadbeat had surprised him with a jab, not much behind it, but it was quick.

He turned his hands over and let the water sooth his sore, torn knuckles. Most of the scrapes had already caked up, but blood kept leaking out the half-inch gash between the middle knuckles of his right hand - he'd caught one of shitball's big teeth. Water ran off his hands onto the plates in the sink. Bits of soggy pink bread spun in pink pools. He took a deep breath and held it. He might just hurl anyway.

"Use the cold water," Uncle Sal harped. He sat at the kitchen table in his silk robe, counting his cash.

"Yeah, I know," Joey said. He closed his eyes and nodded.

"This is it?"

Freakin' guy. "Yeah, that's it," Joey said. He scrubbed at the dried blood on his forearms.

"This is all he had."

Uncle Sal was unconvinced.

"You think I'm lying? He didn't have nothing else on him."

"That's what he told you?"

"No. That's what was in his pockets."

"You alright?"

"Yeah, I caught a freakin' tooth."

"How'd you manage that?"

"Uppercut. Split his lip in half. It was hanging off his face." Joey turned off the water and folded a paper towel over the gash and between his fingers.

"Yeah, Slats is one big, coon-lipped motherfucker."

"Was," Joey corrected. He wrapped a dishrag over the paper towel and around his hand. He pinched the bridge of his nose. It didn't feel broke, just tender. "My nose straight?"

"Come here, let me look," Uncle Sal waved him over. Joey sat beside him at the table. "Naw, a little puffy, it's nothing. You're good, soldier."

Joey inspected his bandage job. He sighed through his sore nose. A pink drop fell from the tip of his nose onto the dishrag. He pressed his left thumb down hard on the rag. The gash throbbed.

"Listen, Uncle Sal, I got to tell you, I don't want to do this no more," Joey muttered.

"You don't wanna do this?" his uncle asked low and slow. "Joey, this is what we do. This is the business."

"Yeah well, I think I came close to putting Slats out of business." Joey looked up, Uncle Sal's thick eyebrows lowered and he frowned.

"Permanently?" Uncle Sal asked.

"No, he was breathing, he was definitely breathing, but I kinda lost my shit after he popped me. I broke him up pretty bad," Joey admitted.

"Joey, you can't be doing that. A good grunt keeps cool in the heat."

"I ain't a good grunt."

"Ah, bullshit! You're a hard, lethal motherfucker. You been training most of your life for this."

"I was training for the Marines, for Special Forces! I was training for 'Nam!"

"Count yourself lucky you missed it," Uncle Sal said.

"I didn't miss it! I got fucked!"

"Jimmy needed you here," Uncle Sal reached and squeezed him on the shoulder.

"Fuck Jimmy," Joey snapped. He swallowed back a hot whiskey burp. He shrugged off his uncle's hand and stood up.

"No, fuck you, Joey. I'm giving you a gift here. Look at me!" his uncle tapped himself on the chest. "I'm freakin' fallin' apart here! You're *my* Special Forces, got it? It ain't fuck Jimmy. It's fuck Uncle Sam! You'll do a helluva lot better soldiering for Uncle Sal."

"I'm no soldier. There's no honor in this," Joey shook his head.

"Take a freakin' seat!" Sal said in a hoarse growl.

Joey sat down. Uncle Sal's eyes got wide and he coughed. His hacking fit bent him over sideways. Joey patted his shaking back.

"I just can't do it, Uncle Sal."

Uncle Sal straightened up and clutched Joey's arm. He caught his breath and rasped, "A soldier does his duty! That's the honor. This is a hard business, a man's business. Get it straight, Joey. This is what we do. This is what *you* do." Uncle Sal looked at him; his chapped lips tight together and twisted to one side. His uncle let go of his arm and smoothed the sleeve of his green fatigue jacket. "Ah fuck it, what I'm saying is... This is what I need you to do. You got me?"

"Yeah, I got you," Joey nodded while his stomach boiled.

"Now sit there and lem'me look at your goddamn hand."

"It's nothing," Joey said.

"Yeah, yeah, let's see."

Joey unwrapped the rag and peeled off the blood soaked paper towel. Uncle Sal bent his stubbly face close and gave it a look. His uncle's skin looked gray and flimsy, like the ash on a butt that needed flicking. His mom's skin looked like that for a while. The cut welled up and blood rolled down between his knuckles.

"That fucker needs a stitch," Uncle Sal said.

"Kill another Sunday at the clinic? No way. I'll get a butterfly."

"A butterfly won't hold it."

Joey rolled his eyes. This was all he freakin' needed! He grabbed the dishrag, got up and went to the counter for another paper towel. He spotted the fancy teacups on the counter.

"Where's the nurse?" Joey asked as he wrapped his hand again.

"She went to get some beers at her place," Uncle Sal said.

"She can stitch me up."

"Maybe. She took Jimmy with her."

"She did?" Joey looked up.

"She wanted help moving the rest of her crap. Said for you to come too. You just missed 'em."

"Where's she at?"

"Here," Sal pushed a scrap of paper across the table.

Joey picked it up. "Waterbury Mews, alright."

"You're going?" His uncle looked surprised.

"Yeah, I'm going."

"Just go to the clinic," Uncle Sal said.

"Waterbury'll be faster."

"What makes you think she'll have stitches?"

"She's a nurse ain't she?"

His uncle grunted. "Just make she sure remembers the beers, soldier."

⇥▆◉ ◉▆⇤

Joey blasted Aerosmith from his 8-track and didn't ease off the pedal until he reached the outskirts of Waterbury. The maples and pines and the long fall grass gave way to newish split-levels and asphalt sidewalks. He took another pull from his flask. The Jim Beam went down warm and fast.

Fuck Uncle Sal and fuck his freakin' business! He didn't need this shit. He didn't need any of it.

Jimmy had it so cush! Always had it so freakin' cush, smoking up his weed and sneaking in the skag; playing him like he was clueless. Like it wasn't obvious! The freakin' kid was doping it, locking himself in the can, forgetting his burnt little foils behind the toilet, under the sink, under the couch - all over the place! Who'd he think cleaned the house? Fairies?

He hung a left into Waterbury Mews and searched for a spot.

Freakin' Sal! Freakin' Numb Nutz! And for what? So he could end up in the joint when one of Sal's sorry fucks got some stones and went to the cops? So Sal could dole him out some extra scratch? And what'd he get to do with it?

Buy himself a naughty nurse? Fuck no, he got to spend it keeping their freakin' house standing. And still he gets stuck being the baby sitter, the freakin' fairy maid!

He passed by her blue Tempest and parked a few spots down the row, facing the street with the apartment building at his back.

He took another swig and stared out the windshield. This freakin' shit had to change. He'd blow Franky and one of his brothers too if he had to, but this shit was gonna change. He drained the last of the whiskey from his flask and tossed it in the back

"Shit's gonna change!" Joey slurred and punched the steering wheel with his wrapped fist.

"Motherfreakin' son of a bitch!" Joey seethed at the pain and held his throbbing fist to his chest. If Jimmy even looked at him sideways he was going to tear his faggot ponytail right off the back of his head; scalp the little shit. He undid the dishrag. A red spot of blood had soaked through the first layer. He rewrapped the rag and crushed it tight in his hand with a grimace. He had to chill out. He breathed in and out his mouth, again. Again. Again.

Joey uncoiled himself out of the Pinto. He knew he was staggering some as he crossed the lot for the faded blue awning above the entrance. Fuck it, no law against drunk. He squinted up at the awning. It was tattered and frayed. The fancy-pants Waterbury Mews logo looked out of place.

"No dressing up the pig," he slurred.

Inside, he pressed the button for the elevator. An old fashioned dial tracked the floors. The hand crawled counter clockwise from three. It was like watching a freakin' sundial. The door opened. At least it worked. It would still be faster than waiting for Jimmy to haul all the naughty nurse's shit down three flights of stairs.

Joey stepped out of the elevator, got his bearings and turned left down the hall, following the numbers to 320.

The woman's scream stopped him on the red carpet. That was no play scream. Joey stood and listened, softly patting his empty jacket pockets. At the end of the hall on the right, a light arched on the rug from an open apartment door. The silence got his heart pounding.

Joey eased to his right and sidestepped softly along the wall to the open door. He took a deep breath and peeked around the corner into the apartment. On the floor by the door he saw the bare soles of a man's upturned feet, and then his jeans...

"Jimmy!" Joey muffled himself with his bandaged hand. "Don't be dead, don't be dead," he mumbled into the dishtowel. Blood flushed through his temples like a hard rain forcing leaves out from a clogged gutter. He blinked. The dim apartment got brighter. Jimmy's features sharpened.

Joey rushed inside the door and dropped to a knee by his brother's side. Jimmy lay flat on his back, facing his way, blood trickling from the corner of his open lips. Joey put his hand on Jimmy's bare chest. It rose and fell.

"Thank you, thank you," Joey whispered. The kid was out cold. A dark red pool had formed on the wood floor under his cheek. Joey checked his perimeter.

"Well now, who's this?"

Halfway down a short hall, a tall, wiry shitball in overalls and no shirt struggled to keep hold of something out of sight. The muscles in his left arm strained beneath dark tattoos. His forearm jerked from side to side like he had hold of a big fish. He looked Joey over, his dark eyes sunk deep in their sockets. His long, scraggly whiskers wiggled under his chin - freakin' Cheesy Jesus.

Joey stood up and flexed his chest, arms bent and ready by his sides. "Who the fuck are you?"

"Whoa there, Magilla," Jesus said with a chummy, brown-toothed smile.

"Joey!" Nurse Bea cried out and lurched into the hall.

Jesus had her by the hair. The nurse was naked from the waist up. Her tits bounced and then jiggled when Jesus jerked her backward. She yelped in pain and reached up to grab hold of his hand with both of hers. Nurse Bea had herself a sweet rack. She stood there, arms up and shaking and Joey had to hand it to her, she didn't have that rabbit's look of fear in her eyes. He knew what fear looked like, that glassy, big-eyed, pleading gape. He'd seen it often enough in the faces of Sal's deadbeats. Nope, the Naughty Nurse had more hate than fear raging from her green eyes, a lot more.

"Like I said, easy there, killer. I got no argument with you. This is between ole Beetle Bug and me." Jesus kept smiling.

"Let her go."

He tilted his beard, "But I just got hold of her."

Joey hardened his fists. "Then I'll just have to run both of you the fuck over."

"Let go of me, Owen! You... you... you lunatic!" Nurse Bea wriggled beneath his hand.

"Do it, Owen," Joey nodded.

"'Fraid not—"

Jimmy groaned and rolled over onto Joey's right boot.

"Hey look it there, ole lover boy's comin' to." Owen reached behind his back with his right hand and pulled out a buck knife with a short, heavy blade. He held the knife up by Bea's cheek.

"Now, like I was saying, I got business with this," he tugged her head back, "what should I say? lady?" The blade glinted as Owen twisted it under her chin. He shook his head and wrinkled his face up in a scowl. "No, that's not right. It's more like nasty, lying, demon slut. What do you think, Beetle? Or what about, say... cum-guzzling Missouri sewer rat?"

Jimmy rolled onto his back. His eyes flickered and he touched his chin. "Joey, dude, that you?"

"Yeah, it's me. Stay put," Joey said and held his palms steady over the kid.

"You see? Lover boy's fine. No harm, 'cept a few teeth maybe. So now, Magilla, if you'll just step aside, me and the lady here, we'll be on our way."

"Tell you what, Owen, I'll pick up lover boy here and we'll be on our way."

"Bea!" Jimmy cried. Joey glanced down. Jimmy looked up at him. "Dude, do something," he pleaded.

"No, dude, don't do nothing. Old beetle Bug and me, we got us some traveling plans."

"Last chance," Joey snarled through his teeth.

Owen swung his straggly beard. "That's it, Magilla. I'm through fuckin' around." He tugged Bea backward by the hair and nicked the corner of her jaw with the tip of his blade. Bea yelped and tears streamed out from eyes gone wide.

"You, you, you slimy fuck!" Bea screamed, struggling under his grip. Blood trailed in a thin, jagged line down the side of her neck.

"Joey..." Jimmy moaned at his feet.

Joey raised his hands and took a step back, bumping his heel against a cardboard moving box. Owen led Bea a step forward and pointed behind Joey with the tip of his knife.

"Glad we got an understanding. Now, you want to toss me that shirt there on the floor? The lady can't be prancing around with her titties shaking for all the world to see. Lord, what if there's children about?"

Joey turned and picked up Jimmy's T-shirt off the floor beside the couch. The kid'd freakin' warmed her up, alright, the little prick. He tossed it over and kept his hands raised. It hit Bea in the chest and fell to her feet. Owen bent her over with his fistful of her hair.

"Get that, will you honey bee?"

Joey clenched and unclenched his fists above his head. The skin on his back bristled and burned. Owen was just out of range. Bea picked up the shirt and balled it in her hands. Owen pointed the blade at Joey.

"You got no idea the favor I'm doin' you boys."

"Like you said, we ain't your concern," Joey said. He lowered his hands.

Owen eyed him while turning sideways to spit on the wall. "No, I said you got no idea."

Joey shrugged.

"Bea? Baby?" Jimmy moaned. He reached out for her.

"Baby's goin' bye-bye," Owen chuckled and led Bea toward the door. She stopped between Jimmy's feet and looked down at him.

"Oh Jimmy, I'm so sorry," she murmured.

"You boys just stay put a while," Owen said, following Bea's footsteps to the door.

Jimmy snagged Owen's leg with his bare feet. Owen mule kicked at Jimmy's groin, giving Joey his shot. Joey lunged forward and grabbed Owen's knife-hand by the wrist. He inverted Owen's wrist with his left hand and palmed the back of Owen's hand with his bandaged right. He applied a little downward pressure and out popped the knife. It was a simple submission hold. Joey pressed a little harder and Owen twisted toward him and groaned.

"Let her go. Now!" Joey ordered. Owen let go of her hair and dropped to one knee. Bea shook her head and jumped forward into the hall. Her heels slipped out from under her on the carpet and she fell on her ass with a thud.

"Hey! hey! cut it damn you! You gonna break it!" Owen pleaded.

"You and me got business," Joey said and bent his wrist further.

"Like hell!" Owen winced.

"See lover boy bleeding there? That's my brother. So yeah, we got business," Joey gave the back of Owen's hand a quick, heavy jolt. He felt the pop and then Owen cried out for Jesus.

"Joey!" Bea gasped, picking herself up.

Joey held Owen by his crooked wrist and turned to her. "Nobody monkeys my freakin' bro!"

"I didn't! I didn't! It's a, it's a favor, man!" Owen yelled.

Joey dropped his wrist and Owen cradled it in his lap. He rocked on his knees right next to Jimmy. Owen's whining gnawed at Joey's every nerve, churned up his insides, turned his mind all foamy and rabid. He jerked Owen up by the bib of his overalls and dragged him into the hallway.

"Joey, don't—" Jimmy pleaded.

"Just gonna show Owen the way out," Joey tried to say, but between the whiskey and his rage the words came out mushy.

"Joey, he's not worth it," Nurse Bea said. She grabbed him by the arm, her grip weak, like a baby's on a bottle.

"No shit," Joey said. He shrugged her off. "How 'bout you stay here and see if you can fuck Numb Nutz all better."

"Hey man," Jimmy protested, but Joey was already out the door.

He dragged Owen down the hall with his wrapped-up hand. The towel kept the buckles and straps of Owen's overalls from digging into his palm. He was pumped freakin' hard, no pain at all. He could drag this fucker all day. He had lava blood and he knew he should take a breather and think, but dragging this shitball felt too damn good.

"Hey, hey! I'm sorry, man! I'm sorry! I... I didn't know it was your brother! I didn't hurt him none! He's fine - you seen yourself! It wasn't nothing personal. I just come for that bitch..."

Joey dragged him past the elevator. Cheesy Jesus would not shut up.

"Hey, you know what? Fuck the bitch - I mean, the lady. It's done, okay? No more business, okay? All done, all done."

Joey pushed open the fire exit door at the end of the hall and tugged Owen to his feet with both hands. "Time for you to go, Owen."

"I'll go, I'll go. You won't never see me again. I swear!" Owen's big begging eyes trembled in their deep, dark sockets like little bunnies in their holes.

"Sounds good."

Joey gripped Owen's overall bib with his left hand and looped his right forearm under his crotch. He propped Owen up on his shoulder. Owen's struggling didn't amount to much, skinny as he was. Joey considered the flight of cement steps and then glanced over the rail. A mattress lay on the ground floor. A trip down the stairs was no good; it might kill the bastard...

"Here we go," Joey propped him up on his shoulder.

"No!"

"Ready?"

"No, no, no, I get it, I get it!" Owen wriggled.

Joey dropped him over the side feet first, aiming for the mattress. Owen's scream cut short when he hit the edge of the mattress with a dull crunch. For a moment he stayed upright, one leg stuck out in front of him, the other cockeyed beneath him. That leg was broke for sure. His black boot jutted up and out from behind his butt like a stubby black tail. Joey leaned over the rail panting. Owen finally slumped over and started up with the screaming again and Joey let out a big whiskey sigh.

Chapter Twenty

ONCE AGAIN, LEGAL was pissing on Eddie's parade. He sat with counselor Constance "Connie" Brown in her office as she reviewed a hardcopy of his presentation, stabbing at one transgression after the next with her red flair pen. They sat side by side at the small, round table in the corner of her office. The worktable was intended to foster collaboration. For here in the Legal Department of Universal Tobacco Company, it was all about protecting company interests through collaboration. UTC was all about team. Never mind that the Legal department was separated from the rest of the building by a 2 inch thick Plexiglas wall, complete with its own security system; that was simply ensuring UTC's collective well being.

It used to be that counselor Cuntstance would slash and burn his documents from behind her desk with her floor-to-ceiling wall of leather-bound legal books spread behind her like burgundy wings of the damned. But a couple years back she too had been offered the opportunity to work with an executive coach. This was the kind of opportunity that you were not permitted to miss. Naturally this was confidential, something the coach always reinforced during his 360 interviews.

"You've been through this, Eddie. You know the deal. My job is to give Connie honest feedback from her colleagues, superiors and subordinates alike, in a non-confrontational manner that is designed to illuminate her blind spots and thus enable her to enhance her efficacy as an employee and her ability to excel as a team player. This has nothing to do with her knowledge or skill set. We all know she's a top-notch lawyer, a real expert. No, this is about her behavior and her development as a leader within UTC."

The coach had sat on the other side of Eddie's desk. In keeping with his carefully constructed charade, the coach had dropped his pen on the desk and folded his hands atop his head.

"So feel free to be absolutely candid," he'd encouraged.

"She's an arrogant cunt," was Eddie's candid feedback. He'd hoped it would be constructive.

So now Eddie sat beside Connie as she slashed a big red X across another page of his presentation.

"Eddie, You don't even have the trilogy on here!"

Eddie cringed. The document was naked. Missing from the footer, in italicized, 12-point, Arial font was "DRAFT DOCUMENT. SEEKING THE ADVICE OF COUNSEL. PROPRIETARY AND CONFIDENTIAL." A naked document was chief among Connie's most reviled peeves.

"Sorry about that, Connie," he shrugged.

"Has anyone else seen this document?"

"No."

"You're sure?"

"Well, just Randy - on my screen," he assured her. "He was looking over my shoulder."

"Of course you showed Randy," she said with condescending glee.

"He liked the idea."

"I'm sure he did," Connie sneered. She turned to the next page and threw up her hands. The slide depicted a small triangle with two capital "A's" inside and an arrow pointing to a stair-step diagram with Fortitude Lights on the bottom step and Fortitude Full Flavored Standards on the top.

"OK, I've seen enough. This is going nowhere. If you have any other hardcopies they need to be shredded."

"Are we collaborating now?" Eddie asked. He knew the idea was dead. He'd salve the wound by driving the bitch apoplectic. Blood flushed into her pockmarked cheeks. She took a deep breath before she spoke again.

"Eddie, I don't know how to collaborate with this. Don't you see what you're depicting here? What are you thinking?"

"I'm thinking about new consumers—"

"Adult consumers."

"Excuse me, adult consumers. I'm thinking about building the brand for the long term."

"Well you're not going to get there like this."

"What's the problem?"

"You have, on this slide, effectively communicated the graduation theory!"

"So?"

"Are you kidding me? What do you mean 'so'? The *graduation theory*, Eddie," she hissed. "You can't do that! You can't have *stairs* for God's sake!" Eddie watched her stab the felt tip of her red pen into his slide. "And what's this triangle?"

"That's AA."

"I see that. What's AA?"

"AA, you know, Alcoholics Anonymous," Eddie said.

"What?" Connie screeched.

"Well obviously, the whole plan is about sampling at AA meetings."

"You can't sample Fortitude at AA meetings!"

"Why not?"

"Because they're addicts!" she shouted and threw both hands up over her head.

"Uh yeah, that's the point," he said with opened palms.

"Yes it is!"

"Look, Connie, everyone in AA is an adult, right? I mean, you've got to be of age to get your hands on the booze, right? And, from what I hear, the incidence of tobacco use is far higher than average - everyone smokes! They can't drink so they do the next best thing, right? Hell, we're doing them a service! We're helping wean these people off the booze! Nobody's out there getting arrested for smoking and driving, right? It's like a public safety PR opportunity! Can't you see it? 'UTC - Supporting the Solution.'"

"What solution?"

"Helping people solve their alcohol problem."

"By smoking?"

"I said helping, not solving."

"Eddie, I don't want to hear another word. You can't sample drunks."

"It's a share grab and a category growth move rolled into one!"

"End of conversation."

"Randy's hot for it. He loves the idea."

"Jesus," she stood up and walked behind her desk to punch keys on her phone.

"Yes, Connie?" her admin's voice sounded over the speaker.

"Get me Randal on the phone please, immediately."

"Right away, Connie."

She folded her hands on her desk. "I'll be having a conversation with Randy. You have some deleting to do." Connie waved him out. Eddie stood and smiled before stepping toward the door.

"You have a great weekend," he said as her phone rang.

"Hello Randal," she said into the receiver. She hit Eddie with a flimsy, yellow smile.

Connie's admin buzzed Eddie out though the Plexiglas door. He lurched quickly across the atrium for Randy's office, his knee aching like hell. His Blackberry buzzed in his pocket. He took the call without looking.

"Oh...hey there," he said, surveying the empty atrium.

"TGIF handsome! Almost quitting time, are you coming by?" Sandra asked. He heard the murmur of Madigan's in the background.

"I can't."

"But I was counting on it!"

"Hey, I'd love to but—"

"Yes, you would," She lowered her voice, "I've got a little party favor for us."

"Oh yeah? What would that be?"

"Guess it doesn't matter now, oh well, more for me."

"Maybe I could stop by for a quickie, no promises."

"Didn't you know? Quickies and broken promises are what makes the world go round," she purred.

Eddie grinned, "Hey, I got to go now."

"See you later maybe."

Eddie hung up and sauntered into Randy's office. Randy had his worn-out Tony Lama's up on his desk. Strips of darker leather crossed over his arches from where he'd removed his spurs a decade ago. He had his phone wedged between his ear and broad shoulder. Randy was six foot four and two-seventy. His face was weathered and scarred. He'd grown up a bulldogger and he still appeared more than capable of tackling a steer. There were plenty of cowboys at UTC, as the company had a longstanding relationship with the rodeo and all things western. The UTC culture idolized the pioneering attitude of the American west. The company was founded upon the spirit of those frontiersmen. That and the huge profit margins. Like most of the UTC cowboys that had transitioned from the corral to corporate, Randy wasn't super swift, but he was loyal to the death. And the team of folks he lead, the ones who were out every day of the year sampling UTC products to adult consumers, were loyal to him. The galoot had power, real power. You want your brand sampled? Then you'd better be in good with Randal L. Smith. Eddie had hoisted many a brew with this fellow.

"Yes ma'am, I'm getting your point ma'am," he winked at Eddie. "I guess you've got yourself a darn good point there. Even so, ain't there any way to get this done? Seems to me to be an idea with some meat on the bone—"

Randy winced and scooped the phone from his ear. He held it at Eddie. Connie's shrill diatribe sounded from the receiver in miniature, as if she'd sucked down a balloon full of helium. The two men sniggered but made no sound. Randy returned the phone to his ear.

"I'm getting you loud and clear, ma'am. I'll be discarding that information directly." He nodded, "Yes ma'am, I'll be sure to tell him when I see him. You have yourself a sunny weekend. Yup, mhmm, will do." He hung up.

"You sure do know how to set that woman off, I tell you what. She was fixin' to have herself a little calf right there in the halls of the Do No Business Bureau."

"She's just scared is all," Eddie piggybacked on Randy's drawl immediately. He was this man's blood brother, at least as far as he was concerned. "She nearly took a switch to me right there in her office."

"Wouldn't that have been a sight."

"Wouldn't be the first time."

"Nor the last, I suspect."

"Yup."

"Mhmm."

"You just hang onto that deck. Maybe run the thought by some of the boys. See what they think of the idea," Eddie said.

"Should I send it along to them? I could forward your email to the regional managers, get their two cents."

"Best make use of the phone on this one," Eddie suggested.

"Right. I'm trackin' with ya," Randy agreed.

"We'll get a little momentum behind this thing and then I'll try for an end around. It's fucking genius. You know it. I know it. The boys'll believe so too."

"Hell yes! The boys'll be all fired up!" Randy picked up his phone. "See you after for a cold one?"

"Can't tonight, need to be back home directly. My little Maggy has a dance recital."

"You're a good man, Eddie. You have yourself a fine weekend. Say hello to the missus and the lil' cowgirl for me."

"Will do. You do the same."

Eddie walked to his office, three doors down, in the corner. Randy would work the phones all weekend if necessary. That was Randy. By Monday, Eddie'd have a groundswell of buy-in from The Field for his idea. Then he could run it by Vic and the two of them would do an end around on Connie - appeal to the G.C. In his two years as the V.P. of Marketing, Vic had taught him one valuable lesson, "Managing Vertically Via Horizontal Alignment," Vic called it. He loved his Ivy League B-school buzzwords. And Eddie had to admit they served him well. Buzzwords in the corporate universe were strong magic. Words like "alignment" and "synergy" and "optics" had the power to transform weasels into kings.

Eddie sat at his desk, scrolled through his emails and decided to make it a trifecta Friday – he'd tee up a little internal alignment, cut out early to knock back a fast one with Sandra, and then get home in plenty of time for Maggy's recital. Hell, he might even score some rare bonus points with Amy.

Chapter Twenty-One

KARL GUIDED HIS chainsaw through the biggest branches of the last pine in the road. The storm clouds had given way to hazy blue humidity, and Sycamore Road had poached itself dry. It was getting on to noon, and that Nellie belly danced in shadows his sun couldn't reach. Sweat dripped off the tip of his nose as he worked the blade. The fog on his safety glasses got too thick. He put the saw down and wiped the glasses best he could with his damp shirt.

Across the way Marcus cut into logs what couldn't fit in the chipper. Just off the road by the edge of the woods, Marcus'd built himself a stack nearly the size of Karl's pickup. The boy had his shirt off. Karl watched him lift a sizable log, a sixty pounder at least, and walk it toward the stack. The muscles across his back rippled and Karl felt proud. And he knew he had no call to be proud that his son was chiseled like one of those stone statues of a god, but the pride welled in him, and filled him falsely.

Karl frowned and put his glasses back on. The streaky lenses distorted the limbs at his feet. He yanked his chainsaw back to life. He goosed the throttle and gunned out the engine bogs. When the chain spun fast and regular he got back to cutting.

Cutting up trees took some thinking, some strategy even. You had to be thinking about where the weight was, and what was carrying it. You cut with a plan and the plan was simple enough. If something was gonna fall or split or roll, best it did so away from you. Same for the saw; if it was gonna catch a knot and bounce up on you, you'd best know it in advance. Respect the saw because it is faster than you, no matter how quick you are on the brake.

A moving chain cut through cloth and skin like an axe through butter. He'd learned the hard way, got himself twenty five stitches limbing with a little Husky one-hander. From then on he only used the heavy saws, the ones that took two hands.

Having limbed the length of the trunk, all that was left to do was cut it up. He worked his saw down the log, taking care to keep his blade tip off the road. He made his cuts about a yard apart and just a little past half way. He rolled the log over with a shove of his boot and finished the cuts through. He killed the saw and set it down but his hands kept vibrating. He took off his hardhat. Sweat rolled in his ears.

Karl walked to the fat end of the trunk and squatted. He rolled a cut log up onto his knee. He had a time of it hoisting it into his arms. His gloves kept the tar of his hands, but the log was oozy with sap, and he felt the rough, sticky bark against his chest and popping biceps. He couldn't smell the fresh pine anymore, though he knew he was in the thick of it. The log was a hundred pounds if it were twenty and he had the thing pinned between the top of his belly and the scars under his chin. He humped it across Sycamore toward Marcus' stack.

Ten feet shy of the wood stack; his arms gave way, and he dropped the log on the soft ground with a grunt. He rubbed the creases in his arms.

"Well fuck you then," he muttered.

Marcus dropped a log on the top of the stack and turned around, slapping sticky needles from his gloves. He tilted his head at the sight of his old man telling off a log by his feet. Marcus wrinkled his wide nose, his mother's wide nose. It was handsome on his face, just like it was pretty on hers. His skin was hers and his almond eyes too.

"Need a hand with that one?" Marcus asked. He looked away, pretending something on the road caught his eye.

"Na, it just slipped," Karl said.

"Yeah."

"How many more you got?"

Marcus thrust a thumb behind him, "that was the last one."

Karl flexed his arms and shoulders and then cracked his neck. He was gonna be sore tonight.

"Could you give me a hand with the ones on the street?" Karl knew what he'd asked. He knelt by his log.

"Sure, whatever."

The damp leaves and grass and needles cooled his knee. It felt fine. He had a mind to drop onto both knees and just sit for a minute, suck in some shady air. Instead, he tugged at the log. He tried to roll it up onto his knee, but it resisted, having settled into the forest floor. He tugged at it again, but it just rolled back into place, like a hung-over head in a worn-out pillow.

"Here," Marcus pushed it from the other side.

The log rolled up his knee, and Karl got his arms underneath it. He stood up, walked it over and dropped it beside the stack. He looked behind him, about to say something in the way of thanks, but Marcus was already crossing the road. He followed behind his son and watched him clutch the cut ends of one of the other hundred-pounders and clean and jerk it up onto his shoulder. They passed each other in the road. Karl stopped on the double yellow lines and turned to watch his son. The boy ambled over with his log and set it on top of the woodpile.

Karl stood in the sun shaking his head, took a breath and walked on to the logs that still needed clearing. He knelt down on the pavement and rolled a skinny one up his knee and lifted it onto his shoulder. His first step was unsteady under the weight, but he got it together. A jagged nub dug into his shoulder. He ignored the pain and held his breath as he passed Marcus.

He lugged it across the street. Marcus loped on by, his strides long and easy, shouldering a log twice the size of his own.

The kid had a knack for teaching him what it was to be weak. Marcus knew the man he had been, and Karl buckled under the weight of all the damn consequences. He'd seen the last beating; he was just a boy then, watching from the top of the stair, thumb in his mouth, fuzzy Mr. Bunny clutched in his skinny little arm. He'd seen his mother screaming and bleeding from the mouth. He'd seen the cops crashing through the door. He'd seen his drunken old man pinned to the floor, bloody; hands cuffed behind his back. Karl knew only a little of what the boy knew, and that was more than enough.

Karl dropped his log on top of the stack with a grunt and followed his son back for another. He made a point to keep his eyes off the ground. Marcus walked toward him, steadying another log on his shoulder with one hand.

"You even feel that thing up there?"

"What thing?" Marcus said as he passed.

But Karl knew enough to be grateful. Kissette had no reason to let Marcus have anything to do with him. What good could he possibly have to offer? Broken ex-con, wife-beater of a father, not a dad for damn sure. Yet she let it happen.

He had enough sober time to know she wasn't doing it for him, though his old mind wanted to believe it. Karl knew that what she did, what she'd always done, she'd done for Marcus. That's all he could know for sure. Why now, why this summer, who knew? That's God's work, and he didn't bother questioning God's work anymore, because his old mind was always quick to come up with the wrong answers.

He propped the second-to-last log on his shoulder and made his way for the stack of wood that was now close to his height and double his truck in length.

Marcus came up from behind and set down the last log. They stood in the shade, side by side by the tall stack of pinewood. Together they looked in the direction of Alec's whining chainsaw. The whine cut to an idle followed by a loud pop of cracking of wood. He heard the leaves rustled and then the heavy thud of a big limb hitting ground.

Karl spoke toward the sound, "I could use some water. You want some?"

"I didn't bring any."

"You can have some of mine."

"Not thirsty."

"You gotta drink water, you'll seize up."

"No I won't."

"Yes, you will."

Marcus dug his smokes and a lighter out of his front pocket. He mouthed a butt out of the pack and lit it.

"I'm not thirsty," Marcus said through the smoke. The rest of the drag slipped from his mouth and nose like cold molasses. He leaned back on the stack of wood, both elbows propped up behind him. He crossed one foot over the other.

"You must be beat," Karl said. "You built this stack like it was nothing."

"Just working," Marcus replied. His swiped the sawdust out of his thick nappy hair.

"There's probably, I don't know, maybe two tons here."

Marcus took a drag.

"You shouldn't smoke," Karl shut his mouth tight, wishing he could take it back.

Marcus looked him in the eye and took another, deeper drag. He blew the smoke straight up into the shade.

"I can't apologize anymore, Marcus. I've got nothing—"

"You don't need to."

"I don't expect forgiveness, you know? But I want it. Know what I mean? My God, how I want it. I'm sorry for the man I was."

"Was?"

"Yeah, was."

"You still look the same to me. Same shame on your face, same ink all over you."

"I ain't the same."

Marcus took a final drag and flicked his butt without moving his elbows off the woodpile. "You're just the same. You don't drink anymore. I get it. Good for you. But you're just the same."

"Not drinking makes a big difference."

"Not to me it don't."

"All I'm saying is, I love you, son," Karl winced.

Marcus rolled his eyes. "Good for you."

Another loud crack sounded in the woods. Alec's chainsaw blared at full throttle before cutting out. Karl felt the wrongness before the screams came.

"Alec!" Karl shouted and ran into the woods.

Chapter Twenty-Two

JONATHAN WAS STUCK on the can, unsure if the storm would ever end. Elbows on knees, he rested between waves of diarrhea. His butt was numb, including the portions that drooped over either side of the thin, plastic seat. Through the open door he followed the soundtrack of the movie playing on his TV.

"Your left! Keep your left up!" the old man growled.

He waited for the next wave, balls tingling. In the quiet of the trough, he brooded. Everything was getting too confusing. Peg had taken away Zella. She carried his dog on her shoulder, promising to call him after she'd dropped Zella off at the pet crematorium. His stomach seized up again. Liquid McMuffin blasted from him in heaving, hot spurts.

Maybe this was how God punished masturbators. Mother said God blinded boys who diddled themselves. But she didn't know what God was up to any more than he did.

In the meetings people talked about "working their programs." He hadn't yet seen a copy of this program. Instead, Francis had given him a copy of Alcoholics Anonymous, a thick blue book.

"Start with the first hundred and sixty-four pages," Francis had said.

A hundred and sixty four pages! Jonathan did his best, but reading was exhausting. He fell asleep after only a few pages. It was like high school all over again. He tried to pay extra attention in the meetings, just like he had in high school. At least there were no tests, and nobody calling him retard anymore. That helped.

The old man shouted from the bedroom, "Protect yourself at all times. Now what is the rule?"

In the meetings people had lots of suggestions. They called them suggestions, but they seemed like rules to Jonathan. A few suggestions came up over and over. If you want to stay sober, it was suggested that you get a sponsor. He hadn't. There was Francis, of course. He was kind of his sponsor. Francis looked out for him, checked up on him, called him. It wasn't official; you had to ask someone to be your sponsor. He hadn't asked Francis, so Francis couldn't be his sponsor, not really.

The gurgling began again. He leaned over and got ready.

They suggested that you go to meetings, ninety meetings in ninety days if you were new. He hadn't done that, but he did have a routine. During the week he made the morning meetings at Our Lady of Perpetual Forgiveness. On Saturdays he slept in and on Sundays he considered going to mass as he slept in.

They suggested that, in the first year of recovery, one should not enter any new relationships and put off any major decisions. If a big decision had to be made, then running it by your sponsor was a must. In the meetings, he'd heard people talk about how their thinking in the early days was "mocus." He'd heard the word often enough to bother to look it up. As far as he could tell, there was no such word. In AA it was another word for confused. And mocus caused all kinds of nasty problems. Mocus brought pain.

Mother was mocus.

He groaned as another cramp gripped him. Poo shot from him with enough force to backsplash in the bowl. Toilet water rained upward. He flushed again, panting and cramped.

According to guys like Francis and King Karl, guys who were celebrating sober anniversaries instead of days, this was the most frightening stage of recovery. It was the stage when they thought they had had things all figured out. It was a time when things seemed crystal clear. The lucky ones stuck to The Program. And so the rule stressed - no big decisions!

"Sobriety accumulates like snow. A dusting is beautiful, but rocks abound beneath its slippery shroud." Francis had explained. Jonathan looked up shroud. He shouldn't have. That just complicated it.

The storm passed. He mopped himself off with wad after wad of toilet paper. He pulled up his pants and duck walked to the sink. He washed his hands, splashed his face and inspected himself in the mirror. He ran his hands back through his hair.

"Thank You God for this sober day. Help me know Thy will today. Help me be Your fearless gladiator," he took a deep breath and puffed his chest toward the mirror. "Thank You for Zella, for her love and company. And thank You for leading me to the woman that brought her peace." In the mirror his jaw dropped.

The miracle! Peg Lohber, Peg was his peace! It was God who had brought Peg to him! God in His mercy. Peg was His instrument of peace. His prayers had been answered. He got down on his knees and said an Our Father, shouting out the "forgives."

Jonathan shuffled to his bedroom. He sat on the end of his unmade bed. The old man and the girl boxer chatted in a diner.

"Sorry, you two are going to have to wait." He got up and shut off the DVD player and television.

He returned to the kitchen, stepped over Zella's cushion and opened the refrigerator. He rummaged through the meats drawer and found a square of cheddar cheese wrapped in cellophane. He stood over the garbage can by the sink and pinched off the dried bite marks. The rest he popped into his mouth and chewed with relief, nature's plug.

This probably counted as a big decision. He should give Francis a call, or maybe King Karl. The Program was very clear. Make a call before any big decision. He reached on top the refrigerator for the folded sheet of paper, the phone list Francis had given him early on.

He swallowed the lump of cheese, "There you are."

He unfolded the paper and read down the list. The names Karl W., and Joe B. and Mike caught his eye, but he settled on Francis. He set the list down, grabbed his cell phone off the counter, scrolled through his recent calls and pressed SEND.

"Hello?" Francis' voice tinkled after the second ring. Jonathan cleared his throat.

"Hi, uh, Francis? This is Jonathan."

"Jonathan! How are you?"

"Well, I'm uh, I'm doing okay—"

"Jonathan, can you hold on for a second? I've got to get rid of my other call, one sec."

The line went blank. Maybe he should have tried Karl.

"Okay, I'm back," Francis said in his cheery girl-voice.

"Um, well, I'm fine. I uh, I kind of didn't expect you to pick up. That is, I was just gonna leave a message."

"Well then we're both fortunate. Everything okay? You looked like you had quite a challenge this morning, what with your mother and all."

"No, I'm fine."

"Methinks you obfuscate," Francis said.

Jonathan flushed. He should have called Karl.

"I'm sorry, Jonathan, that means you don't sound fine to me," Francis explained.

"Oh, okay, yeah, well, I guess that's true. I um, I uh, well you see, I had to euphamize my dog this morning."

"Oh rats, I'm sorry," Francis said.

"She had the cancer. I had to call a vet. She did it right here in the kitch-en," Jonathan sobbed and his stomach flipped. "She went easy, I guess. She was snoring."

"I'm so very sorry for your loss, Jonathan."

"Yeah well..." Jonathan wiped aside the tears. He couldn't keep the shake out of his voice.

"It sounds like you did what you had to do, but that must've been a difficult decision. Unfortunately, sometimes doing the next right thing can be painful. And that can be hard to accept. But that's when we've got to have faith in the act - the act of doing the next right thing, you see? We mustn't make it about our pain. Is this making sense to you?"

"Well..." He should have called Karl.

"You're not drinking over this are you? You know that will only make ev-erything worse, right?"

"Yes, I mean no. I mean yes, I got that. I'm not gonna do that. It's just I have this, I don't know, I'm struggling with this decision—"

"About euthanizing your dog?"

"No, no, not my dog, my mother." There, he did it. He got it out, fearless gladiator style.

"Your mother? Well, yes, your mother, she's a tough one now isn't she?"

"You could say that, yup," he nodded. His stomach settled, probably the cheese.

"You know, Jonathan, I think it's like this. We've all had to come to admit our lives were unmanageable in our own time you know? Believe me, I was a stubborn one. It took me years to surrender and still I struggle from time to time, but that's just what God has for me, understand? We all have our wounds, but our wounds are not permission for us to run amok."

"Yeah..."

"Believe me, I can still get worked up over certain things. But we're human, right? And we're not just simple humans, we're humans with addictions, right? Built-in defects! Complicated humans! But that's just it! We're like fine watches, the more complicated we are the more precious we feel. But in the end, we're only meant for one job, right? To press ahead, one tick at a time. We own nothing, you see? We just press on; our time is up to our Higher Power. In His time, we all surrender."

Jonathan rubbed his head and thought at it hard.

"I'm sorry, what?"

"Your mother just isn't ready to surrender," Francis said.

"I know but—"

"And all you can do is try to be as compassionate as possible."

"That's what I'm trying to do. That's just it—"

"Are you still reading the Big Book?"

"Sometimes," Jonathan admitted.

"Well, this situation with your mother reminds me of the passage where it talks about the people who we feel are doing us wrong. You know the one?"

"I don't think I got to that part."

"Well, it explains how to have compassion. It reminds us that hurtful people are spiritually ill, just like we were. So what I try to remember is that these people are suffering from their own spiritual malady. They have their own soul sickness, no better nor worse than mine."

"She's soul sick, that's for sure," he nodded.

"The point is the suffering. People are suffering, am I making sense?"

"So you mean my mother's suffering, for example."

"Exactly! Exactly, your mother is suffering terribly! To be sure, Jonathan, she makes no secret of it."

"Nope, no secret."

"It's sad really. Can you see that?"

"I see it. It is sad. That's what I'm calling about. I'd um...you see, I'd like to put my mother out of her misery."

"That's very compassionate of you to think that way, good for you, Jonathan."

"Really?"

"Of course! If you can say that and really mean it, you know, not just think it but really feel it and act accordingly, then you're on the right track. Do you pray?"

"I pray all the time."

"And what do you pray for?"

"I ask God to put an end to her suffering."

"Then put your trust in God. That's all you can do. That's all you can ever do."

"Trust in God, yeah, thanks, Francis!"

"See you Monday, then?"

"For sure," Jonathan said, shut his phone. "Trust in Him, for sure for sure," he repeated with soothing certainty.

Chapter Twenty-Three

JIMMY RELEASED THE carb and the cool smoke slipped inside him like melty butter. He settled back in his recliner and watched Greg Brady and his dad develop film on the TV. There was Greg and his dad toiling away, developing one blow up after the next. Jimmy felt electro-shivers buzz up his spine. He wedged himself deeper into the cushions of his La-Z-Boy and savored The Brady Effect.

Most times The Brady Effect came during the sweet moments, moments of forgiveness or tenderness like Carol kissing Mike or Mike ruffling Peter's hair, or Bobby coming to Cindy's rescue in the schoolyard. Baby talk! Baby talk! That motherfucker. He'd have stuck a pencil in that little dude's eye, not very Brady of him. He exhaled and the butter-smoke turned harsh and he hacked. Down the hall, way, way down the hall somewhere beyond the great beyond, the front door slammed. Footsteps clomped his way. Was it Frosty? Was Santa getting a jump on things?

Nope, just G.I. Joey.

"And in comes the workin' man," Jimmy said.

Joey stood right in front of the TV in his slushy boots. "I liked you better with your jaw wired shut."

"Dick," Jimmy muttered. Maybe he should try sucking down Thanksgiving dinner through a straw.

Joey tossed an envelope onto the coffee table. "Pay day, merry freakin' Christmas, bro. You might've shown up for it." The poor guy's heart was ten sizes too small.

"Thanks my brother, I couldn't do it today. I just could not do it."

Joey turned to the screen. "What the freak is this? The Brady Bunch?"

"So?"

"Numb Nutz, that is some deep bullshit."

"It's entertainment."

"It's bullshit," Joey grumbled. Pinned next to his oval name patch was a new, triangular gold button.

"Hey uh, your uni has a fish on it," Jimmy pointed and Joey looked down to his breast. He adjusted the triangle.

"It's a foreman's badge."

"A what?" the words came out papery. He ran his tongue over his parched upper lip. "So, you're like dump cop now?"

"It's a promotion, waste-oid. Franky moved me up to foreman."

"Foreman for what?"

"Managing the refuse."

"The refuse? Bro, you're killing me," Jimmy said with a giggle.

"Yeah, well if you think that's funny, then you're gonna love what else Franky laid on me."

Jimmy exhaled through the perfectly circular hole formed by his lips. His face felt stiff and his head heavy. He was in the midst of a bowling ball metamorphosis. "Oh yeah?" he drawled and followed his words across the room to Joey's red ears.

"Franky says if I stick it out for the winter, he'll hook me up with his brother. He's a trooper down in Delaware or Maryland or somewhere. He said he'd hook me up."

"No way! Confiscated contraband? That is seriously sweet."

Joey shook his flat top. "No, stoner, with a job."

"A Delaware dump? They got like special spilth down there? It is down there right? Where the fuck is Delaware again?"

"Not a freakin' dump job! A cop job."

"What?" things were traveling quickly beyond the pale.

"He can get me a job as a cop."

"A cop? Dude, I thought you were, like, on the flip side of that coin," Jimmy smiled. Coin was a bouncy word. Coi-een, coi-een, coi-een.

"I just do that to keep us afloat."

"It's working."

Joey's face got all twitchy. "Hey, you know what? Forget it! You're like talking to cheese, man. Just keep smokin' that shit, Numb Nutz. That's what you do best. That and fuck skanky old broads."

Hold the phone, this was it!

Jimmy shifted up in his chair with the promise of predestined gratification. Greg Brady and his dad were off to see the coach, photos of truth and justice in hand, his triumph imminent. Jimmy savored the waves of electro-shivers that carried him straight into the commercial break.

"So... What?" Jimmy pinched the bridge of his nose and then looked up at his brother. He'd been saying something about something. "Oh yeah, so what do you got against the Bunch, bro? It's the Bunch, man, you can't not like the Bunch! That's like seriously un-American."

Joey sat down next to him in their mother's chair. The chair had been worn-in all perfect and comfy-cozy from when his mom used to sit in it. She used to sew in that chair, repair jobs mostly. Sometimes she'd sew on patches for fun. Her last summer she'd sewed a smiley face patch on the ass of his jeans. Jimmy wore those things out. Made shorts out of them when his legs got too long. They were still up in his room somewhere. He wouldn't sit in his mom's chair. Neither of them did for a while. But time moves and Joey just kind of eased his way in and took it over. Now the stuffing was all but sat-out from the cushions. The slate corduroy fabric was stained, flat and dull. Joey took a huge, exhausted breath and reached for his bong. The living room went super-bizzaro when his brother pinched an iddy-bit from his frying pan full of sticky buds.

Jimmy watched from his La-Z-Boy - and it was his La-Z-Boy, make no mistake - a new addition to the home. He'd been Johnny-on-the-spot at the dump that particular day. He'd happened on an ancient old boy, his face all gristly and spotty, struggling to yank it out the back of his rusted-out woody.

"You got that, mister?" Jimmy'd just returned from the far fence, chasing chilly white dragons and horses under the icicle trees.

"Do it look as much?"

Jimmy sauntered to the man's side and pulled hard. The recliner toppled to the frosty asphalt. He set it up right. He plopped himself in the chair and pulled the handle, the footrest popped right out. The cream colored upholstery smelled like old man powder.

"You're throwing this out?"

The ancient snorted, and then hopped in his woody and drove off! Total bargain, yes indeedily-do, though it took ten bucks to convince Joey to let him rope it to the roof of his Pinto.

"You put a single scratch on my car with that thing and we'll see just how far I can shove it up your ass."

Callooh! Callay! A yes G.I. Joey style.

Greg Brady was back on the tubular, smiling and giving the gears to Carol. Jimmy curled like a cat into yet another wave of The Brady Effect. What an episode! Beside him, Joey coughed out a thin cloud of smoke. He coughed hard and repeatedly, elbows on his knees, holding the bong between his legs. He didn't move when the fit subsided. He spoke at the floor.

"Goddamn it," he mumbled and then wiped his nose.

"Dude, herb just ain't your thing. You okay?" Jimmy kept his eyes on the beauty of a very Brady moment.

"You know he's fucking her, right?" Joey said.

"What?" Jimmy glanced at his brother and then back to the TV. "Who? Carol?"

"No, Numb Nutz, Uncle Sal! You know he's been boning her all along, right?"

"Bea? I seriously doubt that bro," Jimmy shook his head. The Brady Effect vanished.

"Come on, Jimmy, be real. You think he hired a skank like that just to set his meds out for him? Make his bed? Change the channel? No man, he's hitting it. He's *been* hitting it."

"Did you just call Bea a skank?"

"Jimmy, she's a whore, plain and simple." Joey bit his bottom lip and scrubbed at his hair.

"Hey, dude, what's a matter with you? Take that shit back."

Joey scowled. "Open your eyes, bro. I'm trying to help you here."

"Like balls you are," Jimmy pointed at his big chest, "You're just pissed."

"And how's that?" Joey asked like it was a real question.

"Don't be a dick." Some shit was just not okay.

"Jimmy—"

"Fine, You just can't stand it, that's all."

"Stand what?"

"That she's with me."

"Jimmy, hear me on this one, okay little brother?" Joey put the bong aside. He leaned in close and stared right inside him. "She ain't with you."

Jimmy pushed the lever hard and retracted his footrest. He stood up too fast and kicked at his bong. It cartwheeled across the floor, spraying sooty, yellow bong water. Jimmy regained his balance and bent in close over his brother. He clenched his rubbery fists.

"You're an asshole, you know that? You've always been an asshole! We got something good going. I know it. Bea knows it. So what do I care if you're not too clear on it?" Jimmy stuck his finger in front of Joey's face. "You say anything like that about Bea again and I'll fuck you up, you got it? Don't you fucking do it!" A foamy drop of spit flew onto Joey's cheek.

Joey wiped his cheek. "You got a bad dream going," he poked himself on the temple. "You gotta think, bro. You think Bea's some golden girl? You think a golden girl gets mixed up with shitballs? Like the one who broke your face? What's it gonna take Jimmy? What's it gonna take to wake you up?"

"You should talk! Look at you... Sal's junior goon! King of the fucking dump!"

"You think she's gonna take care of you? You think she's gonna mother you? Tuck you in when you get too high?" Joey shouted.

"Fuck it, man. I don't need your wackado. You got a mother thing happening, that's on you, sorry to hear it." Jimmy dismissed him with a wave. He stomped by the TV in his white socks and didn't look back.

In the hall, cold water soaked his soles as he padded toward the kitchen. He wanted to scream at the framed photos on the stucco walls. Mom's Jesus gear hung among the family photos; Joey and his bike with the red banana seat,

Jimmy on roller skates, the three of them sitting on beach towels, their mom in her pink one piece with the white ruffles, smiling up at the camera. Between the photos hung a wooden crucifix, a picture of Mary and child, and the man himself, palms up with a confounded look, that original Catholic combo of pity and a despairing disbelief.

Jimmy stepped into the can, slammed the door shut and locked it. His mother had called it the "powder room." She'd kept it spotless and dainty for guests who rarely showed, carefully decorated with frilly hand towels; the china soap dish always dry and clean and stocked with little oblong soaps in pastel colors that smelled like the beach and roses.

The powder room had rotted away, just like her.

Three worn toothbrushes and a squeezed-out tube of Crest sat along the sink. Dried toothpaste dollops, some foamy white, others an unused blue, littered the walls of the stained basin. A dirty dishrag, dried too stiff to stink, hung from the stainless steel towel ring.

Jimmy kicked the toilet seat cover down over the brown bowl and sat. The room stunk like piss whether he flushed or not, so he didn't bother. Besides, it was time to ride, high time. It was his brother's ugly jive. All Joey's negativity had set the bad bugs chasing him and he needed to ride, no time for dilly-dally, really, Sally.

Jimmy dug his Sucrets box out of his pocket, popped it open and fished out one of the folded pyramid papers and his one-hitter. He clamped the one-hitter down between his front teeth - thank God he could do that again - and then closed the box and set it on the corner of the sink. From his other pocket he grabbed his zippo and a wad of foil, folded into a flat silver brick. He tore off a piece of foil and then opened the top of the pyramid paper and sprinkled himself out a Dudley-Do-Goodly pile onto the foil. He set a fire underneath that white horse until she reared and bound up his pipe in a smoky, swirling gallop.

Chapter Twenty-Four

BEA TAPPED HER ash into the kitchen sink, staring out the window into Sal's backyard. His grunts into the phone sounded just as dank and icy as the February crust that covered his dead grass.

"Umhm... Yup... Yeah."

Sal hung up the phone and dropped onto the closest chair by the table. Bea turned to him and he looked up at her with a brief, satisfied smile. She blew smoke at the ceiling and then looked down at Sal, even sitting in his chair was an effort. His shoulders rose and fell with his short breaths. His black robe hung off him like a towel on a coat hanger. The satin frayed at the hem. He must've lost fifty pounds since Thanksgiving. He was yellow all over, except when his face got red from coughing, like it was now. He clutched the table and struggled for air between hacks.

Bea watched him with her left arm crossed over the top of her popped belly, holding her right elbow in her hand. She held her cigarette up by her head, pinned between extended fingers. She watched his hands. If he lost his grip, she'd have to hold him in his chair. He'd be a prick about it, try to shrug her off, maybe curse at her between hacks, but that was a lot better than having to pull him up off the floor. Down fifty pounds or not, he was still a lug, and lifting him was a chore. She stood by the sink, took a last drag off her Vagina Slime and dropped the butt in a dirty teacup. The fit subsided. His breathing steadied.

"So what's the news from the Jews?"

"We got'em by the balls. Gonna bleed'em dry," Sal said.

"And for you?"

"I'm sitting pretty." He rolled his shoulders and coughed once. The sound was deep but dry, as if, should he cough something up, it would explode from him like dust from an overstuffed vacuum.

"Well congratulations, Sal. I'm happy for you."

"I bet," he managed between hacks.

"When's the big day?"

"I could cash in right now, today. On the other hand, it could be next week or next year even. It depends."

"Depends on what?" she asked.

"On the number," Sal said.

"Are you saying you're going to hold out?" she flushed.

"It's like this, there's an offer on the table. It's good, a big number. They're looking to settle, check me off their list, right?" Sal sat back in his chair and took in a deliberate breath. The radiation treatments had webbed his wide nose and cheeks with purple spider veins. "But Goldberg says these guys are super fucked, and they know it! There's hundreds of cases like me, maybe thousands - freaking asbestos is everywhere! So this is damage control, get it? I'm damage control."

"So?"

"So? So, that's the beauty of it. Goldberg says we got room to haggle."

"Room maybe..." she frowned.

"Don't get morbid," he growled.

"I'm just trying to be realistic. If it's like he says, then the whole thing's gonna get dragged into court. And then who knows? I mean, you know?"

"What's it to you, anyway?" he paused before pointing a stubbed finger at her with his head tilted to one side. "Worried about your piece?"

"Oh stop it."

"Stop what? You think you're getting a piece, right? 'Course you do. You're a freakin' woman, why wouldn't you?" He raised his arms in conclusion and then pulled the lapels of his robe over his chest. Bea stared at him. He was a long way from the big, scary quasi-Mafioso she'd first met. He sat there in his satin robe looking like a barfly boxer on his way to another beating; hardly a fight left in him save for the defiance in his eyes.

"It's not like I don't take good care of you," she replied.

"Yeah well, that's what I pay you for, keeping the house, doing the laundry, doling out the meds-"

"And what about all the other stuff, *our stuff*? What about that, Sal? You pay for that too? You calling me a whore, Sal?"

"Hey sweetheart, that's your choice. It's not like you don't enjoy it."

"Didn't," she corrected.

He held up both his hands, "Whoa, whoa there, what the fuck is that? Now you gotta get nasty? Maybe I just throw you out on your skinny little ass. How about that? How about that's what you get?"

"Jesus Christ, Sal, who's the one getting nasty? I don't want anything from you, not a thing! If it were just up to me, I wouldn't give rat's ass what you and *Goldberg* do. Take the money, don't take the money, take a chance you hang on long enough for what's behind door number two, whatever."

Sal frowned. He leaned on his forearms, his loose skin spread on the table. "You think I'm doing this for me? You think I don't know? I got the boys in mind."

"That's big of you Sal, real big. Glad to hear you got that all worked out. So you got the boys in mind when you're in the ground and they're stuck with the legal bullshit? That's what you got in mind?" She shook her head.

"Ah, what do you know," he said and waved her off.

Bea sat at the table beside him. She broke the silence with a sigh, "I know I didn't want it to be like this." She put her face in her hands. When she peeked, he was staring at her.

"What gives?" he asked.

"You can't guess?" she sobbed.

"Quit the fucking around. What gives?"

"Sal, I, I, I'm pregnant. I'm *pregnant*. I'm gonna have your kid! Get it? I'm gonna have your kid," Bea dropped her face back in her hands.

"You're what?"

"You heard me," she said into her wet palms. The tears surprised her.

Sal rubbed his chin. "Well, you got to do something about that," he said. His voice was low and ominous, but he wasn't that man anymore. She felt something approaching pity.

"I'm having it," she said.

"But—"

"It's yours, Sal."

"You sure about that?"

"Oh, don't even start," she warned.

"Just answer the question. Come on, let me see your face."

Tears ran down her cheeks in dark blue streams. "You think I'm some slut?"

He shrugged.

"You son of a bitch!" Bea screamed. "You ungrateful, disgusting bastard!" she raised her hand to slap him but held back. She crossed her arms and turned her back on him. "Sorry to disappoint honey, I only fuck one man at a time."

She felt his hand on her shoulder and turned. Sal looked her over, rubbing his chin, mashing his cheeks from side to side. "My kid huh?"

"Yeah, your kid."

"A boy?"

"I don't know. I think so. I...I'm not really sure."

He sat still. At last he turned up his hands, "I'm in no condition, you know? I ain't gonna be around—"

"Well now a part of you will be," she said with a little smile.

"Yeah, I guess so."

"I didn't want it to be like this," she said, shaking her head.

"No, I guess not," his breaths shortened. Bea put a hand on his knee and rubbed his back and as he hacked himself into a deep, dark red. "I gotta lie down."

Bea stood up and positioned herself behind his chair. She hooked her elbows under his armpits. "Okay, on the count of three. One, two, and—"

"Three!" Sal called out in a raspy voice and then the two of them were standing, Bea's muscles straining under his weight. She turned him slowly for the swinging door and the two stepped in unison down the hall. They paused for a breather halfway to the bedroom.

"Homestretch, ready?" Bea said.

"Yeah, I'm good, I'm good," Sal panted.

They made their way down the marble hall, Bea's low heels thudding and Sal's slippers scuffing. Sal tripped forward over the threshold into his bedroom. Bea wrapped her arms around his chest and kept him upright.

"Lift those feet up," she grunted.

"I'm good, I'm good," he muttered. They made it to his bedside. He crumbled onto his sheets, flat on his belly. His back heaved up and down, each breath sounding forced and crunchy, like chalk through a meat grinder. He lay that way for a solid minute until he caught his breath and had the strength to turn over onto his side. Bea picked up the remote from his bedside table, crowded with used tissues and pill bottles and empties. She clicked on TV. Bob Barker appeared, speaking to Kathy from his needle dick microphone. What a gig. She should've gone to Hollywood.

"Price Is Right is on," she said softly. She reached and touched his shoulder.

"Fine." He turned to the TV. "You got a beer for me?"

"You're kidding, right?"

"No I'm not fucking kidding. I want a beer."

"How about some OJ, or soup maybe?"

"I'm fucking dying here woman! Just get me the goddamn beer!"

Bea left the room to fetch him his Budweiser. In the kitchen, she popped open two bottles. She took a few long gulps from hers and left it on the counter. When she got back, Sal had propped himself up on a couple pillows. He took his eyes off the TV to take the beer from her hand. He stared at the screen and sipped.

"Thanks," he said.

"You better?"

"I'm good."

"Sal, honey I don't want to upset you but—"

"Then don't!" he snapped. She looked at the TV. The brunette displayed a price tag beside a can of Cheese Wiz, $2.95.

"Lower," Sal said. The TV audience agreed. He shook his head, "dip shit."

"We got to talk, Sal, this is serious."

He ignored her.

"I'm having the baby."

Sal sat up, sipped again and then blurted, "Higher, you fuck! Higher! Where do they get these morons?"

"Sal."

"Yeah," he said at the TV.

"We've got to talk."

"Yeah, yeah, we'll talk. I got it. You want something for the baby. It's not for you. It's for the baby. Got it."

"I just want to know..."

"I'll take care of it," he said.

"What's that mean?"

"Well it don't mean I'm doing diapers, that's pretty fucking obvious."

"Don't talk like that. I just want to know, you know, how we're going to deal with this. I mean, we've got the boys to think about too, Sal." Bea reached out to stroke his head. The curly tufts of his remaining hair were thick and brittle, as if the radiation only left pubic hair.

"I'll fucking let you know, alright? Why not leave me be and go earn a little."

She yanked her hand away. "You're an asshole, you know that?"

"No shit."

Bea shut off the TV with the remote.

"Hey whadyadoin'?"

"Trying to get your attention."

"Turn the TV on."

Bea crossed her arms and waited.

"I got it, okay? You're having my kid. You want a piece—"

"For him," she corrected.

"Right, for the kid, a piece for the kid. You got it, alright? What else you want me to say? You want me to write it out for you?"

"I want the Jew on it."

"Fine."

"I want to see it in writing."

"Not happening."

"So then how? How am I going to know?"

"You'll know in cash."

"When?"

"When I settle," he said.

"When's that?"

"Soon, satisfied? Next fucking week, alright? Now turn on the goddamn TV and get the fuck outta here."

Bea reached for the phone instead.

"Call Goldberg."

"What?"

"Call the Jew and tell him."

Sal's upper lipped curled. "Alright, fine, gimme the goddamn thing," he snarled.

After Sal and the Jew had it all worked out, she turned on the TV in time for him to catch the final Showcase Showdown. Back in the kitchen, she finished her beer and had another with a smoke. She hummed the refrain from *Muskrat Love* while she waited for his chicken soup to boil. She carried his soup and another Bud back to his bedroom. Outside his door she heard his wet, ugly snore. She turned back for the kitchen and enjoyed his lunch in peace and quiet.

Chapter Twenty-Five

Bea's nerves had set in the moment she'd picked out Jimmy's syrupy Valentine's Day card. She sat in Sal's kitchen and tried to relax with a shot of Johnny Walker and a smoke while she waited for Jimmy to show. She'd been so certain it was Sal who was going to give her the most trouble! But Sal was easy. He didn't notice the extra Diazapam in his noontime bushel of meds. A bomb wouldn't wake him up.

She and Jimmy would have the entire afternoon to themselves.

She unloaded the groceries. She pulled out Jimmy's card, wedged between two sixes of Budweiser. It was a little bent, but Jimmy wouldn't mind. He was easy that way. She liked that about him, nice and simple. She palmed the red envelope on the counter to flatten it. He had simple pleasures. Sex, weed and meat sauce made for a great day. So this afternoon she'd serve the beer in a couple of her big wine glasses, whip up the sauce and soften the blow with some fine dining.

Bea loaded the beer in the refrigerator, leaving one out for herself. She had to watch the hard stuff, especially on top of the mother's little helper. She was pregnant after all and she had to have her wits about her. She opened her beer, shrugged, polished off the shot and chased it. Sometimes you had to make exceptions.

Famished, she bit the heel off the loaf of Italian bread. She chewed as she set out the ground chuck and Ragu on the counter and put a pot of water on the stove to boil. She liked the gas stove, but she wasn't wild about Sal's Formica counters, or the rest of the place for that matter. It had soured for her. She chalked it up to all of Sal's late night hacking and constant grousing. He had utterly tarnished what could have been a beautiful situation. All his luxuries had lost their cache. Just like Jackie-O's pillbox hat and big black sunglasses, somehow the perfectly fabulous had fallen out of fashion. The place made her feel like she had an itch she couldn't get at, and the feeling seemed to have come out of nowhere, like a yeast infection. When the time came, she'd sell the place and find her dream house, maybe on a river or by a lake. And she'd raise her child and they'd go on nature walks and sing songs by a campfire.

She took another bite off the loaf and washed it down with her beer. She tried to swallow the silly thoughts - Jimmy's dreaming was strangely contagious. Sometimes, over the course of the winter, she'd allow herself to dive in and join him. She'd float along beside him in the backseat of her Tempest and talk in terms of "we" this and "we" that and "we're gonna go here" and "our" home and all the good stuff with the fairy tale beginnings, middles and ends. Jimmy would dive deeper though, like one of those sci-fi fish that make there own light in the black depths of the ocean. He'd make his own light and he'd swim for it and she'd swim along, unable to deny just how cold and vacuous the water was. They'd cuddle half nude on the vinyl seat, and he'd go on about their future, clicking one of the seat belt clasps. She'd smoke cigarettes, maybe a little of his weed. He'd smoke up and tell her all about how he planned to get ahead, how his job at the dump was just a temporary gig, a stepping stone, a holding pattern until he found his big idea.

"Oh yeah? the big idea? what's your big idea?" she'd ask.

"I'm not sure yet," he'd say and stroked her cheek with his index finger.

"No idea at all?" his finger on her cheek interfered with the click of her jaw, messing up her smoke rings. They came out like floating stones.

"About what?" he cooed. He traced the line of her jaw.

"About your big idea? No ideas at all?" She pushed his hand away from her face. He didn't notice her mocking, high as he was. She kept at it. The honesty made her feel better. "It's kind of necessary to have some idea, any idea, before you can have a big idea, right?"

"So true," he smiled, "that's what I love about you."

"What's that?"

"You're a realist, you know? That's what makes us such a great team. I'll do the dreaming, you do the reality checks. It's like a machine."

"Jimmy, you know what we're doing here, right?"

He looked over to her, his blue eyes all mushy. "Dreaming?"

"Exactly."

Poor kid, but in the long run, he'd be better off. No better teacher out there than a broken heart. She was doing him a favor. She'd feed him his spaghetti and meat sauce, hand him his Hallmark card with a kiss and give him a lesson he'd have with him always. Like her mother always used to say, all you need is one good beating. Of course, as far as father was concerned, that poor woman was a slow learner. But Jimmy was a quick one. Jimmy was a quick one.

Bea flicked on her transistor radio. She liked a little music while she cooked. Disco cheered her up better than the TV. She shook her big prego booty across the kitchen floor and got herself another beer. She sipped and belched and smiled with mischievous delight. She put the big saucepan on the burner next to the pot, turned the flame on high, peeled the plastic wrap off the ground beef and dropped it into the pan with a thud.

She browned to the beat, shaking her hips and poking the meat around with a wooden spoon, separating it into little chunks. The meat sizzled in its own fat. She stopped her dance to drain the fat in the sink, holding back the beef with the spoon. So it was a little greasy? It was good that way.

That's the way, mhmm-uhuh, Jimmy likes it, mhmm-uhuh.

She returned the pan to the stove, stirred in the Ragu, shut off the burner and put a lid on it. Now that's Italian. By the time she finished her beer, the water was boiling. She dumped in half the box of spaghetti and boogied her way back to the refrigerator. Bea opened the door and pumped her hips, gyrating lower and lower. The burn in her thighs brought to mind the KitKat and old Rocco and Howard, her little butt pirate. Set like she was, she came damn close to pitying those two shits. The only thing pinching her now was her cute white nurse's slacks. She was gaining weight fast and the only thing haunting her now was a vision of shopping for maternity wear, well, mostly.

Sal knew the score now and she couldn't hardly expect him to keep his mouth shut. So today it was Jimmy's turn. It was funny how the kid's mind worked, or didn't; her belly had popped like a Jiffy-Pop pan. The two of them had screwed in the Tempest only the night before last, naked and reckless and loud, the light of the moon so bright you could read by it. She bounced on top of that beautiful boy and he held her hips, rubbed his hands over her bulging belly, but never said a word.

A man knows the difference between pregnant and fat.

This afternoon she'd break his boy's heart right into manhood. And he'd never know the favor she'd done for him. And she'd have to deal with his ignorant lack of appreciation, at least for a while, just until the visiting stopped. And that wouldn't be long now. Sal was running out of steam. She sipped her beer by the sink. Jimmy passed by the window. He spotted her and smiled. She waved back. What a lucky boy.

Bea opened the back door. Jimmy looked tired in his dirty cover-alls. "Wow, looks like we've got ourselves a party," he said.

"Happy Valentine's Day! Come on in!" she beckoned him inside, dancing to the beat.

"Oh, um, shoot," he hesitated. "I thought Valentine's Day was tomorrow."

"It is, I'm just getting a jump on it," she reached for his hands. Jimmy took them and swayed his head in time with the beat. His ponytail flipped from one lean shoulder to the other. The boy could dance. She led him to the counter by the stove and turned down the radio. "Beer?"

"Oh yeah, beer me," he said. She grabbed another can out of the refrigerator. She felt his hands on her hips. She straightened and turned to face him. He pulled her in and kissed her.

"Uncle Sal asleep?" he asked.

"Out cold," she wedged the beer between them. "Let's feed you first."

"If you say so," Jimmy said. He opened his can and slurped.

"You want to shower?"

"Maybe later," he peeked over her shoulder, "what's cooking?"

"Spaghetti and meat sauce."

"You're awesome," he said.

"I know, baby, I know." She turned from him and took plates out of the cabinet. "You wash up."

"Be right back," he walked out of the kitchen. Bea drained the spaghetti and dumped it into the saucepan. She stirred it and then loaded up the plates. What she couldn't finish he would polish off. She set the plates on the table and filled two wine glasses with beer. She sat at the table and waited, pushing the pasta around on her plate. She sipped at her beer. She'd finished half of it before he returned. His eyes were glazed and seemed to have receded into their sockets.

"Phew, sorry about that," he sat beside her and dug a fork into his pile of pasta. Bea winced at the muffled squeaks of his fork twirling against his plate. He stuffed his mouth with a forkful the size of a new ball of twine. She took a deep breath.

"Good?" she smiled.

"Mmmhm," he hummed. He washed his mouthful down with a gulp of beer and followed the gulp with another forkful. His cheeks loaded and his eyes half shut in bliss, she got the ball rolling.

"So, I've got some news."

"Oh yeah?"

"It's kind of big," she said.

He chewed in her direction, eyes opened, brows raised. His eyes were blood-shot and his dark, dilated pupils overtook the pretty blue like an inky eclipse. He swallowed. "What? Is it bad?"

"Well kind of, but no, not really, no," she poked at her spaghetti.

He shrugged, "Well? What?"

"I really, you know, like you Jimmy. You know that right?"

"You *like* me?"

"And you know I'd never do anything to hurt you right?"

"Yeah..." he put his fork down.

"And you know how I never expected you to be exclusive with me? You know, I always said you should find a girl your own age."

"What're trying to say?" Jimmy's face went from pale to white.

"I um..."

"Just say it."

She took a deep breath. The poor kid looked sick. She hadn't expected this, hadn't expected it to be difficult. It wasn't her heart after all. "Jimmy, I'm pregnant."

His jaw dropped. She might have laughed if it weren't for the ghostly hue of his skin, as if his innocence is what gave him his color.

"So we're having a kid?" he asked.

She shook her head. "No, Jimmy, we're not."

"So, you're having a...a, you know a..."

"No, I'm not having an abortion."

He stared at her, jaw still unhinged. "I don't get it."

She reached for his hands and squeezed them hard.

"Baby, it's not your baby," she whispered.

He slumped against the back of his chair, staring at her. She tilted her head and tried to comfort him by batting her eyes. Poor kid, he'd be okay. He was quiet, taking it in, totally understandable. She watched him put a story together.

"So... Whose is it?"

"Well that's the thing, Jimmy. That's the good part, I mean, not good, but in the long run..."

"Whose?" his voice cracked.

"It's Sal's. It's your uncle Sal's," she said gently.

Jimmy nodded slowly. He pulled his hands out from hers and leaned toward her. She braced herself for his reply. He winced, his eyes welling and chin trembling. He started to say something, but drooled instead. He lurched sideways and puked his heart out onto the floor, all chewed up and bloody red.

Chapter Twenty-Six

KARL RAN, GLANCING up in the direction of the screaming. He could see bits of Alec's beige coveralls through the needles and leaves. He hopped over the tangle of felled limbs scattered about the base of the maple Alec was working. Alec's ropes sat coiled by the foot of the tree.

"Sonofabitch! Sonofabitch!" Alec wailed from above.

Karl looked up the length of the trunk. His eyes adjusted to the bright sunlight that streamed down through the hole Alec had cut out of the green canopy. Thirty feet above, he spotted the yellow casing of Alec's chainsaw, and above that he saw Alec's head and then his torso. He dangled upside down, swaying in the air by the safety line attached to his makeshift rope harness. Oil dripped off the saw. Karl stepped to his left to get an angle on Alec's face. Oil pattered onto the rope near his feet, too much to be oil, maybe it was gas.

"Get me down. Get me down quick," Alec moaned.

Karl followed the safety line down the tree. The pattering kept on and there was no smell of gas and Marcus appeared by his side.

"Oh shit," Marcus said, staring up the tree.

"Can you right yourself?" Karl shouted.

"I'm cut. Just lower me as is."

Karl looked down at the rope coils. One red, one yellow, he knew he knew this! His bones shook; that was all he knew.

"Which one?" Karl shouted.

"Yellow! The yellow!" Alec shouted back.

"Jesus Christ," Marcus spat and pushed Karl aside. His boy scooped up the coil of yellow rope. "Oh Jeez," he muttered, handling the rope. Red smeared his hands. His mouth was drawn, and his eyes searched as if he were looking for a sign.

"Blood," Karl said.

"Untie the damn knot!" Alec screamed.

What knot? Karl's mind screamed back, but he got it figured before he had to open his mouth. He stepped around the tree. Five feet up the trunk Alec had drilled in his anchor and secured the yellow line with a double hitch. The line above the anchor was hard and taught. Karl tugged and worked at the stony knot. He pried his middle finger under one of the loops. His fingernail bent backward and separated from its quick.

"Marcus, get over here!" Karl shouted. Marcus appeared by his side, wiping his bloody hands on his jeans. "Get a grip above the knot, right up there," Karl motion with his chin.

Marcus wrapped both hands on the rope, above the anchor.

"Pull on that bitch and get me some slack."

"Dad, let's just cut it."

"If we cut it, all we can do is drop him."

"What the hell are you two doing down there?" Alec screamed, his voice high like a woman's. Alec's fear stoked his own and Karl bit on his lip to settle the quivering.

"Almost got it!" Karl shouted up the tree. "Heave, boy! Heave!"

Marcus propped a foot against the tree and pulled with both hands. The rope gave a little. Marcus got both feet up on the tree. His back curled and strained. He pulled down a few inches of slack, enough to get the hitch loose. Karl freed the rope, left one loop around the anchor and took a few steps away from the tree. He looped the rope under his ass for leverage.

"Ok, let it go, easy as you can," Karl said.

Marcus dropped one foot and then the other as he let the rope retreat back up the tree. Karl took up the slack.

"Okay I got it," Karl said. Marcus let go.

"What the fuck is going on down there!"

"Time's ticking boys!"

"We got you!" Karl shouted back. The rope took on weight and coiled tight around his ass. He fed the line. "Go call 911. Phone's in my truck."

"Okay, Dad."

"And bring back some towels or shirts or something."

"Tourniquet?" Marcus asked.

"No, for calming," he said and hustled the boy along with his chin. "Hurry up now."

Marcus nodded and dashed off. Karl watched him go while he lowered the line. The boy slipped out of sight beyond the cuttings, and Karl felt flushed-out to hollow.

"Eight more feet," Alec called out. "Five. Three..."

The rope went limp. Karl dropped it and ran around the tree to Alec. He lay flat on his back, hugging himself. His coverall top was soaked near black with blood. He face and grey hair were painted red. The pants of his coveralls were tan and dry.

"Push me upright. I got to sit up."

"What's cut?"

"Above my wrist, get me up."

Karl slipped his hands under Alec's armpits and pulled him up as gentle as he could. Alec groaned. Karl propped him up against the tree and held him upright and steady. Alec cradled his left hand in the bend of his right elbow. Over the man's wet shoulder, Karl saw blood gush from the gash.

"We got to tie that off," Karl said.

"You got to get me to a hospital."

"Marcus went to call 911. We got to tie that off now."

Alec looked up at him. Under the blood, the skin on his face was a sickly pale green. "Get to it, then."

"Can you sit up on your own?"

"Ayuh," Alec grunted.

Karl left his side and went for the rope at Alec's feet.

"Oh shit," Alec muttered as he keeled over. Laying on his left side, leaking arm cradled to his chest.

Karl scrambled back with the rope. Dark blood bubbled and spilled out the man's arm. Stopped-up toilets in the joint came to mind, the pulsing well of shit water spilling over onto the cement floor, the helplessness of mopping up with the last of the flimsy TP. He propped Alec up again.

"Alec, you got to stay upright," he said as he looped the line under Alec's armpit. He tied a fast square knot and pulled it tight. Alec cried out in pain but the blood quit flowing.

"Ambulance is on the way," Marcus said from behind. "I brought these." He knelt down in front of Alec, catching his breath. In his hands, the boy had his shirt and a towel from Karl's truck. The boy held them up so they didn't touch the ground. He panted and his face was blotching, the color of worn sandpaper. His almond eyes were stuck open.

"Hand 'em over then," Alec said, beckoning with his right hand. Marcus handed them over.

"Marcus, go get me a knife," Karl said. He said it quiet and slow.

"A knife?"

"I got to cut the rope here."

Marcus looked at the knot tied around Alec's arm.

"Okay, Dad, be right back," he ran again for the road.

Karl wasn't sure if he was wishing or hearing a siren in the distance. He called after Marcus, "If you hear them coming, wave 'em down and bring 'em back here!"

"What about the knife?" Marcus called back.

"If you hear 'em coming, wait for them."

Marcus paused and cocked his head, "I think I hear something."

"Go on, boy," Karl said. "We're fine."

"Ayuh," Alec mumbled.

Marcus nodded and ran off. Karl sat beside Alec with his back against the maple and watched his son disappear into the trees. He wrapped his arm behind Alec's waist and held him close. Karl slouched lower and guided the man's head onto his shoulder. Alec slumped against him, the weight of the thin man light in his arms.

"You gonna be all right, just rest now," Karl whispered through salty lips. A siren rose above the birdsong.

"We all gonna be all right," Karl whispered.

⇥◉ ◎⇤

The sun came from straight overhead and Karl's boot soles felt sticky on the black asphalt of Sycamore road. He rocked slightly from toe to heel and the tackiness underfoot felt both nice and awful. The paramedics rolled Alec and his bloody stretcher into the back of the ambulance. The taller medic had to hunch, near doubled-over, to guide the stretcher inside. Karl raised his hand but Alec was flat on his back with a mask on his face and an IV bag with a mess of tubes on his chest. Karl watched the medic hang the IV bag. The girl medic swung the door shut. She had brown hair just long enough to sweep over her shoulders.

Just long enough for a good, strong grip.

Karl shook the old mind out of his head.

"He'll be at County?" he asked the girl medic.

"Yeah, County, just check-in with the E.R." She bumped the window twice with the heel of her palm and walked for the driver's side. Karl looked at the blood on his boots and pinched his wet lips between dry teeth.

"He's going to be okay, right?" Marcus asked.

The girl paused at the driver's door. "He'll be fine."

She hopped in, shut the door and, with lights and siren blazing, cut a hard U-turn on Sycamore.

The two of them turned to watch until there was nothing left to see. That girl medic was nice, a nice girl. She's got nothing for you and you got less than nothing back. Marcus was right.

Karl wiped his hands down the front of his waffle shirt. It was soaked through with sweat and sticky with blood and tar. He peeled it off and placed it on the hot hood of his truck. He spread it flat and turned back to look down Sycamore, in the direction of the highway. He heard the distant drone of trucks barreling down the road. Marcus stood still, moving only to smoke his Marlboro. They stood in front of his Ford, both of them shirtless now and shoulder-to-shoulder.

"You're right," Karl mumbled.

"What?"

"You're right about me. I haven't changed," he said.

Marcus turned and looked him in the eye. The look was familiar, as if maybe he'd seen it before but forgotten. Marcus looked away, back down the road. He took another drag off his smoke.

"No," Marcus said.

"You think you can drive my truck?"

Marcus shrugged and spit on the road. His son looked back at him and though nothing below the nose had changed, there was no mistaking the boyish delight in his eyes. There was delight there and nothing could hide it, not words, not smokes, not blood or tar. And Karl soaked in what he saw in those eyes, even when the boy looked away. Karl drank in that sight like he was dying of thirst.

Marcus scuffed his foot over pine needles on the pavement. "Sure I can," he said.

"You done much driving?"

"I done some, yeah. Mom's been teaching me," he said and then grinned. "And I drove my buddy's car once."

"Oh yeah? Well, then, all you gotta do is follow me, okay? We'll drive back to your mom's. You sure?"

"Yeah, whatever, it's easy," Marcus shrugged.

"Just go slow and follow right behind me."

"Yeah, I got it."

"The brakes are a little – " Karl stopped. He'd fucked the chicken again. He'd badgered the candy shop look right out of the boy. Karl felt that new thirst, that new kind of craving gnawing at him from the inside. He breathed in deep, sucking in all that God in the air. This wasn't no old mind craving, no killing craving. No, this was a craving for living not dying.

"Sorry, Marcus, it's just new is all."

"Forget it," Marcus said and flicked his butt on the road.

"Keys are in the visor. I'll pull out first."

"That would be following," Marcus said. He stepped around the front bumper on the driver's side. "You want your shirt?"

"Yeah, thanks."

Karl took his sticky shirt off the truck's hood and stretched it on. It was damp, but hot from the sun bake so it didn't shiver his skin. He walked over to Marcus who was settling himself behind the wheel.

"Buttons are on the side," Karl said to the closed window.

Marcus opened the door. "What?"

"Start the engine and I'll show you a couple things."

Marcus started the truck and Karl showed him how to lower his seat, and pointed out the turn signals and pressed the horn and showed him how to turn on the lights and the windshield wipers.

"Okay, Dad, I got it," Marcus said. He rolled his eyes but didn't hide his half-smile.

So he did, so he did.

Karl made his way to Alec's pickup and got in. The cab was filled with clutter, not garbage, just clutter. Coils of rope and worn tools, a chainsaw, a couple spare chains, a greasy can of chain oil, old sooty gloves and a metal box for his invoices. The cloth seats were filthy from years of outdoor work and stunk of cigarette ash. As was his custom, Alec's keys were in the ignition. Karl rolled down his window, started the truck, and looked down Sycamore. He stretched his head out the window but the wide bed with its tall sideboards blocked his view. He had to rely on the rear view mirror. He studied the mirror until he was sure no one was on the road and he pulled out. A horn blared ahead of him. Karl shifted his eyes from the mirror to the windshield and stomped on the brake at the sight of the oncoming car. The car sped by, the driver scolding him with a glare.

"Mind where you're goin', not where you been," Karl mumbled.

He sighed and started away from the curb again. He cut the wheel as far as it would go but the truck didn't have the radius. He didn't want to ride up on the other curb with the chipper in tow. He put it in Reverse and backed up a few feet. In the mirror he saw the chipper start to jackknife. He turned the wheel the wrong way and the chipper came up on the backend sideways.

"Sorry Alec," he said and put the truck back in Drive and rode up over the curb. He glanced into his mirror; the chipper righted itself on the road. He watched Marcus bobbing his head to the rhythm of the music that pounded through the closed windows of his Ford. The boy made the U-turn with ease. Karl smiled, stuck his arm out the window and gave a thumb's up.

Karl led the way down Sycamore. Hot air swirled and escaped out his window. Karl hooked his left hand over the wheel, wiped his wet eyes on the rounds of his shoulders and didn't crave for nothing.

Chapter Twenty-Seven

Jonathan hung up with Francis and looked down at Zella's cushion. He'd have to put that back. He checked the cuckoo clock hanging on the wall - past noon already! The clock didn't chime off the hours any more, and hadn't for years. It had been a gift from his mother on his thirteenth birthday. If his father had still been alive, maybe he'd have gotten a baseball glove or a pellet gun or a skateboard. Instead he got a clock. She'd given it to him first thing in the morning. She'd insisted he hang it right away.

"I know the perfect place," she sipped her pale orange juice from a tall skinny glass and motioned for him to follow her into the kitchen.

The kitchen was in good shape back then and modern too. He held the clock up to the wall by the sliding glass door. His arms and shoulders strained under its weight. She leaned on the counter in her white pants suit and rolled her eyes.

"Oh no, that's too low, Jonathan! What are we a couple of pigmies?" she said and then sipped.

"I can't get it any higher."

"Well then, stand on a chair," she said.

When she was satisfied, he put the clock on the counter and hammered in the nail. He reached for the clock, but she slapped his hand aside.

"Here, let me. It's your present. You just look and enjoy." She hung the clock and turned back to him. "Ready?"

"Sure," Jonathan said.

She rotated the clock's hands to high noon with her manicured finger. A bluebird popped from a little door as two other little bluebirds teetered on the bottom corners of the house. The cuckoo chimed and his mother clapped her hands rapidly in front of her chest.

"Isn't it adorable?" she gushed.

"What are bluebirds doing there in the winter?"

"What?"

"There's snow on the roof."

"So?"

"So, that means it's winter right? What are the birds doing there?" Jonathan pointed to the roof. His mother looked closely.

"Well, right you are, that's a very good point. I hadn't noticed that."

"It's just weird right?"

"Oh yes, very weird." Her face twisted and turned a similar color to the strawberry highlights in her hair.

"I mean, why not make them crows? They stick around in the winter."

Her face screwed sideways. "Are you being serious right now?"

"I'm just wondering."

"I should have known you'd be like this."

"Like what? I'm just—"

"I buy you a wonderful gift and this is the thanks." She finished her juice.

"I'm sorry, Mom. Thanks for the cool clock."

"That's better. And now we'll always know what time it is, right?"

The clock chimed every hour on the hour and it didn't take a week before his mother fixed it so it never chimed again. Since then, the hours sounded off with little clicks of mute, snow-bound bluebirds.

And Jonathan bet none of it would have happened if his father had been alive. Mother didn't talk about his father much. When she did, she slurred. She told him how they met, how she was his nurse, how she had fallen for him despite herself (he was terribly charming), and how he had been very successful in business. Salvino Mancuso, his father, had lived close to town. When they drove by his old house on Sycamore, sometimes she'd point and say, "I swept that porch a thousand times."

Details about his father spilled out of her time to time.

"Whadaya mean you don't like it? Your father loved my spaghetti..."

"It's funny, your father was so tall and lean..."

"You have his hair you know. Of course, he washed his. He wore it in a ponytail, that was the style back then."

"You didn't get his looks though. Your father had a fine, strong chin." She'd let this one slip when she was very drunk, too drunk even to shake her head.

Jonathan built a picture of his father. She didn't have any photographs, blamed it on a fire. He pictured a swashbuckling man with blond hair and full lips and a squared jawed with a sturdy brow. A man built for big business.

When Jonathan learned how to do research at the library during his junior year in high school, he found the man's obituary in the Tartusville Tattler. He zoomed in the microfiche reader on the picture of the round-faced man with the caption below reading, "Salvino Mancuso, 1923-1976." He looked from photo to caption and back again. His father's neck strained over the collar of his dress shirt and he had a slight smirk. His black hair was cut close.

"Oh that was just a bad photo. He was sick," Mother said and sipped her highball.

"His hair was black."

"That was a wig. The medicine made his hair fall out."

"He was fat."

"The medicine made him fat. Be a dear and top me off won't you?"

By then he was pouring drinks for the two of them.

He should get rid of the clock. His cell phone rang and buzzed in his hand, startling him.

"Uh, hello?"

"Jonathan, it's Peg. How're you holding up?"

"I'm okay. Listen...I um, I think maybe we had a misunderstanding."

"Misunderstanding?"

"Well, things got a little weird at the end there," he toed Zella's cushion.

"Well, yeah, naturally."

"I just wanted to make sure I hadn't given you the wrong idea is all."

"You mean you didn't want Zella cremated? Damn, I hope that's not it because I've already been by the—"

"No, it was the other thing."

"The other thing?"

"The thing about, you know, about my mother."

"I'm just pulling together the doses now; what's she weigh?"

"What?"

"A hundred and twenty pounds or so?"

"Who?"

"Your mother."

"Well, yes, I mean no. I mean, yes, she's about that. I don't know, maybe a little less I suppose. She's kind of wasting away."

"That's no problem, rounding up is probably better."

Jonathan cleared his throat. "Look, Peg, I appreciate your help and everything you're doing, but we can't do this. I can't."

"Can't what?"

"You know what!"

"How about I come back about two, alright? The three of us can have lunch together."

"The three of us?"

"Well, yeah," she said, sounding incredulous. Her voice lowered, "I can't wait to meet her."

"No, no-no-no, you're not getting it. Nobody's getting together for lunch. Nobody's doing anything. It's not right. I don't care what Francis says."

"Who?"

"Nothing, never mind. Just forget it."

"Oh Jonathan, you poor thing, you've got your rights and wrongs all mixed up." She sounded choked up. "You're such a gentle soul. I'm so lucky to have crossed your path. But you need to know something here."

"What's that?

"It's not really luck, now is it? We were set up on a collision course! I mean, isn't it obvious? Hasn't that even occurred to you?"

Jonathan rested the receiver on his shoulder and tied to think less. He looked out the glass sliding door. Mother's chair hung motionless above the splintering gray planks of the porch. The trees grew not far from the porch, dense and deep green.

"You there, Johnny?"

"Peg, do you believe in God?"

"You bet your ass I do. That's what I'm getting at here. We're not just a coincidence."

"I know, I know, we're in His plan."

"Exactly," she said.

"And you think this is okay with God?"

"I can't think of a more Godly thing to do than put an end to suffering."

"But isn't that His job?" Jonathan's stomach growled. The cheese plug may not have been enough.

"Are we like philosophizing here? Fine, here you go. I'll get all Socratic on you. Since there's a God, we're His servants, right?"

"Right..."

"Then aren't we supposed to be doing something down here? Or are we just supposed to let people suffer?"

A breeze came up. His mother's chair swayed gently.

Peg continued, "This is Mercy, Jonathan, and I can tell you one thing for sure, God digs mercy. And if it works for my God, then it works for yours. So, I say again, let's have lunch."

How many times had he found Mother passed out on that chair, snoring, glass sideways, still gripped in her hand?

"What about a plan? Don't we need a plan?"

"This is the plan," she said.

"Lunch? Lunch is the plan? What about witnesses? What about the gate-house and the guard and nurse Lucy and, and, and—"

"Jonathan, take a breath," she spoke real slow. "Look, you're having your mother out for lunch, okay? It's no more complicated than that."

"But what happens when I don't bring her back?"

"Nothing."

"You don't think there'll be questions?"

"Of course there'll be questions!"

"And what am I supposed to say?"

"Let's have the rest of this conversation later, in person, okay? In the meantime, go get your mom and I'll see you both this afternoon."

"No. What am I supposed to say? I mean, what am I supposed to say when I'm the last one to have seen her? I'll fry!"

"First of all, they don't fry people in the state of Connecticut. The state uses lethal injection, just like us come to think of it," she giggled. "Seriously, you're looking at this all wrong."

"How's that?"

"Let's say your mom passed yesterday at noon, or last Friday, or New Year's Day or on Super Bowl Sunday, whenever. Wouldn't you always be one of the last to see her alive?"

He thought about that, "Well, yeah, I suppose."

"So that's normal. She's an old lady. She doesn't have a big social life, not even in her fancy nursing home, right?"

"True."

"Then what's to worry?"

"But what about, what's-it, motive? It's no secret we don't get along. I mean, just this morning people witnessed that."

"I got the impression she doesn't get along with anyone, am I wrong?"

"No, I guess not."

"Then what?"

"What about her money?"

"Do you have a copy of her will?"

"No."

"Being a drunk, I'm betting the farm she doesn't have one. Can we just move along now? I have a few errands I want to get to before lunch."

"Are we just going to do her right off?"

Peg laughed, "Jonathan, you're not in the Mafia. It's just lunch. We'll have a few drinks and—"

"I don't drink." There, he said it.

"Suit yourself, your mother and I will have a few drinks and enjoy ourselves. Just go and get her okay? No more talk."

"Okay, okay, we'll be here. See you at two." The line went dead.

He climbed up the stairs and stripped down for a shower. The hot water streamed over his greasy hair and through his creases.

He dried himself and dressed with care. He dug out fresh boxers; sweat pants and a Gold Bond t-shirt. He left the house and faced the afternoon.

He was God's reinvigorated gladiator, squeaky clean and merciful.

Chapter Twenty-Eight

"LUNCH? WHY IN the world would I want to have lunch with you?" His mother huffed smoke.

She ground her cigarette butt into the ashtray on the arm of her couch. She sat tucked into the corner of the white couch wearing her violet sundress and cream sweater vest. Nurse Lisa must have changed her clothes. The dress fell below her knees, only her skinny calves and heavily veined ankles showed. Her red toenails poked out of fuzzy white bedroom slippers. She huffed at the television, stabbing repeatedly at it with her big silver remote.

"Because it would be nice for us," he said. "The rain's gone. We can have a picnic on the porch."

He stood at the door of her apartment, apartment 1709, located at the far end of Sunny Brook Farms' East wing.

"You can have a swing in your chair. Come on, I'm parked right outside," he smiled.

"Well of course you're parked right outside. Where else would you park?"

"I'm just saying, Mother."

"What's the point of telling me that? Do you think I'm losing my marbles or something? You think I imagine you just show up out of thin air?" She stabbed at Erica Kane, and then at Maggie Horton and straight into the heart of Ridge Forrester. She froze with the remote fixed on target, ready for another disappointment.

"I don't think so, Johnny, not today," she stabbed again.

He stepped over to the kitchenette. On top of the small, white Formica counter was a carton of orange juice, a half full jug of Popov and a full fifth of sloe gin. He picked up the jug.

"Looks like you're running low," he said.

"You put that down!" she glared, pointing her remote at him. Her eyes were red and wild.

"I'm not—"

"Put that down this instant!" she squawked, pushing buttons on her remote.

"Take it easy, Mother," he said and held his hands up. "We'll bring it." He noted the fresh scent of his armpit and the pleasing dry hug of his Gold Bond t-shirt.

She tilted her head. "What do you mean?"

"I mean, Mother, that I am not your keeper. I mean that I'm sorry I even tried. If you want to keep on drinking, if that's what's good for you then go for it. I can't stop you."

"You got that right."

"I'm not going to fight you about it anymore, okay?"

"Well thank God for little favors. You know, just because you think *you* have a problem doesn't mean you can—"

"Lay it on you?"

"No, not 'lay it on me' Mr. Smarty-farty. What I was going to say - if you'd let me get a word in edgewise - is that it doesn't mean you have to cure the rest of us, who, I might add, don't need curing." She sat up and straightened her shoulders. "Take a look. What do you see?" She displayed herself.

"I see my mother."

"No kidding. What *else?*"

"Umm, I see my mother holding a remote, and not afraid to use it."

"Ha ha, very funny," she smirked. "Okay, let me spoon feed you as usual. What don't you see?"

Jonathan searched her up and down but finally, tragically, shook his head.

"No glass, Zippy! I haven't had a drink all morning. Just goes to show."

"Mother, you were plowed three hours ago!"

"That was hours ago! I'm sharp as a Ginsu," she snapped.

Jonathan shrugged, "Okay Mother, whatever you say."

"You got that right," she adjusted her aim and stabbed at the television twice more. "You've got this AA thing in your head, Johnny. You're no more of an alcoholic than me." She looked up at him. "Why not just pour yourself a drink and be done with all that hooey? Ex-con faggots telling decent people how to live! What is that? It's insane, that's what that is. It's scary."

"Scary," Jonathan nodded and squeezed his fist around the Popov jug. The sleek, plastic neck felt good in his grip, comforting, like a gladiator with his sword. His mother grinned at him, her thin lips white around the edges.

"Well, isn't that a sight."

Startled, he set the Popov back on the counter. He felt his face flush and beads of sweat covered his body as if he was flooding from the inside out. His Gold Bond t-shirt stuck like wet dough to his belly.

"I say drink up, Johnny boy, because, if you must know, all this abstinence has made you downright unbearable. Mr. High and Mighty, with all your 'One Day At a Time' and 'Easy Does It' and 'One Life to Live' claptrap." She relayed the slogans with a mocking, side-to-side tilt of her head.

In his silent melting, he prayed.

God, grant me the serenity to accept the things I cannot change, grant me the courage to change the things I can. Thy will be done, God.

The prayer didn't sound right in his head. It tumbled in a loop. He'd lost his bearings. His gladiator's chin was made of glass. He looked to lose himself in prayer, but found instead that he was only lost. Her voice came at him from a distance, though he'd discovered himself sitting next to her on the couch.

Whatever she was saying she just kept on saying and saying and saying.

"...It's just not normal, these people and their little covens and all their fake religiousness and hand-holding. I read somewhere that drug addicts in a pinch comb those meetings. Did you know that? For a fix, or a shot or whatever it is they do. I tell you, I believe it. Would you look at the riff-raff in church this morning? And you don't even know the half of it! And, really, a mime? Those people are sick, Jonathan, sick!"

"Yes, Mother," he studied his hands, damp and limp in his lap.

"Well, I'm going to keep saying it until you hear it! Believe me, I know addiction when I see it, and I've seen it." She stopped herself with a sigh and they sat in silence. Jonathan's nerves ate him from the inside until the nothingness in his ears drove him to peer over at her. She stared straight ahead, over the television, at nothing in particular, but something specific all the same. Her thin frown was different. She put a hand on his knee.

"Addicts are hopeless. They die, Jonathan, they die. The rest of us don't."

Jonathan raised a hand, paused and then patted the back of her hand. He cleared his throat and said softly, "Is there something you want to tell me?"

She pulled her hand away, "I'm not in the least bit hungry."

"Well maybe some other time," Jonathan said.

"Maybe, maybe not," she muttered. She threw both her hands in the air and dropped them on her thighs. The remote dropped on her thigh with a hollow pop. "Ouch! See what you make me do?"

He shook his head. "I didn't make you do that, Mother."

"Well, you might as well have, provoking me the way you do."

"I tell you what, how about we bring that bottle along with us and you and I will have a drink on the porch, just like old times."

She eyed him sideways, "Oh really?"

"Yeah, really. I'm hearing you, Mother. I'm reading you loud and clear, okay?" Jonathan stood up and walked to the kitchen counter. His shirt was soaked through.

"Well, that's different. I suppose it might be nice on the swing..."

"It's going to be nice," he nodded.

"If you behave," she snorted and pushed herself up from her seat. He stood up, walked to the counter and grabbed the Popov jug by the neck. Her leathery cheeks folded up in a smile. Jonathan opened the door and held it for her.

"Take that Bitter Truth, too," she said over her shoulder from the hallway.

"The what?"

"The gin, Johnny, the gin."

Jonathan fetched the sloe gin off the counter. He read the label, "Bitter Truth Sloe Gin." He followed her out, a bottle in each fist.

Chapter Twenty-Nine

"HEY NUMB NUTZ! Let's go already!" Joey yelled from the front door.

The sooner they got to Uncle Sal's Easter Sunday suck-fest, the sooner they'd be done with it. Joey's white dress shirt didn't fit him anymore. He cinched up his black tie to keep his collar together. Freakin' shirt and tie bullshit, all of it was bullshit and here he stood, by the fucked-up screen door, knee deep in it. The torn screen flapped over the midsection of the backdoor like it had all winter. One of them had torn it, put a hand or a head through it. It might have been him. One thing was damn sure. He was the one who would end up paying for it, shit, and fixing it too. Numb Nutz wasn't going to cough up a dime, a lung maybe, but no dime. And sure as shit he wasn't going to peal himself away from the freakin' TV to help out. Nope, it was up to him, Joey the Bank, Joey the Super, Joey the Mop. Seems all he did was clean up other people's shit. They'd parade along their merry way like circus elephants, dropping their steaming turds without a look back. And there he was, bringing up the rear, stinking and sweating, scooping shit by the bucket load.

And it was up to him to get rid of - crush it in the compacter or dump it begging and bloody in an alley, or throw it over a freakin' railing - they couldn't give a damn. Up to him to keep Franky's dump running smooth; up to him to keep Uncle Sal's deadbeats paying dues.

He couldn't even catch a break in his own freakin' house! Ever since Nurse Skank had dropped her little B-bomb, he was the one playing mama, Mama Joey. Day after day, drying Jimmy's cheeks and trying to gather up all the kid's pieces and get 'em back together. But Jimmy's pieces were all slippery and warped from all the shit he was on. The kid was high twenty-four-seven now. And not baked high, but FUBAR high, bad high, doper high. His fish eyes didn't belong in his head anymore. They read like the eyes of a striper on ice, all gluey and far down the line.

'Course, what the freak was he gonna say about it? All the shit was taking its toll, drowning him. Some mornings he hurt so bad he had to start right from where he left off, choking back a belt of Beam. And that was no good. That had to stop. He'd done a decent job as foreman. Franky would make good on his promise, but only if Joey had it together. So he'd knocked off the weed three weeks ago. In another few weeks he'd be fully flushed. He'd send in his cadet application to the Staties in Maryland. Franky said his brother down in Elkton was happy to put in a good word.

Elkton couldn't come fast enough. Yeah, he'd had enough alright, had enough of Uncle Sal and that pregnant skank, had enough of trying to reel in his fished-eyed, junkie brother too.

"Hey Numb Nu—" he checked himself. "Hey, Jimmy! Come on, let's just get it over with!"

Through the kitchen and down the hall, the bathroom door opened a crack.

"You go. I'm not going," Jimmy's voice echoed, sounding slow and oily. Then the door shut.

Joey stood there with the sun and his frustration burning up his back. The whole thing was bent so bad, there was no right way to go.

"Mr. Freakin' Clean," Joey grumbled. He stomped back through the kitchen and down the hall, through the gauntlet of his mom's old Catholic crap. He wished he was a kid, just for today. He and Jimmy could just go Easter AWOL. They could give all those two-faced sinners out there something real to worry about, just like Jesus.

But he wasn't no kid and Uncle Sal had made a big thing about having them over for Easter. Maybe Uncle Sal figured that now that he was almost a father, he and God would bury the hatchet. Maybe Uncle Sal figured all it took was to pony up an eleventh-hour spiral ham and some canned veggies and then God would let him wheeze his way right on through the pearly gates. Holy Mother Bea probably had set the table all fancy and formal, with a fine white tablecloth and napkin holders and pretty plates and applesauce and candles. And maybe she'd make everybody hold hands and he and Jimmy would watch her grip the top of Sal's curled, yellow fingers.

And then Uncle Sal'd pull off his oxygen mask and say grace.

"Um... Dear God, tell you what, how 'bout you pay me back for all those dead Nazi's by making sure my kid is healthy and reasonably bright? You know, so he don't get fucked with his whole life. Amen."

And then Sal's porky whore'll smile and pass the limp string beans and the soggy canned corn like her slop was in high demand.

Nope, there was no freakin' way he was going it alone. Joey pounded on the bathroom door.

"C'mon, Jimmy, let's go."

"Fuck off."

The words sounded like they fell out of Jimmy's mouth.

"Look, bro, we got no choice. We owe him, alright? Hate to say it, but we do. He's a prick, but he's a dying prick and he's not making it another Easter. If we don't go it'll stick to us like dog shit on our shoes."

"I think you mean souls..."

"What?" the freakin' kid was sky high.

"Can't die fast enough," Jimmy said through the door.

"Would you just open up? Come on, stop being a bitch." He said it nice, but the door stayed shut. Joey pounded it again. "Open up!"

"Alright, alright!" Jimmy said. The door swung open with a cloud of smoke. He squinted up from his seat on the can. "Okay?"

"Christ man, what're you doing?"

"Having a little pow wow," Jimmy said. His grin had a certain cruelty.

Joey looked down at the rust-stained tiles on the floor and shook his head. "Listen bro, just come alright? I don't want to do this any more than you,"

"Now that's a tall tale."

"Yeah well, I tried to tell you."

"Truism," Jimmy nodded slowly.

"Just come on with, we'll get in and get the hell out, okay?"

"I don't think so bro... Don't think so bro.... So bro... I do not think so... Not so bro-"

"We'll hit the packie for some beers after."

"And the DQ?" Jimmy perked up.

"Sure, whatever you want."

"You promise? In and out?"

"Like a Mexican maiden, bro," Joey assured. He smiled and held out his hands. Jimmy took them and Joey lifted him up off the can. Jimmy was shaky on his feet. He tried a step but fell forward into Joey's arms with a chuckle. Joey pointed to Jimmy's pants at his ankles.

"You're gonna need to pull those up," he said.

"Indeedily do," Jimmy mumbled and put his hand on the sink for balance as he bent over and pulled at the waist of his jeans. They got stuck around his knees. Joey gave him a hand lifting them up the rest of the way. "Okay, I am totally ready."

Joey helped Jimmy into his Pinto. He took a quick nip from his flask as he walked around to the driver's side. Joey settled in behind the wheel, cranked his window down, rested his left arm on the doorframe and pulled away from the curb, slow and steady.

Joey scanned his mirrors as they rolled down Main, Aerosmith playing low on the eight track. He tapped the brakes as they passed by their mom's old church buddies, filing out from the Our Lady of Perpetual Forgiveness. Joey peered through his brother's cigarette smoke at the churchgoers, all prettied up and contrite in their cheap suits and pink bonnets. Jimmy had nodded off. Joey switched hands on the wheel and reached over to nudge him. Jimmy's head slipped sideways against his window.

"Hey man, wake up!" Nothing, the kid looked scary. Joey shook him by the shoulder. "Hey! Yo Jimmy! Wake up!" A string of saliva slipped off Jimmy's hung lip.

"Oh God, shit!" Joey pulled back and punched Jimmy's arm. His blond head bounced against the window.

"Whoa!" Jimmy's eyes flicked open.

"Bro, Jesus..." Joey sighed.

"Have I ever told you what a good driver you are?" Jimmy muttered.

"No, can't say that you have."

"Well, I'm here to tell you brother, you are my driving idol. You're like my highway star."

"You know you got me worrying, right?"

"Hey man, you got no worries, no hurries, no need, bro, no need."

"Jimmy, you gotta cut out the skag."

"I'm putting it down," Jimmy's head bobbed on his rubberneck.

"I'm not fucking around."

"Me neither, Broscious, me neither. I am going to put the shit down." Jimmy rolled down his window and pretended to toss something out.

"That bitch ain't worth it. None of it's worth it."

"I know, I know," he shined on.

"You gotta get over her."

"Oh her," Jimmy paused. He flicked Joey's thigh with the back of his hand. "You ever want kids, bro?"

"What?" Joey glanced at him. His blue eyes were all welled up.

"Kids, you want kids?" Jimmy asked.

"Beats me," Joey said and shrugged.

"I'd be cool with kids," Jimmy's murmured. His chin quivered. "I told her that, you know," Jimmy looked out his window.

"I'm sure you did, bro," Joey said. He reached over and gave his little bother's shoulder a squeeze.

"Even his," Jimmy sobbed into the buffeting wind.

Jimmy's blond ponytail fluttered. Joey strangled the wheel with both hands, biting his lip. Sometimes you just want to go and kill every motherfucker you meet.

⊷⊨◉ ◉⊨⊷

Joey rubbed the frilly edge of the tablecloth between his thumb and fingers. It covered the kitchen table, closer to camouflage than decoration. It was embroidered with fat little angels with freakin' trumpets and bows and the whole shooting match. A powder blue wicker basket was in the center of the table, stuffed with green plastic grass. Five fury, pink bunnies and five purple plastic eggs sat on the tuft of green plastic.

"More beer Joey?" Bea pulled a Bud out of a cooler by her feet. He nodded and she reached over the bunnies, her big belly pressing against the table, and filled his empty wine glass.

Bea sat across from him with Uncle Sal on her left and Jimmy on her right. She had a smile stuck on her face like a Mrs. Potato Head. She wore a loose fitting, long sleeved dress, pink like the bunnies. The cuffs and collar of her dress were trimmed in white patterned cotton. She looked like one of those Thanksgiving turkeys he'd seen in picture books. The ones with the little chef's hats covering the nubs where their feet used to be, or claws, or whatever the fuck.

His uncle sat still, sucking at the oxygen line affixed to his nose. The oxygen tank stood in it's rolling caddy on the floor between his chair and hers. Uncle Sal watched her as she leaned over to saw the gray roast beef on his plate. She sawed and sawed, cutting the meat up into to smaller and smaller bits. Uncle Sal said nothing, just sat there with a scowl festering on his yellow face. Finally, he shooed her away.

Jimmy had edged his seat away from Bea. He sat with his white napkin tucked into the stretched out collar of his black Zappa t-shirt. He stared straight across the table, his eyes and plate empty. Joey served himself a spoonful of instant mashed and turned to his left to offer some to Jimmy. Jimmy acknowledged the bowl with a tilt of his head and Joey dropped a load in the center of his plate. Joey looked from his basket-case brother to his uncle's knocked-up nurse to his tubed-up uncle. He settled on the basket of eggs and bunnies. Easter supper was much worse than he imagined.

"Shall we say grace?" Bea asked.

Uncle Sal shrugged. He chewed and hustled her along with a roll of his fisted fork. She reached her hands out. There were no takers, so she turned her palms upward as if that were the plan. She closed her eyes and bowed her head.

"Thank you, Jesus, for your sacrifice and for our many blessings. May you watch over all the people at this table," she paused, "especially the little one who's on the way. Amen."

Joey cut a slice of his beef and chewed. He chewed and chewed. The meat sucked the moisture from his mouth like a sponge made of salt and the only thing he tasted was the Jim Beam on his breath. He forced a lump down his throat and reached for his beer. He raised his wine glass to her.

"Very fancy," he said and gulped. His belch came up whiskey hot.

"First class all the way for my Batina boys," Bea said. Her face was round now. Her Farrah hair curled around it like the bands of a bonnet. "I wanted to make things special for you. How's the roast?"

"Tasty," said Joey.

"Fine, fine, fine," Jimmy muttered, though he had none on his plate.

Uncle Sal chewed and sucked his oxygen.

"So, how you doin', Uncle Sal?" Joey asked, his mouth filled with another hunk of meat that wasn't gonna go down without a fight.

"Yeah, yeah," Jimmy said.

Uncle Sal eyed Jimmy, and then looked over to Joey. The clear tube pinned to his nostrils drew taught against his top lip. The skin on his nose looked like it was about to come to a boil. He took a deep draw from the tube before he spoke.

"How the fuck you think I'm—"

Uncle Sal turned his head toward Bea and hacked. Joey watched bits of spittle cascade onto her plate. The spasm subsided and he turned back to Joey.

"How's it look like—"

His hacking kicked in again. This time Bea raised her napkin to his mouth. Nobody said a word in the wake of Uncle Sal's fit. Jimmy's fork squeaked on his plate. The kid had a knack for that, used to drive mom up a wall. Joey finished his beer and watched his brother mush potatoes around in his mouth. He needed another beer. He needed another hundred beers.

"Any more beers in that cooler?"

"Nope, there's more in the 'fridge," Bea said.

Joey got up and walked over to the refrigerator.

"Anyone need anything?"

Sal raised his glass. Bea shook her head

"Absolutely not, honey. You can have a sip of mine. I'll have one, thank you, Joey."

"Beer me!" Jimmy shouted. Joey brought a six of Buds back to the table.

"All Buds eh? nice," he remarked to Bea.

"Like I said, only the best for you boys."

Joey popped open two cans and refilled his glass and Jimmy's. He poured the last of the second can into his uncle's glass. "Here you go, Uncle Sal." Sal nodded his head, looking smug.

"That-a-boy," he rasped.

"That's the ticket, Uncle Sal, drink up," Joey encouraged.

Bea shot him a look. "That is not a good idea, Joey. Your uncle's in no condition."

"What's it to you?"

Bea straightened in her chair. "Excuse me?"

"I said, what's it to you?"

"Oh jeez," Jimmy mumbled and buried his face in his hands.

"What sort of ridiculous question is that? I'm, I'm, well, I'm his nurse."

"So you want what's best for him," Joey said.

"Of course."

"And you think that a beer is bad for him."

"Absolutely."

Sal put down his glass and pointed his thick, knurled forefinger at him. "Watch it, Joey," he said ominously.

Joey shrugged him off, "Watch what? What do I got to watch? Look at her for Chrissakes!"

"And what is that supposed to mean?" Bea snarled.

"You're kidding, right?"

"Joey, I don't think I'm liking your tone." She reached for Sal's hand, pulled it under the table and held it there.

Joey felt the fire from his gut shoot straight up the line to his head. He had no problem letting Jim Beam do his talking.

"So we're all supposed to sit here and thank Jesus and make nice and just ignore everything?"

"Ignore what, Joey? Exactly what are you getting at?" she huffed.

"Well, how about the fact that you're knocked up?" Joey glanced at Jimmy, but the kid had his head down.

"I'm pregnant. That's right, so what?"

"And that's a good thing?"

"Of course it's a good thing!"

"Oh yeah? For who? Who's it good for?"

Bea gasped, "Well, for, for, for all of us of course!"

"Oh yeah? For all of us? It ain't looking so good for Jimmy over here," Joey shoved a thumb in his brother's direction.

"Joey, I think you've had too much to drink," Bea concluded. She took her napkin from her lap and placed it on the table. "I don't think this is the time or the place."

"Oh no? Why not? I thought you were just sayin' how good this is for everyone."

"It is."

"I'm thinking maybe that's not it. I'm thinking you having that kid is just good for you."

"Pardon me?" she asked. She covered her mouth and glanced at Sal with hurt in her eyes.

Joey gestured at Sal with both palms up, "I don't think he's gonna be playing much ball with junior. No offense, Uncle Sal."

"Whoa," Jimmy muttered, head teetering from side to side.

Uncle Sal pushed back his chair, sucked in a breath and wheezed, "Hey! Ho! Who the fuck—"

He coughed and coughed. Joey ignored him. "This whole thing is a freaking shakedown. That baby's just a paycheck. Probably not even his—"

"How dare you!" Bea gasped.

"Probably Owen's kid, a little cheesy baby Jesus," Joey said.

"A man you... you... you crippled!" Bea shouted back.

"Whose?" Uncle Sal raised the pale skin where his dark eyebrows used to be.

"Oh really? I didn't hear that. You two still in touch then?"

"Who?" Sal looked at Bea.

"I mean, why not stack the deck, right? You fuck all three of them, some-body's gotta squirt out a winner."

"How can you say such horrible things?" Bea cried. Blue tears ran down her cheeks.

"Then you fuck them over in your own special way - hell I even helped, right? And somehow this makes you not a whore?" Joey put his chin in his hand and studied her. "Nope, sorry, you're quackin' like a duck to me, a fucked duck, a freakin' whore." Joey sat up and shrugged at his uncle. Sal's red face seemed about to pop.

"Jimmy, do something!" Bea whined.

Jimmy moaned and sunk his forehead into his mashed potatoes.

"I mean, I guess maybe you won't always *have* to be a whore. You could get into sales. Like, for instance," Joey pointed to her stomach, "you could sell it. That's probably ten grand growing in there. Well, maybe just five if it's a spindly Jesus knockoff." Joey shoved his thumb at Sal. "Whatever, it's not like this dear old dad's gonna be around to say boo about it."

Uncle Sal stood up with enough momentum to tug the oxygen tube off his nose.

"You get the fuck outta my house!" Uncle Sal bellowed. He backhanded his plate of beef and mashed at Joey. Food scattered across the table. His uncle fell down to his knees, hacking and writhing. Bea dropped to his side, reaching for his tube.

"Yeah, looking good bitch, looking good all around," Joey scoffed and stood up.

"You go to hell," Bea hissed from the floor. "The both of you go to hell!" she cried. She cradled Sal's head to her chest and struggled to clip the tube back in his nose.

Joey yanked his brother up by the back of his shirt. On his way up, Jimmy leaned forward and plucked a pink bunny from the basket.

"We're outta here!" Joey shouted over his shoulder. He gently held Jimmy's arms and led him to the swinging kitchen door. "After you, bro," he muttered. He reached over Jimmy's shoulder and pushed open the door.

Chapter Thirty

JIMMY SAT DOUBLED over on the end of his twin bed, his back to the candle that burned on the top shelf of his headboard. Next to the candle sat his pink bunny, and next to that, his empty Sucrets box, a burnt square of foil and a DQ straw cut in half. The candle was warped and sinking into a pale pool of its own design. Sour yellow light trickled on the walls and sunk into the long blue sea of his twisted comforter. He'd smoked up his entire stash of H and spent the rest of Easter curled under his comforter, head and all, legs bent at the knees so his feet were safely underneath. That was his sweet time, his relief time, nothing could penetrate his comforter. It was Tonka Truck strong. But his sweet time dissolved, as he knew it would. And now it was a Tonka crash of the first order. Among the twisted backhoes and dump trucks, his comforter lent no comfort at all.

"Please God, oh please just let me sleep," he moaned.

No sleep, just images; Bea dancing in the kitchen, her thin, naked body swaying rhythmically in creamy moonlight, Bea's sideways smile with her blond curls tumbling on her powder blue back seat, Bea's belly full of life with promises that were not for him, Bea shaking her head "NO", her full lips spread thin in a scowl, cheesy Jesus shining in his overalls, meeting him at the door.

"Lover boy," cheesy Jesus said and grinned his brown, snaggletoothed grin.

And then came Joey, spit flying from his mouth and then Uncle Sal flailing on the floor like a gaffed blackfish, all greasy around the gills. And the sand worms they used as bait wriggled in Jimmy's stomach and bit his insides with little razor teeth and the aching terror twisted him to the floor. He writhed, gathering days of clothes in his arms and hugging them tight.

"Poor baby..." Bea whispered.

"Pretty boy's got no business working a man's job..."

He reached under his bed for more to grab onto. Felix might keep him afloat. Felix and sweat pants. Oh yeah, sweat pants, nice and cushiony. He gathered the pants to his gut and there, miles beneath the bed, a silver pebble caught his eye. He lifted his head off of crumpled jeans and shimmied under, further, deeper. He captured it in his fingers like one of those tiny spring frogs that hopped themselves into the corners of the garage. He pulled his captive out from under the bed and propped himself up on his elbows. He held his breath as he unraveled the foil. He greeted the dirty white powder with a joy fit for snowstorms on every Christmas morning, past, present and future. But it was Easter of course.

Happy Easter lover boy! Love, God.

He sat against the end of his bed in the sputtering light and sucked up the last of the smoke through his quivering DQ straw. He held the hit and rocked slowly back and forth. The storm passed, but time drained fast from the wasteland. He cracked his neck, first one side, then the other, the bones clicking under his skin like chalk in a fist. It was time to move, time to make it happen. He slipped naked into his Tartusville Refuse Center coveralls and took his time with the zipper up the front. He tied his Keds on his bare feet with a couple of square knots. Jimmy blew out the candle and closed his bedroom door behind him. The hall was dark and still. He toed his way down the hall to Joey's door, and paused. He raised a hand to the door.

Don't be a Numb Nutz

He continued on, avoiding the creakiest steps on his way down the stairs.

Black night breeze flittered under his coveralls like those old ice butterflies and Jimmy walked through his steamy breath for the car. He eased himself into Joey's Pinto. He pulled the door until he heard a click of metal on metal, and then tugged it all the way shut. He sat still, steam escaping his nose in quick bursts. He wiped the windshield and peeked up, searching the upstairs windows for any sign of life in the house.

Nothing stirred. He kept his eyes on the house as he reached under the seat and patted the floor. He sifted through the clutter of wrappers and little bottles. He exhaled deeply, gave up his vigil on the house and bent down further. He swung his hand back and forth beneath the seat, blood filling his head. He sat up and ran the same hand through his thick hair, all the way back to rubber band of his ponytail.

The fucking thing was gone! Not cool, not cool at all.

He searched under the passenger seat. Nothing. He put his hands on the wheel and peeked again at the house. It stared back with dark indifference. He looked to his right and then, with a shrug of a gambler who'd already lost more than he'd ever have, he popped open the door of the glovebox. The striped dishrag was balled inside. He touched it and felt the hard curve of the gun butt. Could Joey really be that stupid? He took out the gun and opened the magazine. It was loaded.

"Yup," he muttered.

He slipped the gun under his seat and started the engine. He backed out the driveway with the headlights off. On the street he checked the house for a last time, not that it mattered, flicked on the lights and rolled on down the road.

He slowed down as he passed the Our Old Lady and the bone yard. In among the rows and six feet down like the rest, his mom lay flat, dry and brittle. God had shown that woman some mercy indeed, took her out of the shit nice and early. He spared her the agony of condemnation. He covered her eyes with a tearing from His infinite robe of every color seen and unseen and smiled on her and touched her cheek with lightning and gave that woman a sweet, merciful break.

The steel fence surrounding the Tartusville Refuse Center was ten feet high with razor wire coiled along its spine, like a mutated metal centipede. He nosed the Pinto up against the front gate, and shut off the headlights and engine. His stomach growled and he almost felt hungry, but not quite, not with all those creepy crawlies just starting to stir, rising up beneath his skin, just shy of waking, just short of feeling. But they were on the rise as sure as the sun; and that shit was just plain factual.

Instead of fencing, the swinging gate doors were made of corrugated metal, and instead of razor wire, a steel sign arched like a monochromatic rainbow across the span. Curling within the arch were metal letters announcing "Tartusville Refuse Center," as if someone might mistake the place for anything else. Jimmy stepped out of the car and shoved the gun in his front pocket. It settled down low, feeling weighty against his thigh. All he had to do was get a grip on top of the gate and he was golden. He climbed up on the hood of the Pinto. He checked behind him, nothing but the yellow hook of moon, low in the sky, just God trolling for bottom feeders.

He turned and jumped with his arms stretched up high. The hood buckled with a hollow pop. Joey was going to go apeshit about denting his hood. His fingers rolled over the edge of the gate, and the rough-cut metal dug into the creases of his fingers. He scurried his rubber toes up the troughs of the wrinkled metal and hauled his torso over with a grunt. The edge scraped along his stomach like a dull blade as he pivoted. He hung for an instant and then dropped hard onto the asphalt and rolled onto his back. He lay in darkness beside the gate. He held his hands close to his face. Too dark to see, he licked at the blood he felt trailing from the first three fingers of his right hand. They throbbed like a son-of-a-bitch already and that throbbing might wake up the worms. The worms would make things much, much worse. He got up, shook his hands and then felt for the gun on his thigh.

Jimmy took long strides across the empty lot, heading for the dark brick hulk of the transfer station. Ghosts of family men in their station wagons rolled on by, chock full of all their family droppings. They lined up to feed the Crusher. He thought they watched with dull wonder, but he'd got it wrong. It was mourning, mourning memories being squeezed into oblivion.

When he said he'd be a good dad, she'd laughed out loud.

To his left was the control room for the industrial compacter, locked tight. He walked through the open bay of the station and up to the four-foot high cement wall that surrounded the Crusher. He peered down into the mouth of the Crusher, down into the dark, rectangular pit. The bottom was twenty feet down, too far to see in the darkness of the station. Jimmy felt the cool emptiness rising from it. Rising from the deep, metal box of nothing, nothing save for the briny stench that wafted up into his clammy face like foul breath. The stench of the unwanted, the broken, the discarded, the putrid, all crushed and plunged into darkness. He planted his angry hands on the wall and hoisted himself up, sitting with his back to its gawking jaw, wide open and poised for prey, like some industrial-sized snapping turtle. He sucked in his breath and dug in his pocket for the gun. His stiff fingers throbbed in painful revolt as he struggled to free the gun from the twist of his pocket. He held the gun in his lap.

This would be so much easier if he were riding high on the horse instead of falling off it. The worms were on the rise, announcing themselves with a chilly sweat that soaked into the back of his coveralls. He shivered, rocking slightly on the wall as he clenched his arms to his sides and his legs together, feet crossed. First the shivers, the shakes would follow with the queasy squirm in his gut. And he'd only felt the worms in his bedroom, just a hint of what was coming down the line. His wriggling insides were on the turn, and all his tubes would writhe in hunger like a clutch of newborn snakes.

He looked out the bay doors of the station. At the far edge of the parking lot, where the woods took over, Jimmy could make out the budded veins of tree limbs coming back to life. And that was the thing, right? Nothing was permanent; everything passed, everything moved from one place to the next, one note to the next. Shit, even garbage kept on the move.

Jimmy sat up and held the gun between his hands. He grimaced as he forced his bloody fingers to curl around the butt, his index finger on the trigger. He pointed the gun, its short barrel bouncing haphazardly along the tree line. He cocked back the hammer with his left hand, pinched his eyes shut and pulled the trigger. It didn't budge. He sighed.

"Safety," he muttered.

He slid back the safety and pointed again. The round blasted in a bright crash of echoes that jolted Jimmy backward. He gripped the wall with his legs to steady himself.

"Goddamn!" his voice sunk into the hard, hollow ringing in his ears.

The snakes hatched Bea belly-laughed and Joey cursed "cunt!" and Sal coughed out a cloud black and thick as coal and a worm poked out from the hole in his mother's red apple cheek, powdery rouge crusted at the black edges and

Jimmy cocked the gun and shoved the muzzle up under his chin and - God he was shaking - and his fucking fingers hurt like a bitch and his skin bubbled and he screamed mean and tugged the trigger. He fell backward into the exploding silence. Weightless, wide-eyed and knowing, he was aware of the hole where his nose used to be and the sorry truth that he'd got it wrong again, fucked up indeedily-do. It hit him, but not as hard as the cement gullet of the Crusher and his bones broke with a crackling belch.

Chapter Thirty-One

EVERYBODY HUDDLED AROUND the grave, some sat, others stood shifting on their feet. Joey looked up from his folding chair at the solid bank of dark clouds. The rain had stopped after pissing down for two days straight. He sat in the mist that hung stone still in the air, trapped under the low clouds like a cold cement ceiling. Springtime grass and new blooms looked dull in the flat light, while all the damp black suits and dresses shimmered. Here and there drops of water slipped down the waxed sides of Jimmy's mahogany coffin. Uncle Sal had bought it. Uncle Sal didn't skimp on the dead. He spent top dollar on Mom's too, at least that's what he said.

"My sister's gonna rest in the best."

Freakin' guy was a real saint when it came to dying. Jimmy's coffin rested on a royal blue drapery. The soaked drape covered the light-duty hydraulic platform lift that would lower him down once Father McMullin gave the word. Four potted bouquets stood by each corner of the grave. Somebody had arranged for the flowers. They were those big, Easter-time flowers, lilies or lilacs something; the ones that looked like big, worn-out fairy queen pussies.

Maybe he should have just ran Jimmy through the compacter when he'd found him, Jimmy and the gun both. The kid had no right to use his freakin' gun. The kid had no right. Father McMullin continued on, standing under his black umbrella at the head of the grave.

"And so we mourn as we must, for we are all God's children and the death of a child reminds us of our own childlike fragility..."

Five folding chairs had been placed on rubber runners by the graveside. Joey sat on the last chair, by Jimmy's feet. Uncle Sal's oxygen caddy stood in front of the seat to Joey's left. Uncle Sal sat hunched over in his black trench coat and hat in the third chair, dead center in front of the coffin. His shoulders rose and fell. His oxygen mask peaked out from under the brim of his hat, fogging and clearing with each labored breath. Bea sat on the other side of Sal, her head tilted down. She held the thick collars of her salt and pepper fur coat up over her chin. Water dripped off the front of her wide-brimmed, dark maroon hat. Attached to the hat brim was a black veil. The two of them stared straight ahead. Occasionally Uncle Sal looked up to acknowledge the words of the priest.

Franky P. and the guys stood on the other side of the grave in a tight knot. Franky brushed off the shoulders of his leather aviator's jacket. He looked from the priest to the coffin and back at the priest. He had a toothpick wedged in the corner of his mouth and sucked his top teeth. The rest of the guys hung their heads.

Franky caught Joey's stare and nodded. He'd stood by his word. Joey was just waiting on the offer from Elkton and then he'd be off to the Academy. Franky had actually come through! Joey nodded back. It was his to buck up or fuck up now. Joey snaked his fingers behind his tie and unbuttoned his shirt collar. Hot air rushed up from under his collar like steam from a kettle. He looked to the priest.

"...The faith of those who mourn and satisfy their longing for that day when all will be made new again in Christ, our risen Lord, who lives and reigns with You forever. Forgive James his sins as You forgive all of us, for we are all sinners..."

Joey grunted. Uncle Sal turned and glared at him, his mask fogging and clearing in silent rage. Joey dropped his eyes. Water beaded on his black shoe polish. His grunt had jumped from his gut, just like the Jim Beam he'd sprayed on the church wall before the mass. The truth just kept surprising the hell out of him.

Father McMullin prayed to God and Joey saw the sameness, he'd been through this before. Of course he had. He shifted, sliding his butt on the cold, hard metal of the chair. He looked over his shoulder, through the few folks standing behind them, to his mother's wet granite marker. The same Easter flowers drooped over the tarnished copper vase planted at the base of her headstone. Father McMullin must've done that.

It all came back; the service in the church, Sal in his charcoal colored three-piece and his freakin' faggy leather loafers with the fake buckles; the all-merciful Jesus and the Lord's Prayer and Almighty this and Eternal that and all the rest of it rolling off McMullin's Irish tongue. He hated the priest that day, spewing all his stinking lies. The stench clung to them all, as foul and plain as dog shit; that special blend of God's mercy smeared all over everything.

"Please rise and join me in the prayer the Lord has taught us," Father McMullin set his umbrella upside down and rose his hands in holy slow motion.

Bea rose up from her seat. She got her hands under Sal's armpit.

"Hold on," Sal grumbled under his mask. She pulled him up. His oxygen line ran out of slack and the mask slid sideways across his hamburger nose.

"For Chrissakes! Wouldya hold on a fuckin' second?" His shout echoed out of his mask, stuck sideways in his mouth.

Father McMullin stood frozen with his hands up to God.

"Sal!" Bea gasped.

"What? I'm tangled up here!" he tugged the mask out of his mouth.

Joey side-stepped over and bent down to free the tube.

"I'll get it. Leave it be, Joey. I'll get it," Sal said.

"Just lift your foot, Uncle Sal."

"I said I'd get it."

"It's under your foot," Joey said. Uncle Sal lifted his left loafer. The gold buckle shined. Joey tapped his right shin, "This one, Sal."

"Don't you fucking 'Sal' me!" he barked and lifted his foot. Joey stood up and Sal righted his mask and then rolled his hand at the priest.

Father McMullin led the mumbling gathering in the Lord's Prayer. Bea stood shaking in her fur. The moment the prayer ended, Bea grabbed hold of the priest and balled and whaled. What a freakin' show.

Joey touched Jimmy's cold, slick box. "Bro," he choked-up and tried again. "I'm gonna miss you," he winced and coughed into his fist and fought back his tears. There was no freakin' way, no way on earth he was giving any of these shits the satisfaction.

Joey double-timed it down the soggy mulch footpath. He caught up to Franky at the arched iron gate. Joey stuck out his hand as they walked into the parking lot.

"Hey, thanks for coming, Franky," Joey gripped Franky's hand hard like a man.

"Hey look kid, I don't know what to say. My condolences, you know?"

"Yeah, thanks... So's everything set with Tony?" Joey flushed. He didn't want to come off so desperate.

"Relax, Joey," Franky patted him on the back. "Tony says it's a done deal, you got the job."

Joey sighed. "Hey, I can't thank you enough, you know?"

"Just don't expect me to call you sir, or officer or any of that shit, cause it ain't ever happening," Franky spat out his toothpick. "Until it comes through, you're still working for me. I'm expecting you back Monday," Franky said. He hit his arm and walked on.

"I'll be there," Joey said to his back and headed the for the front of the church.

⊷═◉ ◉═⊷

They sat shoulder to shoulder in the back seat of the mortician's stretch limo, Uncle Sal and his oxygen tank in the middle. The privacy glass was up and the air was rank with Bea's perfume. The Funeral Home was just a few blocks from the Our Lady of Perpetual Forgiveness. Bea spoke up as they pulled out onto Main.

"You okay, honey?"

"Fine," Uncle Sal said.

Joey looked out his window. They passed the Army Navy store, and then the Castle liquor store. Big yellow stars on the windows advertised this week's deals. JIM BEAM $6.99! (1 ltr. bottle, one bottle/customer).

"Beam me up, Scotty," Joey mumbled.

"That was a nice service," Bea said. She pulled a wad of tissues from the box by Sal's head. She dabbed at her eyes.

"Mhm," Sal nodded. He knotted his arms across his chest.

"Joey, will you be coming over to the house?" she asked, inspecting the black smudges on the tissue.

"Yeah, no, I don't think so," Joey raked his fingers backward along his scalp.

Bea turned to him, "Well, that's a shame. We'd really like you to come. You know, it's times like this when families need to stick together," she pouted beneath her veil.

Joey covered his mouth and coughed.

"What the fuck is that?" Uncle Sal grumbled through his mask.

"What?"

"What, what? The bullshit cough, that's what." His voice was rocky and raw.

"I had to cough," Joey shrugged.

"So, you're not coming," Uncle Sal said.

"Sorry," Joey shook his head. He fended off another tear with a twist of his mouth and scrunch of his cheek.

Bea sat forward in her seat. She set her hands on Sal's leg and leaned toward Joey. Her nails were painted dark maroon, same color as her hat. She sized him up from behind her veil and her fur coat ballooned over her shoulders with each deep, studious breath. Joey watched her smirk, then scowl and then smirk again. The sweet, acidic odor of bellied liquor mixed with her perfume, like squirrels rotting in a flowerbed. Joey cupped his hand over his mouth and checked his breath, nope, not his squirrel.

"It's okay you know, Joey, nobody blames you. Jimmy did what Jimmy did," she reached and patted his knee with her fistful of tissue. "It could have been anybody's gun," she sighed.

Her touch ran through him like volts from live wires. He bent over, balled his fists up between his legs and curled his toes. He looked at her sideways. Her pity congealed in his chest like napalm. He squeezed himself together.

"Yeah, thanks," his freakin' chin quivered.

"It must be so difficult for you, you poor thing," She consoled him with a sad, toothy smile.

Uncle Sal lowered his head. His disgust coming out loud and clear from the hollow of his mask.

"I mean, my God - just the guilt alone!" Bea sighed again. "I know it's normal to feel guilty under the circumstances. I mean, even I feel some sort of, I don't know what really, responsibility? Guilt? Something. And I didn't even have a thing to do with it! So my God, what you must be feeling... Well, it's just awful. I'm so sorry, Joey."

Uncle Sal looked up at the sunroof and scoffed.

"What, Sal? What is it?" Bea asked, her voice drippy.

"It was his fucking gun," Uncle Sal shouted. The mask fogged and bobbed on his face.

She shook her head and swapped Joey's knee for Uncle Sal's. "It was Jimmy who pulled the trigger, honey."

"It was his fucking gun. There wouldn't be any trigger to pull," Sal said.

"Yes, we all know that, but it was Jimmy's decision." Bea dabbed at her eyes.

"The kid wasn't capable of making decisions."

"Sal, that's enough now, honey. That's not helping anyone," she sobbed.

The limo turned onto Imperial. The driver made a slow, wide turn into the parking lot. He inched the limo along, taking care to avoid bottoming-out on the curb. Joey reached for the door handle. Uncle Sal swiped Bea's hand off his knee. He pulled his mask aside and barked at her.

"What fucking dream world are you in? It's his fault! Of course it's his fault! Just look at him," he gestured at Joey, "Come on, look at him for fuck sakes!" He pointed at Joey's hand on the door. "He's running already. He knows what's what!"

The limo stopped. Joey yanked on the handle and swung open the door.

"Joey, dear, don't," Bea pleaded.

"No, do Joey, do. I seen all I ever want to see from you."

Stooped over and with one foot out the door, Joey turned to them. He looked into his uncle's milky, red-rimmed eyeballs. The skin on his face was loose and yellow, the elastic bands of his mask cut sideways along the stubbly folds of his cheeks. He was a dead man in the making.

Joey pointed at him, "You won't."

"Joey!" Bea pleaded.

"You bad bitch, I shoulda let him cut your freakin' throat," Joey snarled.

Bea retreated into the far corner of the limo, her fur coat collar standing on end. "How dare you! How dare you!" She shrieked, but her eyes danced above her smeared lids. She glared at him, her lips curled back from her teeth.

"Get the fuck outa here," Sal shouted and raised his foot. Joey saw it coming. The heel of Sal's loafer caught him on the knee. Joey jumped away from the door. Sal raved away, "You fucking ingrate! You fucking honor-less twerp! I'm done with you, you hear me? Done! Don't come by. Don't call, don't—"

Joey slammed the door shut. He pounded the roof of the limo with both fists, raging, blinded by blood-splashed visions of broken bones and blubbering deadbeats and gouged out eyes and severed digits. He pounded and pounded, the roof buckled under the meat of his fists. And he screamed and pounded until the driver's door swung open.

"My condolences, bro," Jimmy removed his black chauffeur's cap. His hair was perfect.

⊶≡◉ ◉≡⊷

Officer Joe Batina opened his eyes and the glare of the midday sun carved into his corneas. He squinted and looked from side to side. He propped himself up in the grass. He searched his surroundings. His back was stiff as hell and the rest of him was all clammy and cold. Above his head he made out the pockmarked, curve of his mother's headstone. He wiped his crusty lips with the back of his hand and pushed himself up into a sitting position. His brain revolted with pain like a pair of frozen scissors to the eyes. He pinched the corners of his eyes. His sinuses crinkled like plaster between his thumb and index finger.

He checked his wrist for the time. He saw only a silver blur through the painful haze. He rubbed his eyes with the heels of his palms and tried again.

One o'clock.

"One o'clock! Holy shit!" He shimmied backward on his damp blues to prop himself up against his mom's gravestone. He took another look around before reaching into his pocket for his vial. He unscrewed the cap and peeked inside, bracing himself for the onslaught of disappointment and urgency. He tapped out a pile into the wedge he created with the tendon behind his thumb. He snorted at the white mound and his right eye watered.

"Here's to you, bro. May you R.I.P." He snorted the rest up his left lane. "You old S.O.B."

Freakin' God shot - that bad bitch was back.

Joe's thoughts sharpened and missions and resolutions became clear as he exhaled through his mouth. He capped his vial and shook it. He was running seriously low, less than a gram in the can. He'd have to hit the property room and reload for tonight's shift. After that, he was done. He'd call in sick if he had to, but no more night shift and no more drugs.

"Gotta go mom. It's been a visit." Joe stood up. He brushed himself off and caught his breath. His head pained him, but the pains were like fireworks now, a few more bright bursts and the worst would be behind him. He slapped his hat on his thigh and then squared it on his head.

"Say hi to Jimmy for me, alright?" he called over his shoulder and hung a left at the big marble V.M.

Chapter Thirty-Two

MARCUS'S MOTHER WAS gone so Karl double-parked Alec's rig with the chipper in tow in front of her driveway at 124 Railroad Avenue. He swung his stiff legs out of the truck. The tops of his thighs were sore and shaky and he knew he'd be in for a few hard, painful days of getting up and down stairs. He waved to Marcus who looked too young to be sitting behind the wheel. Karl righted the kinks out of his back as he walked. Marcus lowered his window and music rushed out in a thumping attack. Karl frowned and signaled with a slicing motion to his throat. Marcus leaned over and turned down the volume.

"We're gonna have to leave my truck here for a while. You know how to park?"

"Sure, Dad."

"Well, how 'bout you take that spot behind you?" Karl pointed.

Marcus looked back and shrugged, "Okay, no problem. Hey uh, your phone was going off like the whole time."

"How could you tell?" he smiled, but Marcus pinched up his almond eyes.

"There's commercials," he said as if he was talking to the dumbest motherfucker in town. "And it buzzed right across the dashboard."

"Well, give it here then."

Marcus unfastened his seatbelt and reach down into the passenger foot well. Karl leaned in the window.

"Got it?"

"I think it slid under the seat maybe."

"Here, I'll look—"

"No I got it. Here it is," Marcus sat up and handed over his phone.

"Thanks, son," he said. The two stared at each other.

"What?" Marcus asked.

"Nothing. Park it, okay?"

Marcus shrugged and turned to look over his shoulder. He shifted the truck in gear and glanced down at the dash. Karl stepped back a couple of paces and scratched his lower lip with his teeth. The boy didn't have a clue how to park and he wondered what a Higher Power was supposed to do about that. Was it his God mind or his old mind telling him to stop and teach the boy? Shit, maybe it was both minds. But the boy had no interest in being taught; and wasn't he supposed to be learning to live and let live and not impose his will on others? Isn't he standing here watching God's will? It sure as hell wasn't his will. He had no will for watching Marcus ding up his truck or put a pricy dent in someone else's. So it must be God's will getting it done. And if God wants Marcus to fuck up this parking job, then he just had to accept it. Then again, his father had taught him how to parallel park and he'd come to appreciate it, not at the time maybe, but in time.

His phone buzzed. He looked at the number, "RESTRICTED."

"Hello?"

"Karl!"

"Nellie, hey, I was just about to give you a call."

"I've tried you like twenty times!"

"I know, I'm sorry, you okay?"

"No. I'm not okay. I'm really not. I'm not, I'm sorry," she blubbered. His face felt twice baked as his minds tussled on.

You got to stay away from that girl.

But she needs somebody.

But that somebody don't have to be you.

Marcus backed up the truck. He cut the wheel and then stopped and started again.

You got to give what's freely been given.

You don't need to be diddling that girl with your sobriety. It ain't right.

"Karl? Are you still there? Please, I don't know who else to call."

"Where are you?" he said.

"You know the Windsor condos off Tremont? It's like three feet from King's."

"Yeah, I know it." He gritted his teeth, and watched Marcus pull his truck forward for another attempt.

"I'm in 602, toward the back," she said. He held his breath as Marcus backed up again.

"Alright, I'll be there soon, okay? We had some bad shit happen."

"Oh thank you! Thank you so much!" she blubbered. "There's just no one else for me to call."

"I gotta get off now. I'll be there soon as I can. I gotta go," he hung up.

Marcus got out of the truck. He didn't look at him.

"I'm gonna go inside and call mom," Marcus said as he walked up the cement path. Karl followed him. The boy had parked the truck just fine.

"Hey, hold on a sec," Karl called.

Marcus turned and looked at him. "Yeah?"

"Nice parking job."

"Thanks," Marcus said and stuffed his smile into a smirk.

"Well, we got to have something to tell your mother." The words came out feeling wrong.

"Like what you're having for lunch?" Marcus said and then turned and walked up the steps.

"It's not like that at all."

"Whatever."

"It's a woman from the rooms. She needs some help right now," he said to his son's back.

"Whatever."

"I'll be back for the truck in a couple hours," Karl said.

"Whatever."

"You gonna be here?"

"Yeah," Marcus unlocked the door.

"Well then, I'll see you later. I gotta do this program thing, then I gotta swing by and see to Alec."

"You do what you gotta do, right?"

"I'll get a cab back here. Two, three hours tops."

"Whatever you say, Dad."

"Marcus..."

"What?" he opened the door but stopped to look back. His lips were tight.

"I'm, well, I, uh... I'm proud of you, son."

Marcus smiled. "Thanks. See you later, I guess," he said and then shut the door.

"I'll be back in a few hours, promise!" Karl called.

He turned back down the path for Alec's truck. In a few hours he'd sit Marcus down and explain. He'd tell him about what it meant to give to others what had been so freely given to him. He'd tell him again how proud he'd made him. He'd tell him he'd been a hero that day. He'd tell him Alec was getting on fine. He'd see if he wanted to go for a drive. Let him drive the truck for a slice of pizza or an ice cream or something. He'd ask him what his favorite flavor was these days. He'd ask him if he liked ice cream at all. Well shit, everybody likes ice cream.

Chapter Thirty-Three

NELLIE WATCHED HERSELF pull the phone from her ear in the spotless mirror of her medicine cabinet. She fixed her gaze on her painted eyes and pressed the END button on the cordless. Despite his good intentions and contrition, the man was what he was. All the selfless sobriety in the world couldn't alter the fact that Karl was a rapist pig. Facts are facts. This wasn't a matter of rehabilitation or spiritual restitution. Being a rapist was as much a part of him as his left arm. This wasn't a matter of character or circumstance or addiction. It was a matter of makeup.

She'd been careful with her mascara this morning and had been equally conservative with a blue-gray shade of eye shadow. She didn't want to put on a show; God knows she didn't, especially not for an AA meeting. She pulled a dry washcloth off the towel rack above the toilet. She unfolded the bleached white cloth and flipped it in her hand so that the side of the cloth that had been within the folds now faced up in her palm. She set the phone on its back on the side rim of the powder blue sink. Could whoever had built this place come up with an uglier color? Of course it had to have been a man. Only a man could be so completely blind to the tackiness of powder blue porcelain. She turned on the faucet and let the water heat up. She raised the cloth and leaned down to give it a closer inspection. She picked several lint balls off the terrycloth surface of the rag, pinching each little offender between her red fingernails, pinching them hard. She'd make each one bleed if she could, but she could not and so discarded each with a flick of disdain into the toilet bowl. When steam rose from the faucet she stopped her operation and toed the handle of the toilet to flush away the now unseen detritus. She soaked the tip of the rag under the water, feeling the heat at her fingertips. She used the wet tip of the washcloth to wipe the mouthpiece of the phone and when she was done, threw the soiled cloth into the small, mesh hamper positioned under the sink, between the nickel plated legs of the sink and the plumbing that curled from the under the sink into the wall and out to God knows where.

He was a dirty pig who buried and befouled the truth. She turned and un-clipped the plastic rings of her shower curtain. She removed the white terry-cloth curtain and folded it as best she could, determined to keep the fabric off the floor. She did the same with the clear plastic liner. The blueness of the tub soured her stomach. She balanced the folded curtains on the edge of the tub and turned back to face the mirror.

Using both hands, Nellie rolled the scrunchie from off her ponytail. She smoothed the straight blond hair, running her palms from either side of her scalp down to her shoulders. When it was nice and flat and neat she tilted her head and shot herself a sassy smirk before gripping the wig by the crown and pulling it off. She wedged the wig carefully between the tops of her thighs and the front edge of the sink. She inspected her patchwork head in the mirror, turning to one side and then the other. Haphazard little plantings of her auburn hair remained like tufty islands, some as thick as her thumb; others were wispier and lonelier, drifting listlessly in the residual static of the rubber headpiece. She spied a single strand that stuck out sideways just above her right ear. She dug her nails into her scalp at the base of the lone insolent hanger, and yanked it out at the root. She rolled the hair between her fingers before she set it afloat down into the toilet. It landed on the rolling surface of the rising water. She listened to the whine of city water filling the holding tank. When the bathroom fell silent, she flushed again and watched the water spin the bowl empty. In the mirror she spied another straggler, but stopped herself with an enormous force of will. Karl would arrive soon and she wanted to get everything just so.

She left the bathroom, wig and curtains in her arms. She slid open her closet door, nudged a stack of shoeboxes aside and placed the curtains beside the boxes on the wood floor. She slid the door shut. She slipped her wig on and positioned it. Once in place, she cupped her hands beside her eyes like blinds on a quarter horse and hurried through her bedroom door and down the short, narrow hall. The air in the hall felt sandy in her nostrils. She believed she could smell the dust that had gathered on her picture frames since yesterday. This was absurd of course, despite her almost canine sense of smell. Just another blessing that had made her life on the farm that much more unlivable.

Each of the three picture frames, each one of them - one, two, three (each and every one of them!) incomprehensibly askew again, as if her apartment were infested by mischievous little ghosts. She hurried by, her cotton blouse billowing at the shoulders, brushing here and there against who knows what, if anything. On her right was a narrow chest of drawers where she kept her small stacks of cardboard and newspaper clippings and dissection kit and gift wrap and fabric swatches and a tiny spool of chicken wire and seven paperbacks and four paper grocery bags folded tight and tied with twine and one can of Green Giant peas and two cans of Campbell's Chicken and Stars and a half empty box of elbow noodles. The kitchenette was so damn small! No storage at all, just a few ugly metal cabinets above and beside the stove. She scowled and kept her eyes forward and down, so that she glimpsed only a flash of her blood red toenails with each step. She turned left off of the dark wool wall-to-wall carpet onto the mustard colored tile of her kitchenette.

She had told the truth in the meeting. She was a liar of the first order. Unable, it sometimes seemed, to even approach the truth, even for a moment. And the crazy thing was most of her lies started out as truths! But somehow they turned. They piled upon themselves, higher and higher like the dust of dead skin (or so she'd heard) on every horizontal surface of her apartment, on all three picture frames, on the trophies in her freezer. She needed a new freezer. This one would not do any more. It was filled from corner to corner with little bits of the truth and she needed more of these truths, and she would need storage for these truths. And while formaldehyde seemed a sensible option, the liquid was in fact no option at all, stinking, as it did, like some horrid combination of vinegar and earwax.

She toed her way between stains and clutter, careful to avoid the tile cracks. Not so much for the bad luck (could she have any more?) but for the crustiness of what had no doubt gathered in the crannies. Nooks and crannies that looked so good swathed in yummy butter, so homey, so much of mom - the dirty stench of her - with her sweaty hands, black with the shit of pig after pig after pig. Oh those fucking pigs! And her father in the pen, grunting and hollering at his beasts! And her mother's hands, rough on Nellie's shoulders, the callouses scraping bruises that she ignored just like the recurring blood stains right smack in the middle of her bed sheets.

"Wash'em in cold," she'd say with a butt quivering between her lips.

Nellie kept on washing her sheets in cold water even after her father vanished and Peggy took off. But the stains never washed out completely; the dark blotches outlasted them all. When Nellie said goodbye her mother just stared out the sooty window above the kitchen sink, a gray pin-line of tobacco smoke rising up over her head into the dead air.

Burn bitch.

Nellie took a cleansing breath. Today, she resolved, not right now, but at some point today, she would arm herself with a box of heavy-duty trash bags and do a massive, liberating purge. She'd let things go for too long now. She had to face it. No more little distractions, she would set herself on the path to God. This afternoon she would set herself on the path and not look back. This afternoon, as soon as these damned heebie-jeebies passed and she could think straight again and she didn't have to be ruminating the whole time on if or what she was going to drink.

But of course that was a lie! She didn't really ruminate over drinking; she didn't drink that much at all. Well, that wasn't quite the truth of it either. She did drink. But she could purge and drink at the same time. But she couldn't purge and have Karl over at the same time. She couldn't purge with guests.

What a horrible, pathetic thing to be such a slave, crawling before a bottle. She toed from tile to tile and reached for the top door of her refrigerator and checked the freezer compartment. Stacked inside was box upon box, some small and square, the size of ring boxes, others long and narrow. It was a testament to the modern world that there could be a cardboard box properly sized for all her bits. Well, there she goes again. In truth they weren't her bits at all now were they? They were most pointedly not her bits. They were others' bits, little beastly bits. She knew very well that, like truth, it was all a matter of perspective.

Those "others" would hardly consider the contents "bits." She took out a white ring box marked "Mr. Spring Squirrel 4/97" and held it between her hands. The box lost it chill immediately. It was as light as air and if the frozen contents didn't bump about inside, one would assume the box was empty. She opened the lid and nudged at the tiny penis and testicles with the tip of her painted fingernail. No, a squirrel would not consider these bits at all.

She surveyed her collection of boxes, each marked by her tidy, compact black print. In the visible rows resided, among others; "Mr. Whiskers 6/98," "Mr. Chestnut Hare 7/99," "Mr. David ? 4/01," "Mr. Dog 12/03" "Mr. Dog II 2/04," "Mr. Dog III 4/04," "Mr. Krinkles 2/97." She rearranged the cold boxes, eventually throwing her hands up in the air. There simply wasn't room enough for a shoebox! And then she flushed shamefully at her presumption.

She didn't know the first thing about Karl.

"Bullshit!" she said aloud. She closed the freezer door, opened the door below, and reached inside the refrigerator for her chilled jug of Gallo. She put the jug in the middle of her small, square copper topped table. From the cabinet above the sink she took out two juice glasses and placed them on the table by the jug. She hoped he liked white wine.

She knelt down to open the cabinet beneath the sink and pulled out her hand sledgehammer. It had a four-pound iron head and a yellow fiberglass shaft. She touched the cold head of the hammer to her bare chest. Her nipples hardened at the chilly jolt to her skin. She shivered and then hurried back down the hall and into her bedroom. She crawled over her twin mattress and slipped the hammer under the bed. She smoothed the yellow comforter flat.

Back in the kitchen it occurred to her that she might be low on lye, but that was silly, she had plenty of lye.

Chapter Thirty-Four

KARL STEERED ALEC'S rig into Nellie's condo complex, knowing the finest thing by far about the Windsor Condominiums was the sign he passed at the entrance. The sign stood facing Tremont road, tall and proud and full of itself. He rolled down Windsor Drive, passing identical units on either side. The brown stucco buildings were narrow, two-story jobs. Each had a door dead center. To the right of every door was a standard window, most equipped with heavy security bars. The little yards in front of each unit said a little something about the tenants. The family yards were colorful, with yellow Big Wheels and blue pails and red kick balls, bikes with pink tassels, green plastic mowers upturned in the dead grass. One yard had a blue wading pool in front. Shirtless kids in cutoffs darted around and through the pool, screaming like banshees, chasing each other down with water guns.

The yard next door to the pool party was fenced in and showed signs of hard living, all rusted metal and dirty glass. A black and white mutt lay on his back in the dirt, sunning his belly at the foot of a rusted kettle grill. Auto parts, faded beer cans and bottles littered the burnt ground. A folding chair with busted straps lay crooked and sideways next to a damn-sure-to-be empty case of Piels. The door had a hole the shape and size of a steel toed boot some six inches off the ground. Karl rolled by the unit, his attention stuck on the stained sheet covering the front window. He knew all about that sort of decorating. It'd be nailed to the wall inside, or maybe stapled depending on the basehead's calling for neatness. Karl's stomach gurgled but he was not hungry. He rolled on to the back, back to 602.

The grass in the small yard in front of 601/602 was dead and the color of maple saw dust, like the yellow skin on a man whose liver has gone to rot. No amount of water, rain or otherwise, was gonna bring that grass back. On the other hand, the yard was tidy, in so far as it was empty. He pulled over and cut the engine. He bowed his head, folded his hands and pressed them down hard into his lap. He sucked air in through his thick nose.

"Thy will be done. Grant me your mind, not mine." He checked himself in the mirror. He shouldn't be doing this on his own.

Karl locked Alec's truck and made his way up the walk. He had his hand on the knob when he heard Nellie's cry.

"Karl! Karl! Over here!"

She waved at him from the doorway of the next building over, hopping up and down on those sweet honey drumsticks.

"What're you doing over there?" he called back.

She waved him over.

He glanced back at the truck, but decided to leave it. He walked across the yard. Nellie backed into the door and let it close behind her. He followed, reached the door of 801/802 and pulled it open. The entry was empty. A narrow stairway led up to a single door on the second floor. To his right was a door numbered 801. He wasn't so crazy that he didn't hear what he heard. She'd said 602. And where the hell'd she go anyhow?

Don't play fucking games

He had a mind to turn around and give this one up to God.

His feet took him up the stairs to the door of unit 802. Karl pressed the black button under the peephole and heard the bell ring inside. He folded his hands together and rested them on his belly. He shifted on his tired feet, looked down and stuffed his hands deep into his front pockets. Nellie opened the door. She still had on those heels. God, give me the strength to do Thy will. Her belly showed beneath her shirt and that gold ring flashed off her navel, luring him like a spinner bait.

Weak, Godless motherfucker.

⋅→▸═◉ ◉═◂←⋅

Nellie smiled, giddy at the sight of her guest. She clapped her hands to her heart and let out a sigh of relief that echoed down the stairs. She reached for Karl's hands. He had them shoved in his pockets like a bashful little schoolboy.

"Thank God you're here!"

"So, this is your place?" he asked.

"Well, yeah, this is it," she nodded.

"Not 602?" his eyes narrowed.

"My God, Karl! Did you get in a fight?"

"What?" he looked down at his shirt. "Oh, no, nothing like that. We had an accident at work. Hey, I thought you said 602."

"I hope everyone's alright."

"He'll be fine, I think. I got to see him after—"

"Oh Jesus! I'm such a mess!" she moaned. She wrapped her arms around her and squeezed her breasts up from her pink lace bra.

"Alright, it's alright," Karl said. He dropped his eyes like the naughty boy he was.

"Would you look at what I'm doing here?" she waved him inside. "Come in, come in. Shut that will you?" He followed her, closing the door behind him. "Bolt it okay? This isn't Greenwich, you know?"

He threw the bolt. He had blood smeared on the bubbly scars on the back of his head. He turned, shifting his weight from one foot to the other and looked over her shoulder. His breathing was light and quick. He looked terrified. Did something smell in here? She turned and followed his gaze and did a fast inventory. Had she left something out? She turned back to him.

"You okay?" she touched his arm and ran a finger along one of his crude tats.

"That's what I'm supposed to be asking you."

"I'm sorry, I had no one else to call. I'm so fucking crazy, Karl!"

"We all get crazy sometimes," he said with a nod.

"I've never done this before, not exactly," she tapped his forearm. He was here now, here and ready for her. She could give him the whole truth. And he would listen, which seemed so close to being important that she assumed she must just be horny.

"Nellie, you look like you're doing fine. I think I'm gonna go. I got to go see to my boss."

"No!" she grabbed his wrist and pulled him gently. "I mean, please don't do that," she smiled.

"I got to tell you, Nellie, I don't feel quite right about this." He kept his eyes down by her feet.

"Makes two of us."

"No, I don't think you're getting me."

"I believe I'm about to," she let that one trickle on him. He shifted again and then turned for the door.

"Stop!" she cried. He turned but kept his hand on the bolt. "I mean, please stop. I'm sorry. I'm so sorry. You've got to help me. I've been staring down a bottle and the only thing that kept me out of it was waiting on you. Don't go, please. I'll be good."

He sighed and lowered his hand. He turned and looked her in the eye. "Where's it at?"

"It's in the kitchen," she admitted.

"Go get it."

"I, I can't. Will you? I don't want to touch it, not again."

"That way?" he pointed.

"Come," she took his hand and led the way into her kitchen. They stood side-by-side in the doorway and stared at the jug in the middle of the table.

"What's up with the glasses?"

"I thought you might join me. I know, I know, it's crazy. I'm so sorry," her eyes welled up and tears ran down her face. The crying came on her without warning and she lost time. She sat in a chair at the copper table, her face wet and her back to the refrigerator. Karl spoke to her from across the table. His words fell into shape as if they'd shattered in reverse.

"You hearing me? It's the disease. It ain't you."

"I need to excuse myself. Don't go, okay?" she hurried out of the kitchen.

⊷►═◉ ◉═◄⊷

"Why are you whispering?" her sister's voice sounded harsh on the phone.

"I've got a man over," Nellie said, her hand cupped over her mouth.

"A man?"

"Yes, a man."

"Is he..."

"He's fine. He's in the kitchen. I fixed him a drink, though I doubt if he'll—"

"Nell, what are you doing? Where are you?"

"I'm in my bathroom. Peggy, I'm, I'm, I'm thinking bad thoughts, Peggy, very bad thoughts," she whispered, sitting bent over on the edge of her powder blue toilet seat. The waist of her jeans dug into the fold of her belly. The smooth ends of her blond wig cascaded over her forehead and onto her knees. Her hair gave her a wispy comfort.

"Nell, listen to me, you need to tell him to leave. You can't be having men over. You can't."

"Can you come over?"

"Nell—"

"But you have to! I'm losing it here, you know? *I have a hammer!*" she hissed.

"I'm out in the woods here. You're going to have to handle this on your own."

"How can you do that?"

"Do what? I'm not doing anything! You're the one doing things! You're the one with a man in the house and you're the one who's going to ask him, rudely if necessary, to get the fuck out!" Peggy said. She didn't yell. Peggy never yelled. Her sister was cold potatoes, just like the bits in her freezer. She always had been.

"But he's so big, Peggy. He's a big man. You should see him! He's got prison tats and his hands... Huge! And he was a wino, Peggy, a rapist wino and he's in my kitchen and I thought I knew what I was doing but now he's here in my kitchen and I'm all messed up and confused and I want to hurt him so bad and I have the tub all ready and I—"

"You will do nothing of the sort."

"And then he showed up at my door and he seemed to care and I guess I came unglued a little."

"Listen, listen to me," Peggy spoke slowly and methodically. "You are not going to do any of the things that you think you're going to do, okay? You're not and you know it."

"So then he's just going to fuck me?"

"No, you're not doing that either."

"But that I can do."

"We all can do that. No. You're going to hang up this phone. You're going to walk into your kitchen and you're going to tell him to leave. You can be nice if you like. Thank him for coming and tell him you need to be alone."

"But I want to hurt him. I think I can, I really do."

"Sorry, Nell, you're not the type. You're just not."

"Not like you."

"Nope, not like me."

"Why aren't you here?"

"Nell, look, I've got my own thing happening right now."

Nellie raised her head and looked out from beneath her blond canopy, "What thing?"

"The usual."

"Anything interesting?"

"A bitch, I'll tell you about it later. Now get that man out of your place."

"Can I fuck him? I think he wants to."

"Of course he wants to! He's a man isn't he?"

"I think I want to. I think I like him. He raped someone you know. That's why he's here."

"Anyone we know?"

"What? No, 'course not! It was like decades ago and it was some skinny guy."

"So he's gay?"

"No, I don't think so, just drunk. Well, back then at least."

"And you?"

"What?"

"Are you drunk?"

"Do I sound drunk?" Nellie shook her head. "No, I'm totally straight. How do think I got this far?"

"Totally?"

"Yup."

"Then keep it that way. Go tell that man to leave."

"I don't think—" Nellie started, but the connection had been severed. She fixed her wig in the mirror and touched up her mascara with the tip of her quivering finger. She did a passable job. She opened the bathroom door and paused by the bed. She could do this.

She held the hammer and chugged down the hall on her toes. I think I can, I think I can, I think I can...

Chapter Thirty-Five

JONATHAN HELD HIS phone to his ear and propped most of his fanny up on the kitchen counter. Zella's cushion lay untouched near his feet. Outside on the porch, his mother swung in her chair on the deck. She sat in the middle of the love seat with her head back and her arms spread out along the wicker spine, a drink in one hand and a smoke in the other. She kicked her slippered feet for the sky. She exhaled drags from her cigarette on her forward runs. Smoke trailed behind her like steam from an iron locomotive.

Peg finally picked up.

"It's here. You understand?" he cupped his hand over the receiver. "The bird is in the house. I repeat. The bird is in the house."

Peg laughed. He looked at his phone. "You're laughing?"

"Jonathan, you're killing me! But I'm going with it, okay? I think you might actually have a chance at being fun, you know that?"

"This is not fun."

"Well, no, not for everyone," she giggled and then whispered, "I copy. Bird is in the house. Roger that, package in possession. Please validate package contents."

"What? You want me to what?" he hissed.

"Please validate contents, you know, confirm ID," Peg instructed.

"ID confirmed," he muttered.

"Cross-checked?"

"What?"

"Sorry, I'm just messing with you. Listen, I'm running a little behind schedule here."

"What?"

"I'm sorry. It's my sister, family, you know. She's got a little situation."

"And I don't?"

"Jonathan, it's my *sister* and she's in a *situation*. You just have your mom over for a visit."

"Are you kidding me? She's drunk and she wants lunch! That's definitely a situation."

"So? Throw a hot dog at her and let her live it up all she wants."

Jonathan slipped off the counter and stepped in front of the refrigerator. He opened the door, no hot dogs. He shouldered the phone to his ear and took out one bottle at a time and placed them on the counter. First his mother's sloe gin, then her vodka, then the Seven Up, then the Sunny D.

"Maybe we should just call it off," he said. He walked back to the porch door. "Hang on a sec," he held the phone to his chest and slid the door open and stuck his head out. His mother whooshed by on the swing. "Mother, you ready for a refill?" On her next pass, he grabbed the glass from her extended arm. He slid the door shut behind him. "So, yeah, maybe we should just not do this."

"Jonathan, she's there okay? She's there and she's drunk. This whole thing is practically going to play out on its own."

"Maybe we should just forget it."

"Listen, I'm running a little late. That's all this is. We're talking an hour or two, no big deal. I'll bring a pizza with me. In the meantime, just be entertaining."

"That's not so easy."

"Jonathan, feed her drinks and I'll be there soon. Christ, you got to be able to step-up here."

"She's wants me to drink with her, says if I don't she's calling a cab."

"So? Have a drink!" Her tone sounded familiar.

"I can't..."

"Oh, one won't kill you. Make the woman happy, have a drink. I'll be there soon. We'll break bread, eat some pizza."

"You don't get it."

She sighed. "Yes, Jonathan, I get it. Really, I get it. You don't want to drink. You're afraid. I get it, okay? I'll see you in an hour or two, max. Why not do something different today, okay? Be a hero today," she said and hung up.

Jonathan put his phone down and took another tall glass from the cabinet. He mixed two drinks, a syrupy sloe gin fizz for his mother and a strong Sunny Screw for himself. He liked Sunny D better than orange juice. He stared at the drinks on the counter. His mother's voice wobbled through the glass door.

"Is it soup yet?" she cackled.

He prayed.

God, I am Your fearless gladiator. I am an agent of Your peace and Your will. Please give me the strength to see with Your eyes and walk with Your feet. God, I am powerless over alcohol and You know this is not my will. I will trust in Yours. I beg You, help me now. Give me Your strength and protect me from this woman. God protect me.

He took up a glass in either hand and slid open the door. She swung by, complaining out into the yard.

"... in the world can be so important? Get off the horn and *entertain* for God's sake!"

"Let's have a drink," he announced.

She whooped and stopped the swing by dragging her fuzzy slippers. "Now you're talking!" She took the pink glass from him and tipped it at his.

"To a nice visit," she said and raised her glass.

"Yes, Mother," Jonathan wiped his eye and forced a smile. "To quality time," he raised the glass to his lips. She drank deeply from hers, eying him over her brim.

"Well?" she motioned her free palm up and under his glass. "Have at it."

He held the glass close to his chin. The vodka fumes tickled his nostrils and filled him with despair. His hand trembled. She smiled. He touched his lips to the thin edge of the glass, a half moon ice cube bobbed off his upper lip like a frozen fish. He pursed his lips and surrendered with a sip. The vodka burst into his sinuses, followed by a shivery, orange zest. The drink was so very cold! And he drank again, deeper this time and the vodka chill burned down his throat. His mother eyed him, holding her glass just shy of her curled lips.

"Well?" she repeated. "Good, right? Nice right? Am I right?"

She sipped from her glass, pinky extended. She leaned back in the swing, once again resting her arms over the wicker frame. She looked from Jonathan out into the yard and then back at him.

"You see? There is absolutely nothing wrong with you."

"I thought that everything was wrong with me." He was halfway through his drink.

"Not *wrong.* I mean, sure, you do things wrong and you've always said the wrong thing, of course. But *you* aren't wrong. You get me? You aren't wrong. You're just mistaken. It's a mess really. It's, I mean you, that is, is just a messy mess." She stuck her index finger out off her glass and pointed it at him. "That's your problem! You're not an alchy, you're a, you're just a—"

"A mess," he said with a twirl of his ice. He looked over his shoulder at the bottles in the kitchen.

"Yes, exactly! You see?" she turned and shot her feet out and swung.

Jonathan spotted a black squirrel hopping through the tall weeds. Beyond the trees he pictured the lake. God wasn't here at the moment, but He was just a stone's throw away. A stone's throw for God, maybe. Jonathan had no shot of closing the distance. God was out of reach.

Thy will be done, Your will not mine. I am your Gladiator, Our Father Who art in heaven...

Jonathan mouthed his prayer and felt tears welling in his eyes. This was His plan. Have faith in Him. Jonathan sucked down the rest of his drink. The afternoon sun fell weakly on the yard. The morning's brilliant green was gone. The tall weeds and pines and scraggly poplars and maples looked dull and worn. He wiped his eyes.

"Speaking of messes," she pointed a toe at the yard.

"Mother, ready for another?" he asked. He was ready for another. This wasn't cocktail hour. This was the mission. This was His will. This was the mission.

"Oh, I should think so, yes," she said sweetly and extended her glass to him.

"I think we should make good use of this afternoon, Mother."

She swung by, her eyes on the yard as she spoke, "Something's not right here."

"Really?"

"Yes," she slowed the swing and looked up at him. "Where's the mutt?"

"Zella's gone, Mother."

"Run off did she? She was always a fickle bitch."

"No, Mother, I put her down today, remember?"

"You did?"

"Yes, that's why you're here—" he slapped his hand over his mouth.

"Whatdyamean?"

"I mean, um, what do I mean?" he scratched his head. "I mean I wanted you here for company. I was so upset about Zella, you know."

"What'd you do, shoot her?"

"No, I didn't shoot her!" he snapped. He shut his eyes and took a breath. "I mean no, I had a vet come to the house. She was very um, caring, very professional. As a matter of fact I—"

"So you had someone else kill your dog? You pay money for that?"

"Well yes, no, but listen, I really got along with this woman. So I, I, I invited her to come over for a drink and maybe, um, dinner," he waved at his mother. "No big thing, just a get-to-know-you, um, thing," he shrugged.

"I'm sorry, what? Did you just say you invited a woman over?"

"Yes, I did. It'll be fun."

His mother cackled. "You invited a dog killer over for fun? Was it fun the first time?"

"Mother, really, there's no need to—"

"I don't believe this! This is why I'm here? You wanted me to meet some beastly mortician you've got your eye on?"

"No Mother, it's not like that. And she's not a mortician, she's a, a... Her name is Peg. And I don't have my eye on her! She's just coming over to be," he stumbled, "I mean to help me, um... She's just coming over to, you know, break bread with us, okay?"

"What's this? Break bread? What're we, Jewish?"

Jonathan ran back into the kitchen, sliding the door slowly behind him. He put the glasses down and gripped the counter with both hands. He lowered his head, breathed and counted to ten. His grip on the counter hurt his fingers and he counted to ten again. He reached for a bottle. He'd poured before remembering the ice. He fetched a few cubes and dropped them in each glass. His sipped his mother's off the brim and took a gulp of his own. He twitched his head from side to side, straightened his back and shoulders. Whether it was the vodka or God, he was ready for the arena. He slid the door open with his elbow and came out swinging.

"How about you and I get honest about a few things? What do you say, Mother?" he held her drink out for her as he slurped at his Sunny Screw.

She huffed and took a pull from her glass. "By all means, Johnny."

"You, Mother, are an alcoholic."

She rolled her eyes.

"You are also miserable and your misery makes you nasty."

"Oh really?" she scoffed.

"And you act as if the world owes you. And you're stingy and you're mean and, and, and I've had enough!"

"That it?"

"And you need to be in those meetings, Mother. You need to be in those meetings! And you know what else? I've had it with you! I've fucking had it!"

"This is the mouth you use with your mother?"

"This is the mouth I use with this fucking disease!"

She swung on by.

"Oh please, disease! It's no disease. It's weakness. That's all it is. It's your weakness. And if you grow a backbone, you'll manage. And if you don't, you're right, it'll kill you. Just like it killed your father." She paused, stewing with her eyes closed. "But make no mistake, it's not the alcohol that does the killing. It's the shame. You want to be ashamed for taking a drink, go ahead. I chose to be fine with it thank you very much."

"You're not fine with it."

"Says who, Jonathan, you? As usual, you have no clue what you're talking about."

"I think I do, Mother."

"That's your problem."

He took another slug of his Sunny Screw and raised his glass to her. "Yeah, I know about my problem. At least I'm straight up about it. I've learned that much in The Rooms."

"Nobody's straight about anything in that room."

"Speak for yourself, Mother. Everyone tells it like it is in there. It's what it's all about! The First Step!"

"Sorry to burst your bubble, not true at all," she said.

"How would you know?"

"Jonathan, believe me, I know."

"No, come on, what makes you so sure?" He was slurring a little.

She hit the brakes on the swing and glared up at him.

"Okay fine, you want sure? Here's sure, you little prick. Your uncle's in that room. How's that for sure?"

"What? What the hell are you talking about?"

"You know the cop?"

"Officer Joe?"

"Yeah, Officer Joe," she said with a sneer in her voice. "He used to be just plain Joey. He's your uncle. It's a fact. Go ahead and ask him. Though, knowing him, he'll probably deny it. How's that for honesty?"

She pushed off with her slippers and set herself in motion.

"Did he ever lift a finger to help me raise you? No!" she yelled as she swung by, "And has he ever said anything to you? No! He's just another good-for-nothing hypocrite spouting off all his AA gobbledygook! He's a shit. A shit, through and through, a shit like the rest of them."

She gained momentum.

"It's a crime is what it is, sucking the life out of people and making them feel like shit about themselves and talk about their daily reminders and their gratitude for a fucking hard world. Grateful! Right! We should all be grateful. Hey, I bet that little twerp from the back seat is still having a hard time feeling grateful for that, that, that monster corn-holing him, don't you think? Or do you think it's what all-merciful God had in store for him? One day God in His mercy looked down on that man and said, 'I think My poor lost lamb needs some gratitude. Hmmm, what to do, what to do… I know! He could use a good, stiff corn-holing!'"

"Mother, what are you—"

She thrust her feet forward in anger and locked her elbows behind the chair back. Her raspy voice came at him loud and then flew off into the yard.

"One Day At a Time, right Johnny? I mean, from that moment on that twerp knew - without a shadow of a doubt, mind you - a good day from a bad one, right? Have a good one, right? Isn't that what everyone says? Have a good one! Well, I know I'll have a good one, and nobody's going to have to rape me or shame me to know it. Fuck your program, Johnny boy."

"Mother, you're—"

"Raving? Is that what you're gonna say? You wanted to have it out right? You want to have the big airing, right? Well here it is you fat turd, ready or not. You want me to get with the program? Quit drinking? For what? So I can sit and spout off feel-good lies like your dear Uncle Joey? No thank you, not for me."

She tilted her head back and drained her glass. "You think you know so much!" she slurred, pink gin running across her cheek. "You think you suffer so much! you! with this roof over your head and no job and no talent and, and, and, ah... Fuck it!" She threw her glass out into the yard.

"I have a job," he muttered. Drunk and desperate, he could think of only one thing to do. "Get you another, Mother?"

"You bet your fat ass," she hooted.

Jonathan retreated into the house and slid the door shut with a heavy thud. He unscrewed the cap off the vodka and poured his glass full, adding a splash of Sunny D for color. He shut his eyes and slugged.

He choked on his vodka at the loud crack and thunderous clatter. Outside the door, his mother's feet splayed out sideways above the upended chair swing. She lay on her back, facing skyward, her head flat on the deck.

"Oh my God!" Jonathan left his glass on the counter. He yanked open the door.

"Mother! Mother? Can you hear me?" He knelt down and scooped her head in his hand. Blood slid through his fingers like burger grease. Her eyes blinked rapidly and then stayed open.

"I...I...I," she stammered.

"Mother, you're bleeding!"

"I fell."

"Oh God! Get you inside," he said as he lifted her.

"Jeba! Caresull!"

"I'm being careful, Mother." He backed in the door and set her down on Zella's cushion. "Towel and ice, towel and ice," Jonathan scanned the kitchen, towel first, towel comes first.

"How...how... how could you?" she groaned and then she was out.

Chapter Thirty-Six

NELLIE JACKED HIM in the back of his head and knocked God right out his mind. His old mind shouted out some hard truths.

Truth was, if a motherfucker monkeyed you in the back of the head and didn't put your lights out, then your eyes snap open looking for payback. Truth was, pray all you want, walk those twelve steps up and down all you want, but if a cunt jacks you from behind, she's heading for shadowland.

Karl fell back into the darkness and did what came natural; he ducked and shoved his chair back over her toes. He threw his elbow behind him into her saggy gut. She doubled over and he peeled the hammer out of her grip.

`God dropped the hammer to the tile floor.`

Things evened up, but his mind burned with a fury so hot that it singed his God mind into ash. Karl stood up fast, pushing the chair back into her. He was woozy and he felt blood roll down the back of his neck. His fists were hard and jumpy. He caught her on the temple with a right cross and Nellie fell to her knees, cowering. She sobbed but he didn't have much of a feel for what her pains might be.

"Are you fucking crazy?" he shouted. Nellie whimpered some damn thing and that just turned his mind a deeper red. "Speak up, bitch."

"Rapist," she sputtered.

"What?"

She spit on the floor. There wasn't any blood and he wasn't surprised. He didn't hear anything crack when he caught her with the elbow. He just winded her a bit. The thing was, you didn't feel the same shame when you hit a bitch a second time. The first shot could be rough, especially if you weren't really meaning for it to happen from the get go.

Truth was, if the first one lands in her gut or her tit and there's no snap, and no blood comes up, then that's a clean communication. Truth was, if the bitch is dense, or isn't hearing the message, well, that's a different story.

The whole of it was like riding a bike and Karl's old mind only knew enough not to hit her in the mouth. Hit a woman in the mouth and they just tended to get more mouthy, which was funny in a certain way that he knew wasn't right, but then again, it was funny all the same.

Course, the snap inside you wasn't funny at all. You feel that broken soul and you know for a fact that you are the lowest of the low, a cowardly worm with no business calling yourself a child of God or of your own mother for that matter. And maybe it didn't happen every time, but it happened enough to notice that you always had your mother in mind when that shame ripped through your insides. But then you hit again because the rage has you, all of you, and it wants its meat. So you forget about the face rule and knock a tooth across the room so it lands somewhere unusual, in a place teeth aren't meant to be found, like on top of the refrigerator or in your work boot, except you don't know that till later when she's in the other room moaning and you're in the front hall slipping on your boots and something's up in there by your toe and you might just leave it there to see if you can make peace with it rather than have to untie the triple knots you just tied, but you sigh and undo your boot laces and pull it out. And you see it's a tooth, her tooth, and you roll it in your fingers and it fucks you up worse because you laugh at it a little even though you know damn well that laughing is God awful business for certain.

Nellie got her feet under her and stood up, hammer in hand.

"Rapist pig fucker!" she screamed and swung at him.

Karl dipped and countered with another wallop to her temple with the meat of his left palm. Her scalp seemed to slip off as she dropped back down on her knees. And when he made sense of the wig his old mind sputtered and cooled.

Nellie knelt drooling on the floor with her hair all sideways on her head and Karl felt God wetting up that smoldering ash in his mind and molding it back into some semblance of Himself. He'd taken his will back in a bad way, in a way that brought the shame like the forty days of rain, a flood of hatred that he had stored for himself, hatred that ran in underworld rivers just for him. A hatred he'd kept dry in his bones and feeble in God's light until now, until today, when the light when out and he took his will back and he could no longer be denied his shame.

"Karl," Nellie lifted up her empty hands. A few fingernails were missing. "I'm sorry, Karl."

"Me too, I'm sorry too. God knows I truly am." He slapped the wig off the back of her head and she slumped onto tile floor and now there was some blood. Not much, but he saw the steady little drops the moment she lifted her chin.

"You need to stop, Karl. You need to stop now," she sputtered. He squared himself to her, fists ready.

"Don't you get up," was all he could figure to say.

He stood still as a pine. His God mind had hold of him, his mouth, his muscles all of him. Nellie got up on her knees. She wedged her hands between her legs and swayed her head, a patchwork of black scabs and red wispy tufts. Karl's tears soothed his itchy eyes.

Dear God, give me strength to do Thy will.

"I'm sick okay? I know it. You know it. We all know it! I lie. I told you I lie! I told everyone I lie! So what's the big surprise? I had plans for you, big plans. Now you're just going to fuck me, right? You're just going to strip me down and fuck me!" Nellie sobbed.

"I'm not gonna do nothing of the sort."

"Oh bullshit! Fuck it, you hear? Fuck it and cover me up and feed them hogs." Nellie looked up, aimed her buzzing eyes straight at his but missed; missed his rage, missed his shame, missed everything. "I can't, I can't be here anymore. I can't be me anymore. Just do me a favor you fucking good-for-nothing monster! Just get it over with!" She dropped her face in her hands and her shoulders shook.

Karl's fists opened like he was dropping stones.

"Oh my God. Let me get you something. You, you lay still now."

Karl hurried to the sink and grabbed a handful of paper towels and then opened the freezer. The ice try was wedged behind a shoebox labeled "Karl

8/06." He pushed the box aside to get at the ice. Little boxes tumbled onto the floor; a couple lost their tops. He stepped over a little freeze-dried mushroom and slammed the ice tray on the counter. He gathered the cubes in the wad of paper towels. He knelt by her side and set the ice on the back of her head. She flinched.

"Easy, it's just ice. It's going sting at first, then it's gonna get better." He dabbed her head gently with the ice. "Then it's gonna get better," he whispered.

"You see your box?"

"God'll help us both. We just got to let Him," Karl said.

"I can't help it," she sat herself up.

"Whoa, easy, stay put now."

"I can't," she sobbed and spat blood on the floor. He looked down into the little puddle that mercifully gave no reflection.

"I'm so sorry, Nellie, I'm a bad man, but I'm trying, I'm—"

And then he was there on the floor looking up at her and he knew he was not himself and he thought he heard a scream and he tried to tell her he had to get back to Marcus because he promised his son he would and he couldn't let him down this time and besides he wanted to be sure Marcus knew this wasn't what he was thinking it was at all and he was sure he was saying all this but the truth was he was long gone.

⋯▬◉ ◉▬⋯

"Don't you ever do something like this again!" Peggy dropped the hammer by his head. "Now move your ass, he's getting all over the place!"

Nellie's palms slipped in Karl's blood but she got herself up and ran to the bathroom for towels.

When she returned with all her bleached white hand towels, Peggy stood in her scrubs with her hands on her hips.

"He needs a stopper," Peggy said and pointed to the hole in his skull. "Stuff one in there."

Nellie did as instructed. She plugged a towel into the warm wet hole with the tip of her finger. Her finger bumped against something soft and she pulled it out, leaving the towel behind. Blood soaked the towel red.

"Gotta love that capillary action," Peggy said and then turned to look her over, "You're a bloody mess."

"Am I?" Nellie rubbed a knuckle under her eye. She felt sticky all over.

"Help me get him in the tub," Peggy ordered and blew an exasperated breath. "I'll take his feet."

They took Karl from either end, tried to lift him and settled for dragging. Peggy led the way out the kitchen and down the hall. They slid him over the wood floor and onto the tiles of the bathroom. They hoisted his torso up the side of the tub, his neck lolled backward. The soaked towel dislodged and dropped into the tub. They rolled him up and over into the tub.

"Will you do it?" Nellie asked.

"Fuck you."

"I, I don't think I can do it."

"You're the one with the big, bold man killing ideas," Peggy sniffed in disgust. "I got to go. I'm taking a shirt." Peggy stripped off her bloody scrub top. "You've got a serious mess to deal with," she said and stomped out of the bathroom.

"I'll clean it!" Nellie squealed.

"You better," Peggy called from her room. "Find his keys before you start the soup."

"You're really going?"

"I'd say you're pretty lucky I got here at all," Peggy said from the doorway wearing Nellie's favorite blue blouse, the one with the sequins on the collars and a long change pocket sewn to the front, great for a lip liner or a Baggie, or both. "You're lucky you're not dead. Now, find his keys and don't use all the lye. I'll do you a favor and deal with his car."

Nellie dug in Karl's front pockets. She found his key ring and tossed it to Peggy, "Truck."

"What?"

"He drives a pickup," Nellie explained. A skull scab itched and she scratched it pensively. "Yeah, it was a pickup."

"Car, truck, whatever, the point is he drove here and he's not driving out so we have to take care of that for him. I'll be back after dark."

Nellie tugged at Karl, but he refused to roll onto his back. "Oh, shit, I don't think I can get it. I can't."

Nellie wept and her tears dropped onto his soupy red shirt. She shoved him sideways and there was a gurgle and a wheeze from the tear in the top of his skull. She puked in her mouth and swished the thick briny bile around before swallowing it back down. She heard Peggy's rubber souls pad up beside her.

"Here, let me," Peggy said and pressed Nellie aside with a finger on her shoulder. Peg bent over and hauled Karl up by his shoulders, and then dropped him back down with a hard thunk, flat on his back. "Now that wasn't so hard, was it?" She unfastened his belt, unbuttoned his jeans and yanked and yanked until she'd pulled them clear. His undies slipped down easy and there it was.

"Well?" Peggy pulled it upward, gripping the knob of it between her thumb and finger.

"Hmm?"

"Do you have a knife? Or, better yet, just get your poultry shears."

"I have a box too."

"Great," was Peggy's flat reply.

Nellie stared and waited for someone to do something that would help move things along a little because things had just moved a little sideways on her and it seemed like there was something that required tending to but what that something was stumped her.

"Hello? Nellie? Off you go now," Peggy shooed her along with her free hand.

Nellie hustled into the kitchen, which was an utter disaster, but no matter, she'd have at it shortly. Maybe she could do this after all, maybe she could hold it for Peggy, help her lop it off right at the base. She scratched her scalp, which was itching like a son-of-a-bitch for some reason, and thought that that was very doable. She hopscotched her way back between the pools and rivers, holding the shears out to her side for safety's sake.

Chapter Thirty-Seven

THANKS TO THE damn traffic, Eddie limped into the dim light of Madigan's close to 4:00, blinking and ready for a cold one. His knee still bugged him, grinding despite the better weather. Must be more rain on the way. His eyes adjusted and he stepped up to the bar. Sandra greeted him from the far end with a wink and a smile. Eddie sat in the nearest empty stool, pushing it sideways to give himself some elbow-room. He sat between a couple of regular guys, one with mechanic's coveralls, the other wearing a blue wife-beater. Eddie'd left his jacket and tie in the car.

He rolled up the sleeves of his monogrammed YSL oxford and nodded to the men. The mechanic nodded back. The wife beater looked away, to his right, in the direction Sandra and the TV, high up on the wall. The tree of beer taps in the way, Eddie leaned back in his stool to get a better look at his girl. She was chatting with an old timer at the far corner of the bar, half-sitting in her tiny pink shorts on top of a stainless steel beer cooler, her right leg extended over the runner. Eddie sat up in his stool to get an unobstructed view of her smooth calf, tattooed ankle and sandaled foot. Eddie squinted, trying to make it out. She turned and caught him in mid stare.

"Well look who's here!" she called. She lifted her foot off the well and rolled her ankle slowly. "It's a dolphin."

"I like it," said Eddie.

"Me too," said the mechanic.

"Miss," Eddie beckoned her. "Do you folks serve beer in this establishment?"

She pushed off the cooler and strutted her long legs down the rubber runner. She wore a white T-shirt, the V-neck torn at the apex, her tits bursting through.

Her jet black hair was pulled back in a long, shiny ponytail. Eddie took a breath and looked down at his hands. His comfort fit wedding band was yellow gold, just like Amy's. Sandra stopped in front of the beer taps.

"Same way, handsome?"

"Same way."

"You're here," she poured Harps into a pint glass.

"Is that a problem? Do I get a demerit or something?"

"Ha! Hardly," she placed the glass in front of him and leaned over it, her chin hovering above the head. He leaned toward her, until they were nearly nose-to-nose.

"I have a treat for us," she whispered.

"So I've been told. What is it?"

"You'll see. You just sit back and enjoy a few. I'll let you know," she bounced her eyebrows and grinned at him before straightening up. She clapped her hands and addressed the mechanic.

"You ready for another, Mike?"

"Been ready, Sandra. Been here dying for one while you're down there bullshitting with old Bob down there."

"You mean down there-down there? You poor man," Sandra reached for the mechanic's glass. Eddie put a hand over his mouth at the luscious sight before him. She spoke while she refilled the mechanic's glass from the PBR tap.

"Still have that ring on, I see," she pouted.

"Yup."

"Let me see it," Sandra said.

Eddie held his hand straight up, fingers extended. She slid the mechanic his beer and before Eddie knew it, his hand was in hers.

"It's a nice ring, Eddie. Do you like it?"

"Not lately."

"Really? Then why wear it?" she looked him in the eye. "Wow, you have big hands, you know that? So smooth, too," she trailed her index finger over his knuckles.

Time hiccupped. Eddie shifted in his seat. His boxers were getting grabby.

"Mhmm," he agreed.

"You poor man," she grinned, released his hand and walked away.

Eddie sat up straight on his stool and lifted his beer. He downed a third of the glass, took a breath and downed another third. What little he tasted, tasted fine indeed. He set his glass back on the bar.

"That's a tigress right there," the mechanic spoke in a low tone.

"Sandra?"

"Eat you alive, just look at those... Shit, I'm telling you what."

Eddie followed the man's gaze to Sandra's legs at the far end of the bar.

"Used to be this place was dead. Pretty much just be me and old Bob down there and old man Madigan dolling out the booze. Now look at it, place is packed," the mechanic grumbled.

Eddie took a quick headcount, eight swinging dicks, no women.

"Now we get a crowd. It's alright I guess. She's good for business. There's no denying."

"She seems real nice," Eddie said. A workingman clipped his adverbs. And he was just another workingman, working for a living, just like Mike the mechanic here. Nobody in Madigan's was looking for alignment or synergies.

"Oh she's sweet alright. She sweetens right up," Mike took a pull from his glass. "She loves a good suit."

"Come again?"

"You know, she likes the rich ones."

Eddie shook his head and chuckled, "don't they all?"

Mike turned to eye him up and down. "Guess you'd be the one to know," he said and tipped his glass at him. Mike took another long pull and turned away to the TV, wedged up under the ceiling in the far corner by old Bob's end of the bar.

Eddie flushed. He finished off the rest of his beer. He set the glass down at the same time Sandra set down a fresh one. He hadn't even seen her coming this time. She winked and walked off again, without a word. Eddie peered over toward Mike the mechanic. His glass was empty. Eddie reached in his pocket and pealed a twenty from his money clip. He caught Sandra's eye immediately.

"How about a round for these gentlemen here, my good lady?"

Mike stayed fixed on Judge Judy.

"I'm all set, thanks buddy," said the wife beater.

"Me too," said Mike.

"Oh come on boys, he's kind enough to offer, least you could do is accept," Sandra said. She was already at the tap filling three glasses.

"If you insist, sweetness," Mike lifted his new beer off the bar. "Who'm I thanking?"

The wife beater took his and said nothing.

"Eddie Musso."

"Thanks, Eddie."

"And yours?"

"Mike."

"And yours?" Eddie turned to the wife beater, who remained silent.

"That's Sean. He's not much of a talker."

Sean grunted and drank.

"Well, it's my pleasure gentlemen. You from around here, Mike?"

"Am now, grew up in Pelham."

"I'm originally from Binghamton," Eddie said.

"Cold up there," Mike muttered, distracted.

"You got that right. We'd burn wood from September to May, cords of it every season. I split more logs than a fuckin' lumberjack. My father was a pipe fitter," Eddie volunteered, "A real hard ass."

"Aren't they all?" Mike said. "Would you look at that thing?" Down the bar, Sandra reached down into the beer fridge. Her firm, round ass stuck up in the air. With the exception of old Bob, the men at the bar paused to stare, with their drinks temporarily suspended.

The drinks flowed fast and steady and soon it felt like a weekend indeed. Even the wife beater's grunts turned from disdain to morbid amusement when poor old Bob got tangled up in his stool and tripped and fell through the men's room door.

"Is he okay?" Eddie asked Sandra on her next trip back to set him up.

"Bob? oh, he's fine. Doesn't feel a thing that guy. He's clumsy as all hell. I cut him off the first time I saw him fall out of his stool. He bitched such a blue streak, all screaming and yelling that he owned the goddam place and he'd have my goddam job and blah, blah, blah. So I got nervous and called Madigan. Turns out Bob does own the place, a piece of it at least, so that's that. That man should not drink though, that's for sure. He's a total spazz."

Eddie laughed.

"So are you ready to take a break with me?" she grinned.

"Uh, sure. What do you got in mind?"

"Circle around back, I'll see you out there."

"Now?"

"Five minutes," she leaned forward, tits bulging on her forearms. "Don't be late," she warned and then sauntered down the bar.

"Go get'm, Tiger," Mike said and tipped his glass.

Eddie walked out the door into the yellowing light of late afternoon. He closed his eyes and tilted his face slightly to meet the sun. Nothing, not one goddam thing in this world was more wonderful, more sublime than walking out of a bar into daylight. Not the light of dawn, dawn was bad, unless it was like a bachelor party or some other reasonable excuse. This was the perfect light, the perfect time of year, the perfect time of day for a liquid summer's eve.

He checked his watch. It was only 5:25! He'd leave in an hour and be home in plenty of time, even with the tail end of rush hour. Then it was daddy time at Maggy's thing, sporting a nice, mellow buzz. He hung a right, walked along the front of the bar to the side alley. He peeked down the alley, no Sandra yet. He pulled his Dingleberry from the pocket of his khakis.

"Hey honey," Eddie cupped the mouthpiece with his hand.

"Hi, babe. On your way home?"

"Almost, a few loose ends to tie up and I'll be out of here." A horn sounded, then two more. He covered the phone and swore silently. He put it back to his ear.

"Where are you?"

"I just had some shopping to do."

"What?"

"You know, flowers for the ballerina."

"Nice. She'll love that."

"I have a couple emails to send out then I'm off. I'll make better time after some of the traffic clears out anyhow."

"Who's still working? Don't you people know it's the weekend?"

"It's still business hours for the California boys."

"Oh yeah, right. Well hurry home. We need to get Maggy there by 7:30."

"Okay, Ames, will do. Love you!"

"Bye babe."

Done. Beautiful. Mental note - buy flowers. He stuffed the phone back in his pocket and stepped out of the sun into the alley. The bar's backdoor opened and Sandra appeared.

"Hi handsome."

"Hi yourself," he said with a nod, as if he had a hat to tip. She pointed to the metal door near his foot.

"We're going down there, come on."

Sandra opened the trap door and descended. Eddie followed her down the steep iron stairs. The stock room was filled wall-to-wall with cases of beer and booze. She turned as he made it to the concrete floor. There wasn't much room to spare among all the boxes and they stood face to face. She smiled at him as she fingered inside the change pocket of her tight shorts.

"I really hope I got you right," she wagged a brown vial between her thumb and finger. It was the longer size, the kind that comes with the folding spoon for a top.

"Hold my hair," she ordered and tilted her head.

"Aren't you something?" Eddie smiled, her black hair felt silky, her neck warm.

She scooped a heaping spoonful up each nostril in quick succession. This was not her first rodeo. She reloaded and held it out for him. He leaned forward. She positioned the spoon under his nostril and used her other hand as a safety net.

"Go."

He snorted. The coke lit up his sinus with bitter sparkles.

"Go."

He snorted again, up the other side. He stood up straight and sniffed largely, filling his lungs and feeling the powder run its course, up his face, curl under his brain and touch the back of his throat. And he felt good, better than good.

And she smiled at him and he smiled back. And he twitched his head without meaning to and his stomach rumbled. And she was into him and he had a great deal to say.

"That's good bink," he managed.

They obviously had a connection, something more than just physical attraction. She was someone he could talk to. He could see that. It wasn't the beers or the blow. He knew it was something far more profound, on a level that was deeper than he would have thought possible given how little they knew of each other. She was someone that he could relate to on a plane of truth, real truth, not the managed truth of business or marriage or parenting or, or, or suburbing. He pinched his nose, got a good vacuum going, let go and snorted deeply.

"I say again, this is some serious shit."

"I have a good friend. He's big in the business."

"Well, he sells a quality product."

"The best. I'm so happy you partake."

"Listen, Sandra, there's something I've got to say to you. But I'm not sure how you're going to take it. You know, I don't want you to think I'm some kind of flake or something. But I feel like there's something between us."

"Why, Eddie, you're a married man," she scolded.

"Believe me, I know. And you're hot, very hot and it's hard to keep my hands off you, but it's more than that. You're like a kindred spirit, you know? Are you feeling any of this or is it just me? Am I making a total fool out of myself?"

"No, no you're not," she stepped closer. He felt the warmth and fullness of her breasts right through his shirt. She put a finger to his lips and his insides boiled.

"I've got to go," she whispered.

She stepped by him and climbed up the stairs. At the top she turned and smiled at him, beaming over the curve of her tanned ass, "We'll come back."

"I feel like a dope," he admitted.

"Oh my God, don't. If you only knew."

"Knew what?"

"Later, shut the door after you, okay?" She stepped out of sight.

The bar had cleared out some. The mechanic and wife beater were gone. Eddie had the end of the bar all to himself. He sat on his stool buzzing hard and feeing as if he were in motion. His top teeth and lips were pleasantly numb. He scraped at his upper lip with the rough edges of his bottom teeth. On the TV, good old Vanna White walked the white-checkered wall.

Sandra placed a draft in front of him. He reached for it. She touched his hand and beckoned him to come closer.

"Now I'll tell you something," Sandra said. He turned his ear toward her lips. "My pussy is so wet for you right now," she whispered.

He drew back to look her in the eye.

"I'm going insane," she pouted.

Eddie had no reply. Her pout turned into a grin.

"I just thought you should know," she said and made her way back down to the other end of the bar. She looked over her shoulder once before addressing Old Bob. "Ready for another one, honey?"

Eddie couldn't contain his stupefied grin. Real people didn't actually say shit like that. All that stuff in Penthouse was made up so that horny adolescents could bust a nut in their mother's bathroom. He downed his beer.

Drink, drink, sniff, sniff, bink, bink. Blink.

Sandra moaned in the dark, leaning forward, her hands on the iron stairs and her shorts hooked around one ankle. Eddie thrust into her from behind, one hand pulling her head back by her hair, the other holding his shirttail out of the way. She turned and glared at him.

"Harder!" she cried. "Harder! That's right, that's right. Oh no, don't you dare cum!"

He blew sweat off the tip of his nose and held back as best he could until she started to scream.

"Oh yes! Fuck me baby! Harder! That's it! Now!"

He gave one final thrust forward before pulling back and out of her, nearly tripping over his pants. She watched him from over her shoulder as he pointed himself at the floor.

"Jesus!" he groaned and shuddered.

Sandra climbed up the stairs, panting. She pushed open the trap door and made her way back down. Eddie sucked at the fresh air. The little hotbox cooled off. His oxford shirt was soaked through, translucent. He bent down over shaky thighs and pulled up his khakis.

"Oh my God, you are so hot, Eddie."

"Holy shit, you, you, holy shit," he stammered.

His felt a buzzing inside his pocket. He took out his Dingleberry. Eight missed calls, all from Amy. It was 8:20! Maggy!

"What's wrong?"

"I'm fucked."

"I believe that's my line," she said with a chuckle.

"No, that was Amy. I was supposed to be back already."

"Oh boy, okay," Sandra stood and shimmied into her white panties scattered with tiny red polka dot hearts. "Wow, these are soaked," she pulled them off and pulled on her shorts. "Bare backing," she laughed and slapped his arm. "Hey, cheer up. We'll figure it out. Don't worry so much. Things happen, you know? Traffic accidents, emergencies, old friends showing up out of the blue, work stuff, all kinds of things. Here," she tossed her panties at him, "you deserve a trophy."

Eddie caught them, "very funny."

"No seriously, take'em for now, okay? I have nowhere to put them and I don't want to lose them. They're nice."

Eddie pocketed them. "Listen, I've got to call her. I got to get going."

"Baby, you're already late. What's done is done, right? So you're a little late? What's the big deal? It's not like she's in the hospital or anything. You're out with the boys. It's Friday night."

"I missed my kid's recital."

"Oh... Maggy, right?" she paused. "Well, there'll be others. Bring her something nice. You work hard, she'll understand." Sandra spooned a blast up her nose. She dug out another heap and held it up for Eddie. He snorted, the blow dazzling his vision. The taste hit the back of his throat and things seemed more manageable.

"I still gotta call. I can't just go M.I.A."

"M.I.A.?"

"Missing in action," Eddie said.

"I got to get back to the bar before they start swilling out of the taps."

"Be up in a bit."

"I hope so," she rubbed up against him, her t-shirt catching slightly against his half buttoned oxford. "Baby, it's early. We have party favors. It's Friday, TGIF, right?"

She kissed him, licking his top lip and turned to go. He followed the pendulum of her ass up the stairs.

"I'll see you in a bit," he promised.

⟶▣◎ ◎▣⟵

"Amy?" Eddie said. He leaned his elbow on the top stair and peered up into the dim alley.

"Where are you? I've called you like ten times!"

Eddie held the phone from his ear, "I know, I'm so sorry."

"Sorry? sorry? You missed the recital! You missed the goddam recital and you didn't even call," her voice shook. "How's that even possible? How do you miss your own daughter's dance recital? Where the hell are you?"

"I'm stuck in the office."

"Oh bullshit, Eddie. I called the office. I called your phone. Nothing."

"I wasn't in my office," he wiped his nose with a finger that smelled sweetly of Sandra.

"Now you're changing your story?" Amy shrieked.

"I'm not changing any story. I'm trying to explain to you what happened. You want to listen or what?" Eddie sniffed.

"You sound funny."

"Yeah well, I'm pissed. You think I'm happy?"

"No, you're voice sounds funny. What have you been doing?"

"Working," he grunted. He looked at his cum on the cement floor.

"Eddie?" she implored, her voice rising an octave within his name.

"What?"

"What are you up to?"

"What are you talking about?"

"You sound funny."

"Jesus Christ, Amy!" Eddie cupped the phone, took a deep breath and cleared his throat. "Why don't you just say what you want to say?"

"You sound like you've been doing lines."

"Are you kidding me?" He flushed.

"Well, that's what you sound like."

"You're nuts you know that? Nuts. Here I am, dealing with a shit storm on a Friday night and you accuse me of that? What's with you?" He tried not to yell.

"Don't you turn this on me."

"Would you just listen a minute? I was stuck in Wittenberg's office, okay?" he sighed. "Some fucking sales rep went psycho, went walking into the Region Four office waving a gun and making threats."

Silence.

"What?" she sounded stunned.

"Some psycho walked into the regional V.P.s office brandishing a '45 and demanding a raise."

"Oh my God..."

"The R.V.P. settled the guy down enough - salesman that he is - anyway, apparently he got him to pocket the gun and sit down. Fed him a drink or two and got him to talking. Meantime, he texts his admin and had everyone clear out of the office. That's how I heard it from Wittenberg, anyway." He took a breath.

"Where's this?"

"I told you, Region Four office, San Diego."

"Oh thank God! I thought you meant there."

"No. Oh no, sorry honey, this was all going down out in Cali. So anyway, the guy's calm but he won't let up on Jeff."

"Jeff?"

"The Region Four V.P."

"Oh."

"So Jeff says, 'listen, you want me to call someone in Corporate, see what they can do?' The guy agrees and Jeff gets a hold of Wittenberg, who calls me in."

"Why you?"

"Bad luck," he scoffed. "I was just walking by his office when he waved me in. He's hanging on the phone looking like he'd seen a fucking ghost, so, of course I walk in to see what's up. I couldn't, like, duck the guy." Eddie reached into a case of Budweiser at the top of the stack.

"Of course," she paused a moment, "but... weren't you already gone?"

"Yeah well, that's the kicker. I'd already left for the day! I stopped on the Avenue, bought Maggy's flowers, and was just about to head home, when I realized I'd forgot my goddam brief case!"

"Oh, Eddie," Amy said. Eddie pulled out a warm bottle of Bud. He gripped it between his legs and twisted off the top. He took a sip and continued, waving the bottle in the air.

"So, like a sap, I swing back into the garage, run back up for my briefcase and that's when Wittenberg hijacks me. I left my phone in the car. It was going to take me two seconds!" He shook his head in disbelief.

"So what happened?" she asked.

"So for the next, what?" Eddie spilled the beer checking his watch, "two hours, me and Wittenberg are talking to this freaking lunatic. And he's going on and on about how he's getting the shaft and how he's barely making ends meet and all the hours he's putting in."

"Hmm."

"Yeah, no kidding. That's what I'm thinking."

"So..."

"So we let him vent and vent and finally he starts blubbering and Wittenberg and I are looking at each other and he writes me a note to call the San Diego P.D."

"You hadn't already done that?"

"Well, actually we didn't do it at all. A second later Wittenberg gets a text from Jeff saying no cops. He'd handle it."

"*What?*"

"I guess he didn't want to make any waves, just wanted the guy to calm down and leave."

"Eddie, you have to call the cops."

"Yeah, that's what I said, but Wittenberg wouldn't have it. So I just sat there. It was horrible. I was sitting there just waiting to hear a fucking gunshot, you know? I mean, I sweat through my shirt! Literally, I'm soaking wet right now. Anyway, eventually the guy let Jeff back on and Jeff tells us he'll work it out from there and that everything's cool. Probably just to keep the guy, you know, under wraps. Hell, we didn't know what to do. So Wittenberg hangs up and we sit there looking at each other. Then Wittenberg picks up the phone and calls the G.C. on his cell phone. He tells us to sit tight."

"The G.C.?"

"Rob Wilson, the General Counsel."

"Oh."

"So Wilson finally gets there - he lives like a foot from the office - and he makes us relay the whole goddam story. Finally, he thanks us and walks out. Doesn't say another word, you believe that?" Eddie finished off his beer.

"So what happened?"

"I don't know."

"You don't know?"

"No. I'm assuming they arrested the crazy son-of-a-bitch. I'll be checking the San Diego news, I can tell you that much. The fucking guy was bananas. It was scary."

"Oh Eddie, I'm so sorry."

"It's okay, baby. Listen, you have every reason to be pissed."

"And worried."

"And worried," Eddie agreed. He twisted open another beer. "How was Maggy's recital?"

"She was magnificent."

"I'm so bummed I missed it. Can I talk to her, tell her I'm sorry?"

"She's in the shower. I'll tell her. Are you on your way home?"

"I'm on the way to the car but, Amy, my nerves are shot. And you should see Wittenberg. Poor guy's a wreck."

"I can imagine," she sympathized.

"So I think we're going to make a quick stop at Beck's for a beer to decompress. Tell you the truth, I really don't think I can drive just yet."

"Sure, I understand. I don't want you getting behind the wheel all upset. Calm yourself down and we'll see you when you get here. Soon, I hope."

"Me too. My guess is I'll be an hour or two. Wittenberg's still shaking, literally, the guy is shaking."

"Alright, just be safe, okay? Don't drink too much, especially if you're all worked up. And call me when you're on you way."

"Will do. I'm so sorry, babe."

"It's not your fault. I'll see you when you get here."

"I'll make it up to Maggy."

"I know."

"Love you. Kiss Maggy for me."

"Okay, see you soon, love you too," she said.

Eddie pressed END.

That was awesome. He grabbed another warm beer and slammed it down in two passes. He tucked in his damp shirt, climbed the steps and closed the trap door behind him.

Chapter Thirty-Eight

How he could do it?

How he could just leave her there to die? Bea couldn't say.

She touched the back of her throbbing head with her fingertips. Her hair was sticky and she knew without looking that her head was a bloody mess. It was a wonder she'd survived. And what was he doing about it? Where was the ambulance? Why hadn't he carried her to that shitbox Caddy of his and drove her to the hospital? She knew damn well he could've driven with a hand over one eye to keep his lane from doubling. No, nope, that was not his little plan now was it? He was a fat little conniver and she should have seen right through him. And didn't that make it so much worse! All she wanted was to have a nice afternoon with her boy. He'd duped her. Yes, he surely had. He'd played on her sympathies, on her motherly instincts. He'd played her a fool, luring her here with his promise of finally becoming the dutiful, attentive son that she deserved. He'd tricked her and that was the worst pain of all.

She'd given him a lifetime, her lifetime! She'd sacrificed everything for him and what did she have to show for it? A knot on her head the size of a, of a, of a kiwi! That swing had always been in perfect working order. Clearly, he'd tampered with it. How he'd gone from a fat little twist to full-blown psycho was beyond her. She was no shrink and at this point she'd just as soon let the authorities figure him out. She'd diapered him, wiped his rotten ass; clothed him, wiped his snotty nose; fed him, wiped his grimy mouth and when he was older she'd advised him and wiped those larger-than-life pipe dreams out of his head. Like he could have made his mark in Hollywood! Ha! He had as much charisma as a wet fart. And then he got fat and that shut the door on his future because if there's one thing he wasn't going to get far on, it was that little pea brain of his. If only he'd gotten her brains, what a success he might have been!

She winced as she touched her wound again. Blood had congealed her hair into an oval cake. She would not bleed to death. She forced herself up into a seated position. Looking up, the old cuckoo clock came into focus. To her left out the sliding door, she saw Jonathan's big stomach and then his legs and feet prone on the decking. His bulk inflated and deflated in steady rhythm. There he was, Mr. Mastermind murderer, snoring away, her drunk, pinheaded monkey. Bea sat up, her face in a burning twist.

"Jon—" she started but covered her mouth with both hands. She got to her feet and kicked aside the tangle of blanket and cushion with a groan. He'd dumped her on the floor! Onto a dog bed no less! She sighed, a fucking dog bed, a dead dog's bed! As if he was going to kill her like he did that ugly mutt of his. She swiped at the fur on her nice sweater vest. She'd have to get it dry-cleaned. God knows Sunny Brook didn't have a decent laundry service. He'd pay for that. He'd drop it off and pick it up too for that matter, oh yes he would.

She stood, her knees quaking beneath her. She leaned on the kitchen counter, not sure of how to reclaim her balance. She looked out the door and could see more of her son, lying in an awkward position, his torso propped by the upended swing. Sleeping like a baby, murder weapon right there under his nose! Unconscionable! Sociopath! So this is where all that sober time had taken him. This was his sick translation of all that One Day At A Time tripe. Next to him lay her bottle of Popov, empty! She discovered her sloe gin on the counter.

"Happy days, happy days," she declared and took a neat swig. The liquor went down thick but easy and flicked her insides on like a light switch. So Johnny wanted to get honest. Johnny wanted to have his one last vetting with his mother before sending her on her way. She took another sip and capped the bottle. Fine, maybe he didn't rig the swing. Even so, he left her there on the floor to bleed while he clearly had himself a good old time with the rest of her vodka. Where were the consequences? This was the honest living he was after? This was him "working the program?" The Program. What a travesty! A gang of reformed liars all yapping on about truth! And who was telling the truth in there? Any of them? At least she was honest with herself. She loved to drink. She'd always loved to drink, what of it? It hadn't done her in like all of his little loser friends. She'd been getting along very nicely as a matter of fact. Here come the consequences, Johnny. Do them both a favor. At the very least she wouldn't have to deal his preaching for a while. Maybe he'd cool off in jail, get a little more truth. Maybe a little jail time was just what the doctor ordered. He'd figure it out sooner or later. It wasn't the drink. It was the man, or in his case, the boy.

Bea lifted the receiver off the wall and dialed 911.

"Emergency, do you need police, ambulance or fire department?"

"I need the police please."

"What is your name and location?"

"This is Bea and I'm here at my house."

"And where is that, ma'am?"

"In the woods," she said

"Do you know the address, Bea?"

"Yes of course. It's, it's um..."

"Ma'am are you injured?"

"Yes, yes, I, my son tried to, I have a bump you see and I'm bleeding and—"

"Stay on the line, we'll identify your location."

Bea hung up with a disgusted slam of the phone. Moronic civil servants can't even do the simplest thing! All she wanted was the police, not a big get-to-know-you! She took another swig from the bottle. To hell with it, she'd no reason to fret, certainly not from the fat unconscious oaf spread out all over her deck. He'd come to and she'd handle him just fine, make him call the cops on himself! Wouldn't that be a coup?

She staggered out the door and stepped over Jonathan. Her toe tangled in the billows of his filthy t-shirt and she caught onto the railing to save herself a nasty tumble down the stairs. She grunted and picked her way down the stairs with both hands on the rail. Woo-my, she was a little lit. But now there was time to kill and why not make a nice evening of a nice evening? He was stone cold drunk, probably sleep till noon. A nice, cool dip in the lake might very well ease the pain in her head.

She crossed the yard. The long wet grass slipped between her toes and chilled her from the bottom up. She picked her way down toward the lake. There was only a hint of the old path thanks to Jonathan's negligence. Her head throbbed and for a moment she paused to recollect what it was she was on her way to do and decided that she might as well take a dip in the lake.

Chapter Thirty-Nine

EDDIE SAT IN his stool at the end of the bar and finished another draft. Except for old Bob and a longhair throwing darts, Madigan's had cleared out. The Sox were on the TV and Ramblin Man sounded from the jukebox for what, the third time tonight? Sandra had loaded the jukebox with change and punched a series of selections off the top of her head. She'd left the rest of the credits to Eddie. She poured shots for the both of them and danced a bouncy, buxom jig from his end of the bar to the other, shaking her tight ass fast to Rock Lobster, grinding it to When the Levy Breaks.

Eddie threw back the shots and drummed at the smooth, worn bar rail. They were in a Friday night groove. Over his shoulder, the red neon Budweiser sign in the front window reflected against the opaque glass. The pink light of summer sunset had given way to darkness. It was moving toward late night and that was just fine. His Dingleberry hadn't buzzed since he'd hung up with Amy. She knew enough to let him be. And she'd do what she did best, nothing. Besides, the Wittenberg thing was a delicate situation. He grinned and lifted his pint glass. His pinky stuck out and his jaw had the twitchies.

"Barkeep! How about another for a long lost friend?" He twisted his neck to crack it. It needed a good cracking.

"At your service, my lord," Sandra filled a draft and placed it in front of him. She assumed her familiar position, leaning across the bar so that her breasts spilled over her forearms. Eddie leaned forward, zooming in on Sandra's butterfly. Its wings were blue and blurred. The ink had aged.

"Got a bink for me?" he asked.

"For you my lord? Anything," she said and lifted her hand off the bar. The vial came in view and Eddie slipped his hand under hers. In his grasp it felt like encapsulated, pure potential. She squeezed his hand and smiled at him. Her teeth were straight and white, and he now noticed her canines were long. Their sexiness surprised him.

"I told Bob I was feeling sick, told him I had to go home."

"What do you mean?"

"I mean, I want you to take me home and fuck me."

Eddie looked down the bar at Bob teetering on his stool. "So... we're leaving?"

She stroked the back of his hand with the long nail of her forefinger, "Within the next half hour, I want you to cum all over me."

"It's after midnight?" Even long leashes had their limits. A limp fear surfaced from beneath his edgy booziness.

"No silly, it's not even ten," she dragged her nail harder against his hand. "Bob's gonna cover for me," she shooed him along. "Go to it and I'll see you outside."

Eddie palmed the vial and made his way for the can. His hard-on pressed against the front of his khakis as he passed by old Bob. The bathroom was small with dingy wood walls and only enough room for a toilet, a urinal and a sink. He locked the door behind him and got at it. He stood in front of the urinal, pissing down his erection while spooning in the blow. Multitasking. He was a multitasking masterfucker. He trickled to a finish and shook. His boxers had chilly damp spots up and down the front.

The bink did its fast magic and he opened the door, realizing with great relief how early it was. Wittenberg was a mess. Shit, he'd have to be with a guy like that all night, peel him out of the bar, get him a cab, follow him home - babysit for God's sake! It was early. What could she say? Should he just leave a guy like that to his own devices? Just leave him alone? It'd be irresponsible! It was very early. Old Saint Bob had moved his stool behind the bar.

"You have a great night!" Eddie said with a big smile. Bob nodded but kept his eyes on the TV.

Outside on the sidewalk, Eddie followed Sandra down the block. He watched her ass sway, admiring his catch and disbelieving his good fortune in the same thought. She was deep into her thirties, but still a good deal younger and shapelier than he. Her legs were tight from top to bottom, not a single cellulite crater to be found, not even on her ass. He recalled her bent over the steps in the storeroom and he hoped they didn't have far to drive. He'd fuck her in his car if he had to, but more room would be optimal. Optimal, another Vic power word, things were either optimal or sub-optimal. This would be optimal in the extreme, except for the idea of using corporate power language to describe a woman so hot. Eddie couldn't stop the biz speak, his brain was running far faster than he could keep up with and so the corporate cheese popped like orange corn in a copper kettle. Optimal, a paradigm shift, a blank canvas, outstanding optics, consumer centric, Eddie centric, synergy, ideate, accounta–

"Hey, you coming?" Sandra motioned for him to catch up.

"My car's the other way," Eddie pointed.

"Leave it. We can walk," she grabbed his hand. "Come on, Tiger, we have a party to get to."

Optimal.

She walked fast, and led them off the Post Road at the next block. "It's just down here."

"Sweet commute," he said but his jaw stayed in motion long after the words were out and gone, as if he'd fallen into a foreign voiceover. They passed under an anemic city maple, the sidewalk losing light at his feet and gathering it up again in the next step. He felt a tug.

"This is us," Sandra said and hustled up the stairs of the apartment house. She slid her key in the glass front door and they were in. She turned left up the stairwell.

"This way, I'm only on the third floor. I don't bother with elevator. Good for the legs, you know?"

"Have you ever used an elevator?"

"What?"

"Sorry. That was supposed to be a compliment."

"Are you very high?"

"Yes, I believe so. I'm binked up to the brim."

"This shit is the bomb. He cuts it with something special, just for me, or so he says. But you men are always saying things," she said and started up the stairs.

"It's cut with something?"

"Well, yeah, duh! Not saltpeter, though, I can guarantee you that. But I guess you already figured that out," she laughed and took the steps two by two. Eddie followed, expecting his knee to scream at the effort. It did not. There was no pain at all.

"I thought this was puro."

"Oh please, there's no such animal."

She rounded the corner and when he followed she had stopped in the middle of the next flight with her hands on her hips. "You're so cute when you're naive. But I don't like cute so much. I prefer tough." She turned and climbed. Eddie kept pace, breathing hard. He followed her through the door to the third floor hall.

Sandra's apartment was sparsely furnished. She said nothing, just pulled him right by the kitchenette down a short hall and into her bedroom. She flipped a switch and a half-light flooded the room. The bed was made, white sheets painted flat on the mattress.

"So, Sandra, were you in the marines or something?"

"Something like that. You like porn? I love porn," she stepped to Eddie's right. On top of a wide corner table was a large computer screen. Sandra wiggled the mouse on her tabletop and an image appeared on the screen. She clicked through a few open windows. "Give me a sec."

While she clicked away, he took off his shirt and dropped it on the floor. It fell not far from a pink necktie tied to the foot of her bed. He looked to the other corner and saw another tie, this one blue.

Sandra curled in behind him, wrapping her arms around his chest. She scratched gently near his nipples and then her hands trailed downward. "Will you do something for me?" she whispered in his ear.

"Anything."

"I want you to be rough with me. Can you do that?" her hands touched him through his pants.

"Mhmm, oh yeah, sure."

"Turn around."

"Okay," he turned to face her.

"Now, rip my blouse off," she demanded, "just grab it you fucking bastard."

"What?" Eddie hesitated.

"Rip it off me!"

Eddie did as he was told. She squealed as the cotton tore away from her chest. She pulled him close and growled soft and low in his ear. "I want you to fuck me hard enough to hurt me, you promise? I want you to take me from behind. I want you to watch the screen and fuck me better than that. You got that?"

"Anything else?" he smiled.

"No fucking around. Don't you disappoint me and don't you fucking cum and don't you dare fucking stop, no matter what I say. Promise?"

"You're serious?" he looked her over and shrugged. "Okay, I Promise."

"And if I beg you to stop?" she unzipped his pants.

"I keep going."

"No, you fuck me harder."

"Got it."

"Time's a wasting big boy, throw me on the bed."

Eddie did as he was told and threw her harder than he intended. He yanked off his pants and boxers and came at her, erection first. When he climbed on the bed she slapped him across the face.

"Get away from me!" she screamed and tried to crawl away. Eddie caught up to her at the head of the bed and yanked her backward. Sandra spun around on all fours and Eddie turned with her. He chuckled.

"You sick fuck!"

"It's like eighth grade wrestling all over again," he said with a laugh.

"You sick fucking bastard!" she blurted, and then turned back to him. "Yes, yes, do me," she mouthed. She turned toward the screen and called him more names. He entered her, thrusting hard. When she tried to shimmy away, he pulled her back by the hips.

She looked back at him and motioned with her head for him to look at the screen.

On screen, a blonde bobbed atop a dark skinned male who lay flat on his back. The blonde's back was to the camera, which looked down on the couple. It was one of those amateur videos. The man's arms were spread out to the corners of a bed with black satin sheets. His hands were tied down. The woman ground up and down on the man's enormous erection. While he watched, Eddie pounded away at Sandra from behind, ignoring her cries. The woman on screen pivoted above her captive, keeping the dark man's giant thing inside her. She slapped his huge head and then looked up into the camera. Sandra.

"Oh my God...Oh shit!" Eddie wailed.

"Don't you do it you sick fuck!" Sandra screamed.

Eddie followed direction and didn't listen to a word Sandra said. His eyes popped, ejaculating at the sight of a blurry blue butterfly bouncing on the screen. Sandra raised herself upright on her knees, and then turned to face him. Eddie smiled and she landed a right cross on his cheek, knocking him off balance. She hopped up from the bed and ran out the door.

"What the hell?" he yelled after her.

His cheek didn't give him any pain but he rubbed it anyway. He stood up from the bed and pulled on his pants, not bothering with his boxers. He walked down the short hall. Sandra stood nude at the counter of the kitchenette, carving long lines with a gold credit card. He checked his back pocket.

"Hi. Ready for another?" she smiled.

"Is that my credit card?"

"I needed one. A gold card, oo la la," she giggled and batted her eyelashes.

"What'd you hit me for?"

"Oh Eddie, I'm just playing. Don't look so sad."

"You punched me," he said.

"Oh please, the *drama*, it's all in good fun. Here, I set you up," she tapped the card on the counter, "You were an animal," she purred.

Eddie looked from her to the blow. She handed him a rolled dollar bill, one corner folded and tucked in on itself, like a hospital corner. He took the bill and she raised her hand to his head. He flinched.

"Oh, poor baby," she said, and gently touched his cheek. "I might have hit you too hard, I'm sorry."

"Just take it easier next time, okay?" he said as he bent over the cocaine.

"No promises," she whispered as he snorted.

Chapter Forty

"Ouch! Mother, stop—"

She slapped him again.

"What the hell? Stop hitting!" Jonathan rubbed the sting from his cheek. He shook his head and his brain sloshed around like an egg in its shell.

"You wouldn't wake up," Peg said.

Her face came in closer, almost in focus. Her green eyes skipped about in their sockets like water bugs. Her red braid hung off her shoulder and tickled his chest. This was it. Jonathan reached for her face and puckered his lips.

"Ouch! Cut that out!" he rubbed his other cheek.

"Wake up, Jonathan! What are you doing out here?" she hissed at him. "Where's your mother?"

He made a move to sit up. He was already sitting up. He looked from side to side. He was sitting on his porch floor, back against the swing. How'd that come about?

"Jonathan!"

"Hmm? what?" he rubbed his eyes and zeroed in on the Peg in the middle. She looked irritated. That was normal. People who slapped you out of a drunk were always pissed about one thing or another. He raked his top teeth over his coated tongue. He smacked his lips together. "Hey Peg, it's dark out."

"Where's your mother?" she hissed.

Mother! He straightened up. "She, she had an accident! Shit! Shit! Didn't I call you?"

"No, you didn't."

"It's dark. Where were you?"

Peg sandwiched his face in her rough hands. "Jonathan, where's your mother?"

"She had an accident. Swing broke. She was bleeding, bleeding like a pig."

"Where is she?"

"Cracked her head open."

She shook his head like a Magic Eight Ball, "Tell me where she is!"

"Without a doubt," he mumbled.

"Jonathan!" Peg shouted.

"She's on Zella's cushion. I wrapped a towel around her head, towel and ice. She's fine, snoozing away." He blinked. Peg turned to look inside. He could make out only a dark stripe trailing down her neck, as if her tattoo had slithered away and left a black trail behind. "I guess, well, I slipped again, didn't I?" he scratched at the welts on his neck, "tell you what, there are some tipsy mosquitoes out here." Peg glared at him, cheeks red, eyes wide. "Hey, can you get me a glass of water or something?"

"Be right back," Peg said. She slid the door open and went inside. Lights flicked on as she disappeared into the house. Light fell on his yellow belly and his flaking, bare feet.

"Oh jeez," he groaned at the sight of the Popov jug by his side. He picked up the jug and shook it. Still a little fire left. He tilted the jug to his lips and sipped. The vodka went down warm and revolting. He gagged and threw the jug over the deck rail. It disappeared into the dark. He didn't hear it land. Maybe it didn't land. Maybe not. He felt a tickle on his forehead. He shooed the fly, and then shooed another. Three more hovered above a shiny dark spot by his feet. His mother had cracked her head open and he had polished off the vodka and here were the flies. He shook his bare feet and caused a soft, buzzing ruckus.

"Hey! Hey! you're letting the flies in!" he shouted. He rubbed his face and dug his knuckles into his eye sockets. He didn't feel too bad but he was thirsty, plenty thirsty, worse now after the vodka. Vodka wasn't the answer. Time to get up. He rolled onto his hands and knees, sat upright. The porch spun out from under him. Sour saliva flooded his mouth. He set his hands back down on the decking. Saliva poured from his mouth.

"Oh crap," he groaned and his stomach rolled upward and his puke came like liquid fire and blasted against the chair and splashed back over his hands and his shaking forearms and knees. He heaved twice more and then he was empty. He gasped for air and his belly hung, contracting and quivering and dripping. He wiped his chin on his shoulder and sat up on his aching knees. He spat, pressed his hands on his knees and stood. He stumbled sideways. He groped for the light inside the glass door. The door rattled in its track and his hands slipped upward and he gazed through the smeared glass. He steadied himself and peeled his hands slowly from the glass. He stepped inside, eyes on each footstep, into the hazy yellow light of his kitchen. On the floor to his left, Zella's cushion lay empty. The only sign of his mother was a large oval blood stain. He pawed his way along the counter to the sink, turned the water on and sucked from the tap. He rinsed his arms up to his elbows and splashed his face. He rubbed the back of his neck and wiped his belly. His cold, wet hands drew goose bumps. He bent over the dishes in the sink and doused his face again.

"Thank You for this water," he mumbled through dripping lips.

"She's not up here!" Peg shouted. He heard the stairs creak under her fast, heavy footfalls.

He turned off the water and braced himself at the sink. "She's not down here either!" he called.

"I'm right behind you."

He jumped. Mother?

"Jonathan, where the hell is she?" Peg tugged at his shoulder. Her voice and fingers hard as stone.

He turned to her, leaned against the sink and shrugged. Peg's green eyes got thin.

"You need to get a grip, Jonathan."

"I know."

"Drink some water."

"I did."

Peg wore a sleeveless blue blouse with glittering collars. Hands on hips, her tattoos of fanged snakes with scales of green, red and gold curled up and around her muscular arms.

"Listen, this is a problem. We need to find her and that means you've got-ta start using your brain," she poked him hard in the middle of his forehead. "Locating your mother is kind of job number one. So let's think, Jonathan, let's think. Where else might she be?"

He was weak. He was no manly gladiator of God. Spartacus died on a cross. "Peg, I can't do this."

"Christ, not another one," Peg muttered. She rubbed her forehead with the flat of her hand like she was sanding it smooth. "Yes, Jonathan, you can. For fuck sakes, it looks like maybe you already did."

"We're gonna find her and take her to the hospital," he said.

"Like hell we are! We have an arrangement, remember? Remember our deal?"

"What deal?"

"Mercy costs money, remember? You're mother's money to be specific."

"I didn't make any deal!"

"Oh really? Then what the fuck am I doing here? Huh?" she jabbed her same finger at his chest. "We have a thing to do here, Jonathan, a righteous thing, a merciful thing. But it takes guts, alright? Takes some conviction, takes some fucking balls! I brought my balls, Johnny," she pulled a syringe out of the pocket on the front of her shirt and wagged it in his face. "How 'bout you?"

"Peg, I'm sorry. I'm trying to be strong, like a gladiator you know? Brave and strong, but I'm not," he dropped his head. "I'm, scared. I'm a coward, a weak, fat coward."

"No you're not, you just need a little confidence. You know what you need?"

"What?"

"This situation calls for a little liquid courage," she slapped his shoulder and opened the refrigerator. "Anything left from your little party? Ah-ha! How about this?" She held up the bottle of his mother's sloe gin. She checked the freezer. "Looks like that's it. Anything in the cabinets?"

"No," Jonathan said.

"Then it's an easy choice," she unscrewed the cap and sniffed. "Ooof, what is this stuff?" she checked the label.

"Bitter Truth," Jonathan said.

"No shit? Well, here you go Jonathan, bottom's up." She put her hand on his shoulder, gently this time. She reassured him with a big smile, her teeth yellow and long and her breath reached him, sickly sweet like rotten beef. He gagged. And then it was the syrupy smell of his mother's Bitter Truth as she held the bottle close to his lips.

"Just a slug and you'll be fearless and true," Peg cooed.

Jonathan lipped the rim and plugged the hole with his tongue like the little boy and the dyke. He flattened his tongue and sloe gin slid down inside him and his face felt like it had caught fire. He pulled at Peg's wrist and turned away from the bottle.

"That's enough," he wiped his mouth with the back of his hand and spat in the sink.

"You sure?"

"Yes, I'm sure. That's enough."

"Well alright then, let's get to it. She must've wandered outside. You got a flashlight?"

"In the drawer over there," he pointed.

As Peg slid open one drawer and then another, her dark red ponytail swished from side to side and the ink on the back of her neck squirmed in shadows. She fished out the tin flashlight. She flicked it on and pointed the beam out the door.

"Perfect," Peg grinned at him and bobbed her chin like she had a tune in her head. "You got your balls back, Jonathan, I'm impressed. Mercy's not for the meek. "

"Let's go," Jonathan said as he walked past her and out the door. He padded down the porch stairs. He trudged through the yard in the direction of the deer path that led to the lake. The weeds scratched his shins and ankles, and felt cool and prickly on his bare soles. Her flashlight's pale yellow beam skipped against the black wall of woods that lay ahead of him and she howled into the darkness.

"Sooey! C'mon along little girlie! Sooey! Sooey!"

Chapter Forty-One

"I CAN'T WAIT to fuck you all over again," Sandra drawled through lips all gacked-up and akimbo.

"Hey, me too—"

She shut the door. Eddie stood in the hall, considered knocking, but heard a deadbolt slide into place. He shrugged and made for the stairs.

The night air felt fine in his lungs and Eddie dropped into his BMW and set Sandra's goody bag on the passenger seat. She'd sent him on his way with three cans of Bud, and two dollar bills folded and filled with blow. He knew not to keep all his eggs in one basket. He put one bill in his breast pocket and the other in his change pocket - you could never be too careful. Spills happen when you drink and drive and there was no need to put the blow in harm's way.

The ding of the ignition and quite hum of the engine detached him from the dark, silent street. Blood orange light from the dash covered his torso and lap, and he felt discomfited by the exposure. The light settled on him like a phosphorescent shroud of paranoia. He looked around in every direction before dropping the car into gear, his left leg shaky. He lurched the car onto the Post Road and made his way toward the entrance ramp of I95, hands at ten and two, careful to keep his speed steady. The clock read 11:00 pm, totally reasonable.

On the highway he accelerated to 64 mph and set the cruise control. 64 was the optimal speed, any slower at this time of night would raise suspicion, any faster would give cause for a speeding ticket. Nine miles per hour above the posted speed limit was the formula for a smooth ride home. With his speed dialed in, all he had to do was focus on his steering. Straight and steady in the center lane, changing lanes as infrequently as possible. The highway was deserted, but for the occasional truck. A few miles along he settled down into his leather sport seat, turned up the tunes, cracked open a beer and planned.

The trick to all this was to keep on top of the details. It was pure project management. All you had to do was to identify all key actions and implications and put them in a logical, finish-to-start order; run it down like a Gantt chart. First came the story - babysitting poor Wittenberg, mopping up the poor guy's blubbering mess. Story told, finished, check. So what would next week look like? What would be the first consequence in the concomitant series of consequences?

Start first key action: shutdown mode. Shutdown would already be in effect, of course. UTC (more specifically, Rob Wilson and his Legal team) would scramble, taking immediate defensive actions. They would contain the story. There would be no press, no news about a disgruntled employee wielding a gun. That the whole thing would be buried was completely credible. All Tobacco companies, and perhaps particularly UTC, were notoriously tight-lipped, now more than ever. Since The Settlement, all of Big Tobacco had tightened up their practices and perfected the art of the quiet cleanup. It would come as no surprise to Eddie and therefore to Amy, that the matter never breached the walls of the Company. There would be no emails, and minimal documentation, all very believable. The Wittenberg / California affair would be immediately addressed strictly through verbal communications. The disgruntled employee and his shocked boss would be controlled by offers made up of equal parts threat and generous compensation. They would be held to such appeasement by a broad, dually executed disclaimer drawn up behind the bulletproof glass of the Legal Department. These would be the only documents and they would be housed ultimately in HR, protected from discovery by HIPPA or some such act that ensured a citizen's right to privacy under certain mental health related conditions. Okay, maybe he was stretching it here. This was not his area of expertise, but then again, that was just fine. He couldn't know just exactly how they did what they did. And this would only serve to reinforce his credibility with Amy. "Believe me babe, I don't even want to know," he'd say with a shake of his head. She would nod with understanding. Shutdown mode finished, check.

Start next key action: his moral struggle. In the ensuing weeks, any lingering office gossip would dissipate due to lack of new information. Within a month, it would be as if it had never happened. And Eddie would bear unwilling witness to this cover-up, just as he had been an unwilling participant in the traumatic event (a man was held at gunpoint for Christ sakes!). He would feel deeply conflicted. And he would return home from work and speak to Amy about it in a hushed voice, bestowing upon her one internal confidence after the next and she would be satisfied. And this is why she'd never get wind of it at the company picnic or Christmas party or any other company function that required her attendance. Even if Wittenberg cornered her, drunk and stupid and blithering away, he'd not let on and she'd know she was on the inside track. She'd understand better than he knew. So, after dinner one night this week, probably Wednesday, Eddie would shake his head in abject disbelief and wonder aloud what he was doing in such a corrupt business. He would lament over his moral struggle with doing his job and earning for his family and ask Amy what she thought might be the true cost? And she would pity his struggles and when her comforting began he would know that he had successfully completed the project. The Wittenberg / California affair would rightfully cease to be.

The highway hummed under his high-performance Perellis as Duane Allman slid on down his guitar. A yawn caught him by surprise. He wedged his beer in his crotch and pinned the wheel with his knee. He unfolded the dollar bill, steadying his hands on the top of the wheel. He scooped a blast into each nostril with the pointy end of a pen cap. He sharpened right up on his way through Stamford, the low skyline too close to New York City to be taken seriously. He checked the rear view; the road behind him was empty. He smiled, sucked back at the remnants in his sinuses and finished his beer. He pulled the next one out of the bag and cracked it open. He raised it carefully to his lips. A buzz in his pocket startled him and he spilled into his lap.

"Shit!"

Spilling beer in the car was not cool. He didn't need to be smelling like a barroom floor in the unlikely (very unlikely - let's keep it positive here, positive waves only please) event that he was pulled over. It was one thing to spill a little coke here and there, no big deal, unless there was a dog, but there would, of course, be no dog. You don't keep the canine unit out working highway patrol do you? Why would you? Well, this was I95, the main vein for East Coast contraband. It actually made pretty good sense that they'd be patrolling with dogs right now. This is probably when all the mules were driving their glaringly inconspicuous old Honda Accords or Toyota Camrys, trunks loaded with individually wrapped kilos. Man, how awesome would it be to find a kilo? Eddie could see himself jamming a blade into the package, a package with similar dimensions to - and wrapped as expertly as - his dry cleaned dress shirts, starched and neatly folded. He'd heard the stories of waterproof containers loaded with blow washing onto the shores of Amagansett or East Hampton or some other snotty Hamptons' beach and he wondered when his ship would come in. He was lucky that way. He wasn't feeling left out, just impatient. His Dingleberry buzzed again. "What the fuck?"

Of course it was her. Who else would be hitting his work email on a Friday night? Damn, he'd be feeling rough in the morning. He had to make good on the recital. He had to remember to make good on the recital. He had so much to remember. Thank God Sandra set him up so nicely. If he paced himself, he'd have enough to get him through until bedtime tomorrow night. He pulled out his Dingleberry and scrolled up. Storm316 was in his inbox. Sandra. He grimaced. Didn't he remind her, *no emails*? The road ahead was empty. He peeked down.

"YOU ANIMAL"

Eddie smirked at the compliment before a truck blasted by on his right. He flinched and threw the goddamn Dingleberry on the passenger seat and got back to the business of driving. Finish to start relationships, finish the drive home, avoid incident. He was on Route 8, though he didn't recall making the turn in Bridgeport. He put on his signal and changed into the right lane. Route 8 was a two laner and he had no business being in the left one. He rechecked the cruise control, still a rock-steady 64. He scanned his mirrors, no lights, road deserted again. He unfolded his bill; binked-up with a mild pride at his conservative cap-loads, refolded the bill and dropped it back into his breast pocket. That would have to do him for the rest of the evening. Had to get right to sleep when he got home, tossing and turning raised suspicion.

Well, well, well, now there was a B. Now there was a B indeed. His project had a part B. He shook his head in disbelief. Of course it did! Obviously. Okay, fine, onto part B. What to do about Sandra? Sandra, Sandra, Sandra. She was one hot fireball, that's for sure, but he needed to be smart. He had to play this very cool. She was hot and her drugs were good. He snorted. Still, it was mostly the same exercise. Sandra required a degree of containment. No big deal, as long as he was straight with her. She knew the score. He saw that. She knew what they were doing. It was a good time. It was sex and drugs and rock and roll. And that was the long and short of it and she knew it and he knew it and it was all good. All this situation required was a little education. She needed to understand what it meant to email him at work (mental note: next b-card reprint, no email address). He'd call her tomorrow. She was smart. She'd get it. No problem. He rolled along Route 8 and smiled when *Casey Jones* came on. He tapped his foot and sung along absently. He knew all the Dead's stuff.

"...Intrebadunction at seventy-two, the fireman screa… at, at a quarter to ten you know it's driving again! Driving the train, high on cocaine," he sang.

True, he'd been through this with her already. Clearly, the woman had her passions and was no stranger to a good time. Great. But this was her problem, and more to the point, his problem. She just didn't seem to give a damn. She'd phoned him at work; she'd emailed him, despite his specific request to the contrary. Perhaps she wasn't very attentive to details, though the near antiseptic cleanliness of her apartment would suggest otherwise. No, he knew chicks like this. She paid attention, but her attentions were selective. He'd have to do a more thorough job drawing her attention to the realities of their situation. She'd understand. This was a work thing, nothing personal. She might even apologize; assure him it would never happen again. And it wouldn't.

He rolled along. Knee on the wheel, he snorted a couple more cap loads of bink and cracked the last beer. Twenty minutes and he'd be pulling into his driveway. Exhausted and disheveled, he'd take a shower. Smell was a liability.

"Magical Thinking."

He'd heard the term in one of the AA meetings. Some poor jerk jawing about how he had his hopes, like someday he'd be cured and get to sit at the bar and hoist a few with his buds and watch the game on the big screen. "Just a few," the guy kept saying. He was all about, "just a few." And nowadays he'd come to believe that this was just some weird way of torturing himself. And damned if that chirping didn't sound a little bit familiar, damned if that bug planter hadn't stumbled on a nest already big and bustling in Eddie's ear.

To believe that Sandra would lay off the cell phone and email was magical thinking.

An exit sign slipped across his peripheral vision and he absorbed only its oddity. He tapped on the brakes, out of cruise control. Another sign with an arrow approached. SYCAMORE LANE, TARTUSVILLE. He slammed his hand on the top of the wheel.

"Motherfucker!" he shouted. He'd blown by his exit twenty minutes back!

He took the Sycamore exit and decelerated down the ramp and hung a left. In less than a hundred yards, he left the ambient light of the highway behind and the dark road sprung up into his headlights like so many miles of a surprise. He searched for a good spot to turn around but the woods came right up to the road on both sides. He floored it with a roll of his eyes.

Riding shotgun, his Dingleberry buzzed again. He scooped it up to shut it off, another email from her.

"See attachment BURN SCUMBAG"

He scrolled down and highlighted the attachment but it didn't open. He squinted, confused. He didn't recognize the file type. Now she's sending him attachments! Maybe not, maybe it's empty, like a shell or something. Maybe the firewall sizzled it or whatever. Maybe it's a server thing. Maybe it's one of those little image files that come along with some folks' email. Of course, he would recognize a .jpg, or a .gif or .tif or whatever. He raised the screen to eye level and squinted at the little attachment icon. What the hell was an MP4? Was it like an MP3? He tossed the Dingleberry aside.

Eddie glanced up at the road. His jaw dropped at the sight of the big brown hulk dead ahead in the road. He crushed the wheel between his hands. He looked to turn, but there was no turn to make. And then there came a sharp jolt, brittle in the first instant, followed by heavy thumps. The animal took to the air, its antlers crunching like pretzel sticks against his windshield followed by the massive

thud of its body. The impact thrust Eddie forward against his seat belt. The airbag punched his face. He hit the brakes and cut the wheel hard to the left for no
good reason at all. In the spin, he told himself the situation was still manageable.

Chapter Forty-Two

DEEP IN THE dark, Officer Joe Batina's knees bounced furiously and his heels rumbled on the floor of his cruiser. He was parked in a wooded nook off Sycamore, working a speed trap about a mile from the highway.

"What's done is done," he muttered and tilted his head to snort the remains of his stash straight out of the vial. He was so super fucked. He had the whole damn shift in front of him. He sucked the last of it down with the back of his head pressed against the metal perp cage of his cruiser. The puny little blast travelled up his crusted sinus and what little trickled down the back of his throat tasted like pure, uncut despair. He was no coke-head, but this was no way to kick off a shift. Going from coffee to coke was one thing, a bad thing maybe, sure. But going from coke to coffee was like hunting bears with bb's instead of bullets, and surest thing about that little ditty was that the hunter would fall - in agonizing, jaw-grinding freakin' torment - before the beast.

He sat up straight and pawed at his blue tie until it hung loosely around his unbuttoned collar. He'd just have to forget about it, just have to press on through. It wouldn't be that bad. But, it would be that bad. He scratched his fingers through his thick crew cut. He needed a plan, nothing too complicated, a nice, simple plan. He picked up his cell phone off the passenger seat. Who was he kidding? He didn't know any dealers.

He dropped the phone back on the seat. What he needed was an excuse for dispatch, a reason to get back to HQ for a moment or two. Family emergency. Boom, there it is. Denise was having a baby, no, no good. Denise's mother was having a baby and he had to race them to the hospital and... no, no. What the fuck was he thinking? His ex was having a baby? He tried to shake the shit out of his head. Was he really that FUBAR?

No, he had to get back to HQ because he had the shits something awful and he had a thing about public restrooms, a thing about public rest rooms. He was the new guy. What would they know about his hang-ups? There we go. That's the good stuff. The shits. Nobody said boo about the shits. Nobody ever gave a guy a hard time about a Code Brown, right? So now it's just a matter of finding his way into the property room and doing a little shopping. How the fuck's that gonna happen? Did he not just get stonewalled this afternoon by that freakin' officer Dudley-Do-Right? Yeah, but Dudley's off his shift now and maybe Sargent Happy Pants was on, maybe somebody with some freakin' old-school ethics. He'd scare up another couple grams, no problemo. Then he'd finish up his shift and by God; tomorrow he'd get back on The Program, back on his A game. You betcha, hon.

Joe scooped the mic off its cradle and pressed the call button, "Baker-4 to Dispatch."

"Dispatch," came Ramsey's squelchy voice.

"Umm... 10-44."

"Baker-4, 10-9?" Ramsey loved to dispatch.

"Code, uh," he couldn't do it. He'd never hear the end of it.

"Dispatch."

"Negatory, 10-22, out."

"Copy."

Fuck! Fuck! Fuck! Who was he kidding? He wasn't getting into the property room at midnight on a Friday! Fuck! Freakin' fuck fuckers! He was going to have to ride this out. His bouncing thighs rattled the steering wheel.

Working traps at night, the shit job nobody wanted. It was the job rookies pulled for training or screw-ups got stuck with for DA. Yeah, well, no biggie, working traps wasn't that bad, bad if you're jonezing sure, but not that bad, not really. It wasn't like getting thrown out of your house or finding all your shit strewn all over the lawn. Hell, compared to that, not bad at all.

A million years ago back in Elkton, fresh out of the academy, he freakin' got off on working the traps. Back then he was on his program, hitting AA meetings across the state line over in Delaware. He'd got himself out of the racket, out from under old Uncle Sal. No more peeling blood money out of broken fingers. Hell no, he'd found himself some honor with the Staties. He'd buttoned-up, badged-up and become a squeaky-clean crusader. Popping drunks was like doing service.

And it was more fun than fishing, easier too. All he had to do was wait for some dumb-ass to serpentine his way down the road. He'd work it by the book. The perp would pour himself (better yet, herself) out the door and he'd run 'em through the field tests. They'd fail right off, but he'd run them through one test after the next, bite his lip as they mumbled and stumbled along. The drunkest had the highest hopes, convinced they'd just performed the heel / toe ten-step with sober perfection. He'd squeeze the cuffs extra tight and try not to smile while he Miranda'd the shitball.

He rolled down his window and cut the engine and the AC. The warm night seemed to sit out there, while the cold air inside the car rushed over him, through him. He shook his shoulders and imagined headlines in the Tartusville Gazette, *Disgraced Cop Freezes to Death in August!* What a super fine mess indeed, indeedily-do.

Jimmy.

That was Jimmy talking, the kid who didn't say boo at the dinner table, still talking after all these years underground. After all that blood and mash at the bottom of the compacter, a piece of Jimmy was back, fat and miserable, calling himself Jonathan and staring at him from across the circle with those same bathwater blues, that bad bitch dragging him through the ringer all over again.

"So what the hell am I supposed to do about that?" Joe muttered at his reflection in the rear view mirror. His face glowed pink, lit up by the radar's red LED.

What? Shoot her? He smiled. Wouldn't that be something, shoving the nuzzle of his Sig Saurer up under her chin and blowing that red bucket hat right off her withered head. He shook the image aside and fiddled with the radar. But back it crept, like a hungry feral cat, his gun nuzzled up in the naughty nurse's old lady dewlap. He shook his head again. He had to get it together.

Down Sycamore, by the bend in the road, the tree tips lit up in a rising white wave. The light approached fast, running along the tree line. Joe sat up and watched the speed register on the radar. The car's headlamps broke over the black asphalt horizon and the radar flickered 54.

"Fifty-four in a forty-five, fine; run it out, buddy."

He had too much on his mind to bother, what with Jimmy and the empty vial and blowing Bea's brains out and - and how 'bout tossing ole skinny Jesus down that stairwell? Joe grunted. That was some bad business. What was that shitball's name? Nothing but Jesus came to mind, whatever. He had the Property Room mission to be thinking about. No, he'd already figured that through. Well, fuck-a-duck, it wasn't like he was doing it for kicks. Coke was a work thing. He was a boozer, always had been. Anyhow this joker could just speed on by, God bless him; there was way too much going on to bother with a 22-350.

The hum of the engine came up strong and smooth. The car was no beater. Joe studied the lights against the run of the double yellow line as the road lit up between them. The driver kept a good line. Joe sucked the drip from the back of his throat and spat out his window. A boxy black shadow stirred in the wood across the road. The shadow separated from the woods and the stag appeared in relief, its trophy rack lit yellow for an instant before flying through the air. Tires screeched and skipped through a tumble of thuds.

"Dude," Joe gawked.

The car jerked left and then right, veering toward him, lighting up the hood of his cruiser and then the road it had just traveled. The car spun past him, leaving behind a cloud of smoked rubber. The car jumped the curb and stopped cold with a dull crunch of metal on wood. Joe craned his neck out his window, gaping at the taillights that cut through the trees no more than thirty yards from his cruiser.

"Can't ever catch a break," Joe grumbled. He started up the cruiser, turned onto Sycamore and got on the horn, "Baker-4 to Dispatch."

"Dispatch."

"Ramsey, I got an 11-83 on Sycamore, one-point-three miles east of 8."

"10-4 Baker-4."

"Dispatch, Baker-4, 11-41."

"Copy, meat wagon, Baker-4," Freakin' Ramsey.

Joe parked by the fresh tire tracks into the woods. He followed the shaky beam of his Maglite, making sure of his footing. The ruts from the tires made for uneven ground. He walked toward the rear end of a black Beemer, palming his holster. It had plowed into a woodpile. The front end was buried under a heap of cut logs. Dust floated in the indirect light, setting the piney air in motion. Joe aimed his light at the back of the driver's head. The airbag had deployed. He checked the passenger side, no airbag, no passenger.

Nice and simple, thank you, Jesus.

He unclipped his holster and kept his hand close by the butt of his Sig Sauer. The driver stirred. The shattered windshield was bent inward and bloody. The dope was freakin' lucky he had such a sweet ride. The driver's door swung open. Joe pointed his Maglite into the car. He heard the repetitive warning ding and, who was that? The Allman Brothers?

"Whoa, just sit tight there, sir. You've been in an accident. I'm a police officer." The driver froze. "If you can, I'd like to see your hands up on the wheel," Joe approached the driver's door.

Joe waited until he saw fingers curl around the wheel. He stepped beside the door. He scanned the driver, hands first. White male, suit jacket and pants, no tie. The man shielded his eyes, squinting up at the light. Joe skipped the light over to the passenger side, spotting a couple empty tall boys in the foot well. Joe ground his teeth at the thought of having to book the son-of-a-bitch. He scowled and pointed the Maglite back in the driver's face. A long scar cut down the center of the Deewee's wrinkled-up forehead like a river through a valley. Joe blew out a breath and shook his head. He took his hand off his gun.

"Well, Mr. Persistence, how you doin'?" Joe wiped his running nose on his sleeve. "Tell you what, slick, I'd like you to step out of the car please. Can you do that for me?"

⋅⊷⊨◉ ◉⊨⊶⋅

He didn't bother with the field tests. Between the wreck and whatever he'd been hitting all night, Ed Musso could hardly stand up. But he was one of those never-say-die-drunks, going on and on about his bum knee. Joe cuffed Musso and practically had to carry him back to the cruiser. He'd drive slick over to the hospital before booking him. The doctors would get his BAC in the ER. And fuck-a-duck, maybe he could cop a Valium or a Xanax or something.

"Officer," Musso said through the cage.

"Baker-4 to Dispatch," Joe spoke into his mic.

"Dispatch," Ramsey replied.

"I got a 98 in tow. 11-42 on the wagon, I'll take him over," Joe reported.

"10-4 Baker-4. 11-85?" Ramsey replied.

"Most definitely, 10-4, Baker-4 out," Joe said. Hell, if there was a God, maybe he'd find a way into the Property Room.

"Copy."

"Officer," Musso said again, louder this time.

Joe held the mic aside. He checked Musso in his rear view mirror. Musso's upper lip was swelling up pretty good. "What's that you're yapping back there, Musso?"

"I said, couldn't we work something out?"

"Work what out?"

"Officer Joe, right? May I call you that? Is that alright?"

"Officer Batina," Joe corrected him. Christ, this Musso guy was a real suck ass.

"Yes right, of course, Officer Batina. Hey listen; it's been a helluva night. I was hoping you might, you know, given our relationship, that you might afford me, you know, might uh—"

"Might what?"

"Might consider some leniency. What's the sense in just carting me off to jail, you know?"

"No. I don't know," Joe rolled his eyes and bounced his left foot beside the break pedal. He turned to look at Musso. "Why would I want to consider anything else?"

"Well for one thing, I'm not really, like, gonzo you know?"

"Oh no?"

"No, not at all," Musso assured.

"Really?" The freakin' guy reeked! "Sorry to disappoint, Musso, but that's not how it works. This is how it works. You feel those bracelets behind your back?"

"Yes sir, I certainly do."

"Those are, how should I put this? Those bracelets are a sure sign that you, Slick, are under arrest. And, like I said when I Miranda'd you, you're under arrest for driving under the influence. That's another sure sign. See how that works?"

Joe stared Musso down but the guy just tilted his head and stared right back. Joe shook his head. He shifted the cruiser into Drive and pulled out onto Sycamore.

"You know, I couldn't help but notice your jaw, officer Batina."

"How's that?" Joe eyed him in the mirror.

"I don't know. It just seems to be doing that cud-chewing, stuck sideways thing," Musso said with a shrug.

Joe checked himself in the mirror. He rubbed his clenched jaw.

"It just looks like you're, you know, edgy. That's all I'm saying."

"I'd check yourself there, Slick. You been Miranda'd."

"Oh yes, I know. I got that. I'm just saying, you know, your jaw looks like it's working double-time, you know? Listen, I got plenty of respect for the law, don't get me wrong."

"I think you'd better shut your trap."

"Well, all I'm saying is, I've been in that spot where, you know, where you're speaking English but your mouthing Japanese?" Musso leaned closer to the cage. "I saw you this morning. You were bouncing right out of your seat. What I'm saying is... I think we can help each other out, that's all."

Joe slowed the cruiser and crept down Sycamore. He turned around. He had to see this shitball to believe what he was hearing. Musso's face was right up by the cage.

"Lemme get this straight. You're cuffed back there - in police custody - under arrest for deewee - and you've got the balls to imply that I'm under the influence? Do I have that straight, Mr. Musso? 'Cause, I'd be very careful with an accusation like that."

"I'm not accusing you of anything, sir, I'm just talking."

"Are you admitting to me that you have drugs in your possession, Mr. Musso?"

Joe's cell phone rang, startling the hell out of him. He picked it up off the passenger seat. He didn't recognize the number and pressed END.

"Like I was saying, Mr. Musso, are you admitting you have drugs?"

"I don't know that I'm so much admitting..."

His cell rang again. Same number, Joe pressed END. Whoever it was would get the message. "You were saying..." Joe said.

"I'm just throwing it out there that maybe we could strike a deal," Musso smiled.

"I see..."

"Look, officer, tell you what, you never reached into my pocket here and you never took anything, okay?" Musso smiled a toothy salesman's smile; a pretty good salesman, truth be told.

Again with the phone! Joe pulled over the curb onto the grass. There were too many things going at once. Same number, he pressed SEND.

"This is Batina."

"Um... hello? Is this umm, Officer Joe?" Joe could barely hear the guy.

"Who's this?"

"This is Jonathan."

"Speak up, who?" Joe knew it was the kid the moment he asked.

"It's Jonathan, you know, from the rooms?"

"Yeah, uh, hey, how you doin'? Listen kid, I'm on duty at the present moment."

"Yes, well, that's kind of why I'm calling," the kid whispered.

"What's up?"

"You see, I got a little fucked up," he slurred. "You see, I um, I've got a situation here."

"What?"

"Well, it's um... I'm in sort of a situation here."

"I got that. What is it?"

"Oh! Yeah, right, sorry. I'm a little bit fucked up. It's my mother."

"What's the problem?"

"Hey, you know something? You know what? She says you're my uncle..."

Joe closed his eyes. His heart pounded in his ears and the freakin' car was suddenly a hundred degrees. He checked Musso. He'd settled back in his seat. He had a shot of curiosity mixed in with his salesman's smile.

The line was silent.

"Kid? you there?"

"Uh, yup. Well it's bad. I've done something bad and now she's gonna kill her. I didn't know who else to call. Things are a little fucked up here."

"Whatdayamean kill her?"

"Look, I gotta go. She's gonna kill her and I gotta—"

"What? Don't say that if you don't mean it."

"No, I mean it. She's gonna kill her."

"Listen to me kid. Jonathan, you listening?"

"Mhmm..."

"What's your address?"

"52 Lakeside."

"Fine. Hang up now and call 911. Call 911 now."

"You don't get it!" a sob came over the line. "I gotta go. I'm all messed up. She's always right. Mother's always right about everybody. She's always so right!"

The call dropped. Joe put the cruiser in Park and looked back at Musso's.

"What's going on officer?"

"Your phone got a charge, Musso?"

"Yes, sir."

"Then it's your lucky day."

Joe pulled himself out of the cruiser and opened the back door. He gripped Musso by the shoulder of his suit jacket and pulled him out. He stood Musso up in front of the open back door.

"Where is it?" Joe hit Musso's shoulder with an open palm. Ghostly faces of deadbeats floated loose in his memory like dust clouds from a beaten, dirty rug.

"Suit pocket," Musso said and pointed with his nose to his chest. Joe fished inside and pulled out a folded dollar bill. He pocketed it and glared at Musso.

"So, we got an understanding?"

"Absolutely," Musso smiled.

"Not a peep to nobody?"

"Absolutely not, sir."

Joe spun him around and un-cuffed him. "You're on Sycamore Lane, two, maybe three miles east of Highway 8. Call yourself a cab."

"Will do, officer. Enjoy your evening," Musso said and rubbed his wrists.

Joe poked a finger into Musso's chest. "You say boo and I'll consider that a welch. You welch and that makes you a deadbeat." Joe slammed the back door and climbed in behind the wheel. He held the door open and looked up at Musso and spoke low and slow.

"Trust me on this one, Slick. I'm freakin' hell on deadbeats."

Joe shut his door and banged a U-turn on Sycamore, lights on, siren off.

Chapter Forty-Three

EDDIE WATCHED OFFICER Joe Blow-hound screech off, to protect and serve, no doubt. He limped his way back to his car. The Beemer was a big dollar mess; its crumpled hood littered over with logs. Fucking lumberjacks. He unlocked the door and sat on the black leather seat. He set his Dingleberry on the dash, swung his feet in and closed the door. There wasn't any use starting the engine. The car wasn't going anywhere. He sighed and his eyes came to rest on the brown paper bag that lay on the passenger's side floor. He perked up and reached for it. Inside was the last tall boy, intact. He dug in his change pocket for the second dollar bill. He unfolded the bill and scooped out a generous bink. He folded the bill, cracked the beer and gave a nod to God. Good God was he a lucky son of a bitch! He'd gone from utterly fucked to only mildly screwed and he had to laugh.

But there were no cabs and he couldn't count on that cop not changing his mind and coming back for him. Come to think of it, he'd radioed in, hadn't he? Eddie was pretty sure that had happened and that meant more cops and so this was absolutely the wrong place for him to be. Momma didn't raise no dummy. He hopped out of the car and soft shoed it back in the direction of Route 8. Might as well keep it loose. He was a lucky sonofabitch but he still had a mild sub-optimalism on deck. He dialed home and hoped it wouldn't be all that bad. Amy picked up on the second ring.

"Hello? Eddie? Where are you? Are you okay? I must've conked out." Groggy's good; really, could he get any luckier tonight?

"It's only like eleven, Ames. Listen, I'm sorry, but I need your help."

"What? are you okay?"

"Yes, yes, I'm fine no worries but uh, I got into an accident. Well, not an accident actually—"

"You what? are you hurt? Eddie, where are you?"

"Nobody's hurt. It wasn't an accident exactly. I hit a deer and lost control of the car. Anyway, it's dead."

"The deer?"

"No, the car, but yeah the deer too I suppose. So I guess I lied, someone did get hurt," he laughed.

"I'll come get you."

"I tried to call a cab."

"I'm on my way. Where are you?"

"I'm just off Route 8, Tartusville, the Sycamore Lane exit."

"Tartusville?" her voice rose.

"Yeah, had to dump off Wittenberg. What a complete mess. I'm so sorry, honey."

"I'm on my way, sit tight."

"I'll meet you right off the ramp, make it easy for you."

"Honey, don't you think you'd be safer by the car?"

"It's so weird, I was listening to a story on NPR just the other day about statistical evidence to the contrary," he stopped himself. "Give me a ring when you're close, okay?"

"Okay, be careful. I'll be there soon."

Eddie kept to the side of the road, ready to step into the woods at the sight of headlights. He walked at an easy pace down the road, feeling calm and cool in the darkness. The woods loomed overhead, blocking much of the sky and he had to keep a close eye on the road to pick his way along. His Dingleberry jingled, caller blocked. Sandra was going to have to learn the hard way. He drank his beer and watched for the call to drop. He continued on, following the curve of the road and the arrhythmic wale of the Route 8 overpass. He reached the off ramp and sat beside the road with his back against a tree trunk. Amy'd be coming along soon and that called for some maintenance bink, just a couple little blasts to sharpen him up. As he snorted an equalizer up his left nostril, his Dingleberry rang.

"Amy?"

"Hi, I'm coming down the ramp now."

Eddie shouldered the phone and folded up the bill and stuffed it into his breast pocket. He stood, smoothed back his hair and brushed himself off.

"See me?" he said and waved at the headlights rolling down the ramp toward him. She flashed her brights and he hung up. He wondered if he was supposed to have said goodbye. She stopped and he hoisted himself into her Tahoe with a grunt. The Tahoe was a dumping ground for all manner of discarded wrappers and containers; fast food, candy, soda cans, wipes, chocolate bars, empty Poland Spring bottles. It irked the hell out of him. How someone could treat a nice vehicle the way she did was beyond him. It was as if she had no fucking gratitude whatsoever. She really had no respect, none, for all the nice things they were so lucky to have. And he knew now was not the time. In no way was this the time to be casting rocks, stones, whatever. He positioned his loafers between the Happy Meal boxes at his feet.

"God, am I glad to see you," he said and smiled.

"Hey," she said amiably enough, but then looked at him sideways, "Your lip's funny."

Variables jumped in his heart. Was this a cocaine comment or a lipstick comment? He'd washed his face. He went for the big sigh of relief.

"Good God almighty, what a nightmare," he shook his head.

"Eddie," she elongated the hard e in his name with her chiding tone, "why's your lip funny?"

"What're getting at?"

"You look like you've been doing lines."

He dropped his jaw. "You're kidding me right? I've been out here in the woods for the last hour after nearly getting killed by a deer and the first thing that comes out of your mouth is an accusation?"

She scrutinized him, looked him up and down in his seat. He willed himself still. He fought the demands of his lower lip to shift, his pinky to rise, his knee to bounce. The vertebrae in his neck were suddenly askew and in need of immediate realignment. He was carbon-based desperation and his Dingleberry buzzed in his pocket and he silently cursed the goddamn thing.

"Well, you must be totally spent because you sure look funny to me," she said and looked from him back to the road. They rolled beneath the underpass and Eddie covered his mouth with a yawn and let his pinky fly.

"I'm like... delirious," he said through a yawn.

"Long day," she muttered.

"I'm gonna just shut my eyes, okay?

"Sure, go ahead. I'm awake."

"Thanks, Ames, thanks so much," he said. He patted her thigh. "I'm so lucky," he declared before crossing his arms over his chest, shutting his eyes and concentrating on slow, steady breaths through his nose. He lauded his access to full Zen; the buzz of his Dingleberry felt as insignificant as a flea on an elephant's back.

"I'm gonna turn the radio on, 'kay?" she asked.

Eddie maintained his deep breathing groove. He heard the warbling of some pop diva at a whisper's volume, and he knew he had Amy covered. He settled in for the ride, keeping still by concentrating on the drone of the tires and the soul sister's warbling drivel. Down the highway he heard raindrops and then the swish of the wiper blades. Rain battered the roof. Eddie felt for the thin, folded bill in his breast pocket. His bink was safe and dry.

Chapter Forty-Four

Jonathan edged his way through the maple saplings and vines and pine branches. The deer path narrowed to single-file. Peg followed close behind. Her light blazed on the leaves and needles that brushed through his curly hair and dragged along his naked chest like bristles from a dog's brush, sometimes rubber, sometimes wire. He stepped forward and the water lapping at shore suddenly rose above the cicadas' buzz and the peepers' chirps.

"We're here," he said and stepped out of the shadows into the pale light by the lakeside. The water was black and wrinkled by the breeze. He looked up. Patches of spent grey clouds slid beneath big black clouds with sharp edges that crowded a weak moon.

"It's going to rain again," he said.

"So let's get it in gear. I'm going this way." Peg walked away, along the shoreline with the lake on her left. The beam of her flashlight swept in a wide arc from the edge of the woods to as far onto the lake as the light would carry. She rounded a bend. Her beam lit the lake, disappeared, lit the lake again, and then it was gone. She was in the cove.

"Mother!" Jonathan called, "Mother! where are you?"

He walked along the shoreline until the deer path turned inland and the branches grew thick along the shore. He stepped into the water. It warmed and soothed his bare feet. He waded deeper. The bottom was solid underfoot, a mixture of stony sand and leaves. He knew the spot. In the spring it loaded up with spawning beds, little craters guarded by watchful momma bass and sunnies. He waded on until the water cooled and reached the drawstring of his sweats.

He bent over and dunked his head. He trembled as he raked his fingers through his tangled hair. He peed and the warm pool at his middle let him know he was cold. She was cold.

"Mother!" he screamed toward shore. "Where are you?" His voice trailed off into the woods. He heard nothing but the spilling of waves and layer after layer of creatures peeping and buzzing, miles deep.

"God, if I'm not supposed to ask You why, what am I supposed to ask?"

"Hey!" Peg's light bounced down shore, "I found her! Jonathan!" she called.

"I'm here! over here!" he waved.

The light held steady in his direction, a bright spot that twinkled like a star.

"What're you doing out there?" Peg shouted into the wind.

"I'm coming!" He slogged through the water toward the light, his knees pumping under his bouncing belly. Peg held the light on him. In the shallows, he saw her gesturing for him to hurry. The bottom turned soft underfoot. His feet sank through rotten leaves and plugged into muddy silt. His steps sounded with slurps and sloppy farts as he planted and pulled his feet through the mud. He made it to dry ground, bent over and gasped for air.

"Well? come on!" she grabbed his shoulder.

"Is she? is she?" he panted with his hands on his knees.

"She's just around that bend, c'mon!"

"Wait!" he reached for her but missed. He stumbled behind her toward the cove. His head felt as if it had shrunk to half its size. He lurched after her, fighting to catch his breath.

Around the bend she turned and flashed her light at him.

"Right here," Peg hissed. She pointed the light down by her feet. Jonathan made out his mother's figure on the ground, her sundress a dark purple under Peg's twitchy light.

"Mother!" he dropped to his knees by her side. Mother lay on her back, her head and shoulders up on dry ground, her wet hair fanned out on the path. Her bottom half was in the water. Her dress rolled up and down her wrinkled thighs as her legs swayed in the breakwater.

He looked up at Peg, "is she?"

"I don't know."

Peg knelt opposite him and shined her light down between them. His mother's skin was loose on her face like a ruffled bed sheet. Peg pinched her nostrils shut between her fingers. The high-pitched, pulsing drone of insects rang in Jonathan's ears. He bent close to her face.

"Mother?"

Her wrinkled lips parted with a gasp.

"Fuck," Peg muttered.

"Oh God, she's so pale," Jonathan moaned.

"I thought she was dead for sure," Peg shook her head.

"Her head - check her head, please," Jonathan begged.

Peg eyed him sideways. She raked a handful of Mother's hair and pulled her head off the ground.

"Careful!"

"What?" Peg snapped.

"I said be careful with her!"

"And I said, what the fuck," Peg said.

Peg twisted her head sideways. She shined the light on the back of her skull. Jonathan reached out and touched his mother's cold, damp cheek. Her eyelids fluttered.

"You ... you... how," she gurgled.

"It's me, Mother."

"You... dare..."

Peg dropped her head.

"Well now, that's a gash and a half," Peg muttered as she wiped her hand on the ground.

His mother's mouth opened and closed silently, like a fish out of water.

"She's still alive!" he blurted.

"Not for long," Peg said. She reached into her pocket and pulled out a syringe, "Might as well help her along."

"You get away from her!"

"Jonathan, she's suffering."

Peg held the flashlight under her arm. The light flashed on her face as she popped the plastic cap off the needle. Her green eyes glowed.

Jonathan made a fist and hardened it with his rage. He lunged across his mother and struck the side of Peg's face. Her jawbone cracked against his knuckles. The flashlight spun and fell with a splash as she toppled over.

"Get away from us!"

"What the fuck!" Peg ran the back of her hand across her mouth. She stood up and inspected her hand. "Shit!" she whipped her head from side to side, searching the ground by her feet. "Now I've lost the damn needle!"

"I said leave us alone!" Jonathan screamed up at her.

"You know what? You hit like a fucking girl, you retarded little coward," She snarled and then spat.

"Don't you spit on her!"

Peg leaned over and spat in his face. "How's that then?"

"Get outta here!" Jonathan shoved her away with both hands. He bent over and pulled his mother into his arms. Peg fished the flashlight out of the water and banged it on her hand. It flickered on and off and then it stayed lit. She pointed the light in his eyes.

"Fine by me. She can die any way you want, pain, no pain, whatever. But make no mistake, *Jonathan*, she's dead and you killed her. You try and weasel out of our deal, and that's just what I'll tell the cops. Got it?"

"Just go," he said, gathering his mother in his arms. She was cold and limp.

Peg grabbed a handful of his hair and yanked his face upward.

"We'll be settling up soon, retard, real fucking soon." She let him go with a shove, turned and bolted down the path.

Jonathan stood with his mother cradled his arms. He watched Peg's light disappear around the bend. The wind picked up. The first big drops of rain pelted his face until he couldn't feel his tears anymore. Rows of tiny waves popped and shattered on the shore, one after another, like armies of crashing angels. He stepped into the muddy shallows and marched for deeper water.

Black water boiled toward them as the rains rolled in from across the lake. Jonathan waded until his mother floated weightless in his arms. He stopped and turned away from the wind, standing firm and strong as a gladiator, the storm at his back. He curled her in his arms and bent over her. Cold rain spilled from the tip of his nose onto her crown and she blinked.

"How could you?"

"It wasn't easy," he said. He waltzed her from side to side. Fresh water snapped and danced all around them, urged on by wet gusts that chilled his ears.

"So cold," she murmured.

He held her face against his naked chest. He would be her dutiful son. He would love her.

"Me too," he said.

When he dipped her under, she didn't fuss.

Chapter Forty-Five

THE RAIN GOT heavy in a hurry and the cruiser's defroster wasn't worth a shit. Joe had the wipers whipping at full tilt. He wiped the windshield with the heel of his hand, bending over the wheel to get a smeared look at the mailboxes along Lakeside Drive. He cut a left onto the gravel driveway of number 52. His high beams lit up a wet, yellow wall and Joe stood on the brakes. He skidded to a halt.

"What the freak? a wood chipper?"

Joe wiped at the windshield. Yeah, it's a chipper. The rain rattled on the roof. He grabbed the mic, pressed the call button and then paused. What the hell was the kid doing with a wood chipper? Joe looked back through the defogged parallel lines of the rear window. This was 52, right? He held the mic and shifted the cruiser into Reverse. He stopped at the end of the driveway. Yup.

"Baker-4 to Dispatch," Joe said.

"Dispatch," Ramsey's tone had some attitude.

"Baker-4, checking out a 415d."

"Copy, backup?"

"Negative, I'm good. Code 6."

"Copy. Hope you get a keeper this time."

"Baker-4 out."

Dick. Joe cradled the mic and reached for his Maglite. He cupped the flashlight against his window and shined it at the mailbox. This was 52 all right. He pulled back in behind the chipper and put it in Park. Who knew, maybe Bea was in the woodsman business these days. He tilted his head back and sniffed hard at Musso's coke lodged up in his sinuses. He tasted it on the back of his throat. It numbed him up pretty good. Why couldn't they confiscate shit like this?

He paused with his hand on the door. What was he looking at here anyway? This wasn't just some standard DD with a D&D twist. These weren't just perps, these perps were what, family? Shit, was he just gonna jack the old bitch and book her for, for what?

"Fuck-a-duck," he muttered.

And really, what's the difference between a cousin and a nephew? Who freakin' cares? Jimmy don't care anymore. Jimmy can't care anymore.

Outside, wind gusts slapped water and leaves against the cruiser. The rain splattered, waves came heavy against the windshield, then his window then overhead. This was a real freakin' boiler. Joe checked the clock.

It was past midnight, visibility and audibility next to zero, no neighbors to speak of, a deep lake not fifty yards away... Hell, if there was going to be a time, this was it. He could blow the bitch's head off, and if the kid was near as trashed as he sounded, he wouldn't remember a thing. Shit, more likely the kid was already passed out.

Joe sniffed away at his bullshit, and, tasting nothing new on the back of his throat, considered another dip into Musso's blow before his next move. He picked up the folded dollar bill off the center console. He unfolded the dollar, holding it low in his lap. He poked at the flattened powder with the tip of his pinky. It was caking up already from all the humidity. He froze his gums with the white tip of his pinky. None of it made a damn bit of difference to Jimmy, now did it, Numb Nutz?

"Did I not tell you that shit'll kill you? Did I not freakin' tell you?"

Joe sucked in a deep breath. He cracked open his door. Cold rain hit the side of his face. He dumped Musso's coke on the flooding gravel and shut his door. He dropped his face in his hands.

"... I know, I know, this shit is no good," Joe groaned.

He sat up, scratched hard at his flat top and slapped himself on the cheek. He shook his head and slapped himself again. The rain fell straight and steady now, pattering on the roof. Joe wiped his eyes and then gripped the wheel with both hands.

Best he could hope for was to bust the bitch for something. And since there was no law against shredding through a family like a 12 gauge through a watermelon, he'd have to settle for a D&D or something. And 'course none of that was near as good as blowing her brains out, but it was gonna have to do. Joe flicked on the searchlight. It didn't add much to his high beams. The wood chipper blocked most of his view of the house. He could make out only the far corner of the first floor siding and a stone path leading around to the back of the house.

Joe stuck on his hat. He didn't have the shower cap, so the damn thing would soak in a second and be next to useless. Maybe a little head soaking was just what the doctor ordered. Maybe letting Musso off the hook and hauling it up here was exactly what he was supposed to be doing. Maybe he was staring down the barrel of another God-shot.

He opened his door, swept his Maglite beam in the rain and stepped outside. Cold rain pelted his hat and shoulders. He shielded his eyes to follow his flashlight beam. There were no rental stickers on the chipper. He walked along the left side of the chipper and then along the gardener's truck that had it in tow. He had an angle on the front of the house. Raindrops lit up silver in his beam as he scanned the front walk, the door, and the windows. The windows were dark, no lights from inside, no movement. Hell, the both of them were probably dead to the world by now, snoring boozy snores. Then he'd be stuck trying to explain himself; how it was that he dumped a Deewee by the roadside in favor of some wild - what would he even call it? a hunch? some wild hunch.

"A hunch, my ass," he mumbled. He snorted up rain dripping from the tip of his nose. A taste of fresh coke in his throat came from the flush. Hell, he was no Magnum PI. He was a freakin' druggy, plain and simple. So, truly, what the fuck was he doing?

Crunch.

Joe cocked his ear in the direction of what he thought sounded like a boot on gravel. It came from behind him. Did a shadow just shift? Goddamn coke got him all jumpy!

He spun around anyway.

"Hold it! Police!"

He swept his beam across the front end of the pickup truck. Nothing. He shook his wet head and turned back for the house. Freakin' shit is no good, had him imagining all kinds of things.

A clang of metal on metal hit his ears and Joe saw his airborne Maglite tumble away. Pain burst in his left hand and travelled up his elbow. He blocked his head with his right forearm and fist, guarding himself from the direction of the first strike. A second blow smashed flat on his wrist, snapping it. He ducked low and away. The break jolted through him like lightning. He screamed but couldn't hear it. He raised his elbow and the knuckles of his right hand flopped on his cheek, feeling as dead to him as if they were someone else's.

Joe hit the dirt and rolled to get some distance. He looked up and saw the female figure dart toward him, a spade raised above her head. He rolled again but the blade hit him on the left shoulder. He planted his left hand in a puddle, ignored his searing shoulder and got his feet under him. He scurried around the front end of the truck, pawing across his stomach with his left hand for the holster snap on his right hip. His forefinger bent away painfully and uselessly at the snap. He tried with his middle finger; Uncle Sal in his head.

Move or die soldier! Move or die!

Bent over and stumbling, Joe freed his sidearm and pinned it flat to his stomach with left hand and right elbow. He kept his eyes on the ground and made for the headlight of his cruiser. He felt for the safety, flicked it off and got a grip on the butt. He middle fingered the trigger with his left hand.

He heard her closing the distance.

Freakin' bad old bitch! He spun around, landed on his back and aimed between his knees. She came at him, bright white and featureless in the jittery white fog of his headlights. A shovel blade flashed by her head. He popped off three rounds. The shovel fell to the ground. He fired once more, missed, fired again and dropped her. She landed face down, head below his feet.

Joe tried to catch his breath, the back of his head in a puddle, the backs of his ears underwater. His breaths came up short. His lungs wouldn't fill and his heart whaled in his chest. He was gonna have a freakin' heart attack right here.

He gasped and his lungs filled. He lay panting, rain sprinkling his face, not splattering, not so heavy anymore. He lifted his head. The bitch's dark head hadn't moved. Joe lay back again and took three more deep breaths before sitting up with a groan. He propped himself up with his left hand, still clutching the gun. He winced, his left shoulder bright with icy blue pain. She'd cracked his fucking collarbone. He crossed his legs and leaned forward. In his lap, his right hand angled sideways out from his sleeve, lifeless fingers pointing toward his toes. Blood, thinned by the rain, stained his fingers. She'd broke his wrist too. The bad bitch had fucked him all up.

He scooped up his wrist with his gun hand, screaming at the pain. He cradled it in the crux of his elbow and rocked himself, but that hurt worse. Keep moving soldier! Joe uncrossed his legs and got on his knees. He struggled to his feet, drenched and shivering and doubled over at the waist, panting through the pain. He dragged his feet forward through the gravel.

God's big piss petered out into a slow, steady rain shower. Joe looked down at Bea and nudged her head with his toe. The bitch was dead as Elvis, but something still wasn't right - a ponytail? It looked dark, kind of reddish. Was that a tattoo? He stepped his shadow out of the way. Her hair was red. Blood couldn't do that, could it? He toed her head to the side; her ear piercings caught the light.

"Shit. Who the hell are you?"

Goddamn it! An unidentified freakin' owl! Joe shuffled back to the cruiser. He fingered the door open and knelt on the driver's seat. If he sat, he was damn sure he wouldn't be able to get up. And he still had the kid floating out there somewhere. He groaned and reached for the mic.

"Baker-4 to Dispatch."

"Dispatch. What's shakin' Baker-4?" Ramsey could be a snide little bastard.

"Baker-4 requesting immediate backup!" Joe shouted into the mic.

"20?"

"52 Lakeside Drive. We've got a 22-350 and a, a, a 22-372, ah fuck it! Ramsey, we've got shots fired. One dead perp and I'm banged up, down and crosswise. Send a wagon."

"10-4, Baker-4."

Joe spotted motion at his eleven o'clock, back aways from the near side of the house. A figure rose up from the weeds, head first, then shoulders. It made straight for his headlights, a black, drooping cross. No, it was holding something. Joe dropped the mic in favor of his gun. He aimed, resting his left forearm between the frame of his open door and the windshield. He braced himself, his right knee on the seat and his left foot dug into the gravel.

"This is Tartusville Police, identify yourself!"

"Who's that?"

"Tartusville P.D.! Identify yourself! My weapon is drawn. This is no drill, shitball."

"Don't shoot! Don't shoot!" The figure paused by the side of the driveway. It was the kid. Cradled in his arms was something that looked a whole freakin' lot like a body.

"Kid, is that you?" Joe called.

"Yes! It's me, Jonathan! Who's that?"

"Officer Joe Batina. Who've you got there?"

"My mother," Jonathan lurched a step closer into the gray, misty light.

"Listen, kid, how many more are in the vicinity right now?"

"What do you mean?"

"Besides you and your mother, who else is here?" Joe said it slow.

"Well, um, nobody," the kid stammered.

"Nobody else?"

"No."

"Ambulance is on the way," Joe withdrew his gun. He straightened up on his knee for a better look. Bea's head hung over his arm like an open Pez dispenser, mouth gaping. "She drunk?"

"She was."

"How's that?"

"Well, she's not drunk anymore."

"You alright, kid?"

"Yeah."

"You know who that is?" Joe pointed his gun at the dead perp not two yards from where Jonathan stood.

"Who?"

The kid searched about him, lifting his feet as if he'd stepped on something.

Joe shook his head. He spoke slowly, "Caucasian woman? long - red is it? long red hair, tattoos, jeans."

"Oh her, yes sir, I know her."

"Who's she?"

"That's Peg. She wanted to kill my mother."

Joe chewed on that little tidbit. Things were getting fuzzy around the edges. His eyelids were too damn heavy. He shook himself.

"Jesus, kid."

Jonathan stood there looking at his mother in his arms. His wet mop of hair shielded his face. "So, Mother said you're my uncle," he said.

"What's that?"

"She said you're my uncle!" He looked up, his hair hung in his face to his nose.

"Just hang tight, kid, okay? Cavalry's on the way."

The kid whipped his hair back. His blue eyes opened and glimmered in Joe's headlights, those fresh bathwater blues, those big Jimmy blues.

"She said you're my uncle," Jonathan repeated.

"Yeah, well, family's family, kid."

"So?"

"So? So... I suppose you better start calling me Uncle Joey; looks like we're all we got left."

Joe groaned, slid off his knee and fell back in his seat, soaked clean to his core.

Chapter Forty-Six

"Daddy... Daddy?"

Maggy's hand pumped at his shoulder. Eddie eased open his eyes. Maggy looked down at him, a hopeful smile on her little face. He was in the basement den, his decked-out man cave. He peeled his spit-glued cheek off the green leather cushion to check behind her. The TV screen was blank, thank God.

"Daddy, how'd you make this? Can I keep it?"

"What? Oh! hi-dee-hi-Maggy-pie! Morning," he mumbled, wiped his mouth with the back of his hand and smacked his lips together. He smiled at her as she unfolded a dollar bill in her cute little hands. She tipped it to look inside and white powder sprinkled down onto the blue plaid carpet.

"Snow!" she exclaimed with a giggle.

Eddie bolted upright and snatched the bill out of her hand. "That's for daddy."

"Hey!" she whined.

A steely pain like a cold railroad spike pierced his brain from the corner of his right eye straight up his scar along the back of his forehead. He dropped back onto the couch. He checked inside the bill and his sour stomach flipped. It was empty but for maybe a big bump or two.

"Careful honey," he nudged her backward, keeping her sticky bare feet from treading away what few little rocks he might recover. She fell on the seat of her Little Mermaid outfit.

"Ouch! Daddy!" Her wail cut through his head, nauseating him.

"Oh, sorry honey pie. Did you trip? Are you okay?"

"I'm alright," she skulked, rubbing her backside.

"Do me a favor will you, honey?" he forced a smile, breathing through his mouth and feeling sicker by the second.

"Okay."

"Will you please go check on breakfast?"

"Daddy, uh-doy! Mommy's making lunch! Mac and cheese, you want some?"

"Sure. I'll be upstairs in a minute. You go tell Mommy, okay?" Sweet holy Jesus, the idea of mac and cheese lathered him orange around the gills. He pinched at his crunchy, clogged sinuses. "Go tell mommy," he muttered.

"Okay!"

Maggy scampered up the stairs. Eddie felt a hint of dadmiration at her adorable bare feet before setting to work picking little bits of cocaine off the carpet. The remote for the home theater lay on the floor by his feet, lightly dusted by Maggy's little basement snow squall. He picked up The Con, wiped the touch screen with his finger and got a decent freeze. He had personally wired his man cave, not because he was cheap (the AV equipment cost him ten grand) but because he could. The first showing had been "Finding Nemo." He and Maggy had gasped with delight on the new green leather love seat as sea sounds whooshed from left to right and front to back.

He picked and picked but it was futile; he was collecting more wool than anything else. He rolled off the couch onto his hands and knees. It was hopeless. He was counting on that bink! Fucking kid.

And good God was he hung over! Badly hung, horrendously hung and Sandra came to mind and he worried. She'd assured him she was super clean and couldn't get pregnant. He didn't have anything to worry about. He worried some more and his stomach cramped and he picked at little bits of white on the carpet. Slamming his fist on his thigh, he bent down and dabbed his tongue on the carpet, tasting bitter, fuzzy relief.

He sat up and opened the bill and inspected the contents again. There were a couple lines left, he'd make it work. He'd go up and sneak in a vodka bracer. He'd be all right. Footfalls came down the stairs and he looked up. Maggy bent her face down so she could see him.

"Lunch is ready! Come and get it!" She ran back up the steps.

"Be right there, honey."

His wrinkled suit pants and oxford shirt felt damp on his skin and he dreaded the scene above ground. His stomach hated him and his head wasn't coming around from the rug freeze and the pain was causing him to worry. He didn't remember getting home last night, didn't recall anything he and Amy might have said, didn't know if he'd slept on the couch in peace or perdition. And now it was lunchtime and Amy'd been up with Maggy for hours and it was Saturday and she'd probably already been to three activities at least, soccer for sure, and maybe that Gymtastics bullshit thing that he'd hoofed her to now and again.

Christ, it was lunchtime. He smacked his chalky lips, parched actually. He needed something to drink and he hadn't had that shower and he couldn't be sure of what or who he smelled like and he hoped he didn't have pussy crust around his knob. His stomach rippled and saliva streamed over his molars and flooded forward. He swallowed. He just had to make it to the shower. Hit the showers, kid. He just needed a shower, a yak and a shower. He stood up, rocked on his feet and limped up the stairs.

"Just going to shower off, be down in a minute!"

He took the front stairs two at a time, knee screaming. In the bathroom he locked the door, puked and prayed for the water to ease the pain. And it did, a little.

In clean clothes, Eddie walked downstairs feeling fresh after his shower and his tiny maintenance bump. He walked around the corner and into the kitchen. Amy sat at the table alone and watched him approach. She'd covered his bowl with a saucer. That was nice.

"Where's Maggy?"

"Outside."

A one-worder, not so nice; he looked out the French doors. He scanned the stone patio and the lawn beyond, but saw no trace of her.

"I don't see her," he said.

He studied Amy's face, hopeful for positive indicators. She had a concerned look, nothing new or necessarily serious about that. She wore one of her suburban spandex super MILF outfits and had her hair tied back. Maybe the one-worder was an aberration.

"Going for a run?" he asked in his most chipper submissiveness.

"Oh Eddie," she shook her head and the corners of her mouth turned down. She turned away. There was a time when he'd thought the sight of her crying was the saddest thing he'd ever seen.

"What? What is it, Ames?"

"Don't even start," she fended him off with both hands. She didn't have on any rings and he wondered if that was something to wonder about.

"What?"

"Eddie, it's noon," she sobbed. "Don't you get it?"

"Get what?"

"The day's practically over! You're missing everything! Don't you see? You're missing all of it!"

"What am I missing? So I missed one recital! So what? I mean I know it's a big deal and I'm sorry and all, but it's not like murder or something," he pinched his eyes. The spikes of pain reconstituted in his head. His brittle gray matter was too shattered to string together anything sensible. He had nothing for her. "I mean, you know, I was in kind of a life or death situation last night."

"Life or death," she repeated.

The little muscles along her jaw twitched. She got up from the table and walked to the sink. She turned on the faucet and scrubbed at something. This marked trouble. Eddie closed his eyes and breathed into the wave rising up from his stomach.

"Well yeah," he began, and then dropped his hands on the table, palms up, incredulous.

"Yes, well, speaking of life or death, your office called, Constance somebody calling on behalf of Rob Wilson? I don't know, I wrote it down."

"What'd she say?" His innards gurgled. Things were not coming out square, not computing.

"Hmm?" Amy had the water on. Eddie lost himself momentarily in the novelty of Amy washing dishes, but the smug face of Counselor Cuntstance came roaring back.

"What did she say? What did Constance say?" he tried to keep his voice even despite the sudden suspicion that he might have soiled himself.

"She said it was urgent she speak with you today, and so I asked 'on a Saturday?' and she said again that it was urgent and—"

"And?"

"And then she apologized to me in a funny way and just hung up." Amy shut the water off and whipped her sponge into the sink. "As if I needed that!" she shrieked. Eddie jumped. Jesus, the woman was unglued.

"Fuck'em Amy. I won't call them, okay? You're right; they took more than their fair share from us last night! Hell, even ruined my kid's concert—"

"Recital."

"Ruined it! And now this? I hear you, Ames, I'm not going to play their game anymore! Whatever it is, it can just wait." He felt his face heat up.

"What do you mean, 'whatever it is'?"

"Hmm?"

"What do you mean 'whatever'?"

"I don't know! What do you mean what do I mean? I have no idea why they'd be calling me on a fucking Saturday morning."

"Wittenberg?" she turned and crossed her arm over her waist, set her elbow on it and held two fingers to her mouth.

He groaned and shook his head, "Well, yeah, obviously *Wittenberg*, but what the hell else? I mean what else can these people possibly want from me? I'm not the one who went bananas!"

"Eddie, stop, just stop," Amy said and walked toward him. "We're going to have a talk." He hoped for a little compassion but instead she turned and opened the door to the patio. "I've got to check on Maggy."

"I know, Ames. I know," he said with a stiff upper lip.

"I doubt you do, not at the moment," she said and closed the door behind her.

Eddie's thoughts zoomed in on the Absolut in the freezer. He needed some pain relief so he could think straight. Then he could start putting out all the little fires, one at a time, finish the bink, maybe scare up some more and then simply manage through. He'd force down some food, knock back a bracer and get on it.

He straightened up in his chair at the sound of the garage door. Amy must've left it open. Eddie shrugged, lifted his fork and took the saucer off his bowl. A red and white blob poked up from the center of his coagulated orange cheese like a veiny fried egg in reverse. He jabbed at the yolk with the end of his fork, ready for it to pop. It didn't.

He forked Sandra's mac and cheesy g-string up from his bowl and all his little fires combined into a great, all-consuming conflagration.

The shrill ring of the phone jolted Eddie up from his seat. He took a step for the counter, but his bum knee collapsed. He tumbled onto the hard ceramic tiles. He spotted Maggy's multi-colored gum collection stuck beneath the table and the phone rang and plucked at his nerves. He stared up at the ceiling and trembled in his flames.

"Oh Jesus, oh Jesus please," he prayed.

www.ingramcontent.com/pod-product-compliance
Lightning Source LLC
Chambersburg PA
CBHW021311250626
47155CB00002B/488